# The Splendor
# of Silence

The Twentieth Wife

The Feast of Roses

# The Splendor of Silence

INDU SUNDARESAN

WASHINGTON SQUARE PRESS
New York  London  Toronto  Sydney

*For my husband, Uday,*
*again and always*

 Washington Square Press
A Division of Simon & Schuster, Inc.
1230 Avenue of the Americas
New York, NY 10020

Copyright © 2006 by Indu Sundaresan

First Washington Square Press trade paperback edition September 2007

WASHINGTON SQUARE PRESS and colophon are registered trademarks of Simon & Schuster, Inc.

For information about special discounts for bulk purchases, please contact Simon & Schuster Special Sales at 1-800-456-6798 or business@simonandschuster.com.

Designed by Paul Dippolito

Manufactured in the United States of America

10   9   8   7   6   5   4   3   2   1

ISBN-13: 978-0-7432-8367-0
ISBN-10:      0-7432-8367-8
ISBN-13: 978-0-7432-8368-7 (pbk)
ISBN-10:      0-7432-8368-6 (pbk)

# Acknowledgments

I am blessed with a group of writing friends who provide me with a safe haven in which to create my work. They nurtured my first two novels and have done the same for *The Splendor of Silence*. I am deeply thankful to all of them and especially to Phillip Winberry and Janet Lee Carey for taking the time to read the entire manuscript.

My agent, Sandra Dijkstra, is similarly another blessing, encouraging and supportive of my efforts. I would be remiss not to mention others at her agency who, over the years, have worked as hard on my behalf and are all brilliant in their own way—Elisabeth James, Taryn Fagerness, and Elise Capron.

My publisher, Judith Curr, and my wonderful editor, Malaika Adero, make every contact with the business side of writing a pleasure. This they have done from the very beginning, and I am grateful to have found a home with them.

Many thanks to Rei Shimizu for translating the Japanese soldier's words in the last Burma scene in this novel.

And finally, as with my first two novels, I spent many happy hours in the stacks of the King County Library System and the University of Washington's Suzzallo and Allen libraries, immersed in their superb collection of books, maps, and narratives that gave me a firm sense of atmosphere, place, and society in 1942's India and Burma.

April 1963

*Somewhere Near Seattle*

# At the Cabin

S am painted the stairs that zigzag down the cliff's face to culminate at the beach. He had asked Olivia what color she wanted, and she had said red, so he painted the stairs Victoria Red—the same color as his breathtakingly expensive 1950 Crown Imperial limousine. Olivia was seven that year, and remembers lying on the sand in the hot sun, looking up as her father meticulously painted his way down. Having cornered himself and her on the beach by nightfall, they jogged up to the cabin, careful not to bump against the railings, but leaving footprints on the paint-wet wood. Olivia still has those red-soled shoes, but now, fourteen years later, fourteen Northwest summers and winters have stripped the paint, bleached the wood, weathered the railings into an old woman's face.

A gust of wind grasps Olivia's hair, yanks it loose from the collar of her coat, and sets it flying. One strand whips over her mouth, soaks into the tears that fall down her cheeks. She looks up the cliff in the approaching darkness and imagines that she sees a light in the window—one her father has lighted in welcome. But Sam died five days ago; he will never come here again. Elsa the dog nudges against Olivia's shins to remind her that it is cold here, and begins the climb up the seventy-nine steps. Olivia slowly follows, hands in her pockets, shoulders hunched about her ears.

Once Sam said to Olivia, "You look like your mother." She had just washed her waist-length hair, and drowsy from the bath, had laid her head on a pillow in front of the wood stove and fanned the strands out to dry. Sleep fled. "I do, Papa?" she asked. "Did you love her?" "With all of my heart; I still love her, as I love you." "Tell me about her. Tell me about my mother." "Later," Sam said. "Later." He always said later.

Olivia would then gaze intently in the mirror, trying to find her mother in herself—in her ebony hair, her curved eyebrows, even the elongated shape of the blue eyes she has inherited from Sam. Her Indian side and her American side.

They came to this cabin from Seattle each summer to while away the long daylight hours when Sam did not have to teach. He would write and she would fish desultorily in the chilled waters of the cove, or read, or throw sticks for Elsa until he was done for the day and they could go to the store or the library. She did not lack companions her age in the neighboring cabins, but she did not want them; she only wanted summers unadulterated by anyone but her father. On most weekends though, Grandma Maude would come to visit, and they would eat dinners by candlelight on the outside deck as the day died, and the night was born in skies of jewel-like stars.

On other nights, they would build a fire on the beach, huddling together in a blanket while Sam told her stories, and Olivia would fall asleep, warm in his arms, not awakening until morning, in her own bed. Sam's stories were mostly of India—rajas atop caparisoned elephants, camel markets in the desert, bazaars in a riot of colors, the chug of a train journey, the fire of curry in his belly. Every now and then, very late at night, when it was quiet and the rains came to scatter mellow gold drops in the light on the cabin's deck, he would be reminded of his first trip into Burma in April 1942 and into the thick of the war, and those were stories of packed, impenetrable jungles, stone pagodas, the slick of sweat, the crackle of gunfire, the pain of death.

By the time she reaches the cabin, the rain has begun again; the skies have turned a mottled gray, a muted thunder rumbles over the Cascade Mountains, over the bejeweled city of Seattle, and disperses into this sheltered cove in the Puget Sound. Olivia lights the fire in the stove, removes her coat, and rubs her cold hands together. Then she drags the enormous mahogany leather trunk from the front door to the rug in front of the stove. The knuckled brass fittings on the trunk gleam gently in the light from the fire as Olivia lifts the lid. The trunk arrived five days ago from India—a twenty-first birthday gift for her, from whom, she is yet to discover. On the same day this trunk came, her father died, so she now has to discover its secrets for herself.

She tugs at the silks at the very top and the fragrance of jasmine and smoke eddies around, let loose from its imprisonment within the trunk. The materials melt under her hand, the colors as vivid today as they must have been when they were woven—the pale lilac of early lavender; the pink of roses heavy with fragrance; the yellow of near-ripe mangoes. Olivia hugs the cool silks to her chest, wondering how anyone could drape these long lengths of cloth around themselves and still manage to look elegant. As her mother must have once. The only aromas from the fabrics are of mothballs and sandalwood—there is no hint of the real, living woman who once wore these saris, whom her father loved so much, whom Sam continued to love, but whom he could never talk about. Not even to their child, not even to Olivia.

She reaches in. An enamel-etched casket holds tiny silver anklets, blackened with age, their bells tinkling like faintly heard wind chimes. A black cord is coiled inside a palm-size wooden box inlaid with old ivory. It is too thick to be broken by hand, and is hung with little gold charms—a few golden beads, a coin with a dog carved on it, and a minute gold cylinder, scarcely larger than Olivia's fingernail. She strings the cord with its frayed edges around her throat and it barely fits. So it is not a necklace. Then what?

There are photographs in a transparent envelope. Letters. A wooden doll. Three carved wooden monkeys that fit in the palm of her hand. Olivia takes out one of the photographs and gazes at the woman in it. She has a thick swath of hair, sharp collarbones, a gentle face, a sweet smile. Who is she? Is she. . . . She looks again at the photograph, yearning to see something in the woman's face that she, Olivia, also carries in her own face. But there is little resemblance for the woman's face is thin and long, and Olivia's is broad, rounded. They both have long hair, black as thunderclouds, though that is too little of a coincidence to claim as ancestry. The woman's skin is smooth, as though things have not yet happened to her in her life. She half-smiles and yet a little edge of discontent seems to lift the edge of her mouth. There are no colors but black and shades of gray, so no way to tell the color of her blouse, or the sari *pallu* that drapes over the woman's left shoulder. Her neck is bare; tiny gold studs glow in her ears, and there is a flash of what looks like a diamond in her nose. Olivia turns the photo over but there is nothing behind it, no name, just a date and a place. RUDRAKOT, MAY 1942

Where is this Rudrakot? Will the letters tell her? A thick, unopened envelope lies against the side of the trunk. Framed against the light from the stove is a sheaf of papers inside, and the darkening brown blotches of glue along the flap.

On the envelope is one word. Nazeera. Something about the name is familiar; the *sound* of it is familiar. Olivia has heard it somewhere, at some time, but this memory lies stubbornly buried inside her. She carefully peels back the flap of the envelope and takes out the letter. Her heart crashes and thuds. It is addressed to her, as Olivia. Here is some person calling her Olivia. Who then is this Nazeera? The memory surfaces suddenly in a blast of three names—Olivia, Nazeera, Padmini. They are her names, ones she was born with, ones she has never used, for herself or with others. And here, in the writing in this long and looped hand, *must* be the stories that fill all the silences in her life, the stories Sam never told her, the ones he saved for a later that never came. Here they are then.

Outside the cabin, the storm dies as suddenly as it was born, extinguished into the womb of the Cascades, but night has crept up on the heels of the storm. The fire in the stove spits out a bit of ash that ebbs into oblivion on the stone hearth. Olivia leans against the trunk, its treasures scattered around her, holds the papers up to the light, and reads.

> *My dearest Olivia,*
>
> *I wonder, even as I set ink on paper, if you will ever read this letter. If you are reading it now, I wonder who you look like, what you know already of us all, if you know anything at all. What has Sam told you about us?*
>
> *So many questions. But all I hold in my memory is a baby of smiles, a dimple on her chin, lashes so long all the women around envied their length and called them cow lashes. It sounds odd, but this was a compliment then. Have you seen a cow's lashes? They are enormous, like the tassels on a woman's sari. I am sorry, I ramble on when I want to be to the point and succinct . . . but I also want to tell you a story.*
>
> *All stories start with a little telling. Interest evoked, questions asked, the first nugget unearthed and brought forward, shining bright on the palm of the narrator. Here, this is for you. From me.*
>
> *I am an unlikely narrator of this story; you will see that when you know it all. I am the last person who would want to write to you, but*

*by the end, you will also see why I want to be that person. I put down events as I know them. Some things I know of from having been there, but most came to me from other voices. Where I have detected malice, I have cut out its evil heart. I want to tell you, truthfully, or . . . as truthfully as I can, what happened in Rudrakot in 1942. I do not believe that anyone else will speak of this silence that hangs over us. They have not, perhaps, the courage.*

*For me, there are some stories that defy all silences. This is one of them.*

*Sorry, but I will settle down now to the actual telling. You must forgive my ramblings, my self-absorptions. I have been brought up to consider myself important, so reveling in the sound of my own voice is a . . . an occupational hazard, even a genetic predisposition, if you will. Never mind, a fresh pen and here goes.*

*All stories have their beginnings, not always evident as such when they happen. I have looked back over the years and thought, Was it then . . . or then . . . when? Even as I search for this beginning, I must tell you that this story spans a mere four days in May 1942. But you must not think of these as a* mere *four days, for you know, don't you, my child, that those four days were just a culmination, a climax toward a meeting that spiraled our lives out from that moment in time. Oh, we had histories before that May; we have had histories after that May. But you exist, as a reminder to us all of those four days in Rudrakot. I write to you. Our histories are linked, will always be. You exist, my dear, because of that May in Rudrakot.*

*Your father, Sam, came into our lives and threw us into turbulence. He came wounded, a bird with a broken wing, from Burma. Has he talked to you of his first foray into the war, as the British and Indian forces retreated when the Japanese invaded Burma? He did not tell us, or perhaps he told us—some of us—and we did not stop to think of why he had been there, and so who he was, or might have been. For, you see, everyone was fleeing Burma, but Sam had gone into that country and come back out alive. That in itself should have been a warning to us that Sam Hawthorne (how easily I use this name) was no ordinary man. Perhaps you, my dear, can excuse the events of those four days upon your father's injuries in Burma; perhaps that was why he was ready to fall in love with your mother. But I cannot. I choose not to. Sam was never really honest with us; he could not be, of course . . . but still.*

*I still say us, and him. Yet he is part of us now. As are you.*

*You see how much I have vested in this story. Oh, it is barely told yet, so you will see how much I have vested in this story. Then perhaps, you will excuse me too. For I was not entirely honest either.*

*So . . . where do I commence?*

*Here then. For our story began, of course, when Sam came to Rudrakot. . . .*

May 28, 1942

# The Kingdom of Rudrakot

SOMEWHERE IN NORTHWESTERN INDIA

# One

*Every station had separate dining-rooms for Hindus, Muslims, and for Europeans . . . Many towns had separate stations, one for the Indian town, and one for the European . . . cantonment . . . Indians who did attempt to travel first class often found themselves in the humiliating position of being thrown out of the compartment, either by brute force or by the stationmaster.*

—E. M. Collingham, *Imperial Bodies*, 2001

*A* cold moon washed the skies as the single, black caterpillar line of the night train to Rudrakot cleaved through the Sukh desert. The train's headlamp, fiercely ablaze like Shiva's third eye, illuminated the way across the glistening steel tracks—a triangle of golden light amidst this background of silver and shadows.

It was not the only thing that moved in the desert night. Vipers and kraits coiled out of their daytime stupor and went in search of the rats and mice that burrowed into the hard ground; the fox slunk with equal stealth in search of the same prey, and far enough from the train, stayed to watch as it crossed his field of vision.

The supernatural too was alive at night in the Sukh, claimed to be real, and believed to be impossible. The Sukh was the birthplace and, now, the death place of kings and warriors. Despite its inhospitality, its unwillingness to nurture, to welcome them on its soil and sands, these kings and warriors had lived here through generations and centuries. Their tombs (the memories of their demise anyway—the Sukh kings were Hindus and so were cremated) dotted the vast landscape, wedded into the rust colors of the desert. Some small, some mammoth, invariably constructed of red or caramel sandstone. Stories were built upon these tombs, of little snatches of lovelorn songs, of figures clad in the white of ghosts, or of the tempest of a thousand horse hooves near the tomb of a valiant raja felled in battle.

The fox waited patiently for the passing of the lighted carriages of the train before crossing the tracks. After its sound receded into the distance and night came to claim the desert again, his ears angled toward the noise of tiny feet scrambling in the dark, and he whisked away toward it, hungry and slavering.

From the train's vantage, of course, there was nothing much to be seen. Most of the carriages had their shutters down, but one, the fourth bogie behind the steam engine, had one of the shutters open, and a man leaned his head against the bars of the window.

Of the three occupants in the bogie, Sam was the only one not yet asleep. A cloth sling lay tight against his right shoulder, cradling his arm into his chest, but the pain had flared up again, mocking the aspirin's efficacy. If he stayed very still, difficult to do so in a moving train, the pain dulled into something manageable. It had been only two days since the military hospital doctor in Calcutta had reset his dislocated shoulder and promised Sam relief almost immediately, but Sam had been so long with his arm out of the shoulder socket that relief did not come easily. He concentrated on the telegraph poles whipping past in a rhythmic tempo, *whoosh*, silence, *whoosh* . . . forever, the sounds and silences born of the train-sired wind. The telegraph poles stuck close to the tracks, as though afraid of striding out on their own into that hugely flat earth.

Sam willed sleep to come and erase the fatigue of his body. He had boarded the train to Rudrakot at Palampore early this morning, had spent the previous night bumping along a dusty dirt track in a jeep from Delhi to Palampore, and before that had flown on a military transport plane from Calcutta, westward to Delhi. He had not slept in more than two days. The plane to Delhi had had no luxuries—Sam was strapped into the sides of its cavernous belly, buffeted by the winds, kept from being thrown about and smashing his shoulder further only by the belt that held him. During the drive to Palampore in the ancient, barely running jeep, the driver had considered every pothole in the road a personal challenge, and Sam had not dared close his eyes, afraid that he would wake with his head wrenched off his neck and settled in his lap. Since boarding the Rudrakot train, he had stared at his traveling companions wide-eyed and had fended off Mrs. Stanton's overly invasive questions as best he could without being too impolite.

Rudrakot was not an entire twenty-four-hour journey from Palampore, if the train began on time at one end and ended on time at the other, without reckless stops. And so Sam learned one of his first lessons about India during this long, sleepless day as the sun bleached the desert into a whiteness and sent its heated fingers into their compartment. The train stopped at *every* village on the way from Palampore to Rudrakot, every forty-five minutes or so. Just as it had begun to pick up speed from the last, unscheduled stop, it began to slow again, and Sam listened gloomily to the screeching of the brakes, the slowing of rhythm, and felt the growing heat in the compartment as the breeze dropped. The ceiling fans clanked obligingly, but they were really useless, and sleep was impossible.

But the night train to Rudrakot was the only way to get there; it was too far out into the desert to drive, too small a kingdom to have a commercial airfield, and the only regiments garrisoned there were army regiments, who brought in their men and supplies by rail.

With his eyes closed, Sam listened to the chug of the train, and a sudden, shattering, long and hollow hoot from the engine. He leaned out farther into the air, and let the wind push against his hair. The sweat from his day's journey had long dried. But dirt still rimmed his collar, perspiration stained half-cups of brown under the armpits of his khaki shirt, his skin was gritty with soot. Sam licked his cracked lips, and tasted the coal and smelled the fires from the engine up front. His shoulder throbbed again, and Sam clenched his hand into a fist, drawing the ache down to his palm and holding it there until it abated. Only a few more hours, he thought, and then he would be at Rudrakot. This dirt, this journey, this lack of sleep would be worth it. He could rest his shoulder then . . . but, no, he could not rest his shoulder then, he had only four days left of his leave at Rudrakot. And so much to accomplish.

His holdall lay under his seat, and Sam nudged it lightly with his heel, wanting to be reassured of its presence. There was a map of Rudrakot in that holdall, a map Sam had seared in his mind. The town itself, curved around the edges of the lake. The army regiment quarters in a shaded cantonment avenue. The mighty fort built into the hill behind, looming over the town, melding into the browns and reds of this forsaken earth. The lake in brilliant blue, like a wedge of sky, its waters winking in the sunshine. Beyond the lake, across from a colossal stretch of nothingness, a large tomb of pillars and stones called simply Chetak on the map, and then beyond that, the march of sands westward into an expanse of desolation. And here, somewhere in this desert kingdom, his brother, Mike, had gone missing.

Their mother had once said begin your search at the beginning, where you first remember losing what is lost. So Sam was going to Rudrakot. Maude's advice had come to him at an earlier time—when he was in boyhood tears at having misplaced his precious baseball cap—and had served him well just a few years later at the cabin.

Mike and he had clattered down the stairs to the beach to watch the birth of a winter storm. Clouds banked over the cove; the wind whipped the waters into frothy waves that grew to mountains midway, ebbed, then expired along the sand. There was a curious and exhilarating blue quality to the light around them, as though crystals of ice hung in the air. Seaweed glistened on brightly white driftwood. Gulls soared and hummed above, wings aspread. Mike, seven at that time, trotted away along the edge of the water, clambering over the logs of wood, and Sam followed him as fast as he could. He had been distracted and overwhelmed by this fury of nature, and yet heedful, in some part of his head, that he had to keep an eye on his younger brother. Lightning forked along the thickly gray sky and Sam waited, listening for thunder. It came, booming and loud, setting the earth shaking.

"Listen to that, Mike!" Sam had yelled, opening his arms wide to embrace the storm. "The skies are hungry. Listen!"

He looked toward his left and did not see Mike anywhere. The clouds had completely covered the north entrance to the cove by now, dulled the light, brought night where day was, and Sam strained to find his brother.

The tips of Sam's fingers began to freeze and he put his hands under his armpits.

"Mike!" he shouted. "We should go in. Mama will worry."

But nothing moved on the logs deposited haphazardly on the beach by previous tides, forming castles and goblins in the dying light. Sam clam bered up a rock, zipped closed the front of his jacket, and searched around him. Where was Mike? He had been here, near the log pile they had named Buckingham Palace, and then here, near the Eiffel Tower, and there, and then where?

"Mike, this is not funny. Come back now."

Lightning crawled over the skies again, and Sam put his hands around his mouth. MIKE. MIKE. MIKE-Y. Until he was hoarse and panting. The sea roared in anger, crashing in huge sprays around him. His heart banged in his chest and a sudden chill ate away at his bones.

"Mike," Sam whispered. "Where are you?"

And then a cold hand touched his leg. Sam whirled around.

"Ha!" Mike shouted, pushing a stick of bleached driftwood at him. "Got ya."

Sam slithered down from the rock, scraping his ankles and shins, and grabbed the front of Mike's sweater. "Don't ever do that again. *Never*. Do you hear?"

On the night train to Rudrakot, Sam remembered the dread that had ensnared him when he thought he had lost Mike, for what had seemed like an eternity, each moment as lucid today as it had been that day. And here, in another continent, another time, now when they were both grown men sent to India to engage in a mighty war, Mike was lost again, this time through no artifice of his own. And no amount of shouting would bring him back. Sam would not let himself think that he could not find Mike, and that was why he was on his way to the desert kingdom Rudrakot, to search for his brother again. To the place where he was first lost. To the beginning.

An arrow of heat plunged downward from Sam's shoulder into his arm and he jerked back from the compartment window and fell heavily onto the bunk on his left side, crying out from the sudden pain. Whiteness filled his gaze, his ears roared, and Sam clutched at his shoulder.

"Captain Hawthorne!"

Sam gasped. "Yes, Mrs. Stanton." And then in a more resigned tone, he said, "I apologize, a sudden pain."

"Your shoulder hurts?" she asked, her tone sleep softened from its daytime raucousness.

"Yes," he replied, surprised. She was being solicitous? Why? He had been nothing but rude to her, well, barely civil anyway.

"Well." She clicked her tongue. "It's the war. War hurts, Captain Hawthorne."

Ah, Sam thought, righting himself on his bunk, there was never a truer statement, and it was astonishing that she of all people had considered it.

Adelaide Stanton had a flowered cloth cap tied to her head, to keep her curls in perfect order overnight, yet little wisps of graying hair pulled out from under it. Her printed cotton nightgown was the most decorous Sam had seen; the tightly buttoned collar rode up her thin neck, the folds of cloth diffused tentlike over her body. He had been bestowed with the tiniest flash of skin around her ankles when she whipped her feet onto the bunk and settled her blanket over herself.

"Would you mind shutting the window? The noise of the wind disturbs me greatly."

"Of course, Mrs. Stanton." Sam pulled the shutter down. The air in their compartment stilled. Sam put his nose to the slats of the shutter and heard the soft whistle of the breeze outside. He breathed deeply, drawing the air into his lungs, closing his eyes as it lifted the hair sloping over his forehead and cooled that first effect of closeness. A minute later, Sam rose to switch off the lights, and the blue-tinted globe of the night-light came on.

On the bunk above Mrs. Stanton, his back straight even in sleep, the black of his coat still uncreased, was the Indian gentleman. He slept in his clothes, unlike Adelaide Stanton, who had changed in the adjoining bathroom. He wore a white *churidar*, tight about his shins, a fitted black coat with a mandarin collar, a gold watch on his right wrist, and leather sandals that were now under the bunk. He had not moved in four hours; he did not even seem to breathe, his form as rigid in sleep as it had been when he was awake.

Early that morning, at Palampore, Sam had been the first inside the bogie, desperate for the quiet of a bunk where he could lie down.

He had pulled himself upright when the Indian gentleman paused at the doorway. The Indian though was so diffident, he almost melted back into the corridor again upon seeing Sam. His demeanor seemed retiring, but nothing about his clothing or his person was—his *sherwani* coat was made of a fine and thick black silk, exquisitely tailored; his hair was cut well, his nails manicured. After a moment, he came into the compartment and nodded, his expression watchful. They said good morning to each other, and Sam added, "How are you?"

"Well, well, thank you," the man said. "My seat is here." His voice was firm, yet with an underlying hint of a quaver, backed by defiance.

"I'm not in your seat, am I?"

"No, no. This," he said, pointing to the bunk opposite, and the seat near the door, "is mine. Thank you."

And then Mrs. Stanton appeared. She hesitated at the doorway, ticket in a sweating lilac-gloved hand, three coolies behind her sporting a variety of baggage.

"I'm sorry," Mrs. Stanton said, "but I believe you have my seat."

She was looking toward the Indian, who jumped up from his seat and reached into the breast pocket of his long, black coat. She was not actually looking *at* the man, not meeting his eyes, that is, but placing her gaze at the first button of his coat, just below his well-trimmed beard.

"I do not think so, madam," he said with an abbreviated bow, not proffering his ticket to her though. "Everything is quite correct here."

Mrs. Stanton's face congealed into a grimace. She was at that indeterminate age that some women achieved once they reached forty, not really aging more until they were seventy, when what little freshness youth provided had long gone, when ideas and prejudices were firmly settled. She had not even glanced at Sam, though perhaps from the corner of her eye, and registered, somehow, that Sam was not Indian. But he looked Indian to a casual, uneducated glance, for now at least, his skin charred by the Burma sun he had trudged under for weeks, his hair a glossy black, his eyes a deepening blue. The color of his eyes was misleading, for Indians too had blue eyes, or green or hazel, an unfortunate legacy of indulgence and lack of self-control on the part of Mrs. Stanton's countrymen. Yet she somehow knew. Something in the way Sam sat, in his manner, proclaimed him not Indian. Mrs. Stanton had no casual, uneducated eye in India. She *knew*.

"The native carriages are at the back of the train," she said. "Please find your way there. This is my seat. There can be no possibility of a mistake here."

The British conductor hovering behind Mrs. Stanton's vast figure, with a "May I?" edged through the narrow doorway to look at the Indian's ticket.

"It's quite all right, Mrs. Stanton," he had said, and cleared his throat in that uncomfortable silence. He held the little pink rectangle of cardboard between the tips of his fingers, and Sam saw the name MOHAMMAD ABDULLAH stamped on it, along with FIRST CLASS, BOGIE 4.

It would have been quite all right if the matter had stopped there.

"I'm sure," Mrs. Stanton said, the pale yellow feather in her purple hat quivering with the movement of her head, "this gentleman has been issued the right ticket. But this is not his place. Surely you realize that?"

"You are welcome to sit beside me, madam," Mr. Abdullah said. "But I have bought, and paid, for this ticket. There is no possibility of a mistake here." He echoed Mrs. Stanton's words, but his voice was so bland, his expression so unmarked that Sam saw the underlying sarcasm only in a little smile that touched his lips within his neat, graying beard.

Mrs. Stanton seemed to grow until she filled the doorway with her obstinate presence. And when she spoke, she did not look at the man, but at the conductor. "I cannot be asked to sit in the same compartment as this man. There must be another seat in this bogie."

Her words roused a flurry of worry in the poor conductor, who mopped his brow, and cleared his throat even more. Sam, still seated near the window, had not said a word. He had merely watched the three of them, frozen in a tableau of stubbornness—Mr. Abdullah, unyielding to all influence; Mrs. Stanton, equally shut from everything, but simmering in anger, her breathing harsh; and the conductor, sighing and repeatedly patting the pocket where his handkerchief reposed. The conductor had taken Mr. Abdullah out into the corridor and Sam heard him talking, entreating, pleading. At first, his voice was persuasive, and then raised and threatening, but Mr. Abdullah's voice was always tranquil in response. "This is my seat," he had said. "She is welcome to go elsewhere." The train had waited, because Mrs. Stanton insisted that it would not leave Palampore until Mr. Abdullah left her compartment.

The tags on Mrs. Stanton's bags read CALCUTTA-PALAMPORE-RUDRAKOT. On the Calcutta to Palampore train, Mrs. Stanton had sat uncomplaining with Mr. Abdullah. But there she was unknown, just anybody. On the Rudrakot train, she was someone of consequence. She knew the conductor well; he got his little packet of Christmas biscuits and an envelope of rupees from her as baksheesh. He was under her patronage. She could hold up the train if she so wanted. This was *her* train—the train of those like her who owned and ran Rudrakot.

Sam leaned forward to rest his elbows on his thighs and stared fixedly at the floor of the compartment. A little crowd of coolies had grown outside on the platform, along with some pointing of fingers and some asking of questions in Hindustani and Urdu, and Sam could understand only bits of that. What a bloody memsahib she was, he thought. *The* memsahib of the British Raj, so typical, so true to what she had to be—imperious, disdainful, blind to any color of skin but hers, fearful even behind that mask of rudeness. He also experienced a well of irritation at Mr. Abdullah, with his quiet voice, his gentle insistence, his *expectation* of such behavior. Sam would have wrung Mrs. Stanton's skinny neck by now. His shoulder throbbed.

Mr. Abdullah and Mrs. Stanton had fallen silent, each inflexible, until the train blasted its horn and pulled out of the station after thirty minutes. All the immense built-up drama deflated into futility, because Mrs. Stanton's influence over the night train to Rudrakot from Palampore could bear the weight of only half an hour. For anything beyond that, she would have to be someone and something greater in the British Raj.

She sat then, finally, her bags and hatboxes littered under the bunks, her knitting by her side, and the train moved into its measure without a word spoken in the carriage. And this was Sam's introduction to the India he had not yet seen for himself because, though he had been in the subcontinent since February, all his time thus far had been spent in Burma dealing with the Japanese invasion. With his own attention caught by the war, the Indian nationalist struggle for independence from the British had only briefly imprinted itself upon his consciousness. Ten or fifteen years ago, the Rudrakot train would have stayed at Palampore at Mrs. Stanton's command and Mr. Abdullah would have been forcibly removed to the back. Much had changed since then—the world war, the insistence on a free and independent India—and so, in 1942, Indians often traveled (when they could afford it) in first-class carriages, some journeys conducted, as this one promised to be, in total silence.

The day passed, slowly, with the stops along the track, the white heat of the sun, the blessed death of it by evening, the coming of the night. Sam and Mrs. Stanton went to dinner together, beckoned by the call of the bogie *chai* boy, who popped his head deferentially into their compartment and said, "Dinner is served, Sahib," to Sam, and then added, "Memsahib," to Mrs. Stanton. Mr. Abdullah, the boy ignored, knowing he would have his own food with him, that he had permission to occupy their compartment, but not to sit at the table in the dining carriage. Progress had stepped, gingerly, into their compartment, but did not yet dare step over the threshold into other parts of the train. Sam and Mrs. Stanton sat across from each other, for such as it was, they knew only each other, and he learned that the best way to keep her from asking questions was to ask them of her. He knew precious little about her by the end of dinner, because he had not listened to her answers.

They returned from the dining carriage at nine o'clock to the aroma of curry and spices. Mr. Abdullah was just stacking the layers of the round steel vessels of his tiffin carrier, which had been filled in the waiting rooms at Palampore with rice, *chapattis,* and chicken curry, and from which he had surreptitiously nibbled throughout the day. She wrinkled her nose, but Mr. Abdullah did not seem to see it. He was scrupulously polite and climbed up on his berth, turned on his side, and went to sleep.

When Mrs. Stanton had also closed her eyes, Sam took out his map of Rudrakot and traced all its possessions with his finger. The cantonment area. The native town. The lake. Chetak's tomb. He had four days of leave before he had to return to his regiment. Would it be enough to find his brother? It had to be. Any alternative answer to that question was too terrible to consider. So it was love for Mike and for his mother that drove Sam Hawthorne to Rudrakot.

What he did not know then was that love, of another kind, fulfilling and cherished, would bring him back here, and would eventually occupy his life. Would give him Olivia.


As the train cut through the night toward Rudrakot, Mila sprawled on her stomach, her face flattened against the pillows. Every now and then, she twitched and her eyelids fluttered, her sleep sprayed with dreams she could not stop. Somewhere, a conscious part of her watched the pictures in her mind and told her it was only a dream, that it meant nothing. There was the mocking face of the madam of the Lal Bazaar, Leelabai, her appraising eyes, her too-knowing gaze upon Mila.

*She* is going to teach us, an Indian girl? Teach us what? Girls are good for only one thing, Missionary Sahib, you should know that. Or perhaps not, your God does not allow you the normal pleasures of a man. What a cruel God you have.

Leelabai was soft and dumpy, dimpled at her elbows, with skin pale as ripening wheat, her hair balding at the part on the crown of her head. Her guttural voice was fed by the harsh smoke of the *hookah* she smoked incessantly. Mila had almost departed then in disgust, but Father Manning had put a gentle hand at her elbow and said softly, "Look at the women. And then leave if you want to."

So she lifted her eyes for the first time to the women—some only girls with childhoods barely brushed out of their expressions. They were all caricatures of any real women Mila had known, caricatures of herself even, their faces powdered white, quarter-inch-thick *kohl* lining their eyes, its curves elongated to their hairlines, mouths red with *paan*, beauty marks to ward off the evil eye painted on a chin here, a cheek there.

Mila woke shaking, exhausted, her breathing ragged, with a sudden sting of tears behind her eyes, the images of her dream hanging before her. She had not known that such places existed until Father Manning had taken her there, and once she had visited the Lal Bazaar, she was not able to stay away. So Mila went twice a week, listened to the women's shrill laughter and to their bawdy jokes, heard the hurt lodged somewhere deep within them that they could not be her, privileged and clean—that they had never been able to be her, and would never be her now, for they were fallen women.

She sat up on the bed and put her feet on the cool mosaic floor. The previous day's heat had lost its edge, but only a little, enough to transmute into a deceiving semblance of coolness. Though the fan whirred overhead, Mila had woken in a sweat, her skin damp on the undersides of her breasts and the nape of her neck under her hair. The outside *khus* mats covering the windows of her bedroom had been drawn up by a servant and the sky beyond was saturated with the beryl blues of predawn. Mila had lived in Rudrakot for most of her life, and yet had never tired of the tranquility of this time of day, or been overwhelmed by the waiting vastness of the desert outside that would receive her. She had once been awed by its immensity, when she was a child. Around Rudrakot, the Sukh was a desert not of sands, but a hard, pounded ground of dirt stretching out for miles. Trees and scrub dotted its arid countenance where they could find hold, but they were so sparse, so thirst ridden, their leaves and branches grew into a spinelike hardiness. But there were ways to survive in the Sukh, shelter to be found in the shade of the little hills and hillocks formed of its slowly eroding surface, water to be tapped if one only knew where to look, journeys to be made with a surefootedness led by the sun during the day and the canopy of stars at night.

And in the view from Mila's bedroom window, well into the horizon, one small hill was adorned with a hundred-year-old tomb. It housed a massive, square sarcophagus, ten feet by ten feet, large enough to provide that eternal rest for five humans lying side by side. The tomb was called Chetak, after its occupant, so beloved in life that, in death, he warranted this magnificent creation of stone. The enormous sarcophagus covered the remains of an enormous body. Not human. Chetak was a horse, of the four-legged kind.

The fright from the dream had melted away, and Mila titled her head to listen for sounds within the house. She had woken at this time—the cusp of night and day—ever since she was seven years old because this was what her mother, Lakshmi, used to do for Mila's father, Raman.

Lakshmi had always opened her eyes before Raman, reached down the bed to touch his feet lightly in the darkness, as a wife was taught to do, asking for a daily blessing from the man who was her master. After Lakshmi died, Mila would awaken to listen for her father's rising and his going down the stairs to the well for his prayers. Mila did not have to sweep the courtyard, wash it down, draw the rice flour *kolam* to welcome visitors at the front door; there were enough servants in the house to do this. But the rules of engagement between men and women were laid out such that Mila had felt, without ever being told so, that a woman in the house had to rise before the men. In the early years, when she was merely seven years old, she would knock softly on her father's door with a, "Papa, it is time to get up," her limbs loose with sleep, her long hair tangled in knots, her short petticoat (which she wore under her frocks) crumpled. Raman would carry his child back to her bed, his heart touched by this devotion, and Mila would be asleep again before he put her down. He scolded her so much Mila understood that she did not need to waken before her father— it was a wife's place, not a daughter's, or at least not a child's responsibility. But this did not stop her from getting up before he did, though now she stayed in her room, waiting to hear his footsteps pass her door.

This morning the top floor of the house was quiet. One of her brothers, Kiran, snored delicately from the room on her right. Ashok, younger than she, the youngest of them all, was a room away on her left, and he would not have been merciful to Kiran had he known of the snoring. Ashok would have stomped around the house trumpeting like an elephant—but he was only sixteen, and so young enough to find this sort of thing terribly amusing.

Mila brushed her teeth in the bathroom without glancing into the mirror above the porcelain sink. The toothpaste was chalky and bitter, made of the *neem* tree's fruit and leaves. It reminded her of the time she had tasted the walls of the corridor outside her room just after they had been brushed with a wash of slaked lime. Mila had felt an irresistible urge to lay her tongue against the dripping whitewash to see if it tasted as good as it smelled. She had placed her fingertips on the wall for support, leaned inward, and touched the tip of her tongue on the gritty coating as her nose was crushed against the surface. The taste was abominable, and Mila had backed away hurriedly, swallowing that stinging flavor, wiping her fingers on her frock, just as Kiran climbed up the stairs. He said nothing, just grinned, dabbed at her white nose, and made sounds of retching.

When she came out of the bathroom, she paused by the photographs on the wall between the windows that fronted the balcony. Jai, ruler of Rudrakot, was in each of them, glorious in his royal finery. Rudrakot was now a princely state in British India, and Jai's title, inherited as it was, had little meaning other than to bestow pomp and circumstance upon him. But this minor inconvenience had never stopped him from considering privilege to be his birthright. In one photograph, he was on his beloved horse, Fitzgerald, saddle and boots indistinguishable from the horse's ebony coat, Jai in his ICC uniform of salt white jacket, white turban, all rimmed in light blue and gold braid. In another, Jai was with Lord Wellesley, governor of the Bombay presidency, and was turned away from the governor just a little, head up, chin ferocious, arrogant as usual. In the third, Jai had been captured during one of his famed White Durbars, held on the night of *purnima*—the full moon—more shadows than light on his thin, sharply planed face.

Mila touched this last photograph lightly, the glass cool under her fingertips. Jai had been away at the Imperial Cadet Corps for sixty-two days, and by her counting, it would be at least another month before he returned. He had written her eight letters so far, which she had read with a deep sense of happiness, for in them, he had been candid, open, passionate—attributes difficult to posses when they came face-to-face because of

an inbuilt shyness in both. As Mila stood by Jai's photograph, she heard
the first splash of the brass pot into the well. She went out into the balcony
and leaned over the edge.

The sky above her lightened, skewered with skeins of tangerine, but
the backyard, thick with the arms of the banyan tree, still held the ebony
of the night. And there, amidst that gloom, Mila saw the gleam of the
well's whitewashed wall and heard Raman's voice, soothing and mellow in
praise of God.

Mila bent down until her chin rested on the concrete parapet. She
would pray with Papa, she thought, but she could not concentrate. A tu-
mult of sound crept into her consciousness—the crows cawed, the *koyal*
cooed maddeningly, water splashed from the well, the soft, morning
voices of the servants rose behind the house. The racket never seemed to
bother her father; his focus was complete in the midst of chaos. In the distance, she heard the short and sharp hoots of the night train to Rudrakot.
Still balanced on just her toes and chin, her body bent at the waist, she
watched the steam from the engine dissolve as a tiny slice of the sun
brightened the horizon just beyond Chetak's tomb.

This train would bring Jai home to his kingdom of Rudrakot, though
when, Mila did not know. Jai was never very specific with time; he did not
have to be because, as in everything else, time adjusted itself around him.
Jai would travel, of course, *with* the train, not *on* the train, his own bogie
shunted to the back. He would merely use the engine to pull him to
Rudrakot, but would endure none of the discomforts of travel. Jai's bogie
had hushed custard apple carpets, Louis XV sofas and giltwood chairs,
teak and brass appointments, a gold-plated sink in the mirrored bathroom.
Even, at one end, his own kitchen and bar. His own palace-uniform-clad
servants, in white turbans and coats with silver-braided sashes. Gaslight-
shaped lamps that picked diamonds out of shimmering cut-glass de-
canters. Mila had traveled in Jai's bogie only once, with Papa and her
brothers many years ago, and she had been astounded by how easily Jai fit
into his surroundings, lounging casually on the French damask of the
sofa, barely distressed as his wine sponged into that precious fabric when
the train braked. The conductor and driver had come later to apologize for
the train's shudders, with promises to never let that happen again.

Mila listened to the *chug-chug* of the train, and wondered who came to
Rudrakot today, traveling in a much more common way. She lifted her el-

bows from the balcony's ledge and straightened her back. It did not matter. This night train to Rudrakot would bring them no visitors. Nothing would ruffle the calm of their lives, nothing would break the routine . . . until Jai came back home.

Sam woke as the train pulled into Rudrakot at the first shine of dawn. Of the birth of the sun over the flat edge of the earth he saw nothing, for his window looked out toward the cavernous platform. He raised the shutter as the brakes squealed on the tracks. Both Mrs. Stanton and Mr. Abdullah were already awake. The Indian was seated cross-legged on his bunk, hunched against the curved roof of the compartment, his head dangerously close to the fans. She was dressed and finished in a white voile dress printed with lilacs, dog-skin gloves on her hands, her curls coaxed back into place on her skull, her bags packed, the nightgown stuffed in with her knitting.

There were little boys and old, wizened men along the edges of the platform, staring solemnly as the train trundled by. They all had their hands raised into the air, fingers splayed in the Churchillian V. Their stances were overcasual, free arms looped about each other's waists, weights depending upon one foot so their hips stuck out. It was an odd gesture, one Sam had witnessed at other train stations during this journey, but never up this close. He began to laugh, and the weight of the last few weeks lifted.

The men and boys had their palms facing *inward*, not outward, with two fingers, the middle and the index, up in the air. If one of them tucked his index finger out of sight, it would mean something else altogether. Surely, Sam thought, filled with delight, it was a mistake. Or was it? Would the vast, uneducated Indian masses, with their unwashed faces and their ragged clothes, show the finger to the first-class compartments normally occupied only by the British?

The platform crackled with a sudden life. Coolies lined up where the bogie doors were to stop, one after another, four or five deep, their turbans and short coats a brilliant red, white *dhotis* wrapped around their waists and tucked between their legs. Even in the gathering heat of the morning, steam blew from the cauldrons of *chai* makers, wafting the aroma of cinnamon that made Sam think suddenly and yearningly of his mother's pumpkin pie. Men and women who had slept through the night in neat rows along the platform, in anticipation of the train, sat up on their haunches to watch it unload its bellyful of passengers. Vendors shouted out their wares, hoping for a hungry passenger who could not wait until he reached his home in Rudrakot. There were crisp golden *samosas* and persimmon-colored *jalebis* wrapped in newspaper, and toted in wicker baskets aswarm with flies. Water bearers carried earthenware pots atop their heads—Hindu bearers for Hindu water, and Muslim bearers for Muslim water—covered with steel plates, long-handled cups hooked on the side. To the India-uninitiated, this raw, unboiled water was a silent invitation to cholera and dysentery.

Mrs. Stanton leaned out of her window and pointed at a coolie. "You! *Andhar aao. Jaldi!* Now!" and he obligingly fought his way into the carriage to their compartment and began to pile her luggage onto his head, his shoulders, slung on his arms, settled on his thighs, wherever he could find a place so he did not have to share his burden and thus his fee. She made him drop all the bags on the platform outside the bogie, around her feet.

Sam waited until Mr. Abdullah had also left, then pulled out his holdall and tried to hoist it onto his good shoulder. He almost collapsed with its weight, so he settled for dragging it behind him down onto the platform. Here and there, uniformed officers from the Rudrakot regiments, both Indian and British, turned to glance at him with a mild curiosity, but no one approached him. Mrs. Stanton still waited in front of the bogie, glancing at the watch on her wrist. There was clearly no one to meet her, and she had expected someone. Sam almost offered his services and then stopped himself. He would be damned if he would help this hellish woman. The crowds milled around her in a tightening circle; the coolie sat by, spitting out *paan* near her feet, a few bright red spots sprinkling on her lilac shoes; people fell against her as though by accident, knocked her bags about; and still no one came to receive Mrs. Stanton. She began to droop.

A bevy of little boys appeared from nowhere to surround Sam. "Sahib, baksheesh!" "Please, Sahib, some baksheesh." "You like dance, I do dance." And then an incongruous flailing of arms and legs was followed by "Hip, hip, hurrah" in strident voices. They pawed at him; he fought them off as well as he could, then reached into his shirt pocket for a bunch of coins, which he gave them, one by one, placing each *anna* coin in an upturned, blackened little palm. They all looked the same to him, bright-eyed, sweet-faced creatures, with a great deal of cunning and slyness all at once. With the money tucked into their torn shorts and shirts, the boys melted away to go bother someone else. But one boy gave Sam a solemn look and shook his head when he proffered the coin.

"No, Sahib," he said, and then ran along the platform and behind a newsstand.

Sam instinctively followed him, hauling his bag. When he got there, the boy, not more than eight perhaps, was standing with his back against the wall, his hands looped behind. He smiled at Sam, looked down at the hand holding the *anna* coin, and said nothing.

"Take it," Sam said.

"You American, Sahib?"

"Yes. Take it. Go feed your family with it." He did not have the energy to care what they did with the money he gave out, but he still gave. It made him feel as if he was doing something; it appeased his conscience.

"Three *annas,* Sahib," the boy said. There was a grown-up look on his face, despite his vagabond appearance. He had not bathed in many days, clumps of filth matted his hair, his face was patterned with dirt, and his teeth were yellow and rotting.

"Three *annas?*" Sam grinned at the boy. He had some skill at negotiation despite having begged for the money. "Two," he said. "My final offer. Take it or leave it."

"I have sick sister, Sahib, please, Sahib."

Sam took out another coin and placed it next to the one in his hand. "Here."

"More for three *annas,* Sahib. Whatever you want. I touch, two *annas.* You touch, anywhere, three *annas.*"

Sam's stomach turned. Shit, he thought, oh, bloody shit. Why.

Just then, the birthing sun sent a shaft of sunshine ducking under the platform's roof and over Sam's shoulder to light up the child's face. The wall behind the boy was red-streaked with *paan* juice and tumultuous blossoms of urine that spat out a stench. Newspapers flapped on their racks, spilling out their surfeit of war news, so many killed, Burma fallen, deaths and destruction, a damnable party at some club in Calcutta, the music accompanied by the bawling of blackout sirens. The boy waited. Something, tiny, countless, moved in his dirty hair, lifting strands of it in the sunlight.

Sam recoiled and the boy's brown eyes flickered with fear, but he retained his smile. Long moments passed and Sam felt sweat pool within his palm, the coins clammy against his skin. Who in hell was he to stand in judgement on this boy? Men wanted this, they paid the boy well for it; he had it to offer . . . he had little else to offer. Perhaps he really had a sick sister at home. Perhaps his mother and his father did not know, or did not care where he was now. Perhaps he had no mother or father. Oh, shit.

Sam reached into his pocket and took out another coin. He set the three of them down on the ground in front of him, and then turned and walked away quickly. The boy whimpered, but Sam did not look back again.

Outside the platform, after having surrendered his ticket stub at the gate, Sam hired a rickshaw and dumped his holdall onto the seat. He was in a bazaar of some sort, foul, disorganized, with overflowing gutters on either side of the muddy tarred road, cows lounging in the center, whipping at flies with their long tails. Something nudged at his shoulder and Sam swung around rapidly, his left arm protecting his right. In front of him, at his very nose, was an enormous head with big, gentle eyes, long lashes, and a thick-lipped mouth that moved in gum-chewing fashion. The camel sniffed at Sam, blew its stinking breath into his face, and then righted itself to its full height. The camel driver, seated in the cart yoked to the beast's back, laughed. "He is curious, Sahib. He has not seen American sahib before, only British. Many British here."

So much for being invisible at Rudrakot, Sam thought with disgust. It was as though he was carrying a banner proclaiming that he was foreign, that he was American. How did everyone know even before he opened his mouth?

"The Victoria Club, Sahib?" the rickshaw puller asked.

"No, I'm not staying at the club."

An enormous and stately Daimler Double Six honked. Sam saw Mrs. Stanton, gracefully and joyously upright, in the backseat. A Union Jack fluttered on the bonnet. As the limousine went by, Mr. Abdullah raised his hand in salute to Sam from the front seat, next to the chauffeur. Sam stared at the squat backside of the brown car. The same car had come to pick them up? They knew each other, then. Why that performance on the train?

When he was climbing onto the rickshaw, a man came running out of the station, dragging the tearful boy behind him, the wet cutting twin rivers through the dirt on his face down to his chin.

"Sahib," the man shouted, *paan*-colored saliva staining one side of his mouth, as though he had been bloodied in a fight. "You don't like this one? He is stupid. Another one? Younger? Older? Or you want girl?" He cuffed the boy on the head; the boy ducked and cried out, trying to yank his thin arm away from the man's grip.

Sam whipped his head away and said to the rickshaw puller, "Take me to the political agent's house. *Jaldi.*"

# TWO

*. . . I had just returned from a ride and went into Father's study to greet*
*him . . . He had been talking to a wealthy landowner . . . [who] was very*
*old-fashioned and did not believe in freedom for women . . . "Is it neces-*
*sary," he asked, "to let an Indian girl behave in the uncouth manner of*
*the English? Why is she being educated according to foreign standards*
*and being given so much freedom? Do you intend to make her into a*
*lawyer like yourself?" . . . As I entered . . . Father asked me if I would*
*like to read law.*

—Vijaya Lakshmi Pandit, *The Scope of Happiness,* 1979

The door to Mila's room swung open while she stood in the balcony
and she knew who it was without turning—Pallavi, who had been
with their household since her mother and father had married. These past
ten minutes were usually the only fragments of time when Mila would find
herself alone during the day, when her thoughts were her own.

"Are you awake?" Pallavi said softly, bringing with her the fragrance
of a sweet morning chicory coffee. She peered around the Japanese screen
at the doorway and proffered the tray she held. "Come in, my dear. Coffee, omelet with cheese and chilies, two slices of toast, three curls of butter. Come, eat, you are a growing child."

Mila came from the balcony to stand at the doorway, one arm laid
along the cool brick wall. She rested her head against the door frame and
looked at Pallavi, half amused, half annoyed.

Pallavi held the tray well away from her waist, her nose slanted away from the aroma of the eggs. If Raman had allowed her to have her way, she would have had the cooks make *dosas* and chutney and *sambar* for breakfast, not eggs that could have been born into chicks and hens someday. But Raman had explained to Pallavi, many times and with a great deal of patience, that all of his children were to be fed as much eggs and meat as they wanted to eat, that it was healthy for them, that there was no room for argument here, that this was, in effect, an order. So Pallavi had rearranged the kitchens after Lakshmi died (this Raman allowed her, for she was family by then), banished the nonvegetarian cooks to another kitchen house that she inspected for grime every morning, bought special pots and *kadais* for their use, and tried to limit the plates and *katoris* into which the eggs and chicken curries were served. In this last she was not entirely successful, for the best china in the house was used at all the home parties, so she settled for scouring them herself, after they had already been washed by the servants. She put the tray down on the bed, beat the pillows, and set them up against the wall.

Mila plunged back into the bed, pulling up her sari around her thighs. The sheets were refreshing again, after having carried her warmth all night. It was finally and thankfully a little chill this morning. May in Rudrakot was the month of death by heat. Only the monsoons—if and when they came—would assuage Rudrakot's scorched heart. The Sukh desert was testament to the fact that the monsoon rains did not always bless Rudrakot—the ifs were as important to Rudrakot's residents as the whens of the temperamental rains. For there was no river that ran through the city, and the wells, tapped deep into the earth, were not always reliable, as the water table lay very low during the dry season. There was the lake, dug out of the clayey soil four centuries ago by a Rudrakot king, that served as a catchment for rainwater, which could sustain Rudrakot for perhaps three years of missed rains.

Pallavi placed the tray on Mila's knees and yanked at her sari to cover her legs. She then surveyed the clothes flung around the room and started a gentle, under-the-breath clucking. She kept her back toward Mila, firmly, but every now and then Mila saw her twist her mouth, or raise her eyebrows, or whistle busily through her teeth. All this as she picked up and folded Mila's chiffon sari, cast upon the chaise longue in undulating waves of sea green; shook out the crumpled petticoat; and stumbled over the heeled shoes lying upside down under the chaise. She shook her head vigorously at the shoes. Pallavi had her little superstitions and one of these was that shoes *had* to be stored upright or a scolding was in order from an elder. When she was a child, Mila had believed this superstition with all of her heart. One rare admonition from Raman, who never thought Mila could do wrong, sent her to her *almirah* in search of that errant shoe or slipper, sole side up, to be blamed for Papa's loss of temper and for her consequent tears.

Mila ignored Pallavi as she chopped her omelet into precise squares. But she was not oblivious to her morning mutterings, and an edgy skin of discontent descended upon Mila. She had been thus for two months now, easily irritated, not knowing why, not really wanting to be so. She burned her mouth when she sipped the coffee, and involuntary tears blurred her view of the tray with its *zari*-embroidered place mat and the gold-edged white porcelain plate.

"You are going riding this morning?" Pallavi asked, and Mila nodded in reply, not trusting her voice. They spoke to each other in a strange alloy of Hindi, Tamil, and English, strange only because there were no rules for such language. Over the years, Pallavi had picked up enough English to use it well, which did not mean that she always did. Pallavi could not read or write in any language, though she could now recognize some letters of the English alphabet and unerringly set out place cards at the home buffets. *White soup. Oysters en brochette. Braised chicken stuffed in the Mogul manner. Mutton cutlets. Ginger soufflé.* She could match these words with the dishes.

When she was in one of her frequent tempers—Pallavi's tolerance lay tight beneath her skin—she lapsed into a torrent of Tamil, and all the family scattered to the corners of the house until she had subsided. It did not matter to any of them that Pallavi was a mere servant in the house— she had been for many years now in the place of their mother.

Pallavi had come as a servant to Mila's mother almost thirty years ago, when Pallavi was eight, as part of Lakshmi's dowry, and had stayed on, not even returning to her parents' village for a holiday as time went by.

There had been talk though when Pallavi turned sixteen—the year Mila was born—of an alliance with a farmer in the village. Raman had read out the letters that Pallavi's father had hired the village scribe to pen, but in the end, it all fell to nothing. The boy married elsewhere, and

Pallavi's father did not again incur the expense of having the scribe write a letter for him.

"Don't you want to marry, Pallavi?" Raman had asked her the year Ashok was born, four years after Mila. "Do you not want your own children?"

"What will you do without me?" Pallavi had said. "Who will look after these three children who are so like mine already?"

This conversation was a couple of months after Lakshmi's death, for she never really recovered from giving birth to Ashok, gave in to an infection from the childbirth, and nothing anyone could do saved her life. When Raman finally began to return to the world, take up his duties, think about his household, he also had thought of how to deal with Pallavi living with them. It was considered incorrect to have a young woman at home without the blessing of the lady of the house. The gossips chattered. Raman had dismissed all of their sewer talk until he could no longer. To him it was incredible that anyone would dare to think such thoughts—Pallavi was so intrinsic to the fabric of his house, a little sister when she came to him, a friend to his wife, one who loved his children, now a mother, for they needed a mother. Raman would not marry again. He had no interest in a companion for himself, merely a mother for his children, and they had that in Pallavi. When he was very lonely, when he missed the smoothness of a woman's skin, when he yearned for a gentle touch, Sayyid brought him a woman from the neighboring village. She came in the dense of the night, stayed for a few hours, and left with some money. Raman knew her name, but not much else. He had a need; she fulfilled it. A name to call her by, when he wished to speak during such times, was enough. He did not think anyone else needed to know, so he told no one, and he made sure no one found out.

He did not encourage Pallavi, after that first tentative alliance, to think of a marriage; selfishly, yes, but also knowing that she was really happy with them. Now Kiran, Mila, and Ashok were all of an age to find their own homes, to make their own happiness in other places, and Pallavi would be equally welcome with any of them, or with him, Raman had thought when Lakshmi died. He *had* thought ahead to this time.

Pallavi knew all of this—in her there was no fear of being rendered useless by time or by circumstances. She did not have what were considered normal ambitions for a woman, if a woman could be said to harbor ambitions at all. She was content where she was.

"Eat your toast," she said to Mila, pointing to the edges scattered on the plate.

"I'm full," Mila said. "No more. You must think I'm a camel."

"You are too thin. What man would marry someone . . . ?" Pallavi paused then said, "Never mind. Eat your toast. Get dressed." She shook Mila's white shirt and jodhpurs at her.

Mila clambered out of bed, and started to unravel her cotton sari. She smiled at Pallavi's frown. "I know it is crumpled, dear Pallavi," she said. "But I slept in this sari; it will crumple, you know."

"Mine does not."

"That is because you sleep like a statue; where you lay your head down, a pit forms, for you press down on the pillows all night."

"And a lady must sleep thus, Mila. How many times have I told you this? You must lie straight, you must not move when you sleep, or move but lightly. A disturbed sleep speaks of a disturbed mind."

Mila shook her head and refused to answer. She pulled her sari away from her, untied her petticoat, unhooked the buttons of her blouse, and then held out her arms for the sleeves of her white shirt. As she dressed, a peculiar mixture of pride and disapproval grew on Pallavi's round face. Mila could almost see her thoughts written in the air above her well-oiled head. *So well these English clothes fit her. Makes her look almost like a boy. My Mila is daring and courageous, like a boy. Like a boy? Who wants to look like a boy? She should be wearing a sari. At least it is early, perhaps no one will see her. Raman should not let her go out like this, riding a horse.*

"What is the necessity to ride a horse when it is not necessary to go anywhere on it?" she asked, letting her thoughts spill into words.

"Because, my dearest Pallavi," Mila said, "it is what elegant people do. I'm going out to eat the air, to refresh myself, to ride with grace and dignity, to kick my heels into the waler and allow it to race on the *maidan*. More important, to see and be seen."

"I hope no one sees you like this," Pallavi grumbled, tucking Mila's shirt into the waistband of the jodhpurs. "Like a boy."

Mila skipped around the room, evading Pallavi's hands. "I can do this."

"Okay, okay," Pallavi said. "When you come back, you must sit with me while I go through the contents of the storeroom to see what we need from the *mandi*."

"Why?" This Mila asked merely for the sake of asking, for the sake of being contrary. Whether it was that she was tired from a lack of sleep, or just antagonized for no reason, she did not know. So she said again, "Why?"

"You have to learn, Mila. How can you be married without knowing how to run a house? If your mother were here, she would have taught you; now I will teach you." Pallavi's face grew heated.

"You know I will not need these skills," Mila said obstinately, lines gathering over her eyebrows. She wandered around the room picking up her gloves and her riding whip. "I will have plenty of servants."

"I know," Pallavi said somberly. "But you must know how to run a house, even if there will be others to take up your duties. The servants will cheat you, charge you more than the market price for the *dals* and the *atta*. What will you do then?"

Mila sat down in the chair by the door and pulled on her boots.

"Do that outside," Pallavi said. "Too much dust here."

But Mila continued to tuck her feet into her boots and yanked at the zipper, which slid through their silence with a hiss. "I have to go," Mila said. "Before it gets too hot outside."

They heard a flapping of wings and a gray-and-black crow, its avaricious eyes glinting in its head, came to settle upon the balcony ledge. It peered at them through the door and opened its mouth in a mammoth caw. Once. Twice.

"Look," Mila said, "that means we will have a visitor."

Pallavi ran to the door and waved her arms at the crow. "Shoo. Shoo."

The crow moved a few inches to its left, on its feet, and cawed again.

"*Shoo,*" Pallavi shouted at the crow and it flew away, protesting all the while.

"Three times it cawed," she muttered as she came in again. "That's not a good omen. We will have a visitor, but this is not good, Mila."

Mila smiled. "Oh, Pallavi, that's just a superstition, you know that."

A frown puckered Pallavi's brow. "You will see," she said, then she asked, "When is Jai coming back?" Their argument was still unfinished, but they also knew that it would continue sometime in the future. Thus their conversations always went, disapproval on Pallavi's side, stubbornness on Mila's, and unended thoughts on both sides, persisting forever, almost as if they needed something to talk about.

"I don't know," Mila said. "Ask Papa."

"Mila . . ." Pallavi's voice stopped her at the door. "Be careful when you go out. I don't like your being away from the house like this, without an escort, without your papa or one of your brothers. Be careful, don't talk with strange men."

Mila rubbed her face wearily with one hand. "I do not talk with *strange* men, Pallavi, only the ones we know."

Pallavi sighed and gathered the tray from the bed. "Come back and make your bed."

"You do it," Mila said as she left the room.

The household was well astir when Mila went downstairs to the front door, but there was no sound from her brothers' rooms. Ashok would wake later, in an hour. Kiran had rarely woken before noon since his return from England.

The waler, one of Jai's early gifts to her, was standing at the front door, gently snorting at the delay and shaking his head at the syce's attempts to hold him still. Sweat already glistened on his skin; later, when she had ridden him hard, they would both be drenched. He stood fourteen hands tall, terra-cotta brown with a well-tended gleaming coat, his mane and tail a shining black. The horse whinnied when he saw Mila and nudged at her closed fist. She opened her fingers and offered him the raw, in-shell peanuts and he swept them up with his rough tongue and then nuzzled in Mila's neck and blew little puffs of breath into her hair.

Mila climbed into the saddle and dug her heels into the horse's side.

"Let's go, Ghatoth," she said to the horse. The two syces mounted their own horses and followed her.

A long, unbroken tarred road linked two ends of Rudrakot's habitations, well away from the reaches of the railway station, and it was here, ten minutes after Mila had left the house, that one of the wheels of Sam's rickshaw deflated into a flat. The tire screamed over the heating tar and Sam tilted to one side along with the rickshaw.

The rickshaw puller jumped down from the cycle and, under the gaze of the wakening sun, pulled the conveyance to an edge of the dusty road.

"What now?" Sam asked tiredly, getting down also to view the damage. They were half a mile from one set of trees, and at least that distance from the shade at the other end, and there was nothing to be done but wait while the flat was repaired. Sam knew where he was headed, to the political agent's home, but for him that was as yet simply a name and a place; he would not know how to find the right house even if he set out along the road. He moved toward the west side of the rickshaw, sat down under the meager shade of its awning, and lit a cigarette. The rickshaw puller removed the vehicle's padded seat and reached in. Sam watched as he took out a tiffin carrier, a threadbare towel, a can of water, a collapsed pillow for afternoon naps, and a cloth pouch in which to keep his earnings. Below these treasures was the access to a wooden plank, which the man prized out, and underneath was a set of tools—an air pump, a large metal bowl, a bottle of filthy water, some lengths of thin rubber, a pair of scissors, and some glue.

The man deftly undid the tire from its rim and pulled out the rubber tube. He filled the tube with air from the pump and Sam could already hear the sibilant hissing of escaping air before the man poured water into a metal bowl and ran the length of the tube through it, piece by piece, until the water bubbled. Then, with his finger over the spot, he let the air out and with a rough stone began to shave at the rubber of the inner tube.

Sam leaned back against his holdall and contemplated his cigarette. It was quiet here this early in the morning, and deserted. The road ran through the middle of this relative wasteland with no trees to shade it, no mile markers to distinguish it, and yet it had to be the main artery that led from the station to the residential area. Sam had slept with his chin ensconced in his palm on the way here, and remembered little of what he had seen when he had been jolted awake every now and then. He threw his cigarette away, and it went spinning into the air and landed in the dirt. At that moment he heard the steady *clip-clop* of horses' hooves. Sam rose from the side of the rickshaw and came out into the road to look toward the farther bank of trees. Three riders broke from the greenery and came riding down the path. As they neared, Sam could see that the one in front was a woman, an Indian woman, and he experienced a twinge of pleasant surprise. He had not seen too many upper-class Indian women out and about without an escort, or with only two syces as companions. He realized it was a strange observation to make in India of all places, of course, but all of Sam's social encounters so far had been at the regimental messes, or at hotels in Calcutta—in other words, with the *British* constituents of the British Raj. There were plenty of Indians to be met in the cinema houses or in the bazaars, but they were not the type to be invited into the gymkhana clubs or the hotels, and of the few who could gain entry, Sam had not been introduced to any. He would have talked with Mr. Abdullah on the train, but Mrs. Stanton's onerous presence had dampened those efforts.

The woman had come closer by now. She rode well, her back upright, her gloved hands holding the reins loosely. Sam put a hand up to shade his eyes and squinted to see her better. There was a loveliness about her, an elegance he could not describe even to himself. Her skin was a lush and creamy brown, her shirt collar a lustrous white against her neck; the khaki of her pants and the gleaming roan of her horse's coat married into the background of the desert behind her. Even as she neared, Sam could not see much of her face, for it was shadowed by the wide brim of her *sola topi*. He wondered if she would talk with him; he wanted her to talk with him, so he raised his hand and said, "Good morning."

Her eyes fell to the reins in her hands and then she touched the rim of her *topi* with her whip and said, "Good morning," as she passed by. Sam listened to the lingering sound of her voice, low and sweet, and repeated her tone, with the emphasis on the first word, *good* morning. He had seen more of her by now, her eyes, her mouth, the slant of her chin, the muscles flexing her slender forearm. He moved to the middle of the road and watched her ride away in the direction he had come from and willed her to turn back, to turn around, to do something that would be more of an acknowledgment of him.

It was an interminably long time to Sam, but in actuality only a few seconds, before Mila reined in her horse and swung its head back toward Sam.

"Is there anything I can do to help?" she asked.

"I'm headed to the Civil Lines," Sam said, reaching out to grasp the horse's bridle. "Is this"—he pointed toward the trees from which Mila had emerged—"the right way?"

"Yes." She smiled then, for the first time, and a lone dimple deepened the skin of her cheek. Sam felt his heart stop and smiled back at her. He was no longer tired, his shoulder did not ache, he did not care that the temperature was steadily rising around them. He wanted to ask her if she lived within the Civil Lines and, if so, where, and if he could come to call on her.

She pointed to the rickshaw with her whip. "I see that the puncture is almost fixed. You should be within the trees and in the coolness soon. It isn't always this hot here, you know."

"You don't seem to feel the heat."

"Not very much," she replied. "I've grown up here in Rudrakot. The desert lies in my skin; I don't know that I could really live anywhere else." Color rose on her face as she spoke and she looked away from Sam, offering him a glimpse of her ear and her hairline. "You should be all right now."

"Is this all of Rudrakot?" Sam asked desperately, gesticulating around him to the trees and the desert.

She turned back. "What you see here, well, from the station to here, is merely the town of Rudrakot. The entire princely state takes its name from the town, the two are indistinguishable, but the state goes beyond here, into the sands of the Sukh." She pointed southeast, to the low-lying hills. "Those are the Panjari Mountains. Both the names are misnomers, optimistic misnomers." Mila laughed. "As is Rudrakot's own name."

"Tell me," Sam said.

Mila studied Sam's face, as if to decipher whether he was serious about wanting to know all of this. She was not used to talking with strangers— particularly a man—and had already engaged in a far longer and, to her, more intimate conversation than with any other person she had just encountered. "My brother Ashok would be thrilled to give you the history of Rudrakot. This might seem like an odd thing to say, but he is fascinated by America, and so would demand an equal rendition of your country's history from you in return."

"I will be glad to talk with Ashok anytime, but he's not here, you are," Sam said, greatly daring, not knowing if she would think him rude.

She lifted the edge of her *topi* so that it sat back on her head and Sam could see her more clearly. "The *panjari* is the bird's nest on a ship's main mast. It is said that one of Rudrakot's early kings trekked to the top of these hills, which only range about five thousand feet into the sky, and, overwhelmed by the cool, fresh air, named these the Panjari Mountains."

The mountains had begun to glow now with the golden touch of the sun, and though Sam was used to the mightier Cascade Mountains back home, to him this chain of hills in the distance looked enormous compared to the flat of the desert around him.

"And Rudrakot?" he asked.

"Rudrakot was originally Rudraksha-kot, named for the rudraksha tree."

"The seeds are used for rosaries," Sam said. "I've seen the *sadhus* wear them."

Mila looked fully upon Sam then. "You are unusual," she said. "I don't know many people visiting India who would have taken the trouble to be so observant."

Sam felt a flush of happiness and said, "The rudraksha tree represents the tears of Lord Shiva, and 'rudra' is Shiva's name, and 'aksha' means tears. Lord Shiva is said to have come out of a deep meditation, and upon opening his eyes, peace and happiness so overwhelmed him that tears ran down his face and fell upon the earth. At each place the tears drenched the ground, a rudraksha tree sprang up."

He watched surprise flood her face and said, "I should confess; I teach South Asian languages back home . . . especially Sanskrit."

"Are you visiting Rudrakot for long?" Mila asked. "My father would be absolutely delighted to meet you."

"Not very long," Sam said. "So why Rudrakot?"

"Many years ago, we claimed this as the origin of the kingdom—as the sacred ground upon which Lord Shiva had wept for joy. The name was then shortened to Rudrakot, now to mean the abode of Lord Shiva, not merely of his tears, even more ambitious than the original name, as you see. What had not mattered to the kings who named the land was that no rudraksha tree grew in or around Rudrakot. When we are questioned about the absence of the tree that gives the place its name, you will find us vacillating, with perhaps . . . at one time . . . maybe . . . or but, of course, there *was* a reason, now just lost in time and legend. The rudraksha tree grows only at the foothills of the Himalayas; the Sukh desert could never nurture it." Mila began to laugh. "Perhaps that is why Rudrakot shortened its name—the nonexistence of the tree is obvious; Shiva's presence at Rudrakot could not be suspect. For God only shows Himself to those who believe."

"Sahib," the rickshaw puller said behind them. "We can go."

Mila's laugh turned into a lower, more self-conscious sound. She bent down to pat her horse's neck and soothe him. For the past five minutes, as Mila and Sam had talked, Ghatoth had fallen into a steady restlessness, his shoes clicking on the tar road as he shifted his feet about.

"Thank you," Sam said. "I will remember this story forever." And the voice and the face of the storyteller, he thought to himself. If only he had more time in Rudrakot, he could find out who this woman was, he could . . .

He stood back and raised his hand again. "Good-bye."

She nodded and rode away.

Twenty minutes later, Sam reached the political agent's house and paid off the rickshaw driver. When he looked down at the ground, he realized that he was standing on an elaborate design—flowers and squares and hexagons, drawn upon the dark earth in rice flour; this was a welcome *kolam*. He lifted a foot and saw that the lines of the design had dissolved under his weight. Sam stepped carefully around and climbed the steps without smudging the design. It seemed a shame to destroy it, yet he knew that a smudged *kolam* was the sign of a house well-visited, a house where people came to ask after the owners' health, a house that was welcoming and open—it was almost obligatory for the visitor to step into the home with little grains of rice flour clinging to the soles of his feet, but Sam did not have the heart to disturb it so early in the morning.

At the top step, Sam was raising a hand to pound on the door when his shoulder began to throb. He dropped his holdall, letting it tumble down to settle in a fine mist of dust and rice flour, the *kolam* distorted beyond recognition, and leaned against the wood door, his eyes closed, his knock unfinished.

April 1942, a Month Earlier

*Somewhere in Burma*

*T*here has been no rain for an hour, but the teak forest stubbling the lower hills holds moisture in its dogged embrace. It is not monsoon season yet, or so the meteorologists declared in the report that Sam read in Assam. *The monsoon in Burma is southwesterly; rains blanket the country from May until October of every year. It sometimes rains every day, and every night, with no respite. September will bring relief—the rains shut down, like a faucet turned off.* A little, oft-overlooked footnote, which Sam did not miss, added: *A few showers are possible in April, but the months of December to April are definitely the dry season.*

Sam sprawls against the base of a tree, where he has thrown himself when they stopped. Twenty minutes pass and the three of them do not speak, and in the silence they harness their fleeing energies. Sam slouches into his chest, his chin touching the front of his shirt. He inhales and exhales with an effort, as though teaching himself to breathe again. His lungs draw in the damp air of the forest, the putrid stench of his mildewed socks, the stink of unwashed perspiration. His breathing then falls into such a quietness that bluebottle flies buzz busily around his face and eyes, enticed by the rankness of his skin. If he stays still long enough, they will lay their eggs into his skin, uncaring that he might still be alive.

A sharp cry breaks through the silence. A monkey perches almost upside down on the lower branch of the tree that shelters Sam, gazing at him with hard, bright eyes. Sam moves his right hand to his side and lifts the Winchester up and at the monkey, the butt of the rifle against his stomach. They gaze at each other for a few long minutes, until Sam deliberately curls his index finger around the trigger.

The monkey protests, swings up on the branches, chatters madly, and pelts a hard berry in Sam's direction before jumping onto another tree, then another, until he is gone.

"They are wicked," Marianne Westwood says, fatigue smudging the normally sharp edges of her voice. "It would have clawed your eyes out while you slept. I have seen a man mauled by a gang of monkeys near the village. They even ate parts of him."

"You're awake?" Sam turns to the woman leaning against a teak trunk on the other side of the all but blurred trail. He smiles at her through the dull green light of the forest. Above them, the sun has come to ride the skies again, but here the trees cram themselves into any space possible, depositing tiny and tender green saplings with a ferocity fed by the nurturing damp and warmth. Their branches meet on top, linking arms with each other, battling for a glimpse of the sun, and so the bottom of the forest is in perpetual shade.

Marianne nods. "I can't sleep."

"I hoped to frighten it away without you noticing," Sam says. "You would have wanted to keep it as a pet. And," he says, his tone lightening, "you've given me enough trouble already."

Her eyes come alive through the grime on her face. They are bright, like the monkey's, but hers are a blue washed into paleness by the hand of time. Marianne Westwood has labored under the Burmese sun for the last twenty-five years as a Baptist missionary in northeastern Burma where the Kachin live. She was married when she came here, but malarial fever took Joseph away during the first monsoon, and Marianne stayed on. She lived in a *basha* set atop teak posts at the edge of the Kachin village, made them construct a new *basha* for a church when the old one that Joseph had built disintegrated in the rains one year, learned their language, translated the word of God into their tongue. The Kachin children came to Marianne's Sunday school, listened to her exhortations to think of her god as their own, and called her prettily, in their lilting voices, "Marie-annne." The children, with their masses of glossy black hair chopped at their jawlines, their ready smiles, enchanted her. They also loved the chicken curry she made for them after Sunday school.

When Colonel Parsley sent word that the Japanese were in Burma, and that she should find her way to Myitkyina for a flight out to India, she decided to stay with her beloved Kachin.

"Just how many of them did you manage to convert?" Sam asks. He knows her history by now; they have been together for five days. He also knows of her stubbornness, her will—these he has read about in a report. When the Japanese came to Burma, Marianne Westwood, formerly of New Jersey, all but forgotten by any who knew her as a child, suddenly became a POI—a person of importance—for she was the only American missionary in Burma who would not leave. Her hair is cut short, shorter than Sam's, close-cropped to her head. It is almost all white too, a blaze of noncolor against skin brushed with a palette of browns over the years. She wears, incongruously, diamond earrings in her little and perfectly shaped ears.

"Not a one," she says with the smile of an imp, which sheds years from her face. "I'm a terrible failure. In that first year"—she looks down at her hands—"it seemed as though Joseph was going to have some success. They listened so politely, were so patient with us . . ." She turns to her right and gently shifts Ken's head from her shoulder, where he has been resting it in a pooling circle of sweat that is soaked into her shirt.

He jerks awake and sits up. "Sorry, did I fall asleep?"

"Every time we halt, you fall asleep," Sam says with a grin. "It must be a propensity of the idle—this ability to sleep at every stop."

"Don't tease the poor child, Captain Hawthorne," Marianne says as she rubs Ken's face with the back of her hand.

"The poor *child,* as you call him, flew his plane into a hillside and so he's here with us instead of back in Assam, drowning himself in beers with his buddies. It was a good thing I parachuted out first." Sam mock-glowers at Ken. "I should have left you by the crash site; my orders were only to bring Marianne out."

Both of them ignore Sam, and Marianne Westwood leans toward Ken and says in a gentle voice, "Does your leg hurt?"

"Only a little, Mrs. Westwood," Ken says, his voice aching and youthful, and at the same time with an edge of laughter directed at Sam. She bends over to check on the rancid bandages around Ken's foot and ankle. While she is thus engrossed, Sam swats in the air at Ken, and then sobers into silence as the boy winces at Marianne's touch. What lies under that bandage, Sam does not even want to think about. It has been five days since he last wrapped that foot; the dressings should have been changed every day, at least every day, if not every time they were drenched by the rains. But they are right now guardians of their very lives; a foot seems a little enough sacrifice.

Ken is not even supposed to be here with them. He piloted the plane that dropped Sam into the Burmese jungles in his mission to find and coax Marianne Westwood to safety. And just as Ken was lifting off above the trees, in a strange perversity of nature on an otherwise calm day, a massive wind buffeted the plane and plunged it into the hillside. Sam, watching that explosion of fire and heat, his heart crashing, sees a parachute struggle to open in the sky as Ken comes down. The forest mostly cushions his fall, shatters only his right ankle. The navigation officer in the plane is not so lucky. Sam drags his body from the crash debris and buries him in a shallow grave. He does not weep even as Marianne sings out a few prayers into the clean forest air, even though this is his first encounter with death in the war.

Another ten minutes, Sam thinks, before they have to move on. At the last supply drop, they had instructions to head to the Chindwin. By Sam's calculations, a hundred and fifty miles of mountains, bush, rivers, monsoon forest, and contingents of the Japanese army lie between them and India . . . and freedom. And there are just three of them. Ken is almost incapacitated by his smashed ankle—they cannot carry him, so he walks on broken bones, with even the idea of pain long anesthetized. Under the surface of her good humor, Marianne carries, imprinted on her for life, pictures of the Japanese slaughter of the entire Kachin village that she had once called home—she could have better handled walking on two broken legs and shattered ankles. But she does not complain, and Sam is grateful for that little consideration because he has been given the responsibility of bringing her out of Burma, according to his orders, in merely a bodily whole. He does not have charge of her emotions, which, in any case, will take years to heal if they do heal at all.

At least, Sam thinks, he is not injured. Yet. Toughened by his training, toughened even by his own self, Sam never lets himself think that India is a distant and unattainable possibility. They *will* survive. They *will* reach safety. For a reason more important than merely his own survival.

Sam watches Marianne coo over Ken, who is enjoying the attention. He shifts against the tree trunk and bangs his hand over his shirt pocket to swat a whining mosquito that is trying to burrow through the plastic and cloth to his skin. He reaches into the pocket and draws out a bundle of papers, enclosed carefully in the clear plastic wrapping of his cigarettes. The handwriting is familiar, still as unformed as a child's hand. Here are

Mike's tales of this distant desert kingdom called Rudrakot in northwestern India. Here in these other letters, also written by a familiar hand, are his mother's fears that Mike might be . . . Sam leans back against the tree, his heart exploding. He was given his orders to rescue Marianne and the news that Mike was missing on the same day and with no time to even turn his head away from Burma and absorb the news. Missing, he thinks of Mike as missing, does not dare to even think of that other word.

"What is it?" Marianne says softly at his shoulder. And it is then Sam realizes that his fingers scrabble over the cellophane covering the letters. He stops.

"Nothing," he replies. "Nothing."

Ken lifts his eyelids with an effort; he is tired. "Is it a love letter?"

Sam smiles, thinking how much easier it is to let them think this. "Of sorts."

"Have you ever been in love, Sam?" Ken asks.

# Three

*Declaring himself Indian first and a Brahman afterward, he told the conference he would not follow any custom of the Brahmans, however sanctified by age and authority, if it came in the way of his duties as a true Indian . . . in independent India, there continue to be few Indians but many members of the various caste groups—a sad commentary on our national life.*

—Vijaya Lakshmi Pandit, *The Scope of Happiness,* 1979

The political agent's house at Rudrakot was built in the style of a British back-home house, with only some allowances made for India. It was a long, serene, whitewashed building in two stories. Three low stone steps led up to the front door, and the style here was so much home and so little India that the door stood naked, embedded into the wall—no portico, no cool, slender-pillared porch sheltered the front entrance to the house. Carriages, phaetons, rickshaws, and cars stopped in the blasting heat of the desert sun; the door itself, painted a warm red, swallowed the westerly heat and spat it out in the evenings in the faces of callers. An architectural mistake, of course, one that was much lamented but little addressed over the seventy-odd years of the house's existence.

A compound wall encircled the front of the house with wrought-iron gates on two corners. A half-moon driveway started at one gate and, swinging near the house, ended at the other. There was a fountain in the center of this semicircle, resplendent with plaster cupids who spouted water out of their pursed mouths when the rains came. During the dry season, they were frozen in disgusted pouts, feeling perhaps quite as silly as they looked.

The front door led to an entrance porch. To the right was the dining room, with windows along the width of the eastern and western walls. To the left were the political agent's offices—a room that was an actual office, light and airy; a small washroom for the most important visitors; and an antechamber for those who had to wait for the agent.

All the actual living was done upstairs. The top story of the house, seen from the gates, sat on only two-thirds of the bottom story—it ended somewhere above the dining room in a huge and open verandah. Here— in the pillared, roofed-in verandah—was the concession to India. No English home could boast so much open space for outdoor living; the weather would not support it. The stairs to the second story climbed from the entry hallway and came to a small landing upstairs, then cleaved into corridors running along the house on both sides, to drawing rooms and six bedrooms with attached baths.

Toward the back a verandah wrapped itself around the lower story, its roof the balcony of the top story, looking out into the lush garden with its banyan and tamarind trees. Here Mila had stood earlier in the morning, looking down upon her father praying at the well.

The servants slept in separate buildings behind the house, tucked behind the trees, which also had the offices of living for the masters of the main house—the kitchens, the storeroom, and the storage room. Also to the back was a huge, steel-girdered shed that housed the two cars, a jeep and a Morris Cowley; their chauffeurs; and a phaeton. The cows for milk, the horses for riding and for drawing the phaeton, and the chickens for eggs had their own sheds too, and each animal had its keepers. A cowherd milked the cows every morning and grazed them in the scrub near the lake; three syces exercised the horses and accompanied Mila on her morning rides; and Pallavi fussed over the chickens, rustled through the straw for breakfast eggs and encouraged her charges to be obliging or they would find themselves in the pot for a home buffet.

Raman drank his morning cup of coffee in the upstairs verandah, which faced south. When he had first come to Rudrakot, this verandah was a bare square of cement with a low compound wall around it. He had the concrete pillars erected, and a thick thatched roof of straw and dry palm fronds put on top to keep away the sun's glare. But over the years he found the roof to be impractical. It disintegrated during the rains—sparse as they were—and after the monsoons, every insect in Rudrakot, along with the ever-present yellow geckos, found its home there. Kiran and Ashok loved this, quite naturally, and spent all of their time catching beetles and grasshoppers by poking sticks into the thatch and gathering up their spoils by the handful. Mila hated it, also quite naturally; she had not her brothers' fascination with either the insects or the geckos that left their tails wriggling on the floor as they tried to escape.

A brick-and-mortar roof was also impracticable, so Raman, after years of hits and misses, came up with the idea of a wooden skeletal frame for the roof, covered now with lightweight *khus* matting knitted of fragrant river rushes. This dried swiftly after the rains, kept direct sunlight off their faces, and gave out a pleasant aroma. The idea was so successful that Raman had *khus* mats installed along the pillars too, rolled up in the mornings and let down in the afternoons. Raman had been at Rudrakot for fourteen years, well beyond the time of any political agent's duties. As a member of the political branch of the Indian Civil Service, he should have moved all over the country, but he had been here for most of his life as an ICS officer, and for a reason. So there had been time to experiment with the verandah roof's vagaries, to understand them, and, finally, to appease them.

He raised the coffee cup to inhale that first, sharp scent of coffee beans, and saliva rinsed his mouth in anticipation. It was quiet around him. The sparrows tittered in the bushes; the busy gray-and-black crows cawed out morning greetings; the tamarind tree's leaves rustled quietly in a gentle breeze from the lake. He set the cup down on the saucer, and let his mind rest for a while. Raman had woken early, as usual, bathed and said his prayers, and heard Mila depart for her morning ride. The boys were not awake yet; Ashok would get up soon, for his tutor came in at nine; Kiran was rarely a presence in the house before noon.

At the thought of his eldest son, Raman began to fret mildly, and then pushed away the worry. This was his time for solitude and calm, the rest of the day would churn out in all directions and fritter away any quiet he might have. Like his daughter, Raman also had demands on his time and his energies all through the day, and yet, because he was a man, he had more freedom.

His coffee cooled. Sayyid, standing behind his master's chair, took away the cup and saucer and filled a new cup with some more coffee from a steel jug that sat among the glowing embers of coal in a brazier. Raman liked his coffee hot, not just hot, but boiling hot, so his tongue was scalded each time he drank. That meant every sip had to come as though directly from the stove. In the early days, he would invade the kitchen quarters behind the house, and drink his coffee leaning over a blazing mud *chula*, setting down his steel tumbler over the fire between sips. The servants chattered in protest to Lakshmi at this irregularity. Every stove was needed; there was water and milk to boil, coffee to make, tea kept ready if wanted, spices to roast. Besides, Raman's being in the smoke-blackened rooms threw them into a frozen silence, with hands suspended over chopping and cleaning and cutting until he left, because the sahib had no place in the kitchen, and they did not quite know how to get on with their duties while he was there.

So Lakshmi, knowing Raman would not change his ways, ordered a brazier from the bazaar and came up with the idea of the live coals, the steel jug, the ten empty cups filled just before Raman wanted a sip.

Raman was on his third cup when he heard the banging on the front door. "See who it is, Sayyid," he said.

"Yes, Sahib." Sayyid bowed and went downstairs. He came back in a few minutes and said, "An American sahib wishes to see you, Sahib."

"This early? Tell him to come back at nine o'clock; I will be in the office then."

"Yes, Sahib." Another bow, another retreat, and then Sayyid came back again. "He says it is not official business, he must speak with you, and now."

Raman sighed. He had learned to guard this half hour in the morning with a lover's jealousy, as he had learned, over the years, to guard his nightly sleep, and he gave up either only for Jai and for no one else. Jai was demanding enough as it was, the others came during office hours, or dragged him from bed only for absolute emergencies. He considered insisting that the man wait, but relinquished that thought almost as soon as it came to mind, for Raman could deny almost no one. It was a weakness in one so often petitioned, he knew, but so carefully ingrained in his character, he realized it and did not any longer fight it. Raman also considered putting on a shirt, rubbing a hand over the hair on his chest, but this he was able to resist—if the American wanted to see him outside of his office hours, he would have to take him as he was. He told Sayyid to bring the man up.

When Sam came into the verandah, Raman rose from his armchair and offered him his hand.

"Good morning," he said. The other man's shake was tentative. But why? He had come seeking him, to his house. Sam recovered himself soon enough and his eyes crinkled at the edges when he smiled.

"Good morning. Sam Hawthorne . . . I was told to come to the political agent's home in Rudrakot. Colonel Eden's orders."

"I see," Raman said. "Won't you sit? Sayyid, some coffee for the gentleman. Or . . ." He looked at Sam. "Would you prefer tea?"

"Coffee's fine, thank you."

"What can I do for you, Mr. Hawthorne?" Raman asked.

"Actually, it's Captain Hawthorne. Third Burma Rangers, U.S. Army," Sam said, accepting a cup from Sayyid and nodding his thanks. "I was hoping to talk with the political agent."

"Ah," Raman said. He sat back to look upon the young man in front of him who had very easily mistaken that just because Raman was Indian, he could not, naturally, be the political agent. What did he consider him? A peon? A secretary? There was, however, nothing offensive in his guest's manner. He had an engaging smile and an evenly browned face. His eyes were a startling blue among all that earth color, the hair a glossy, India ink black, too long in the front for an army man. Sam had to, every so often, toss his head slightly, or swipe the hair from his eyes. It was not an unmanly gesture, and yet Raman had not seen much of it before, as used as he was to the straitjacket rigidity of the officers of the British Indian army.

Somehow, that lack of insistence on protocol made him American to Raman. His accent rang strange too, true, but not unpleasantly. Raman wondered what he was doing here in Rudrakot.

"May I ask, Captain Hawthorne," he said, "how old you are? If it is not a too terribly invasive question?"

"Not at all," Sam replied. "But I'm sorry; I don't know with whom I am talking . . ."

"My name is Raman." And so Raman deliberately kept the information from Sam yet another time.

"Just that?" Sam asked before he had the time to think. It was not a rude question in itself, but the manner of asking it denied etiquette. But Raman let it pass, for it told him more about Sam than his appearance had. He did not need to know how old Sam was anymore; in Raman's mind he could not be more than twenty-five, or twenty-six at the most. But a few years older than Kiran, though he seemed to possess more of himself than Kiran did. His eldest son was a restless, unhappy creature, especially now. Raman shifted in his chair, and as he had earlier, tore his attention from Kiran to Sam.

"My name is just Raman," he said. "Do you know something of Indian names, Captain Hawthorne?"

"Sam, please. Please call me Sam."

"All right," Raman said, surprised and somewhat pleased. It was not less than he had expected from an American—for all of Raman's ideas of Americans were based on what he had been told by friends who had traveled to that country. So he had expected this openness, this immediate and somewhat rash friendship, because Sam did not know who Raman was, yet insisted upon a familiarity that was, because it was so unusual to Raman, charming.

"And yes," Sam added, "I've been in India long enough to distinguish between different names, not very well though. My batman taught me that the name could point to many different things: religion, of course, though it's easy enough to tell from a name whether you are Hindu or Muslim, also what your caste is, what part of the country you come from, in some cases what languages you speak." Sam grinned. "I must admit that it was all quite confusing, I understood that much from what Ramsingh told me, but not enough to actually use any of it."

Raman smiled at this much information. Sam had come to Rudrakot on the night train from Palampore; his clothes and his person held that iron-and-metal smell of railway travel. He had also come here, in the not-so-distant past, from some war front, or some training camp; the color of his face and hands gave that away. Sam Hawthorne had taken the trouble to talk with his batman about the origin of Indian names.

"You have an erudite batman, Captain Hawthorne," Raman said. "I don't know many men in that class of life who would choose to engage their masters in conversation other than the shine of polish on their shoes or the ironing of their uniforms."

"Ramsingh was certainly unusual, sir," Sam said. "I do not employ him anymore. He was assigned to me in the barracks in Assam and is probably serving another captain now. But you were saying . . . about your name. . . ."

"Ah, yes. I digress a lot; my children tell me this constantly," Raman said, bending his head toward Sam in a little apology. Both of their coffees had cooled in the conversation, and Sayyid, still standing behind Raman's chair, was but an unnecessary adjunct, for neither man had, for several minutes, reached to the little rattan table by his side that held the coffee cup. "I too, as you so well know from your astounding conversations with Ramsingh, had a much fuller, more descriptive name. It was indeed so expressive, in all of its components, merely three, but such an eloquent three, that it told the hearer, just upon introduction, which village I came from, what my actual name was, and what caste I belonged to."

Raman had leaned forward in his chair, and Sam did the same now. Raman was uncaring of his quiet morning being shattered, and Sam's shoulder, which had throbbed into pain on each rut in the road during the rickshaw ride, was quiet and on its best behavior. "The other aspect of my caste name," Raman continued, holding up his hand and ticking off all the oddities of the name he had been bestowed with upon birth, "is that it gave away, quite specifically, the language I spoke, or that ubiquitous name for it called a *mother tongue,* and what community I came from."

"That's a lot of work for a three-word name," Sam said, amusement evident in his voice. "I think other . . ." he said pausing for a brief moment, "other Hawthornes might be able to trace some connection with my family. And so we would know we have a similar ancestry, perhaps, but my name means nothing more than that. Why *did* you have such a name, sir?"

Raman smiled with delight. "Ah, I see you understand. I gave away two parts of my name and shortened the third. So I am, as you see, in front of you, merely Raman."

Sam laughed at his enthusiasm. "How does one give away a name? Doesn't it belong to you, from when you are born? Did you put notices in the local newspapers saying you were 'merely Raman,' from this day forth and so on?"

Raman nodded energetically. "Yes, and that was exactly it. I took away my caste name, my village name, slashed away half of my actual name.

But I did not put a notice in any papers, or announce it publicly. I did this more than fifteen years ago, Sam, and by sheer persistence, I made people think of me as Raman."

"You still haven't told me what your name was," Sam said.

Raman rubbed the top of his head in a rueful gesture. This young man was very smart, and very persistent. But Raman was persistent too—it had taken him many years to get people to think of him as merely Raman, but now they did, not remembering what his actual name was. "Murugankoil Ramanathan Iyer."

"The first is your village . . . ?" Sam asked, ticking off the names on his finger, as Raman had; he waited for the other man's nod, and went on, "the second is your name . . . the third identifies you as an Iyer . . . a Brahmin from the land of the Tamils. You speak Tamil, and you are also a Shaivaite, a follower of Shiva; the other sect of Tamil Brahmins are Vaishnavites, followers of Vishnu."

Raman had been following this discourse with a light of absolute enjoyment in his eyes. He had no idea how Sam knew so much, or had taken the care to know so much. *This* was an army man? "You see why I got rid of my names?"

"Yes," Sam replied. "Not because you do not honor them, but because they take away the mystery of who you are, because they assign a place in life to you, because they burden you with certain expectations to be fulfilled. I see why."

They stretched across the rattan center table between them and shook hands. The sun had broken beyond the height of the tamarind outside and bathed the southern half of the verandah in a clean oblong of light. Dust motes rode lightly upon the beams of the sun and Raman felt a kinship to Sam he had not felt before with any other man.

"The taking away of my caste name had more to do with just what expectations were required of me," Raman said. "I felt it set me apart. We have had, Sam, as Brahmins, a somewhat shameful history of neglect and domination of our fellow humans. I abhor the caste system; my name marked me out as an oppressor—I discarded it."

They reached simultaneously for their coffee cups, which Sayyid filled. They drank in silence and then Raman said, "Rudrakot is very far from the war, Sam."

"Yes, sir," Sam replied, brought into alertness again. He sat up in his chair, and touched his right forearm in what he thought was a surreptitious gesture, but Raman's eyes followed the movement of his hand.

"An injury?" he asked.

"Yes, sir," Sam said, "In Burma, last month."

"Hmmm. . . ." Raman's gaze grew reflective. "I did not know the Americans were in Burma last month, Sam."

"We were, sir," Sam replied, and then waited. What a lot of secrets he had to keep. He could not talk of Burma, aside from skirting around the periphery of it, and he could not talk about Rudrakot or why he was here. Sam's shoulder began to grow uncomfortable in his body. The bones seemed to swell, the skin writhed as though tickled by a hundred unseen fingers, a fist came from out of nowhere to punch him in his clavicle. Sam took a deep breath and held it for as long as he could, not willing to feed the pain any more oxygen. He let it out finally when Raman began to speak.

"I see. What can the political agent do for you, Sam?"

"I have a letter for him, sir, from Colonel Eden, he's—"

"—in the governor-general's council in the Bengal presidency," Raman finished for Sam. "I know him well. What does the letter say?"

"I am . . ." Sam hesitated. "I am looking for a place in Rudrakot for the next four days of my leave. Colonel Eden recommended that I stay with the political agent."

"Why?"

Sam understood that question well enough, but tried to divert his response anyway. "Colonel Eden thought the agent might not mind billeting me, sir."

Raman shook his head gently. "I mean why are you here, Sam?"

So here it was then for Sam, his first attempt of many over the next few days at a stellar subterfuge in response to a direct question. He thought about his answer, not really wanting to misrepresent himself to this man for whom he felt a sudden affection merely because they had conversed about Indian names. But it had been a conversation not about the war, not about Burma, or death or dying, and so was of immense value to Sam. He was not trained for the war in his civilian life; his mind did not bend toward destruction, but rather the vagaries of societies, the wills of men, their eccentricities. He was, though, trained for deception—in fact, since he had volunteered for the war, that was all Sam had been taught.

Sometime during this last half hour, Sam had started to address Raman as "sir." There was something about him—not his appearance, for Raman was just barely clad, as though he were newly risen from bed—that invited the title. Also, Sam was now army, and in the army he had been taught that when in doubt, append the salutation of respect.

He said with a rueful little smile, "I have been ordered by the army and by my doctor to rest my arm and shoulder, sir. I thought Rudrakot would be an interesting place to visit. Perhaps I can tour around the state a little, see the sights, the fort, even the horse's tomb beyond the lake. . . ."

"Of course," Raman said. "As our guest, you must avail yourself of all that we have to offer."

Sam searched for suspicion in Raman's expression, but the other man's face was open, friendly, welcoming. The first hurdle passed, he thought. Many more to come for sure in the next few days, but he would overcome them all too, and then he would leave Rudrakot, and no one would remember that a U.S. Army captain named Sam Hawthorne had ever been here, lying about everything so completely that even his name was false. What Sam did not know that May morning in Raman's verandah was how untrue these thoughts were—for he would be inextricably linked to Rudrakot for the rest of his life.

He asked, "When will I meet the political agent, sir? Will he be in his office soon?"

The man opposite him, bare chested, with a head of still-black hair receding quite far, a cloth of white known as a *veshti* around his waist (his only vestment), his feet without slippers, made the most astonishing announcement of this morning to Sam.

"Why," Raman said, "I am the political agent. I thought you knew that."


Sam's surprise, his assumption that Raman could not be the political agent because he was Indian, had been born in his subconscious, and was not entirely unfounded. For until Raman, no other princely state in India had had an Indian political agent or resident.

Jai was the reason Raman was at Rudrakot, which already had a British resident. The two titles—political agent and resident—were equally interchangeable, and in most of the independent kingdoms of the

British Raj, there was only one or the other. The political agent himself, by whatever name he was called, was the heavy hand of the British Indian government upon the princely kingdom's grudging shoulder. The British East India Company had created the post many years before India had come under the crown of Queen Victoria. The political agent's influence had few limits; he advised the ruler on agricultural policies, taxes, revenues, court ceremonies, and even arranged marriages between kingdoms.

In 1858, Queen Victoria stepped in and declared herself empress of the Indian empire, and transferred all powers to her viceroys, governors, and civil servants. The princely kingdoms each made their own treaties with this new empress in England, and allowed the continued presence of a diplomatic official in their kingdoms under the name of a political agent, who was either a member of the heaven-born Indian Civil Service or a high-ranking army officer.

Sam's inadvertent inference about Raman had come from his ability to assimilate nuances in his atmosphere, and from his unconscious understanding that this was a prejudice that came from both sides—Indian and British.

The princes, many of whom considered themselves descended directly from the sun or moon or some other celestial body, would not countenance an *Indian* as their advisor—the British they could tolerate even though they considered the British beneath them, casteless, temporary residents of their lands who deposited their faith in foreign Gods. The position of a political agent was supposed to hover over the prince in hierarchy—in actuality, the princes considered themselves superior (for the reasons mentioned before), and the British considered themselves superior, but each played the diplomatic game with polite words and gestures and formal rituals and neither was hurt by the deception. An Indian political agent would not fit in this grand scheme of things. By the very virtue of being a lay Indian, he would be inferior to the sun-descended prince; by virtue of his position in the kingdom, he would be above the prince as a representative of the British Indian government.

Raja Bhimsen, Jai's father, had disdained such distinctions. Knowing he was going to die of cancer, Bhimsen had used his generations-old royal inheritance of trickery and guile to bring Raman into Rudrakot as a mentor for his son in the years to come. Bhimsen had met him in England while Raman was there to sit for his civil service examinations, had introduced him to liquor and meat, had seen him resist both initially and then exercise moderation—had seen in the young Raman a man of steady character and calmness, all of which he thought Jai would need.

The deal he struck with the British Indian government was that Raman's posting to Rudrakot would be for his life, or as long as Jai needed him. The return Bhimsen gave was allowing the Rudrakot Rifles regiment to construct a field-punishment center beyond Chetak's tomb for defectors from the army. Atrocities were committed at the punishment center in the name of discipline and training; army traitors entered its gates only to disappear forever from the world of the living. But Bhimsen shut his eyes to everything. He had Raman and he died peacefully, knowing that his son would be well looked after.

Very early after Sam had volunteered for the war, he had had bestowed upon him another name. Why? he had asked his colonel at the training camp in Virginia, wasn't his name good enough? Yes and no, the colonel had replied, for Sam was to be part of a fledgling, invisible force, so early in the stages of its conception that it was best for all of them to carry names they did not own. This was so that no one, friend or enemy, would be able to tell who they really were.

All that subterfuge, which Sam had considered unnecessary, not so much like making war, but *playing* at war, had its advantages. For because of that name, no one initially connected Sam Hawthorne with his missing brother—Second Lieutenant Michael Ridley of the Rudrakot Rifles regiment.

# Four

*You occasionally met Indians at dinner parties—very high-class Indians.
I was allowed to go out with Maharajahs—there was something about
their being very rich that overrode the colour thing.*

*We made lots of friends with Indians, but it didn't get any further. I
mean to say, I don't think that if our sons and daughters had been anxious to marry each other, any of us would have been at all pleased. I
mean, the prejudice was as much with them as it was with us.*

—Anton Gill, *Ruling Passions: Sex, Race and Empire*, 1995

*M*ila had come home while Raman and Sam were talking, still me-
andering down the convoluted paths of the name explanations.
She threw her reins to the syce and ran up the stairs, heading for her room.
At the landing, she paused, stripping off her gloves. Papa's voice rumbled
from the verandah, interspersed with another man's voice, more youthful.
She tarried there, head slanted toward her left, thinking that he sounded
like the man she had met on the road earlier that morning. The doors to the
verandah were open, and the morning's rising heat filled the door frame.

Pallavi backed out of Ashok's room and shut the door.

"Who's with Papa?" Mila asked. "He doesn't like early visitors.
Nothing's wrong, is it?"

Pallavi came down the corridor, shaking her head. "No, nothing wrong,
I think. Some man wanted to see your papa, Sayyid let him in, and he is
there now. I didn't want to intrude or I would have gone to see who it was."

"I'll go." Mila moved and Pallavi put a hand on her shoulder.

"Look," she said, pointing at Mila's crisp white shirt, with its sweat stains on the back, under the armpits, encircling her neck. Mila's hair lay slick against her head, and little lines of sweat streaked her face. "Don't go like this, my dear, what will your papa say when he sees you unwashed and wilted?"

Mila bent to put her arms around Pallavi. She rubbed her sweaty face into the curve of Pallavi's shoulder, against her blouse. With her voice in Pallavi's sandalwood-scented skin, she said, "Papa won't say anything, Pallavi. You will."

Pallavi reached up on tiptoe to grasp all of Mila in her arms. She grumbled about her smell, about the perspiration, but even as she muttered, she managed to give Mila a little kiss on her neck. It was the soft peck of a chicken, all but lost in the rest of the clucking. " . . . and wearing those pants," Pallavi ended. "Why wear pants? Go take a bath, change into a sari. You are a woman now, so old you should have been married five years ago."

Mila withdrew her face from Pallavi. This too was a familiar refrain, and Pallavi was right, here in any case. Mila did not know too many women her age, twenty-one, who were not married and did not have at least two or three children. But then, marriage had never really seemed important . . . until now. They stood in the middle of the landing, Mila much taller than Pallavi, much more slender, thin really, with the biology of her youth, thin also because she could not keep her arms and legs at rest, as Pallavi said a lady should. A little prick of exasperation began to build in her. She was hot, she was tired, all she wanted was a bath and to go back to bed, for her night's sleep had been frayed on both ends, with the party last night, and the early riding this morning.

"Enough, Pallavi," she said. "I'm not that old, you know. And I am going to get married one day."

"One day, one day. When, may I ask? Why all the waiting? Are you not fine enough as you are? Why the riding lessons? I need to talk with your papa."

"I am not taking *lessons*," Mila said, holding herself up so that Pallavi seemed much shorter; she had also settled, seemingly, into the flecked mosaic floor of the landing, digging herself in like a besieged soldier. "I ride better than any other woman I know, and most of the men of our acquaintance."

"And a fine skill that is." Pallavi's voice shook with her climbing vexation. "Is it going to help you bear children? Do the books teach you this?"

"I'm not going to fight," Mila said quietly, drooping over Pallavi.

"What is it you do not like now? What happened?"

"Nothing." Pallavi pulled the *pallu* of her sari around her shoulders and went down the stairs. "I have to see to breakfast. I do not know what has happened to this household today. There is your papa, still talking to some man. When is he going to come to eat, when will he go to his office. . . ."

Mila backed to the landing windows and sat on the thick wedge of the sill. She heard laughter from the verandah, and strained toward it, but the words were too obtuse for her to make out anything. She leaned her head against the glass pane and looked out over the front of the house. She was strangely lethargic and exhausted after the ride. Sleep would deplete the weariness of her body, but the agitation, somewhere in the area of her chest, had lingered for almost two months now. Perhaps Pallavi was right; it was merely time for her to marry, to have children, and to settle down into the routine that was every woman's lot. But that would mean no Papa, no Pallavi, no Ashok, no Kiran . . . although he had been away for so many years now, he was almost unknown again. Kiran had returned from England a stranger. He was charming, he was funny, he was elegant and eloquent, but he too was somehow dissatisfied, and in her unnamed fraught state Mila picked up that his laughter was edged with irritation, that his confidence wasted away behind the bluster. Much as she felt.

She sat back on the sill and pulled her knees up under her chin, still listening to the sounds from the verandah and still not able to discern the whole of the conversation. She had always eavesdropped, without a sense of shame though, for she had always been curious. When she was nine, she had heard whispers behind the *rath-ki-rani* bush at the club one night. There had not been much talking after that, just the hum of sighs and breathing, and mouths meeting. Illicit, of course, in the grand tradition of an affair—a Rudrakot Rifles captain with the wife of a major. She had seen them fused into each other, the woman straddling the man, his hands under her skirt, cupping her buttocks, their mouths merged. Nothing more—forbidden trysts rarely found completion on stone benches behind bushes—and this Mila realized only later when she thought of that evening. But there had been something spellbinding that moonlit night—the hotly scented white flowers amidst glossy green-black leaves, the tableau of mind-losing lust, the sweep of silk over skin, the groans of unfulfilled desire. Leaning out from behind a tree to watch, Mila had tripped and toppled to the dirt. She had picked herself up, dusted off her frock and elbows, but the two people ensconced in the fragrant embrace of the *rath-ki-rani* did not notice her presence, so engrossed were they in each other. Surely, the young Mila had thought, this must be love, this absorption, this blight of all else but the beloved, this rapture.

A year later she had asked Papa—and only once, since most people did not talk to their parents about love and such nonsense anyway—if he had loved Lakshmi. And Papa had said, "Of course, she was my wife."

"But you did not know her before you married her?" Mila had asked. By then she had observed the British officers pursuing the women who became their wives, seen them stepping out with each other, and thought that this was how courting was to be. She was ten that year, and this conversation had taken place at dinner, with Pallavi leaning toward their side of the table with a scandalized air. She told Mila later that one did not talk with one's parents about *love and such nonsense,* and that it was wrong to have even initiated the topic. But this was after Raman had taken the care to answer Mila.

"I did not know her, true," he had said, "your grandmother chose her for me. But I fell in love with your mother, and it turned out all right."

"And what if you had not loved her?" Mila asked.

Pallavi sucked in air between her teeth, and shouted at Sayyid, "Get the buttermilk, Sayyid. Sahib's rice is cooling."

"I would have learned to love her; it would have been a tempered love, perhaps not the furious and fierce one it was, but one more vested with calm," Raman said with a smile.

"I think I want a love like yours, Papa," Mila had announced. Raman grinned at his daughter, and hoped, in his heart, that she would find a love much like his had been for Lakshmi. He was enchanted by the question and not at all embarrassed. The only two people at the table whose skins mottled with discomposure were Pallavi and Kiran. They knew what a furious and fierce love was—Pallavi because she had slept in a room close by theirs while Raman and Lakshmi were married, Kiran because he was fourteen already, and Jai had taken great care to initiate him—not physically yet, for now it was all wonderment and chatter—about the marvels of *love*. A misused word in Jai's and Kiran's context, but still one that had some resemblance to the love of which Raman spoke.

Mila had asked the question because the year she turned ten, Jai, who was seventeen, got married. His marriage was arranged, of course, by Raman himself. The bride, the wife-who-was-to-be-loved, was the princess of Shaktipur. Jai had not seen her at the betrothal ceremony, and his first sight of his wife would be at the official viewing, after the wedding. He had been told by his *diwan*, his prime minister, that she was beautiful, and his *diwan* had been told so by the Shaktipur *diwan*. Neither of the men had seen the princess, but each was equally assertive of the merits of her beauty. Jai had come home to moan and pout to Raman about this strange state of affairs. Mila had stood at his knee, literally at his knee, for she was leaning against his legs and watching the curvings and swivelings of his beautiful, discontented mouth, fronted by a neat, clipped mustache. Why did he have to marry? he had asked Raman. Because, Raman explained patiently, Rudrakot needed an heir, and he had to provide one or the line would die. Why couldn't he see her, damn it, before the wedding? Because it was not done; he knew this, surely?

That night, at dinner, Mila asked Raman what love was, and if he had ever possessed it, for it seemed poor Jai was doomed.

Still sitting on the windowsill, Mila wondered why she thought of Jai's marriage to the princess today; there had been, if she so wanted, plenty of other opportunities to think of it. Now the marriage was an old one; they had three children, the younger two boys, an heir to spare for Rudrakot. Jai had never talked of love for the princess of Shaktipur, and now, Mila would not ask him. She heard her father and his guest rise from their armchairs in the verandah and step over the door frame into the corridor. Mila stood up. Before she could head for her rooms, Raman came down the corridor and saw her.

"Mila," he called out, "wait, my dear. I want you to meet Captain Hawthorne."

Mila turned to her father, and saw a tall man following behind him, his stride long and easy, clad in the omnipresent khaki of the war, his figure all but blotting out the light through the door frame from the verandah. He had to duck his head under the door frame and almost stumbled over the six-inch threshold in the doorway, built to deter snakes, or rather to contain them to the room they found themselves in. She felt that she was smiling even before he neared—it was the stranded stranger. Why had he come to their house? To see Papa? Sam put out his hand without hesitation, and Mila gave him hers in return, thinking that this Captain Hawthorne must be special indeed for Papa to allow him to intrude upon his coffee hour.

"How are you? Since my father forgot to introduce me, I must tell you that I am his daughter."

There was a long moment of silence, which stretched so far that Mila found it difficult to hold Sam's steady gaze upon her face. Then Sam cleared his throat and said, "I gathered as much." For someone who had expounded at great length upon the qualities of the rudraksha tree, he seemed to have given in to a paucity of language. His teeth flashed a startling white in his sun-browned face.

Their crow-heralded visitor, Mila thought suddenly, the one who would bring them ill luck. But how could Sam Hawthorne be that man?

"Captain Hawthorne will be staying with us, Mila," Raman said. "Will you see that a room is prepared for him?"

"Sam, please," Sam said. "I have already convinced your father to call me thus; perhaps you will give me the honor of doing so too?"

"Yes, of course," Mila said. "I am Mila. Well . . ." She hesitated. "Not Mila exactly; I have other names, but everyone calls me Mila."

"Is this your father's doing?" he asked.

Raman roared with a delighted laughter, and slapped Sam on the arm before turning to go down the corridor to his room. "Yes, it is my doing, Sam. If I can meddle with my own name, I have no reason not to do so with my daughter's."

They watched him head away, and then Mila turned to Sam. "If you wouldn't mind stopping in the drawing room for a while, I will see that your room is made ready."

"I'm glad," he said hurriedly, and then paused to consider his words, "that you . . . live here, in this house; we can now talk longer about Rudrakot and its history. I hope this is no inconvenience."

She shook her head. She had been curious about him, but now she wanted to leave, to go wipe her face and hands, to change into something else, something more becoming, a sari. Sam Hawthorne was not one of

Papa's usual strays. Raman had a delectable propensity for inviting strangers into their home, to stay, at times, as long as they wanted. He liked people, he enjoyed investigating their minds, he had the same curiosity Mila had. And the ICS, being a social and sociable service, afforded many opportunities for unlooked-for house guests. But Sam Hawthorne was already different. He was American, and *that* made him different. Not the first American she had met, but still different from all others. He was unsettling, with a gaze too intense, a demeanor too focused . . . on what though? Why was he here, Mila wondered, but she would not ask him. She hoped that he would stay long with them. But she could not ask him that either, in case he understood the question to reflect their impatience to have him leave. Not done.

They both tarried in the corridor outside the drawing room, suddenly plagued with shyness, heedful of themselves and of each other, not quite knowing what to say or how to say it.

Sam lifted his right hand to gesticulate and begin a sentence, but Mila began to talk almost as he did and he stopped to listen, his eyes fixed upon her face.

"I hope you have a wonderful time here at Rudrakot, Captain Hawthorne," she said with a smile. "It is not often that we have American guests at our home. Ashok, my brother, he will be thrilled, and you must please not mind it if he asks you too many questions about your home."

"I won't," Sam replied. "It will be a pleasure for me. Bring on all of your brothers and I will be happy to talk with them. But . . . can I repay your . . . and your father's hospitality in some other way also?"

She laughed and rested against the wall, her hands clasped behind her. The collar of her white blouse strained over etched bones at the base of her neck with a little dip between them. A slender gold chain rested its excess length in that dip. Mila smelled of a just-risen sun, still cool and fresh. Sam saw and felt all of this and yet seemed not to see any of it. He leaned against the other wall of the corridor, and from the way they were positioned, their feet were just a few inches apart, Sam's scuffed army boots more gray with dust than black, Mila's riding boots with their three-inch heels still shiny from all of Sayyid's ministrations with a brush and polish.

Mila had forgotten her need to flee from Sam; like him, she too wanted to be here and nowhere else, but for her the thought was merely instinct. She did not know that she was flirting with Sam, inviting his gaze upon her face and her neck, searching his own face for a smile or a crinkle of skin around his eyes.

"We had a young army officer here whom Ashok pestered so much with all of his America questions that he preferred to leave Rudrakot itself. I hope that you will stay, Captain Hawthorne."

Sam was still staring at Mila with a grin on his face, and in the midst of that haze of joy, the question finally searched for and found his brain. "I have only a few days of my leave, but"—his voice dropped to an overcasual tone—"who was this man? Was he American?"

And Sam waited for the answer with his heart banging in his chest. Something though, about the way he had posed the question, about what he had said, or left unsaid, rose to curdle the air around them.

"Yes," Mila said as she straightened from the wall. "But you would not know him. America is a big country, isn't it?"

She led the way to the drawing room, waved him to a chair, gave him a quick smile, and ran out of the room, leaving him suddenly stunned and out of breath.

Sam sank into the stuffed armchair and bent his head. He was tired; his mind was playing tricks upon him. He had left Mila at the road and pushed her firmly out of his mind, thinking that he would never see her again, that the encounter had been one to remember and cherish. He raised his hands to his face, and spread out his fingers, palms downward, and watched as his hands shook slightly, trembling in midair. Mila. What a lovely name, whatever her other names might be. Swept away by an exhilaration he could not identify, because he had never felt this before, Sam still wondered if he was merely being stupid. And all at once, he compared her to his other loves, if such a word could be used with them. He had dated many women, and there had been one . . . her name even escaped him now, who when she knew he was going to India and Burma, had offered him marriage. They liked each other, she had said (they had), they were both reasonably attractive (they were), and if he never came back, at least he would know he had had her. Everyone must marry at least once. But something in Sam rebelled against this arrangement without sentiment or emotion, even though he was too academically trained to think of sentiment or emotion as being attractive. And he did not think of marriage in terms of at *least* once, he thought of it as at *most* once. And so that had ended, the most serious relationship Sam had ever had. With that woman, he had hiked in the Cascades, kissed in the rain, fumbled at her clothing on the sofa in his apartment.

He sat in the drawing room waiting for Mila to return and thought of her without realizing that he thought *only* of her. Trivialities really. She was not very tall; her head came up only to his shoulder. A drop of sweat had run down along her cheek and dispersed wetly into the collar of her white shirt.

When he remembered this second meeting later, he realized that he had seen her like an artist studying his subject limb by limb, hair by hair, and for Sam this was an astonishment, for he usually saw the entireties of people—what they said, how they used their hands, what matter was contained in their brains. Asked what his mother, Maude, had worn when she left the house, he had never remembered much, not even an impression of a color. But this is what he remembered of Mila that morning. When she had turned to meet him, her eyebrows had lifted into the narrow expanse of the skin of her forehead and created fine lines of questions. She had a tiny mole flanking the outer edge of her right eyebrow. Her hand was easy in his grasp, her grip was firm, not insipid, and her palm fitted around his warmly. He followed her into the drawing room and noticed the creases in the khaki of her jodhpurs where they were tucked into the top half of her boots, from where they blossomed into exaggerated, wide, buckram-enforced curves around her thighs. He saw the curve of her breast under the thin white shirt, the plunge of the collar in front, drowned in the aroma of her skin without being anywhere close to her.

And despite that near reference to Mike—or at least Sam thought it must have been Mike that Mila mentioned—he did not think of Mike. He did not think of his mother's letters from home, or of his purpose in being here in Rudrakot, or even of the four short days he had to accomplish what he had come for. He listened instead to the sound of her fading footsteps, and hankered for her to return.

# Five

*I was neither Englishman nor Indian, but it was not a national matter. It looked to me as if the whole globe might be in the war before it was over . . . It might be America's business, too, before so very long. The world had shrunk. India was no longer far away from anywhere. What with the radio and the Quiz Kids, we talked in New York . . . Gandhi was no stranger to us . . . I found myself tingling with a kind of impotent impatience. Europe was aflame, the sparks were flying in India's direction, but the politicians would not help man the fire engine!*

—Post Wheeler, *India Against the Storm,* 1944

Sayyid came to lead him to his bedroom, not Mila, and upon entering it, Sam saw nothing in that room—not the gossamer white curtains on the windows and the door leading to the balcony, not the malachite green mosaic floor or the burnished teak furniture; Sam saw only the bed.

He touched the cool sheets, bent to rub his face against the clean soap-nut smell of the fabric. An immense weariness overtook him; his limbs turned to water, his legs folded beneath him, and he barely heard Sayyid asking when he wanted breakfast. One moment Sam had his nose against the fragrant *dhobi*-washed pillowcase, the next the bed reached out to yank him into its inviting embrace. He fumbled with the alarm clock on the bedside table in those last few moments before he slept. Sam slept with his boots on, on his face, just as he had fallen, and did not move the entire morning. His dreams were manacled with images of Mike, of their childhood together with their mother, and, briefly, of the father he had not known. George Ridley had left his wife and children, unable, quite simply, to bear the burden of a family. Maude herself was silent to a stillness about the husband she had once loved, but there were lingerings of their father's presence all around the house, in photographs tucked into the flaps of albums, in a letter laid facedown at the bottom of a box under Maude's winter sweaters.

Little by little, Mike and Sam had pieced their father together—a salmon and crab fisherman in Alaska, a man who preferred the seduction of the wild, the cold, the raw land up north, who had abandoned their mother after a few years when the sea called out his name so insistently that it shut out everything else. The photographs showed a prematurely white beard on a startlingly immature face, a wide smile, and burly shoulders. Even then, when he was ten or eleven or fourteen, Sam had wondered what had attracted them to each other, kept them together for as long as they had been married, since they had so little in common. Their childhoods had been varied, their manners different; Maude was a reader, George had read very little, for he had grown up on the docks in Juneau, surrounded by the aroma of fish, schooled in fishing and little else. On winter days, when the snow lay softly on the shoulders of the Olympic Mountains out to the west, Sam would go to the pier at the cusp of night and watch the sun slip behind the mountains. Then his gaze would drift north and west, where he thought Alaska was, where his father was, and Sam would wonder if he thought of them all. Through the fog of no news, they had heard that George Ridley had married an Aleut woman and fathered a daughter. After that, they had heard nothing more.

Mike was born three months after George left, when Sam was four, and his memories of the events of that time were as lucid as when they had happened. Maude wearily hunched in the rocking chair, her feet firmly on the floor, still pitching the chair, the baby asleep against her breast. Maude clucking over Mike, her nose buried in his little tummy, his giggles of rapture as he clutched at her hair. Sam had felt as though he was being deserted again, this time by his mother, for a tiny, mewling, demanding creature who took all of her time. He had refused to look at Mike, to hear his gurgles, to notice that his gaze only followed Sam when he was in the room. And then one day he looked at his little brother, who smiled and spit at him, and Sam fell in love.

They grew up alike, Mike an adoring shadow of his older brother. They climbed the same trees, hid in the branches of the plum while Maude shouted at them to come inside for lunch, and hugged their mother all around, their arms linking her waist, their faces smothered in the cool linens of her summer dresses. On the rare winter days of snow, when school was called off by a mere whitening on the roads, Sam and Mike filched a tray from Maude's kitchen and sledded down the slope near the house, arriving at the bottom in a wet, cold heap of happiness. Mike was the one with the outward passion—he shouted, drummed his fists on the floor, threw his body around on the furniture, in moments of distress tore at the rugs like a puppy. Sam was quieter, more thoughtful, amazed by Mike's antics, even more astounded that they brought results. But even then, very young, he understood that they each had their ways and their peculiarities, that these vagaries made them unique. Maude was a painter and was absorbed in the afternoons in her studio atop the house with huge daubs on canvases gleaming with colors splattered haphazardly to Sam, but perfectly understandable to Mike.

When the war had come three years ago in Europe, Mike, then only eighteen, chafed in the safe confines of Seattle. There was a war on, he would tell Sam, and they were doing nothing to contribute to justice. These were the words he used—*truth, honesty, integrity, conviction*—there were no shades of gray in Mike's world, no place for guilt that could not be atoned for, no hiding from his own flaws.

Sam, more patient, had been content to wait for America to go into the war; he knew that the waiting would not be long, but not Mike. He had joined the American Field Service and taken ambulances out to the war front in France in 1940, and then, sometime the next year, he wrote to them to say that he was in India, training for a British Indian regiment. Times of war were forgiving; all Mike had needed was a sanction from the U.S. embassy in Paris and a nod from the India Office in London to join an Indian army without losing his American citizenship. Four months later, Second Lieutenant Michael Ridley joined the Rudrakot Rifles as an emergency commissioned officer. *We are all pristinely white here—the Rifles are a British regiment, and we live unhappily across the road from the Rudrakot Lancers, an all-Indian regiment, right up to their commanding officer, who is, if you can believe it, some sort of prince. Do you remember reading about the struggle for freedom, Ma,* Mike had written to Maude, *well, it's alive, well, and kicking here . . . though too slow for my liking. These Indians are too quiet a people, steadily persistent though, and I just don't understand Gandhi's nonviolence movement—whack the hell out of these sorry British bastards, I say, and they will leave India. Or better yet, refuse to engage in the war—after all, it is not an Indian war, but a British one. Why should Indian regiments, fighting on behalf of the British Raj, die in droves on war fronts like Egypt and Libya—poorly clad, ill equipped, shabbily trained, fighting an enemy they do not even recognize as their own?*

This letter was written in February 1942, by which time Sam was already also on his way to India. For one month, Sam had tried to make contact with Mike, but his letters had been unanswered, his phone calls dropped by one of the myriad operators who would have linked him from his base camp in Assam to Rudrakot. The day before he left for Burma to find and rescue Marianne Westwood, he received Maude's frantic letter. Mike was missing, considered AWOL from the army, which, like all armies, blew minor infractions out of proportion and labeled liars murderers. The Rudrakot Rifles had closed their files on him for now—the war was on, Burma had fallen, there was no time to search out errant officers. *Find him, darling. I'm only grateful that you are in India already.* But Sam had had to put his mother's pleas away and go into Burma, and all through that journey with Marianne and Ken, he had seethed with the desire to be in Rudrakot.

The alarm on the bedside clock beeped for five minutes before its sound delved into Sam's sleep-fogged brain. For a moment, he could not tell where he was. The white-washed expanse over his head, the fan hiccupping through its revolutions, the quiet around him at this time of the day bespoke almost all of civilized India. He had been in so many places over the last four days that this could be any one of them. And then he remembered his morning conversation with Raman, remembered meeting Mila, and an ache began to grow within his chest, for then he also recalled why he was here at Rudrakot. His shoulder had stiffened with the rest, the bones seemed solidified under his skin and Sam shrugged gently to loosen the hardness. His stomach rumbled, as though glad he was finally awake.

On the table beside his bed was a tray covered with a thin film of cloth. Sam lifted it and found a plate with a domed aluminum lid, a pot of tea in a Devon teapot, one cup and saucer, a fork and a knife clad in the folds of an ivory napkin, and, most incongruously, a wilted red rose laid alongside the plate. He was almost afraid of lifting the dome to see what lay underneath, for the aging of the rose told him that the tray had been by his bedside since shortly after he had fallen asleep. Two eggs from Pallavi's chicken coop blinked their unbroken yolk eyes at him, the fat still runny around the edges, since it was too hot for the butter to congeal. There was also a slice of potted meat, decorated with a wilted sprig of coriander leaf. A toast rack also stood by the tray and two pieces of bread, now dry and flaky, disintegrated onto the table's shiny surface. The tea was at room temperature, which was to say that it was not cold, but not as hot as it ought to be, and slivers of creamy milk and tea swirled from the spout into the teacup when Sam poured. He dusted his eggs with pepper and salt. Ever since he had come to India, Sam's taste buds had blossomed under the care of the army cooks who with no finesse had fed spices into the dishes by the handful. In the beginning his stomach had revolted; a thin flame of heat had burned around the periphery of its lining until Sam could *feel* the throbbing shape and size of his stomach within his torso. That burning had finally settled into a dull ache, and then had miraculously vanished.

The eggs melted in Sam's mouth. The toast broke into a thousand shattered pieces of baked dough and he sponged up every minute piece with his wetted forefinger. He even wiped the teacup out with his finger and held it, cup upended, over his mouth until the last drop of tea slid out onto his waiting tongue. Sam was still hungry. He walked over to his holdall, unzipped it, and rummaged around the sides for the two chocolate bars. Still sitting on the floor, he ate the chocolate, not slowly, not savoring it, but in a sudden rush of hunger.

Sam had chosen to awaken in the middle of the afternoon—his watch told him it was a little after one o'clock—because this was the time of rest and sleep in India and for what he wanted to do, there would be no prying eyes to encounter.

He went into the bathroom to brush his teeth and wash his face, and then came back to his holdall. He dug around the bottom of the bag and came up with a *dhoti*, a long piece of cloth, about five feet by three, muddied and browned beyond its woven-white color. Sam had dipped the *dhoti* in the river behind his barracks in Assam and then, without rinsing out the mud, had flung it on some bushes; it had dried in less than half an hour, the sun eagerly eating up all moisture in the cloth. He laid the *dhoti* on the floor, and then brought out a *kurta*, also dulled from its former color to look aged and worn, its sleeves torn and frayed at the edges where they would fall upon his wrists. Another piece of cloth, navy blue and white, he deposited near the *dhoti* and the *kurta*. And then Sam began to dress. He took off his pants and his shirt, folded them, and stuffed them under the mattress. He knotted the *dhoti* skirtlike around his waist. Bending over, Sam reached for the back of the *dhoti,* drew it up in front, over his crotch, and tucked the end into his waist. Then he ruffled the edges along his legs, pulling them down until his knees were covered.

The only mirror in his room was above the chest of drawers and Sam had to climb up on the bed to look at his efforts. The *dhoti* fit snugly around his waist and over his body. Mr. Gandhi's loincloth, Sam thought, this is what it was, a piece of cloth woven around the body, easily washed, with no seams that would come unraveled, no stitches to pick up or to lose. He donned his *kurta,* rolled up the sleeves above his elbow, and then tackled the blue-and-white turban cloth. Sam had watched peasants tie on turbans with a great deal of ease, with concentration and no mirror, at most a river's reflection to look into. So he did the same, and as he worked, slowly and laboriously, he let his mind go blank and turned from Sam Hawthorne, U.S. Army, into a simple Indian peasant.

The cloth he wrapped around his fingers until it was twisted, and one end he set at the middle of his forehead. Still holding the end in place on his forehead with his left hand, Sam used his right hand to twirl the cloth and wind it around his head in larger and larger circles. The last bit he tucked into the side, above his right ear. The turban, so wrapped, left a circle of emptiness on the top of his head, where his hair shone black and shining. Sam smoothed down the shine with some talcum powder, and then spread some powder over his eyebrows and the stubble on his face. He did not need to worry about the color of his face or his hands; he had a farmer's tan from Burma, but his legs and his feet were still sickly pale from having been encased in pants and damp and mildewed socks. He reached into his holdall again and brought out a compact of dull brown powder that had come from the United States—there was no *brown* makeup powder to be found in India, only white. He broke the compact powder into little pieces, and went to the bathroom to make a sludgy mess in his hand with some water. This he rubbed over his legs and his feet. The water would soon dry and the powder would fall off, but by then Sam hoped the dust outside would muddy his legs.

There were a pair of worn leather *chappals* also in his holdall; Sam took these out and slipped them on his feet, and then slipped them off again. If he truly was to be unnoticeable, he had to be barefoot, as Indian peasants and gardeners and coolies often were. Why, even Sayyid, butler in the house of the political agent, for all of his uniform finery of a white jacket studded with brass buttons, red cummerbund, and red turban, had had no slippers on his feet when he led Sam to this room.

Sam opened the door to the balcony and paused at the threshold, listening. But it was an afternoon quiet that hung over Raman's house. The gardens below and behind the house were deserted, the servants in a deep slumber, the sun beat down upon them all, victorious at having driven all living beings, human and animal, indoors.

He went along the length of the balcony softly, down the spiral concrete stairs to the gardens, and walked along its length to the back where there was a little iron gate set in the concrete wall. Sam opened this gate and held his breath, but the hinges did not creak. Before he closed it behind him, he took a rusty spade from where it leaned against the wall, set it upon his shoulders, and started along the back of Raman's house toward the cantonment area and the grounds of the Rudrakot Rifles. To the beginning. Where his brother was first lost.

As Sam wended his way through the scrub and bush behind the houses and then, with an eye on the sun, bore northwest behind the Civil Lines, the day wore on in the field punishment center, still and onerous, bearing the weight of a summer holding its breath in anticipation of the rains. Heat mirages shimmied across the desert, drawing distorted images along the horizon—the blue of water, the green of palms, the slow sway of a camel caravan—none of which existed, of course, in the arid emptiness of this dismal earth.

The sun burned, unforgiving and harsh, over a squat building of red sandstone. It was built in a square, with a courtyard in the center, and cells fronting this yard without the cover of verandahs. The cells were tiny, six feet by six feet, the floors bare and filthy, a hole in ground at the far end for a latrine, their every corner visible, like pens for caged animals on display. There was a well in the courtyard surrounded by a low brick wall, covered with wooden shutters. A silent, struggling row of men knelt in the hot sun, their heads bare and drenched in sweat.

"Again," the guard said, and he flipped the box of matches into the air.

One man watched the matches twirl and fall into the dust, and cringed as the sun hit his eyes and scorched his face. He bent from his knees, and scrambled slowly in the red mud with his fingers, blowing on each match as he picked it up, and then rubbing it against his dirty shirt before he slid it carefully into the box. He counted in his mind . . . one . . . two . . . three . . . four . . . as the matches stacked up inside the little box. His fingers were raw with blood from a lashing across his knuckles the last time he had lost a match. The box held forty-five matches. Forty-five. Michael Ridley had lost count again. His brain was too tired for even this simple math, starved of food, famished for rest. He had even lost count of how many days he had been here. Months? Maybe a year? He had no idea where he was. In the two months Mike had spent at the Rifles barracks, he had seen no building like this prison, or nothing that looked like this on the inside. What it was camouflaged to be on the outside, Mike had no idea.

He had woken one night to a fist jammed into his mouth, and before he could struggle, his hands and feet were tied, his mouth gagged, a blanket draped over his head. A horse had borne him here; he had been flung over the saddle, his face smothered in the thick of the blanket, thudding against the horse's belly. His own stomach and ribs had been banged raw by the riding, and when his feet and hands had been untied, blood had strung its way painfully into his veins again. In the beginning, so long ago, Mike had demanded a trial, asked for one, begged and pleaded, ducking his head from the careless, swinging wallops from the guards' *lathis*. The guards had taken away his food, taken away his water, taken away everything but his will to live. Once also, the iron gates in the middle of one of the walls had swung open during the day to let in the water lorry (it mostly opened at night) and they had all leaned their heads hard against the bars, twisted their necks, thrown their visions to the outside, to that world beyond. But a burl of cinnamon mud in the maw of the sky was all they had seen. Brown and blue. A tree in the very far distance like an opalescent pale mushroom. The heat haze lifted then and something else, a building, a monument, came into almost sharp focus for Mike. But it then disappeared so quietly in front of him that he could no longer capture its image in his exhausted mind. What had it been? A temple? Surely he had seen it before?

Forty-four. Only forty-four matches, Mike thought. He dug through the dirt again, praying, oh God, let me find the last one, oh God, please God. The dust rose to choke him, fill his nostrils, burn his eyes, but he kept looking.

"Time's up, chaps, hold up your boxes."

The guard went past the line of prisoners, counting the matches in each box, until he came to Mike. "Didn't find them all, did yer?"

Every interminable day had been like this one, with games and tasks that had once seemed stupid, when his brain could still reason so, but no longer. There was always the hope that if he counted all of his matches right, they would let him go beyond the iron gates of the entrance, that that would be the reward. His brain had tricked him into thinking so, had made an enemy of logic. Mike bowed his head, waiting for a blow . . . something . . . some punishment. His knees burned in the hot dirt. Anger came roiling over him all of a sudden. Where was Sam? Why had his mother not tried to find him? He hadn't written to them in months, and letters went astray because of the war, but did they not wonder, or care? Where was Sam? At some European war front—a beribboned and decorated officer?

He hunched into his chest, sobbing softly, his mouth parched and open to the salt of his tears. The pot went spinning into the well, thwacked into the water, gurgled with fullness, and came swinging up the pulley. He closed his eyes as the guard flung water at the men who had found all of their matches, and heard their thirsty slurping as the drops came their way. A drop splattered near his knee and kicked up dust. With the sun beating down upon him, Michael Ridley felt a blessed coolness. He still cried, still tasted his tears, absorbed that moisture back into his body and listened for the next soft drop of water in the dirt.

# Six

BRITAIN THE CRADLE OF DEMOCRACY. *Although you'll read in the papers about "lords" and "sirs," England is still one of the great democracies and the cradle of many American liberties . . . the British enjoy a practical, working twentieth century democracy which is . . . flexible and sensitive to the will of the people . . .*

—War Department, *Instructions for American Servicemen in Britain,* 1942

*And by now, my dear Olivia, you have met a few of the main players in this stage I have created for you. But as you will see, the setting also matters. Mila lives in one part of Rudrakot—the elite part. Toward the reaches of the desert, away from the civil and cantonment lines of the city is—in the parlance of the British Raj—the black town. In other words, only the natives inhabited this part of the land, linked to the cantonment by a bazaar street. Mila and her family were also "native," of course, but they were one of the few, privileged families to find their residences situated within the Civil Lines of Rudrakot. Times were, my dearest Olivia, when even this little invasion would not have been possible. But it was 1942, and there were now more Indians in the civil service, more Indians with wealth and power, more Indians demanding freedom from British rule. The encroachment into the once-inviolable Civil Lines was inevitable. For all her entitlements,*

81

*Mila never forgot that she was Indian—different in skin, understanding, and disposition from most other people in her neighborhood or at the Victoria Club.*

*I say this because here is your father, Sam, tumbling headlong and rashly in love with your mother. And here is Mila, her equanimity already shaken by him (though she does not know it yet). For the first time in her life, a man who is not Indian has stirred an interest within her. For the first time also, she is considering Sam in the light of a lover, of a love that would last her for the rest of her life.*

A lull, heavy and silent in the heat, extended over the bazaar. The shop fronts were shuttered with gunnysack matting, cows dozed in the shade of awnings, and stench flew upward from the gutters filled with viscous, black, and now drying water. Nothing moved in the afternoon heat—in the houses atop the shops, windows were closed, and women slept on the bare cement floors, heads laid on arms and hands, glued to their skins with drops of sweat. The bazaar was called such, "lal," or red, after the color of the uniforms worn by the officers of the Rudrakot Rifles, who were half of the patrons of the Lal Bazaar. It sold an item of necessity to men in army regiments, to men all over the world—sex. The houses fronted the little, crooked street, painted in brilliant pinks and blues, much like the saris the women draped so casually as to reveal everything, their faces painted in livid lines in the same colors in the evenings, blue around their eyes, reds outlining their mouths.

At one end of the bazaar was a house set away from the street. It had a small compound in front sheltered by a gracefully growing banyan tree. And under the shade of that banyan, fifteen pairs of arms and legs moved in unison. The boys and girls, most in their teens, were all clad in white *kurtas* and *churidars*, indigo sashes around their waists. Their teacher, a youth of seventeen, still smooth faced, shouted out orders in a singsong voice, "*One*-two-three-four. One-*two*." And his fifteen pupils obligingly followed in jumping jacks, twists and turns, bending from the waist to meet their left foot with their right hand and their right foot with their left, the girls' long plaits swinging down over their backs to the dust and up again.

Inside the two-story house, Vimal Kumar stood near the window, looking down upon the exercising, sweating group. He was a slim, intense man, not much older than the group outside, but he had been elected their leader almost from the beginning. He wore the same white *kurta* and *churidar,* but he was cool inside the room even though there was hardly any breeze from the ancient, creaking, ceiling fan.

Vimal turned back to the room, his delicate hands clasped behind his back. There was a wooden table in the center, with four chairs, three of which were occupied by two men and a woman. His eyes burned into them, bright with fervor, his back straightened, and he whipped his head so that his hair slung over his forehead. The other three stared, their breaths shallow. They all shared the intensity of Vimal's expression, their faces blank canvases of focus and nothing else, their gazes fixed hungrily upon him. They waited for him to speak.

"Will they be able to keep this up much longer?" he asked, with a nod over his shoulder. "It is hot. Blastedly hot."

The girl spoke softly. "They will have to, comrade. We can meet for the next hour, no more, and they will exercise until we are done."

A little smile touched Vimal's perfectly formed lips. "Mahatma Gandhi asked us to give our lives for our country; I don't believe this was what he meant."

One of the men shifted in his seat and said, "The police will not come into the house as long as they see the exercisers outside, comrade."

Vimal Kumar sat down in the fourth chair and laid his hands on the smooth and bare wood of the table. He wore a gold ring on one finger, his left index, engraved with an etching of the goddess Lakshmi, the goddess of wealth, and a gold chain with a coin around his neck. Vimal had been adorned with many more ornaments upon his birth, since his father was one of Rudrakot's leading dry-goods merchants, for the black town, of course—a British merchant ran the store in the cantonment area. But over the months of being the unheralded head of the underground nationalist movement in Rudrakot, he had slowly divested himself of each piece of jewelry. He had worn earrings at one time, and those had gone into the fund plate to buy this house and compound in the Lal Bazaar. The silver watch with diamond studs had gone into another collection plate, at a meeting one night when he had stripped it off his wrist and flung it onto the plate with a, "Money means nothing to me, comrades, freedom is worth all I have now, and all I can give in the future!" That speech was so impassioned, so moving, that merely looking upon the handsome Vimal on the platform, sweat soaking into his *kurta* until it stuck to the lines of his chest, his hair plastered to his well-formed skull, his mouth spewing words that brought chills up the listeners' spines, money and jewelry piled onto the plate. That night they collected forty watches, a thousand rupees, fifteen gold chains, fifty bangles, nose studs, earrings, anklets—all for the cause. That night they also collected the hearts of most of Rudrakot's young.

Vimal had nicked his finger while slicing a green mango the day before. The wound on the pad of his left index finger was quite deep, but no longer bleeding, with only a lurid red gash to show where the knife had slashed through the whorls and circles of his fingertip. He looked down at his finger ruefully, and the three around the table reacted together in reaching out toward him. The girl wanted to lift his finger to her mouth and kiss away the hurt. The two men wanted to slice his mangoes for him from now on and bear the burden of any future cuts. Vimal noticed their movements and smiled into himself. He had always had this power over people. All leaders, he thought, had a personal charisma, an almost sexual energy that consumed their followers. In Mahatma Gandhi's case, this last was not quite true, but he still possessed a strange and awe-inspiring power in his quiet voice, his studied sentences, his use of just-adequate language. The one aspect of the Mahatma's teachings that Vimal had never been able to fully understand or accept was the concept of nonviolent resistance. It seemed too futile for him, too much like waiting too long and not wanting enough for the cause.

From the outside came the shrill cries of the exercise leader, one-two-three-four, and Vimal leaned into his comrades. "I have heard news."

They all waited, looking into his beautiful face with adoration.

"Since Burma has fallen to the Japanese, the British have shown themselves to be grossly inadequate. They were thrown out of Burma and fled back to Assam like pariah dogs, tails between their legs. And the *goras* were given first preference for evacuation, leaving our Indian comrades defenseless against the Japanese in many cases, or leaving them quite simply to walk out of Burma and Malaya into Assam. Do you know how far that is? A thousand miles."

Vimal's voice rose into the silent room to drown out the steady clank of the ceiling fan. He moved his hands as he talked, blood flooding into the clear skin of his face. "The refugees from Burma walked into Assam to camps in search of assistance and food, and they were divided into two groups—the *goras* on one road, the Indians on a parallel road. A white road, my comrades, and a black one. Which group do you think received the best aid, the best medications, and the best supplies? One *gora* even took his billiards table while our brethren were left to perish on the roadside."

The three listeners flushed and their eyes glowed. "I know we are too far from the war frontiers, that the first Japanese threats are to Assam and Calcutta and Madras and parts of Ceylon, but are these cities fortified? Are they capable of withstanding an assault from the Japanese? Are they then capable of defending the whole of India?"

"No," the three breathed softly.

"Our British government, too craven and cowardly to defend our motherland, is now ready to take flight. Do you know what the government has decided to do?" Vimal demanded, pushing back his chair to stand up, his palms on the table. "A policy of scorched earth, they call it. They are going to bomb all the docks in Calcutta and Madras, destroy the local infrastructure of industry and buildings, all in anticipation of a Japanese takeover. And this is the country they consider the jewel in their crown. Since they cannot defend her, our Mother India, they seek instead to destroy her!" He spat on the floor, and the three spat along with him. "The Mahatma has written in condemnation of this. But I say we should go further than mere words. We have to show them that we will not stand for this willful destruction of our property and of the livelihoods of our people. We must do something!"

He strode around the table in quick, short strides, panting from all the shouting. Outside, the exercise leader had increased the volume of his cries to muffle Vimal's voice. *One-two,* he shouted.

"What shall we do, Vimal?" the girl asked, her question accompanied by the slapping of hands against thighs in the compound below.

Vimal stopped and his breathing slowed, his chest heaving. "Nonviolence is not the answer," he said slowly. "I say we return violence for violence. Attempting to destroy our docks and our buildings is an attempt at violence against our people."

He shook his head. "I shall have to think of something." He glanced at one of the boys. "Can you make a bomb, Parekh?"

The boy nodded eagerly. "Of course, Vimal."

"When?"

"In a day."

"A day. . . ." Vimal rubbed his chin and then looked at them again. "Do you know where Colonel Pankhurst is right now?"

"The British resident?" the girl asked.

"Yes, don't confuse him with the political agent . . . ," Vimal said, pausing, an idea registering on him, and then went on, "that chap is Indian, not on our side, a staunch imperialist of course, but perhaps he can be brought to reason. . . . Colonel Pankhurst is the resident and he is out on a tiger hunt right now in the Sukh. Can you believe this? Our borders are being threatened and the resident is away on a pleasure trip."

"The bastard," the three followers said simultaneously, and Vimal turned away to disguise a smile. Colonel Pankhurst, that poor shit, was actually in Delhi in deep conference with the viceroy, most probably on Rudrakot business, but such tedium would not foment his followers into action, hence the little lie. The mention of Raman's name set his head aflame with ideas. Why had he not thought of Raman before? Vimal's father and Raman were old acquaintances despite the difference in their social stations, because Raman chose his friends where he found them. And yet Vimal knew that there was never a man more loyal to the British cause than Raman—a born-and-bred ICS officer.

The other three had begun chattering, their voices rising and falling in passion, cursing the British resident, cursing the government, decrying Gandhi's lethargy in only demanding but not taking freedom from the British. Vimal did not listen to their talk; he wandered to the window and gazed out into the deserted street of the Lal Bazaar. The boys and girls below whipped themselves into a perspiring frenzy at the sight of his beloved figure at the window, all eager to please him, all heedless of their own comfort. Such was his power. Such, he knew too, was his power.

It had been Vimal's idea to buy this dirty little house in this bazaar of filth. The British Indian army, the Rifles regiment specifically, which was an all-white regiment, had petitioned for and received permission to construct the Lal Bazaar. Half the women, on one half of the street, clearly demarcated, were allotted for the use of the Rifles; the other half were for the Lancers, an all-Indian regiment. Neither group of men wanted to be contaminated by women who slept with the other kind, though the Rifles were the first to demand this demarcation. The Lal Bazaar, then, was a sanctioned street of brothels, ruled over by two madams, attended to by two separate physicians, British and Indian. It was—the British government of India had determined—a necessity for their men, so they provided it helpfully, along with their mess kits, their canteens, their turbans and hats, their revolvers and swords, their stirrups and uniforms. But the bazaar was also, most naturally, the bastard child of the army. An unfortunate necessity, and so rarely patrolled, little acknowledged except in times of emergencies. And so, Vimal Kumar, leader of the Freedom for India movement in Rudrakot, had brought his band of freedom fighters here, under the noses of the men who ran and policed Rudrakot.

The police inspector had bothered them only once, when one of the girls had fainted in the heat and a little crowd of prostitutes had gathered around, awash in cheap perfume, raucous voices, and useless advice. The inspector had asked where the girl was from, and Vimal, in a moment of brilliance, had mentioned a side street in the poorer section of the black town, and not where she actually lived, within the Civil Lines, the daughter of a rich Indian lawyer. The inspector ordered them to take her home, and to keep their physical activities to a minimum in the afternoons. They had nodded respectfully, shrieking with laughter inside at the poor sod's red face and the bracelets of white skin on his neck where the sun had not touched. So they confined their exercising to the times when the sun smoldered over Rudrakot, confident the inspector, even though he was British (and so by definition insane), would not come out in the heat to check on them.

Vimal thought of Raman again. For a few short years, Ashok and he had studied mathematics and English with the same tutor. Ashok Raman had been a shy little boy, as enamored of Vimal then as were the members of his movement now. Raman had two other children though? Kiran and Mila. This Kiran chap would be of no use; he was too much like his father, too much in love with the British and their ways. And the girl, not her either. If he approached Ashok, he would have to be careful of her. From what he remembered, the girl had been imperious, mothering of Ashok, *smothering* of Ashok; she would not be so easily led. Vimal had been irritated by her indifference when she had looked past him in their study room. No matter, he thought, he held no grudges. She would come under his influence, as all others did, if he but exerted himself. It was Ashok he wanted to see again.

Now he had to reestablish contact and deposit a viper in the political agent's breast, one ready to uncoil and strike, and Raman would not even know that he had nurtured it.

# Seven

*[It would be imprudent for the British]* *to descend from the high place*
*which the genius of the Englishman has rightfully won, and endeavour to*
*persuade the people of India . . . that they are intellectually or morally*
*our equals, and that to them have been confided by fortune those secrets of*
*government which in the modern world, are the inheritance of the Anglo-*
*Saxon race alone.*

—Sir Lepel Griffin, *Fortnightly Review,* October 1883

*M*ila lay in her bed listening to the soft sounds of the lethargic afternoon. She could not sleep, so she thought instead of Jai's last letter from the Imperial Cadet Corps. He had gone back to the ICC as an instructor this time, fully vested as a King's Commissioned Officer, or KCO, and his students were all, like him, princes and noblemen connected with the princely states.

When Jai had first joined the Indian army, king's commissions were not bestowed upon Indians—no matter that he was a prince, that he held a royal title, such as it was. But all British officers of the Indian army had king's commissions simply because their skins were white, even though their origins might be dead common. Jai could only manage a viceroy's commission, or a VCO. The unspoken fiction was that all ranks, VCO or KCO, were equal. But it was evident that the VCOs were black Indians, and the KCOs were the white British, so even a British subaltern considered a high-ranking Indian officer subordinate to him because of the color of the Indian officer's skin.

The VCO had not been enough for Jai and for years Mila had heard him complain about the unfairness of this rule. "Here is yet another differentiation between Indians and the British in India," he would say. "I am an army officer, I command a regiment, my men and I will fight and die for the empire—why do I deserve less?"

To murk the waters of these arguments further, Jai's Rudrakot Lancers was a regiment raised by his father, Raja Bhimsen, and was quartered in and wholly maintained by the princely state, with no burden of responsibility on the British Indian government. As such, the Rudrakot Lancers, though ostensibly part of the Indian army, could not really be governed by these rules in the Indian army. For the British government considered that the princely states enjoyed a certain degree of autonomy within the boundaries of the Raj, and asked that Rudrakot in turn recognize the suzerainty of the king in England.

Ten years ago, in the 1930s, these stringent color rules had begun to bleed at their edges, especially in the princely states. Jai shouted, fought, wrote impassioned letters to the viceroy and the king, and, as an afterthought, exercised a little diplomacy too, at Raman's exhorting. After much of this wrangling and petitioning and politicking, Jai got his cherished commission from the king. But he knew that he still could not rank over a British officer, even with his KCO—the color bar in India was indeed a hard line to cross. Jai still had to be satisfied to be the commander of his all-Indian Rudrakot Lancers. But wars, like this one and the Great War before this one, had a way of equalizing all prejudices, for a bleeding and dying soldier is a bleeding and dying soldier, no matter what earth he spills his blood upon, no matter what color that blood is. In the end, all was ashes and dust. Death was the great leveler, and before this war ended, Jai suspected that he might well be put in command of an all-white regiment.

Mila could remember the day, two months ago, when the news of the commission had come. The ten-year period of waiting, the immense yearning for that commission had taken away none of its charm. That was the day Jai had approached Raman about another matter. Mila had liked Jai immensely before; it was difficult not to like him despite all of his eccentricities and his tantrums. His heart was open and he was impeccably honest—but then two months ago, there had come an inevitable shifting in their relationship. It was something she had anticipated for a while, but its coming to pass had still been mildly shocking, as though her life had been decided for her.

She missed Jai's presence here at Rudrakot. If a Rifles officer (bestowed with his KCO well before Jai) refused to salute Jai, or ignored his presence, as had been done before when Jai had held a mere viceroy's commission, Jai, fire headed as usual, would plunge into a temper and Papa would be called in to mediate and pacify, as he had done all these years. There was little quiet when Jai was around; even this Sam Hawthorne could not have come unnoticed into their house and slept for so long without a visit from Jai, imperious, demanding, wanting to investigate the visitor to Rudrakot.

At the thought of Sam, Mila pushed her pillows away and laid her ear against the wall dividing their rooms. How long he slept, this American. Did he mean to spend all his time here in bed? She had heard no noises from his room for a long time. She had flitted by his closed door in the corridor many times in the morning, seen the line of light under it that meant the door to the balcony was open. She had even stepped out into the balcony from her own room and looked to the left, but had not dared walk past that open door to peep inside. Would he never waken? Where was he from? Why had he come here? Papa had said little about him, only told Mila to look after their guest, as he was going to be busy for the next few days. Ashok was thrilled by the visitor; he had asked the same questions and Mila had had no answers, so he flounced off to his studies with a strict admonition that the *minute* Sam Hawthorne woke up, Ashok was to be told. She flattened her face against the wall, but the brick and mortar beneath kept its silence. She thought she heard a snore. And then her day came up to her, all that fatigue, that tension, that blistering heat, that lull of the afternoon's calm. Her eyes closed, and she slipped down to curl onto her bed.

And so the afternoon passed that May in Rudrakot. The natives, except for Vimal's army of exercisers, crept into their houses and slept the heat away, waited for the sun to die in the arms of the coming night. All over the Raj, all over India, the natives followed this policy of hibernation on summer afternoons. So the days were always split into two sections, the early mornings and the late afternoons and evenings. If they all did not sleep, they "took rest" after lunch, ensnared in desultory conversations and caustic hand-rolled *beedis,* their movements slow and unhurried—hands to mouths, a considerate drag, a reflection on the taste, a flicking of ashes, the same repeated again. In many ways, this slowing down was a wise policy, more efficient certainly, and more considerate of irritable tempers and simmering bloods.

Sam took the beaten mud path around the fringes of the town. On one side were the huge bungalows and mansions of the Civil Lines, on the other, the shacks and shanties of the servants who served the sahibs and memsahibs. Over the last few months, Sam had sat outside his barracks, or lingered in the bazaars in Assam, to watch the peasants walk, and now he duplicated that walk and manner as best he could.

His head was angled to his chest and he kept it down for two reasons—one, that he was expected not to stride about, chin in air in a very sahiblike fashion; and two, because he could not, as a servant, meet a master's gaze. Though the Burma sun had painted its ochre hues upon his skin so he could pass for Indian, nothing could take away the telltale blue of his eyes. He could very well be an Anglo-Indian, half British and half Indian, invariably the product of a liaison, for it had been decades since Anglo-Indian marriage alliances had been sanctioned by Raj society.

The shift in thinking had come after 1858, when Victoria became queen empress of India. The British officers in the Indian army, the civilians in the civil service, the industrialists and traders had now become the masters of India. If they wanted to marry, pretty English roses, especially those a little long in the tooth or short in the purse, shipped themselves out in aptly named "fishing fleets" to marry them and create a little England in this heathen land.

But men, it seemed, would be men. And Indian women were not that often unattractive, no matter what color their skins were. So the British pleasured themselves and begat children most often outside the bonds of marriage, children whom neither society, Indian or British, wanted to claim as their own. They were called half-castes, or Eurasians, both derogatory and embarrassing names. *Anglo-Indians* had long been reserved for the use of the British in India, but had only lately been appropriated for the use of . . . well, the true Anglo-Indians—the ones who could, somewhere in the past, trace an ancestry to a Briton and an Indian.

Sam, then, could have been Anglo-Indian, but he could not have been Anglo-Indian and been a gardener in the regiment grounds because the two (profession and race) did not readily mix and would cause suspicion. He had to keep his head bowed to the ground. He also had to remember that if someone talked to him, he had to respond to the earth and not raise his head.

His bare feet burned in the mud, and with each step he drew clouds of dust around himself. He had slung the spade over his shoulders and looped his arms around the wooden haft with his hands falling near his face. Surprisingly, his right shoulder did not protest much; the heat, the fluidity of his muscles, the warmth on his skin had loosened the pain.

The shacks that housed the servants petered out into a hot, dusty plain just past the Civil Lines and the homes of the rich in Rudrakot. Sam saw a stand of trees in the far distance, and a metalled road that cut across the plain and vanished into the foliage. Somewhere in the middle of this road, his rickshaw had broken down earlier that day. In the distance, skirting above the trees and the deserted landscape, was a hill of some considerable size. Looming on that hill, in every sense of the word, was an ancient fort. The battlements that snaked their way in loops and curves along the slopes of the hill were massive and built of huge blocks of red sandstone thrust one upon the other. There were tiny window holes cut in squares at uneven places along the face of the wall, but they were too high to be reached by a marauding army struggling its way up the hillside. From this vantage, Sam could see the dun-colored palaces and mansions that perched precariously on the knife-edged summit of the hill. He saw minarets and domes topped by tarnished brass finials and the triangular steeplelike roof of a temple festooned with pillars. Below, trees and crawling bushes dotted the hillside, keeping the land from sliding down. Though the fort palace absolutely dominated the slice of sky above the road, Sam had not even noticed it when his rickshaw stopped.

In the dull of the afternoon, Sam heard the roar of an engine and searched around him for a bush to hide behind. A jeep broke out of the green of the trees ahead, a tiny, moving insect at first, heralded only by the noise of its engine, a sound that moved cleanly across the land to meet Sam. As the jeep neared, Sam shuffled his feet, lowered his eyes, and tried not to flinch as the tender skin of his soles rested on the heated dirt. The jeep passed by him in a roar of petrol fumes and red dust. An Indian *jawan* was driving the jeep, an officer from the Rifles regiment, a major, by the markings on his uniform, sat upright and beside the driver. They did not even glance at him.

Thirty minutes later, he trudged into the stand of trees, and rested for a few minutes against the trunk of a tamarind, wiping the wetness off his face and his arms. His *kurta* clung to his body, and perspiration ran in lines down his inner thighs to his ankles. The compact-powder makeup Sam had slathered on his legs had muddied and puddled and muddied again, and his whole body was awash in sweat. Sam moved away from the road that went into the center and toward the outside perimeter of the regimental headquarters. Here, at the very back, there were no gates into the regiment, the neatness and precision that adorned the front entrance had given way to the cookhouses and quarters for the servants of the regiment and their families. All the buildings were of one story with flat roofs, once whitewashed upon first being built, they all now carried a soot-covered countenance. Sam stepped quietly into the path that meandered between the cookhouses. Hens pecked in the dust busily, unfazed by the heat. An aroma of stale meat and blood hung about the yard. For the most part, everything was silent as the servants slept in the afternoon. A cur, its fur dotted with beige and white, tied to a bicycle with a length of hemp, lifted its sleepy head and snarled at Sam. He did nothing to respond, did not kick in its direction, or throw a stone at it, and the dog dropped its head back down again. Its nostrils twitched and Sam knew that his body smelled different to the dog. A baby cried as he passed the servants' quarters, and continued to sob and hiccup, but no one woke or came to call out to Sam or to demand of him what his business was here.

Just beyond these quarters was an underground water tank, reached by a series of steep steps and landings; the water level always determined which was the last step to stand upon to dunk the pot in the water. The well provided water for the whole regiment, and the roof above was to keep the sun from evaporating that precious resource. The regimental *dhobis* had set up their business around the water tank, and rows of clothes lines stretched out into the sunshine, the cloth already stiff with drying. There were whites of underwear and undershirts, the browns of khakis, the reds of the Rifles's dress-uniform jackets, and their socks and handkerchiefs. It was an almost bucolic scene and Sam wondered if he would really find Mike amidst all this domestic rusticity.

The NCOs' barracks stretched on either side of the path; these had tiny verandahs in front of the rows of rooms. The doors to the rooms were open, and here and there a half-asleep *punkah* boy looked up at Sam as he passed, lying on the verandah with the *punkah*'s rope tied to his toe. When he waved his foot around, the *punkah* moved the heated air around the room.

Next came the officers' quarters. These too were barracks, and tiny houses consisting of one and two bedrooms, a bathroom, a kitchen, and a drawing room were scattered around the barracks. Each little house for the married officers of the Rudrakot Rifles had its own garden, a handkerchief-size plot of land, a slew of roses in red clay pots on the verandah, the odd jasmine vine valiantly attempting to clamber up to the flat roof. There were two men in their undershorts and shirts lounging in wooden easy chairs on the verandah of the barracks to Sam's left, their feet swung over the extended arms of the chairs. A folding table stood between them and on it reposed two frosted glasses of beer. The men's heads cocked in Sam's direction when they heard the soft thud of his feet, but he kept his eyes away from them. Here though, in these barracks, Mike must have lived.

There had been only two letters from Mike after he had arrived at Rudrakot, and none of them described his living quarters, or what he ate, or even the officers who were his companions, with whom he drank and played billiards. Mike had spent one and a half pages on the story of a regimental cook who had almost died as the result of a beating. An officer had shouted at the cook one day, and for the next three meals, the cook had spit in the officer's chicken curry and used his urine to water down the gravy. But the matter had gone well beyond mere irritability in the heat; the cook's legs were broken, the bones in his fingers shattered, his very livelihood lost because he could no longer hold a knife to carve a chicken or chop vegetables. When the resident, Colonel Pankhurst, had heard of this incident, as he almost invariably had, through an anonymous letter written in shabby English by an Indian servant (the language gave it away), he had notified the viceroy, and the viceroy had sent the regimental commander and the second in command on forced leave without pay for two weeks. *It doesn't seem enough,* Mike had written, *what is a spot of urine in chicken curry (well cooked, I might add) compared to an inability to walk or hold any object in one's hands again?*

Sam passed by the unshaded parade grounds, the polo field that was bare, without a hint of grass, the offices of the commanding officer and the paymaster. Here was the regiment in its full glory. There was no grass anywhere, but the terrain was swept, and lining the roads were stones painted red and white after the regimental colors; the flags on the main flagpoles were freshly laundered and limp in the breezeless air. A pariah dog wandered about, this one so light-headed in the heat, it lacked the gumption to even bark. Sam peered into every open window, saw clerks asleep at their desks, heads on folded arms, and guards dozing at their posts. The few who did notice him saw a *mali*, slowly shuffling through the dust from building to building. Every now and then, to lend himself authenticity, Sam flung his spade into the dirt and dug up the hard ground, flattened it with his bare feet, and then moved on.

There was not much left to investigate at the end of an hour and a heavy weight bore down upon Sam's heart. If Mike was here, where was he? There was no sign of a prison, or any building that looked like a prison. Here was only a benign regiment, the flags, the snoring administrative clerks, the offices of the commanders, why, even the two officers lounging in their smalls in the barracks.

Sam turned back the way he had come and dragged his feet to the path behind the regiment. He had to talk to someone now, one of Mike's friends or acquaintances. The regiment itself told him nothing, everything here was too perfect, too calm, certainly not the regiment of wartime, but one comatose in the summer heat, waiting for something to happen. As he passed the barracks, one of the officers yelled, "Boy! *Ek aur shandy lao.*"

And the "boy," who served them, an old man in his seventies, hobbled out of the barracks with a tray, an open bottle of beer, a glass stuffed with ice cubes, filled halfway with lime juice. The beer gurgled into the glass, and Sam stopped in the shade of a pillar, suddenly thirsty, his throat parched, listening to the crack and spit of the ice cubes in the glass. He had never liked shandies, preferring to drink his beer undiluted, but now, his tongue curled in his mouth around the sweet-sour lime taste of a shandy. He watched as the officer, a young man with seemingly no bone in his chin and a fold of flesh in his neck, took a deep draft of his shandy and placed the glass on his chest, where the cold of the ice condensed and ran down into his navel.

"Damn," he said in a weak voice, "this damn glass bleeds. Boy!"

The old man came running out, and stood in front of the officer. "Sahib?"

"This glass pisses me off. You understand? Get me a new glass. Now."

The old man touched his hands together, his fingers interlocking. "Sahib, all glass will go to the bathroom. It is ice melting, Sahib."

The officer flung his glass out into the scrub beyond the verandah. There was the hard sound of glass breaking and a hiss when the dry earth soaked up the shandy. "No argument, you hear? Go get me another glass and make sure it does not piss. *Jaldi*, or I will whip you."

"Yes, Sahib," the old man muttered and backed into the doorway.

"You are a shithead, Sims," the other officer drawled from the depths of his chair. "The boy is right, all glass goes to the bathroom; ice melts in this damn heat. Why make a fuss? It's too much damn effort."

Sims turned to his companion. "I'm bored, Blakely. Bored shitless to death. All we do here is sit and eat and drink. I should never have joined this regiment; there were better offers elsewhere."

Blakely lifted his neck from the chair. "Go elsewhere then, damn you, and see if that doesn't get you into the war." He leaned back. "I'm content to be here. I don't want to die, victoriously or otherwise."

A mocking smile lifted the edges of Sims's mouth. "This from an army officer? Sedition, I tell you. Have you no pride in your work? No allegiance to the king?"

Blakely sat up to fling off his shirt and then winced when the wicker of the chair seared into his sweating back. "I'm glad the king pays my salary every month." His expression became moody. "And Susan spends it just as fast as I can deposit it in the Mussoorie bank account. There she is, cool in the hills, away from all this bloody heat, and I cannot even go to visit her now because of that damn cook. Why did you have to beat him nearly to death? We all agree that he deserved a whipping, but you should have done it discreetly, left no or little scars, not damn near killed him."

"Sorry," said curtly. He put a cigarette into his mouth and shouted around it. "Boy, lighter *lao*!"

"He's gone to get your nonmelting shandy," Blakely said.

The old bearer came back with a fresh tray and a new glass of lime juice choked with ice. His hands trembled as he poured the beer into the glass and then proffered it to Sims. "Sahib, you drink. You put it down. I wipe." He gestured at the tea cloth on his shoulder. "No ice melting, Sahib."

Sims muttered to himself, took a deep mouthful of the shandy, and then handed the glass back to the bearer, who assiduously wiped the bottom and the sides of all condensation. When Sims indicated the table and the lighter, the bearer picked the lighter up and started a flame that he held carefully under Sims's cigarette.

"Go now," Sims said irritably. "Enough. Go."

The bearer bowed, placed the tea cloth on the table, and went back into the barracks. For the next few minutes, the two men were quiet, drinking and smoking, and occasionally wiping their chests and foreheads with the towel.

"When does Susan come back?" Sims asked.

"I don't know," Blakely said. "When she wants to, when the money runs out, I suppose. I stop depositing money when I want her to come back. She spends too much time at parties and balls and gymkhanas at Mussoorie, spends too much damn money too, with all the new frocks she *needs*, not just wants, but needs. And this year, I cannot be there; thanks to you, none of us is allowed to go to the hills for our leave. So here we are, bachelors again, roasting in the plains."

"You complain too much."

Blakely sat up in indignation. "And what would you know, Sims? No woman has chosen to marry you yet."

Sims grinned. "I have it all, my friend. No wife, but plenty who want to be one for a night, or for a few nights. All the pleasure and no pain."

Blakely moaned. "Yes, and so you keep reminding me." He shook the cigarette tin and spilled the cigarettes onto the table. Picking one up, he lit it and filled his lungs with smoke. "What was her name . . . the girl you knew, the one who was so accommodating . . . Rose?"

"Rosalie." Sims ran the edge of his palm over his bare legs, sweeping the sweat onto the verandah's floor. "Rosalie," he said again, his gaze thoughtful upon the heat haze beyond the barracks. "The boys had a ditty for her."

"Do tell."

Sims slurped up the rest of his shandy and set the glass down on the table. When the bearer stepped through the door to refill his drink, he waved him away. "I want a clear head tonight. And there's more drinking to do at the club."

"Sahib," the bearer said, not understanding all of that, but moving away beyond the door's frame and out of their sight to sit against the wall in case they needed him again, or changed their minds, as they were wont to do.

"I once knew . . . ," Sims began, and then cleared his throat. "I need to stand for this." He stood up to face Blakely, and Sam saw that the wicker chair had posted tiny, circular patterns of red on the skin of his back and the backs of his thighs.

> *"I once knew a girl called Rosalie,*
> *Who said 'how do you do' so very prettily.*
> *On the floor she held sway*
> *Swains leaping into love night and day.*
> *Proposals though she awaited eagerly,*
> *Most men were content to skip over fleetly."*

Blakely roared with laughter. "But why?"
    Sims held out his hand. "Wait, you must wait. I'm not finished.

> *For Rosalie, hide them as she may,*
> *Her fingernails gave her away.*
> *And in the end, all knew that it was true,*
> *Rosalie was only four annas in the rupee."*

The two men bent over with mirth, laughing at their own cleverness. Blakely was actually crying, wiping his eyes, coughing over his cigarette. "That was priceless, Sims," he said, his voice rasping in his throat. "How long did it take all of you to figure out that she had a touch of the tar brush? Did no one come close to marrying her?"

    "One officer did; he wouldn't believe us when we told him of her ancestry. You should have seen her, Blakely. Skin as white as cow's milk, as creamy as whey, eyes as green as slime in a water tank. Auburn hair, and not from a bottle. She wouldn't take that poor chap to see her parents or her brothers and one day he followed her home and saw them for himself. Two days later, we heard that some thugs set upon her and cut up her face with a shaving blade. That was the end of Rosalie; she never came to the dance hall again. A good thing too." Sims's face hardened. "She had tried to pass herself off as one of us, but was nothing but a half-caste."

Around the verandah and alongside the wall of the barracks, Sam leaned on his spade. Talk such as this he had heard many times before, perhaps too many times before, and it caused a ruffling anger to grow within him. He had understood the mean and cheap rhyme about the poor girl called Rosalie. *Her fingernails gave her away.* This was the myth among soldiers, that Indians who looked British because they had some white blood could never hide the darkening skin around their fingernails, or the ridge of browner color in the half-moons of skin. It was prejudice of the shallowest and most petty kind, practiced on both sides. As much as the British had brought their color consciousness into this society, the Indians Sam had met in Calcutta or Assam, sometimes in the Grand Hotel, sometimes in clubs, had also been surreptitiously proud of their color, especially when it seemed as though they would bleed white if pricked, *without* the aid of a British ancestry. The color bar was everywhere, and this Rosalie, if she really existed, had paid for it, perhaps more so because she was Anglo-Indian.

Sam moved so that his eyes were level with the verandah's floor. Sims and Blakely were still laughing, without a sound now; the heat had robbed them of even their laughter. And if this joke was funny, it was funny no longer, because it was so oft repeated. The two men had talked about the cook's beating; why, Sims was the very man who had beaten the cook. Had Mike mentioned his name? Or any connection with him at all? Had he known him?

He peered at the two men to commit their faces to his memory. The sun had begun to cast longer shadows on the ground and Sam knew that it was time to return to Raman's house and slip back into his room before the servants began to stir from their afternoon sleep. He hefted the spade back on his right shoulder, and at that moment, the pain returned in a full, blossoming anger, sending fire through his muscles. Sam cried out and dropped the spade. It thunked onto the ground, lifting a fine sheen of dust around his feet. The two men in the verandah moved with an astonishing speed down the slick concrete floor; Sam heard them before he saw them leaning over the parapet.

"What are you doing here?" Sims shouted.

Sam raised his head to look at them, and then ducked, wiping the sweat from his forehead. "Sorry, Sahib," he mumbled, his voice hoarse, falling into a singsong intonation. He moved slowly, tiredly, his back hunched, to pick up the spade and turn his back on them.

"Who is it?" Blakely asked.

"Some *mali*, listening to us. What are you doing here?" Sims shouted again.

"Sorry, Sahib," Sam said again as he moved toward the bushes and the NCOs' quarters.

A pebble sang through the air and nicked Sam on his leg, but he kept going. An argument he could not have with these men, and he hoped they hadn't looked into his face too closely. Still maintaining his slouch and scramble walk, Sam shuffled away. More stones littered the dirt around him.

"Damn," he heard Blakely say. "I must have had too many shandies; I can't even get a clear shot at the bugger."

As he walked away, more swiftly now, Sam sneaked a look back at the men, and found them leaning over the parapet in a wet, sweating exhaustion. All the way back on the dirt path, he thought about what he had heard, the men he had seen, tried to remember if their names sounded familiar. But no, it was not their names that caused some forcibly buried memory to stir within him.

It was the name of the girl. Rosalie.

April 1942, a Month Earlier

*Somewhere in Burma*

They smell the village first. Before they see it, before they even know it is there. Sam's map shows a green, jungly void here in the Kachin hills, just forests unbroken from the eye of a mapping plane above. But they *smell* the village and know it has to be an entire village, not just the remains of a single human, but many. Men, women, children.

When that awful stench rises up the hillside and hums around them, Sam, Marianne, and Ken crash to a halt where they are on the track. That first horrid breath of carrion decaying ambushes them. It punches into their lungs. They cough violently into their hands, bend over from the waist to squeeze out that smell from their bodies. When they straighten, Marianne reaches out a shaking hand for Sam, who is ahead of her in their single-file walking, and the other hand to Ken, who is behind her.

"It cannot be," she whispers. "Say it cannot be, Sam. Not again."

Sam tears his gaze from Marianne's face and down to the glistening brown and green leaves on the forest's floor. He hears Ken hobble closer to Marianne, grasp her arm into his chest, and lay his head on her shoulder. For comfort. Sam can say nothing, his tongue grows thick, glues itself to the top of his mouth, and tears prickle at the back of his eyes. As they stand there, linked together in the slowly dripping forest, the sun comes out somewhere above them, hews through the monsoon clouds, sends glittering spears of slanting light between the leaves and branches.

Marianne begins to cry. Not again. Not again, she says to herself.

Sam straightens his back, swabs at his eyes, and ties his filthy and damp handkerchief around his nose. "We must go see," he says.

Marianne holds him back, not letting go of his hand. "No. Let us go around. There must be a way around. Why do we have to go through the village?"

Sam begins to trudge down the track, his boots gathering leeches from fern fronds. It is only when they cut away a tiny triangle of his flesh that he even knows they are there, feasting on his blood with surgical precision, feeding poison into his body to keep the blood thinned, and flowing. But he does not feel their bite, does not feel them plop onto the ground, fat and satiated, gray with pleasure from the feed.

"There must be something in the village we can salvage, Marianne," Sam says, more to himself than to her. "We have no food left; we have to go through the village."

"I'm not coming," she says, and sits down on the ground, pulling Ken, whose hand she is still clutching, down with her. The leeches drop off from the trees onto their heads, wend their way around their collars and slide inside.

"I'm not coming either," Ken says now. His face is discolored, ash on his cheeks, salt around his mouth and his eyes. His ankle is swollen, the skin straining against the bandages that are drenched in blood again. The leeches on Ken's shirt and his khaki pants move downward, enticed by the scent of fresh blood.

Sam bends to whack at them and knocks them to the ground. He takes out his tin of cigarettes, shoves three in his mouth and lights them all together. That first draft of nicotine gladdens his lungs, and the air around them is so still, so humid that the smoke hangs over his head in a mist. Sam gives Marianne and Ken a cigarette each, then sets his, lit end smoldering, against the leeches on his legs. They shrivel in protest and drop off, one by one.

"Aren't you afraid of the Japanese smelling the smoke, Sam?" Ken asks, his face more drawn in fatigue now that they are at rest, even so briefly.

"It's doubtful that they can smell anything beyond the death of that village."

"I'm not going there," Marianne says again. She too is tired, but there is something else in her eyes, something Sam has not seen before today. Fear. Marianne is afraid of confronting a scene much like the one she left behind in the Kachin village where she lived for so many years. There, every death was of someone dear, someone she had laughed with, taught the scriptures to, kept safe from the menace of the white man. They had been her children, given to Marianne by her god. And in the end, they had taken care of her, given her the gift of her life. So Marianne sits stubbornly amongst leeches and dead leaves, her heels dug into the ground, upwind from another, shattered village that has not survived the onslaught of the Imperial Japanese Army.

Sam squats on his haunches, his knees creaking. "Tell me," he says. He cannot order them to move. They are not children; they are not even army. Well, Ken is, and Sam outranks him. But the rules do not seem to apply here anymore. Sam will not leave Marianne and Ken on the hillside to forage through the dead village on his own. He does not know what he will find there, who will still be living, who dead, what terrors await to haunt future dreams for many years. He does not know if the Japanese still linger, if he will come out alive. He does know though that they have to scavenge for food. From their last supply drop all they have left is a can of cherries in heavy syrup, a can of cream to go with it—not enough to keep them alive. Sam also cannot leave them alone here even for a brief while, no matter how stubborn they are, how pigheaded; he is their guardian and he must either stay with them or take them with him. He chooses to take them with him. Since he also cannot order them to lift their behinds from the forest floor and follow him, he will coax them.

"Tell me," he says again. Gently.

Marianne's eyes fill with tears. She shrugs the thick straps of her haversack from her shoulders and pulls it onto her lap. From inside, she draws out a whittled teakwood pipe and a dried plantain leaf full of a powdered substance, much like tea leaves. She stuffs the pipe, sets it smoking with the lit end of her cigarette, and inhales. As the opium races through her lungs, into her veins, it dulls the sharp edges of fear on her face. Her blue eyes, washed out and overexposed to the Burma sun, glaze over. The opium smacks its calmness into her with even just that one draw, for Marianne, like Sam and Ken, is hungry, is tired, is weak from the rain and the blinding heat. She offers the pipe to Ken. Then to Sam. And they both clasp it gratefully, even Sam, despite his best intentions—and he does intend to go into the village, come what may—wants the blessed relief of a few hours without worry.

A grinning idiocy comes over Sam. His mouth widens and his ears seem to grow funnel-like on either side of his head. He can hear every drip of water in the hush of the forest.

"Have you?" he asks, feeling his lips stretch over his teeth.

Marianne lifts a slow gaze to his and then shifts on her buttocks to face Ken.

"Once," Ken says. "I've been in love only once, Sam." He had asked Sam this very question, once, so many days ago, and it is only now Sam thinks to ask him back. But Sam has mulled over this word, this *love*, not wanting to think of the other word, *death*, in relation to his missing brother, Mike.

"Who . . . ," Sam begins and then pauses to consider the pictures of emotion Ken displays so violently across his youthful face. The effect of the opium takes away all pretense of civility Ken might otherwise have shown—his mouth twists, he heaves from his stomach, his fists clench into bloodless stumps at the ends of his wrists. Sam almost shudders at this sudden and unexpected ugliness. Ken is the ideal of an all-American boy—thinly muscled, lean jawed, clean shaven, with an easy manner and a beguiling, faultless smile. But some passion lurks beneath that surface, pulled out by Sam's innocuous question.

"What is her name?" Sam asks, more out of curiosity than anything else. He watches Ken with care, leaning forward. Marianne does not see any of this, for she is humming a tune and examining her fingernails with the studied attention of the very inebriated.

Ken turns from the bright scrutiny of Sam's blue eyes and rests his chin against the tree trunk behind him. His voice comes out sour. "What do names matter? It was a pretty enough one. Rosalie."

# Eight

*One hard-pressed Resident, Sir Bertand Glancey, had travelled hundreds of miles to talk to one of the Princes about a problem. He was very put out to be told that his Highness could not be disturbed. He protested that he had come a long way and eventually the Maharajah appeared. "Ah, Sir Bertrand," he said in a state of excitement, "we are having a very urgent Cabinet meeting."*

*The Resident, appreciating this sort of priority, was suitably impressed.*

*"Yes," went on the Maharajah. "There is a most interesting item on the agenda; we have three canaries and we are trying to decide which one sings best."*

—Ann Morrow, *The Maharajas of India*, 1998

*T*he same sun that blistered Rudrakot flamed harsh and white over the Civil Lines and the cantonment of Meerut, about three hundred miles east. Northeast of the city was a large, wholly tented compound that simmered along with Meerut. This was a military compound, so the tents, though white, blazed with the care of scrubbing from a hundred servants; the mud paths between the tents were swept and blighted of vegetation, stones lined the paths, dabbed with red, white, and green paint, liquid in the heat.

Inside the tents, it was as though India had stepped back three hundred years into the traveling tents and entourages of the great Mughal kings. Oils of present, past, and future kings (or in this case, princes) of the princely kingdoms in India adorned the walls. Canvas tarpaulin mats had

been laid on the ground, these then covered with jute mats, and these further clad with Persian carpets in grasshopper greens, coconut browns, or
chameleon reds, depending upon the whimsy of the prince. Unlike the divans and bolsters and low beds of the Mughal kings, furniture of every
modern and ancient English kind abounded—secretaires and writing
desks, chairs and tables, four-poster beds, a lot of which would have been
not just welcomed in the best of British homes, but desperately vied for.

It was here, so far away from Rudrakot, that Jai had spent many
months. This was the headquarters of the Imperial Cadet Corps, a concoction of Lord Curzon's brain. Curzon, viceroy of India at the turn of
the century, had sought to birth a military school in India for the sons and
male members of the Indian elite, and by that he naturally meant the
princes—the natural nobles of the country.

In the quiet dull of that afternoon in May, Jai lounged in a wooden
armchair with curved legs and blue damask upholstery. Blue was the pre-
dominant color in the tent. The sheets on his bed, placed on a raised platform, were of a light blue silk; the coverlet was a darker blue-and-puce
brocade; the carpets were a rare Persian white, with a blue-and-gold
weave in the pattern. All the furniture was in gleaming wood, mahogany
and a dark, rich walnut—the Queen Anne bookcase with its marquetry
inlay and an opalescent oyster veneer; the table at which he wrote his letters and corrected his notes; the sofa and armchair in an eighteenth-
century Chinese style. Jai had his feet propped on an occasional table and
a blank writing pad rested on his knees.

A cool breeze swirled around the tent, repelling the immense heat of
the sun, as a rectangular *punkah* swung back and forth, pulled by rope by a
boy seated outside. This was the time for a siesta, but Jai, restless as ever,
had never yet closed his eyes in the afternoon unless it was on a day when
he was ill with a fever.

He was a tall man, leanly muscled from all his years in the saddle. Horses
were Jai's first love. There was no time in his life when he could not remember the scent of a stable, the nicker of pleasure when one of his horses saw
him approaching, the sigh when he ran his hand along their corded and muscular necks. Because he was a prince, the heir to Rudrakot, Raja Bhimsen,
Jai's father, had frowned on his sleeping in the stables at night, but no other
power on earth had kept him from his horses for every waking moment.
Riding horses almost from the day he could walk—first his Shetland ponies,

and then the walers—had burned Jai's skin to a dark ochre. His cheeks were pitted by a childhood bout of smallpox, which he had fought and vanquished, but which had left its mark upon him. He had a strong face, cut in sharp angles; a slanting, clean-shaven jaw; and a trimmed, thin mustache, more a darkening above his well-formed lips than a mustache.

He moved his right hand and dipped the pen into the inkwell by his side, then, holding the nib against the rim of the glass, drained the excess ink. When he put the pen to paper and began drawing in broad strokes, the mane, forelock, glittering eyes, and flared nostrils of his favorite horse, Fitzgerald, took shape quickly. Jai shaded in the area on Fitzgerald's forehead, and left a tiny star of white unmarked. Then he tore the paper from the pad and let it fly loose into the tent, where it wavered in the breeze from the *punkah* before settling on the floor. His hand hovered again over the paper, his pen dropped blotches of ink upon its unmarred surface, but he could not sketch again.

Jai sighed and put down the pen and the pad. Reluctantly, he picked up Captain Cameron's carefully worded note. *I am afraid, my dear Jai,* Cameron had written, *that the young maharaja of Kishorenagar has been . . . how shall I put this . . . misbehaving. Would you talk with him, old chap? Might be better coming from you. He looks up to you, you know.*

Such were the burdens of responsibility. When Jai had first joined the ICC, he had been a student here, schooled in the best traditions that the corps could offer, given first his viceroy's commission into the Indian army, then, with a lot of trouble and effort, his king's commission. The ICC had only twenty students at any given time. The students were restricted to the nobility and the royalty in India, and even so, a student had to be nominated by at least two or three prominent men, his lineage researched, his bloodlines tested. There was no question of an open examination, no question of anything as common as *merit* to decide the applicant's fitness in joining the ICC. With all these restrictions, then, there were never very many students here, and so no necessity for a staff of more than three officers—a British commandant, a British adjutant, and a native adjutant. It was the last of these three that Jai had been invited to be for this term in the ICC. As a military school, the ICC was to teach as many subjects as possible, but very soon, arithmetic and algebra gave way to history (of England), English literature, dictation, and some Greek and Latin.

The native adjutant was not considered qualified to instruct in any of these subjects, naturally, so Jai's job was to drill the cadets every morning and to teach them to ride properly and like gentlemen. It was a dubious honor at best, Jai thought, gathering the papers Cameron had sent to him along with the note. Procrastinating again, he picked up the silver bell on the table and rang it. Even before its soft tinkles had faded into the dull gloom of his tent, the flap lifted, letting in a lean shaft of the outside light.

"*Huzoor?*" the servant said.

"Get me a lime soda. Make sure it's cold. Lots of ice."

"*Ji, huzoor,*" the servant said, bowing and retreating, allowing the coolness to return.

The minutes passed, interminably, it seemed to Jai, who was used to the fleet-footed servants at his palace in Rudrakot. Here, he knew, the servant had to trek across the heated earth to the mess tent, place the order for a lime soda, put the glass on a tray, and bring it back. At Rudrakot the distances to the kitchens were surely as long, Jai thought irritably, still waiting. If only he could have brought his servants, but the rules at the ICC allowed only three ponies (maximum) to be brought for the drills and the polo fields, not servants. It was a wise precaution, for otherwise the cadets would arrive with full entourages—uncles, cousins, and servants—all deemed an absolute necessity, given masking titles of secretaries and aides-de-camp. An entourage, then, was not encouraged, but one *diwan* could come along, and all the princes had brought with them at least one advisor.

Knowing he could delay his reading no longer, Jai picked up the first letter from the maharaja of Kishorenagar to a young cadet at the ICC, the son of a noble from another princely kingdom. He had to force himself to read the letter. This was a love letter, no, perhaps not a love letter but a letter of seduction. The young maharaja—he was only seventeen—eulogized the advantages of male friendships, suggested that the women in the *zenanas* were a necessity for the continuation of the lineage, but it was among men, hard-riding, hard-drinking and unsentimental men that true amity could be found. Kishorenagar said that when the officers of the ICC were abed, every night at midnight, a group of them met in his tent to watch the *nautch* girls brought in from the bazaars at Meerut, and once the girls left, there were still entertainments for the rest of the night. Would this cadet join them? If he did now—and this was implied more than written outright—there was an opening after they all graduated from the ICC, at Kishorenagar for a *fauj bakshi*, a military commander of the infantry. The tent flap lifted and the servant came in. He meticulously wiped his bare feet on the mat at the entrance and then deposited the tray with Jai's lime soda on the table next to his armchair. The glass was covered with a fine net in silk thread weighted at the corners by silver beads.

Jai nodded, and when the servant left, he drank half the glass in one big gulp, the tart and sweet taste singing in his mouth, the coldness of the ice soothing the fever within. After half an hour of reading the other letters, some from the maharaja of Kishorenagar to other cadets, some from other members of that group, Jai rang the bell again.

When the servant appeared, he said, "Bring the maharaja of Kishorenagar here."

The servant balked, though not visibly, just enough to show resistance. His head bowed but he did not back out of the tent at once. He lifted his gaze to Jai's feet, and he brought his palms together in a salutation.

"The Sun God rides high in the sky, *huzoor,*" he said softly.

"Now, Ramlal," Jai said. "If he is asleep, he must be wakened. I want him here in fifteen minutes."

When the servant had gone, Jai drank the last of the now-warm lime soda and put down the glass with shaking hands. Giving orders came naturally to him, for he was born to be the heir of Rudrakot, and yet Kishorenagar was no minor princely state. The population of Kishorenagar was three times that of Rudrakot, the land acreage at least twice, even including all the waste desert land that Jai ruled over. But more than these obvious markers of supremacy, the British government of India had awarded Kishorenagar an eighteen-gun salute at all official functions, and Rudrakot, because it was tiny and relatively poor, had only a thirteen-gun salute. The young maharaja of Kishorenagar then, although only seventeen, would expect, and get, a proper amount of respect from Jai. Under any other circumstances.

The tent flap lifted again, and this time Jai had to put up a hand to shade his eyes from the glare. Kishorenagar stood there, mutinous, rubbing sleep out of his face. He was not a handsome boy; he had a bulbous nose, thick eyebrows that met in the middle, a small and growing belly under the pristine white cotton of his *kurta*. When he spoke, it was with the clipped English accent he had acquired from having spent the last five years in London in pursuit of . . . generally nothing. "I can hardly believe the servant's message. You *com-manded* me here?"

Jai was equally curt. "Come in and sit down, Kishorenagar." He used a shorter form of his title, and so the name of his kingdom, to address the maharaja. Employing his actual name (and he too had many, like Jai) would have shown a degree of familiarity that was not encouraged at the ICC. Since most of the cadets, if not all, had some title or other, this is how they were addressed and urged to address each other.

There was something in Jai's voice that propelled the maharaja into the tent, and he stomped in with clouds of dust, not bothering to wipe his feet on the mat. The flap remained open.

"Ramlal," Jai said quietly. When the servant appeared, he said, "Go to the mess tent. I will call for you when I want you." The servant bowed and began to retreat. "Wait." Jai turned to the prince. "Are any of your toadies outside?"

"I don't know what you mean." The maharaja's tone was icy.

"Ramlal," Jai said again, as the figures of four or five men blotted the door to the tent behind the servant's shoulders, "there must be no one outside the tent for the next half hour. Not one single person, is that understood?"

"*Ji, huzoor.*"

"You are being ridiculous, Rudrakot." Now the maharaja's voice was full of spite.

"When you are here," Jai said slowly, holding the young prince's gaze, "at the ICC, you will address me as Major Jaikishan."

The boy headed to the sofa opposite Jai. He lounged casually; none of the fight had left him, but there lurked some fear, some nervousness as he picked with his thick fingers at the fabric of the sofa's upholstery. Jai let him sweat for a while and then brought out the letters and placed them on the table between them.

"Captain Cameron came by these yesterday and sent them to me."

Kishorenagar's eyes darted to the table and his face blanched. "They are not mine."

"I think the authorship of these letters is easily established. You have signed them yourself."

"It is a forgery."

"A very good one, then, for I can recognize your handwriting."

Kishorenagar made a sucking sound with his mouth and then stuck his tongue out in distress. He took a deep breath, cunning marking his face now. "You would have no opportunity to read my dictation or my essays, Major, you teach us foot drills and riding." He sat back on the sofa. "Unliterary pursuits."

Jai rubbed his face slowly, damping the anger as it rose within him. He had expected resistance, bravado and some brashness, from the young maharaja. And perhaps some insinuations about their respective positions in the royalty ladder, but not insults. He bit down on the words that came swelling up. Kishorenagar sat watching him, his eyes screwed up and sly beneath his brows.

"Captain Cameron recognizes your penmanship, then, Kishorenagar."

"Oh." The prince was quiet. Then he said, "But it is nothing. An attempt at play, a way to pass time while we are here."

"You are here to learn to be an army officer, Kishorenagar," Jai spat out. There were many and better ways to handle this situation, but Cameron had enlisted Jai's help because he had thought that the reprimand would be better coming from another Indian, an Indian prince. And Jai, as much as he knew he seethed at insults, also knew that at some time in his life he had to learn to control his temper—perhaps this was Cameron's way of giving him a chance. But Jai's anger was not to be stopped, especially at this insult to his beloved corps. Why could Kishorenagar not see that this was a privilege, being here at the ICC? He asked him.

The maharaja sat up and crossed his legs in his best drawing-room manner. "What you do not see is that we are, none of us, allowed to sit for the examinations at the Royal Military Academy at Sandhurst, for if we did, and if we passed out of Sandhurst, we would have to be granted king's commissions, right?"

"We get them now, Kishorenagar, or rather, you would get one if you were able to give up these bad habits and graduate from the corps."

"To what avail, Rudrakot?" the maharaja said with a sneer. "Can you command British officers, or will you just return to your tiny kingdom and reign over your all-native, all-black Lancers? What use is a king's commission under such false pretense?"

What an audacious bastard he was, Jai thought, a little calmer now. He recognized that Kishorenagar's arrogance was reflected within himself also—like this prince, he had always also believed that he was here by some divine right to be king. Under the British Raj, the concept of divine right, of an *absolute* right to rule, was laughable. Arrogant or not, the maharaja was correct—Jai had his king's commission, but until he had the right to command *any* battalion of the British Indian army, it was pretty much worthless. The anger rose again within him, not just because Kishorenagar had pointed out this truth, but because it *was* the truth and it had troubled him for many years.

"Yours is not to question, Kishorenagar," Jai said. "You are here to train to become an officer in the Indian army, to hold a commission signed by the king-emperor himself, to be a facet of the British empire, to be a worthy representative of that empire. Your job, your responsibility is to rise strongly to the defense of the empire."

The maharaja of Kishorenagar clapped his hands languidly, slapping flabby fingers against one another. "Well done, old chap," he drawled. "You do us all proud—it is a speech fit for a king. You *are* a king, are you not, Jai? One can never be too sure, you know. My mother still resides in the *zenana* quarters of my father's palace. I look like my father; I have his eyes, his nose"—he tapped his nose gingerly—"even his damned receding hairline." Kishorenagar stroked the top of his forehead. "I am my father's son, not some usurper who makes claims to the throne. *I* should be the one giving the speech of kings."

Jai's voice went quiet. "Just what are you insinuating, Kishorenagar?"

"Nothing," the boy said, sitting up now, knowing somehow that he had gone too far, said too much. "Nothing, Major. Permission to leave, sir."

"Stay," Jai said, with as much inflection in his voice as if he were talking to a dog. He picked up Cameron's letter again. The words, *masturbation and sodomy*, swam before his eyes. *I'm afraid the young maharaja is guilty of both; make him see reason, will you, Jai?* Before the boy had come in, Jai had been prepared to reason with him. All boys in boarding schools indulged in this nonsense at some time or other. When Jai, at sixteen, had been at school in England for one brief year, he had been approached three times and had rebuffed each of these proposals. Not because he had been disgusted, but because he had already been with a woman, and unlike the boys in his school, knew what women had to offer. There had been no need to experiment with members of his own sex.

His first experience in lying with a woman had been when he was fifteen. His *diwan* had brought him the girl and had left her in his bedchamber, naked on his bed. She had been irresistible, and he had never felt even a shred of guilt about it later, knowing somehow that this was what men did. He had never told Raman about it . . . why, he could still not fathom, though this inculcation into manhood (as long as it was done discreetly and well) would be something both the political agent and the British resident would approve of as a necessity for a prince. But Jai had always wanted the respect of Raman the man, the father figure, and did not somehow think that this was the way to earn that respect. Jai had been married at seventeen, the same age as this young maharaja, who was betrothed, but not yet married. God help his young wife-to-be, Jai thought. This boy is a bastard.

"I am leaving now." A little bluster had returned to the maharaja's tone, now shirred with disrespect again.

"Yes," Jai said simply, refusing to react. "Pack your bags. I want you out of the ICC by sundown."

"You are joking."

"No," Jai replied. "There is nothing remotely humorous about this. You have constantly defied the rules of the ICC, you have come here under false pretenses; you have been unwilling to conform. The filthy habits you indulge in"—Jai's upper lip curled—"which I am loath to even give name to, have blackened the name and reputation of the ICC."

Jai had always thought the young maharaja of Kishorenagar to be a vapid, unthinking young man, but now he saw a terrible malevolence marking his pudgy features. "There will be repercussions, Jai," he said in a growl.

"So be it," Jai replied with a forced nonchalance, turning away again to his papers. "The scandal of your dismissal from the corps will be nothing. We have a standard to uphold here, and in giving you permission to leave the ICC, we are maintaining that uprightness for which the corps is known."

The maharaja of Kishorenagar jumped up from the sofa and staggered toward the entrance of the tent. He would say no more in his defense, this also Jai knew, for they were both princes, not used to explanations or excuses. But he did say something when he turned at the doorway, the flap lifted, the sunshine outside casting his body in a silhouette and smudging his features. "There will be repercussions for *you*, Jai. I will remember this insult for a long time."

When he had left, Jai rose from his armchair and stumbled blindly around the tent in circles, bumping into various pieces of furniture, cursing as he tripped over an occasional table. His hands ached for the smoothness of Fitzgerald's reins, he wanted to bury his face in the sweet aroma of the horse's coat and mane, feel the pounding exhilaration of a ride even in this dense afternoon heat. But he had to stay here, within his tent, stay and pretend, as though this conversation, Kishorenagar's insults and allusions, had not almost taken the life out of him. Would he never be free of his past? How had Kishorenagar, as young as he was, the impudent and swaggering puppy, known? How had he dared to repeat what he had heard?

When Jai finally sat down again, reaching for the drawing pad with a desperate yearning, hardly able to hold his pen steady in his fingers, he was saturated with sweat. Leaning over the pad, he began to draw with an urgency—the line of a finely carved brow, the curve of a neck, the liquid eyes, hair the color of a moonless midnight, all taking shape in a matter of seconds. Little drops of sweat ran down his cheek and dripped onto the sketch, blotching the lines, making the ink run.

The young maharaja of Kishorenagar had an instinct for knowing when to tell the truth. Or to put it another way, Kishorenagar knew the stories and tales and gossip about the royal houses in India that usually lurked only in the recesses of the old-timers' minds. He had had a lot of time in London to listen to these stories from his *diwan* and the other members of his entourage while he was dressing to go to a ball or to the park or to the theater. So when he had suggested kinks in Jai's lineage, he had been speaking the truth.

Jai was not Bhimsen's natural son, but was the child of a cousin a few times removed, who was precariously pendant on a distant branch of the family tree. Jai's original father was a minor chieftain, but the family were, and this was important in the adoption process, Rajawats—a line from which kings and princes could be safely adopted. Hindu law recognized the necessity of the carrying on of the male line, or the frailty of the human condition in not being able to supply that male heir, and considerately provided loopholes such as this one—any child, male or female, adopted into a family and brought up as their own, would become their own. The bloods would merge, the histories would become one, and they would be, in *everything*, born of the parents who nurtured them. Such was the forgiving and providing nature of the law.

Bhimsen brought Jai to live in the *zenana* with the women of his household, and declared him his heir—Jai had the right to be *king* of Rudrakot after him. The British resident initially balked. Bhimsen had adopted Jai in 1917, when he was three, when Rudrakot was still a princely state in the empire, bound to bow to the vagaries of the Raj.

When India first became part of the Raj in 1858 and Queen Victoria took upon herself the title of empress of India, the independent kingdoms retained their sovereignty, though it was at best a tenuous claim to *king*-ship. Although allowed pomp, circumstance, and an elaborate ritual of the pretense of royalty, the kingdoms were now merely princely states. Their rulers were rulers only in name, tightly controlled by the India Office in King Charles Street in London, six thousand miles away; the viceroy in Delhi; the governors and governor-generals of the provinces where their princely states fell; and the British resident or political agent.

The rulers kept for themselves their native titles, whether raja, which meant king, or maharaja, which meant a great king. In English, they were called "princes" and addressed simply as "Your Highness."

The *majesty* all belonged to the queen-empress of India. And she lived in England.

In the early years of Victoria's rule over India, princes who could not produce heirs invariably lost their lands to the greater British Raj, with the kingdom annexed and absorbed under the "doctrine of lapse."

But by 1917, when Jai was adopted, a little man come recently from South Africa had started to rustle up some not inconsiderable trouble for the British. He was educated by the selfsame system the British had set up to create the brown sahib in India—one in taste, accent, education, manner, and deportment British, and only in the color of his skin Indian. His ideas, initially founded on the asserting of rights for the Indian in India, had now reshaped themselves most dangerously into *thinking* that India was for Indians, and that the British should leave. The man's name was Mohandas Karamchand Gandhi.

So when Bhimsen brought Jai to the palaces at Rudrakot in 1917, the British resident visited, looked grave, shook his head, wrote to the viceroy . . . and did nothing. He did not demand Rudrakot dissolved because of a fear that anger would lead the princes and their subjects toward the nationalist movement. On orders from up high, the resident did insist on some compensation for recognizing Jai as heir, and Bhimsen agreed to raise a cavalry regiment for the British Indian army. And so the Rudrakot Lancers came into being.

In return, Bhimsen asked that the number of his guns be elevated from eleven to thirteen. This was another example of Bhimsen's tenacity and persuasiveness, because the Lancers were raised in return for Jai as heir, but Bhimsen managed to get an extra two guns by pretending to do the British government the *favor* of raising the Lancers. And this was how he did it.

Once Jai was crowned heir in a grand durbar at Rudrakot, with the British resident attending, Bhimsen took an inordinate amount of time ordering the walers from Australia and training his soldiers. The horses were finicky, the men were prone to sickness, their uniforms were not ready, the instructing officer was on a constant holiday due to an illness in his family . . . and so it went. Once his gun salute was raised to thirteen guns, the regiment was magically in commission, almost within a month, after a four-year delay.

In Rudrakot, few people remembered (or if they did remember, chose to forget) that Jai was not born of Raja Bhimsen. He had not seen his biological parents since he was adopted; and though he had met his older brother three times in the last twenty-five years, on state occasions, it was a bond that had been frittered away from disuse. The palaces at Rudrakot became his home, he was addressed as the *rajkumar,* the heir to the throne, and very soon the child Jai forgot that he was anything but entitled to Rudrakot.

When the young maharaja of Kishorenagar had said that his own mother had been part of his father's *zenana,* he was referring to this part of Jai's past. Even though Jai had ruled Rudrakot for the past fifteen years now, since he was twelve.

As the bugle sounded over the white tents of the ICC at Meerut to signal the end of the afternoon siesta, Jai rose from his armchair, exhausted and limp with perspiration even though he had been under the *punkah.* The carpet around him was littered with pages torn out of his drawing pad, which had now been reduced to the stiff, outer cardboard, no papers left on the pad.

A woman gazed out of each of the sketches with half smiles, a laugh, a pout. Her hair raged behind her in the wind. In each sketch, her gaze was direct and candid.

Every picture was of the woman Jai loved—Mila.

# Nine

*One of the greatest stumbling-blocks here is the personal relationship between the British and the Indians—between whites and coloreds. At the best we're patronizing. At worst—and that's pretty often—we're arrogant and domineering . . . Any British Tommy thinks he's a perfect right to go into a shop and call the proprietor a thieving black bastard. Maybe he is too, but would he stump into a British shop and call the proprietor a "thieving white bastard"? Even white children draw away from Indian kids as if they'd the plague—which maybe they have got. But don't forget the Indians didn't ask white children to come to their country. The Indians feel aliens in their own country, just by the way we treat them.*

—W. G. Burchett, *Trek Back from Burma*, 1943

*A* little after six o'clock Sam stood on the front doorstep, in full view of the waning westerly sun, and cursed the architect who had thought this was England. In the morning when he had arrived at Raman's home, this part of the house had been a gleaming white, still cool in the shade, with a hint of the moisture in the air that had been birthed during the night. Now the air around him was dry enough to flake into pieces, Sam's mouth parched, and his skin seeming to leach moisture into the seeking heat.

Seeking the relative freshness behind the tamarind tree's trunk, he flung his cigarette to the ground and trod it out with the heel of his shoe. He took out his handkerchief, swabbed his forehead with it, and then raised the *sola topi* Sayyid had given him and mopped up as much sweat as he could from his hair. The *topi* was a blessing; it was a round pith helmet of sorts with a wide brim, like a safari hat with a buckram rim, constructed to battle the Indian sun. Sam had brought only his Burma Rangers cap, which left the back of his neck exposed.

The return back to Raman's house earlier in the afternoon had been relatively easy, as Sam had entered the gate at the bottom of the back garden just before the servants had begun to stir from their afternoon's rest. He had cautiously passed by Sayyid sitting on his *charpai,* a jute-knitted bed, feet on the ground, shoulders hunched, still nodding in the last vestiges of sleep. But Sayyid had not seen him. Looking up at the house, Sam had spied Mila in the balcony and had melted behind a jasmine bush, his heart pounding. But Mila, like Sayyid, seemed asleep on her feet, her back bent at an incongruous angle, her chin and arms resting on the parapet, her eyes closed. Sam waited, and finally she rose to straighten her back, glanced in the direction of his room and then went inside her room. He had run up the outer stairs without pausing, knowing that this was probably his only chance to enter his room undetected. There, he had stripped off his clothes, folded them, and stowed them away at the bottom of his holdall, then padded naked to the bathroom for the relief of sitting in a tub filled with water, tepid and warm as it was. When Sayyid had come in with a tray of tea, to find Sam in the tub, he had said nothing, merely bowed, set the tray down on a table at Sam's elbow, and retreated to start unpacking Sam's holdall. At which, of course, Sam had shouted out through the silk curtains that he could do that himself, thank you very much.

From his vantage point behind the tamarind tree, Sam watched the front door of the house open and shut numerous times as messengers and peons flitted in and out, some carrying cotton bags filled with papers and files. They all looked the same to Sam, nondescript men, young and old, clad in khaki shirts and shorts and Nehru caps, lawyers' briefs tucked under their right arms. In those briefs were the lifeblood of the Indian Civil Service—letters, memos, and documents authenticating the mundane, endless details of the machinery of the mighty Raj.

A chameleon scampered up the tree trunk to one of the lower branches. Fear and surprise sent colors racing under the chameleon's skin in blotches of reds, yellows, and greens. Sam watched it hide from him, slung over a branch, its scaly tail hanging over one side. He settled back

into waiting . . . and dreaming. After the bath, and after drinking the hot
*chai* and eating a couple of *samosas* fried to a flaky perfection with a ginger
and coriander chutney, Sam had wandered out into the balcony for a cigarette in his shorts and a shirt that he had not bothered to button. And there
Mila had found him.

"Will you join us for a fair, a *mela*, at the Victoria Club, Captain
Hawthorne?" she had asked, somewhat shy, a half smile directed at his
bare chest. Sam had buttoned his shirt and said yes, mesmerized by the
masses of hair that had come loose from her plait and framed her face, and
by the glint of the thin cord of a gold chain around her neck. "In two
hours," she had said. "Outside the front door."

It was still too bloody hot for a *mela* of all things, but the *mela* was a
church fund-raiser for a new music organ, to be purchased by the sweat of
all their brows. Now Sam knew why there was even this form of entertainment at Rudrakot at the peak of summer, when normally by this time
everyone would have fled to the hills. Because Sims had beaten the cook
and almost killed him, and Colonel Pankhurst and the Rifles commander
had decreed that the regiment would not get its normal summer leave. And
not having this form of escape, they all had to be entertained somehow.

He heard the roar of the jeep in the garage then, and it swept over the
gravel drive from the far side of the house to the front. Mila was driving.
A pale green chiffon sari floated around her like a cloud in the sky, and in
the little seat at the back of the jeep a young man mock-fought with the
*pallu* of the sari, hollering above the din that he was being strangled by
fabric. They came to a halt in front of Sam, and Mila wrestled her sari
from Ashok.

"Do get in, Captain Hawthorne," she said, jumping out from her seat.
Her slippered feet raised a little puff of dust. "I need to fix this or Ashok
will keep yanking at my sari and complaining that he can't see." She layered the top half of her *pallu* over her left shoulder, wound it around her
neck and over her head to cover her hair, and then brought the extra
around her once more and tucked it into her waist. This she did deftly, as
though from long years of practice, and when she finished, the sari
swathed her slim figure and concealed all her hair, leaving a rectangle of
smooth brown skin above her eyebrows. "There," she said, and put her
sunglasses on again. They were large, oval, and a deep black. Ashok was

dressed with an open-necked white linen shirt, crisp fawn-colored pants, a white silk ascot blooming at his neck. Sam felt shabby beside all this finery in his Burma Rangers uniform and his boots.

"This is my brother Ashok," Mila said, gesturing with her head.

What an attractive family they were, Sam thought. Mila looked nothing like Raman—perhaps she had more of her mother in her—and Ashok was a leaner, younger version of his father. Yet they looked alike. Perhaps it was the color of their skins, so perfectly matched in their neighboring faces, the bronze of the earth. Perhaps it was their eyes, the outer edges curving upward into their hairlines, thickly lashed. Mila's eyebrows had definition, like the arches of bows; perhaps once, without the aid of artifice, they had looked like the smudges of hair above Ashok's eyes. They both had the same strongly shaped faces, and the same manner of slanting their heads. Mila's nose had a little bump at the bridge and her sunglasses perched precariously on this bump.

A smile split Ashok's young face and he thrust his hand forward eagerly. Sam clasped it and felt the slenderness of his fingers, the smallness of the hand in his. Why, he thought, for all his grown-up clothes, Ashok was still a boy. How old was he?

"Hello," he said, and to his surprise, Ashok replied with, "Seattle must be a wonderful place. I say, do you get a lot of snow there?"

"Mostly in the mountains," Sam said.

"Ah, the Cascade Mountains. But also in the Olympic Mountains, no? West of Seattle?"

"Yes," Sam said. "But that is quite astounding—how do you know all this?"

"Oh, I know more," Ashok said. He rubbed his hands and leaned forward. "Are you getting in?" Then, not waiting for Sam's answer, he went on, "Seattle is a hundred and twenty-five nautical miles from the Pacific Ocean, on the Puget Sound, between Elliott Bay and Lake Washington. It is situated a hundred and ten miles south of the Canadian border and lies in King County. Mount Rainier, the highest peak in the Cascade Mountains, is ninety miles south of Seattle. Have you seen it, Captain Hawthorne?"

"All the time," Sam said. He climbed into the jeep on the passenger side. "That is, all the time when it is not raining. We have a saying in Seattle that when you don't see Mount Rainier, it is raining—"

"And when you do see it, it is going to rain," Ashok finished for him with a tremendous peal of laughter.

"Enough, Ashok," Mila said with a smile. "You will bore our guest."

"But no," Sam said. "All this is very interesting; how do you know these facts, Ashok? I've lived in Seattle all of my life, but I haven't memorized how many nautical miles lay between Seattle and the Pacific."

"I just know." Ashok had an air of seriousness and erudition.

"Papa gave Ashok an *Encyclopaedia Britannica* for his birthday a few years ago, so my brother is now a walking fund of knowledge—most of it useless for life, but useful only to impress our visitors," Mila said, speaking over Ashok's little noises of protest. "Shall we go?"

Sam nodded. He turned back to face the front of the jeep. The windshield was up and locked in place. There was a handle welded onto the side of the windshield pane on the passenger's side. Sam had a few seconds to wonder what it was for before he found out.

Mila jammed the jeep into reverse, spun the tires as she backed up the jeep, thrust the gear into first, and slammed on the accelerator. The gates were shut at the end of the drive. The two watchmen dashed to unlatch the gates and had barely run them open before they sped past, with the watchmen still clinging to the wrought iron on its outward swing. A blast of the horn and, without waiting to see if there was any traffic to worry about, Mila turned onto the road. Sam clung to the handle on the side of the windshield pane.

"Mila's a maniac behind the wheel, Captain Hawthorne," Ashok yelled in his ear. "She taught me to drive."

"Remind me not to get into a vehicle again with either of you, then," Sam yelled back, his voice snatched by the wind and carried away behind them.

"I'm not that terrible," Mila shouted. "Jai taught me to drive; you should see him. It's a wonder he's still alive. It's a wonder anyone in Rudrakot is alive, considering the way he plows through the streets. There," she said, shifting down and slowing, "is this better?"

Sam leaned back on his seat finally and let go of the safety handle. Ashok seemed to have worked out a system for being stable; his hands were clenched around the leather of his seat, his feet were jammed apart against the floor; his ascot, though, was still in its place, snowily resplendent.

"I'm used to Mila, Captain Hawthorne," he said, grinning. "She likes to race out of the driveway usually, but has no courage to continue her mad driving outside."

"This from someone who has no driving privileges."

"And why not?" Ashok demanded, his head between the two of them. "I'm sixteen, not a child. Jai was driving when he was twelve. He taught Kiran when he was fourteen. Why can't I drive?"

"You do drive," Mila pointed out. "Just not when Papa is around."

Sam listened to them banter and quibble, with a soreness in his heart, as they drove along the avenue that sheltered all the houses in the Civil Lines of Rudrakot. Mike and he were perhaps the same number of years apart as Mila and Ashok, and their arguments had once—foolishly—involved knives. This was many years ago—Mike had brandished a kitchen knife and then laid it back on the counter, and Sam had leapt for it and then leapt at Mike. He had chased him all over the house in a murderous rage about something he could no longer remember. Their mother, horrified beyond appeal, had banished them from the kitchen for three months and quarantined them at home for a month. It was the only time Sam could remember having been so angry with Mike. He had never lost his temper again. It had sobered them both.

He raised his head and breathed in the aroma of the sun-fired flowers of the *prakrit* trees along the avenue. Mike had been here along this very road at one time. This afternoon's search had led nowhere, but no matter, if Mike was in Rudrakot, Sam would find him.

Ashok and Mila had fallen quiet, voices tired of competing with the jeep's engine roar. They were the only ones on the road, and for Sam this was stunning, this hush, this emptiness, this lack of human presence, so used was he to that other, teeming India where even his thoughts did not seem to belong to him. Wealth and opulence bought open spaces and silence. The houses were all, like Raman's, set well back from the avenue. The trees canted obligingly toward the center of the road, linking their arms on the sides, until it seemed as though they were driving through a wondrous sun-dappled tunnel of greens and golds.

As they passed by the houses, someone stepped out from behind a tree. Sam saw him first and then he thought that Mila saw him too, for her hands wavered on the wheel and the jeep swerved to one side. The man held their gazes until both Sam and Ashok turned their heads to look back at him. The man's *kurta* and pajama glimmered a serene white in the shade, his skin glistened with sweat, his hair lay built up in thick curls on his well-crafted head. At the *kurta's* opening at his neck, his collarbones jutted out, sharply defined under his skin. An Indian David, Sam thought, perfection bestowed upon each muscle, each line on the face, the brightness of the eyes. Who was he? And why did he look at them like that? There was no paraphernalia of trade or business surrounding him, no boxes of silks or curios, and no pots of water to indicate that he was within the Civil Lines to sell something. Mila's shoulders had tensed. Ashok turned to the front and dropped his eyes, a flush riding on his young face. And that moment passed in silence.

"Who was that man?" Sam asked.

"That's the vicar's house," Mila said in response, and Sam followed her finger to his right. A watchman drowsed upright on his stool in front of the gate, his brown turban bobbing as his head moved in sleep. There were two glass-plated signs, painted writing on them, embedded into the concrete gateposts. One read 12 ALBERT AVENUE, the other THE SEXTONS. The gate itself was hung with a black metal letterbox with the words LAETITIA SEXTON painted on it.

"What an unfortunate name for a vicar," Sam said, allowing himself to be diverted from his question.

Mila laughed. "It bothers Mrs. Sexton quite a bit. The vicar doesn't seem to care; he has lived with this name all of his life. Laetitia acquired it only through marriage."

They had passed the house now, and Sam got a small glimpse of stately white pillars, plush lawns, an empty garage shed, and pink geraniums in pots on the front porch.

"It's a beautiful home," he said. "Vicars live well in India."

"Not all vicars," Mila said. "Only the Rudrakot vicars. There are not enough British here in the civil area, so they'll take anyone they can get, even vicars."

"Why *even* vicars?"

"Mrs. Sexton's father," Mila said, "was a fishmonger in London; marrying the vicar has brought her up considerably. Under any other circumstances, she would not have been accepted in Rudrakot society. Perhaps she would not be accepted at home, in England, but here . . . the British cannot afford to be choosy."

The road curved out of the trees and into the blazing sun. To their right was the lake, its waters blue bright in the light, mesmerizing in contrast to the brown and red hues of the desert. Sam shaded his eyes with his hand. Another jeep broke out from the trees ahead and onto the road, and as it passed them, the man driving raised his hand. Both Mila and Ashok nodded and Sam waved. Now, in his own clothes, in his own skin, in a jeep, by Mila's side, he was no longer invisible—as he had been when he had walked here in the afternoon.

They drove out of the sun into the cantonment area.

"The home of the Rudrakot Rifles," Sam said, and then wondered if he should have exhibited knowledge of this. But Mila and Ashok did not react.

"On the right," Ashok said. "The Rifles are a British regiment. On the left are the Rudrakot Lancers. An Indian regiment."

Sam looked right first and then left and it was like looking at images in a mirror—the two regimental headquarters looked alike, the same red-and-white-painted stones along the pathways, the same whitewashed facade of the barracks, flags hanging limply on the airless, treeless, sun-drenched *maidan* near the sentry houses. Sam now remembered stories from Mike's letters of the pranks the officers of the Rifles regiment played on those of the Lancers—jackal carcasses strung on the barbed wire in the middle of the night, a cow let loose to deposit dung at the base of the flagpole, the stones along the drive upturned to their muddy sides. With an immense stroke of luck earlier in the afternoon, he had stumbled correctly around the living quarters of the Rifles, Mike's regiment, and not the one right opposite it.

"The Rifles came here once the Lancers were brought into commission."

"Why? It must be a great drain on resources."

"Have you heard of the Sepoy Mutiny of 1857, Captain Hawthorne?" Mila asked.

Sam nodded. "A little. Mostly what I've read."

"Well, since then, since the mutiny, as it was called, was started within—and was largely contained within—the ranks of the army, the British try to maintain a one-to-one ratio of British soldiers to Indian soldiers. It's a show of force, a deterrent to further mutinies. It is called the

Cardwell system, after the man who invented it." She paused. "The presence of the army in Rudrakot is relatively new—Jai's father, Raja Bhimsen, first raised the Lancers about twenty years ago; the government brought the Rifles here soon after."

The road stretched before them, metallic black with clean edges, and the two regiments garrisoned on either side balanced each other's might.

Mila said, "The Cardwell system is meant to station British soldiers only within India's borders. At the borders, the northwest frontier, for example, there are fewer British soldiers for every Indian soldier. The threat comes from within, you see, not without."

*And what do you think of the politics of this prejudice,* Sam wanted to ask. Mila had recited the facts like a history lesson, with little change in her demeanor, little expression of disdain. She had shown no rancor. Here is the British regiment, Captain Hawthorne, and here is the Indian regiment. One is meant to keep the other in order. British. Indian. Mila was Indian, living in her own country, ruled by a foreign hand. For the first time, Sam began to think of what this must mean.

"How do you know all of this?"

She gave him a fleeting smile. "We know a lot because of Jai."

"Who's Jai?"

Ashok and Mila began to speak together, went silent together, started to laugh together. "Poor Jai," Mila said finally. "Here is someone in his kingdom who does not know who he is. He will be crushed, devastated. We must not tell him."

"Jai is the prince of Rudrakot," Sam said, smiling too when he realized what he had just said. It was akin to blasphemy, to not acknowledge the presence of a sovereign in his own kingdom.

"Jai commands the Rudrakot Lancers, Captain Hawthorne," Ashok said from behind. "So he is the only one who can go into the Rifles' mess halls and their club. The main club, the Victoria Club, is another matter, though. A whole other bomb just begging to be detonated."

"Why?" Sam asked. Mila had stopped talking, but she was angry; he could sense that. She listened, driving slowly now.

"The Rifles, before they came here, were not used to sharing their club with an Indian regiment. They insisted on separate tables at first, separate sections of the club for their use . . . but they forgot that they were the second occupants of the club. This is why Jai goes over to the Rifles regiment to dine with the officers and the men. He wants them to see him often, to realize that Rudrakot *is* the Rudrakot Lancers."

"Jai is Indian too, isn't he?"

"So he is," Ashok said with a grin. "The men don't forget this. Jai is dark as the heavens in a thunderstorm, Captain Hawthorne. But he is royalty. Every drop of his blood has more value than the whole of the Rifles put together. It is an undeniable fact. It is an unpleasant conundrum for the noncommissioned British army man, the Tommy. He will not take orders from a blackie, but damn if that blackie could not buy him and his county out from under his feet."

It was an astonishingly lucid thought for a sixteen-year-old, and Sam felt an admiration for Ashok. In Seattle, Sam had heard on the radio of the conditions in India and of the freedom struggle. But it was not until he had come to the Indian subcontinent and seen this discrimination at work that he had begun to fathom the real cause of the ferment. The British had so long held themselves aloof from Indians, built up so much animosity, that there was no middle ground for compromise for the Indian nationalists. The British were not welcome in India anymore—there were *no* circumstances under which they could stay on or share India.

Ashok said, "Did you see the washrooms at the railway station?"

Damn, Sam thought, knowing what was coming. It was something he had heard for the last few months from almost every Englishman and woman in India the moment he had opened his mouth and his accent had placed him as an American. And he had heard this in some form or another everywhere—at clubs, in shops, on railway station platforms, within the barracks in Assam. *You talk of equality and civil rights, Captain Hawthorne; tell me, are all people equal in America?*

The Indians he had spoken with had only made it a little easier. To them, he had been representative of FDR and openness and generosity, swung and placed at the other end of the pendulum, much, in some senses, as Raman had seen him earlier this morning. Sam was uncomfortable in both roles, of being from a dominating race in his own country and of being considered so impartial—neither was true.

Ashok repeated his question. "Did you happen to notice the washrooms at the railway stations, Captain Hawthorne?"

Sam nodded.

"They must have been marked 'Europeans Only' and 'Indians Only.' " Ashok paused and leaned forward. "Tell me, Captain Hawthorne, was that distinction not much like home to you?"

"The land of the free," Mila sang, "and the not-quite free."

# Ten

*My father was among the few black members of the Delhi Gymkhana Club. This was only for show; Indians who had been knighted were regarded as wogs acceptable to the British. But the Gymkhana Club and other clubs which started taking Indians made conditions very difficult. You had to be interviewed. Your wife had to be there with you. Now my mother couldn't speak a word of English.*

*Whites-only places like the Delhi Club remained a symbolic reminder of the alien and humiliating side of foreign rule. The last of them, the Breach Candy Swimming Pool in Bombay, excluded Indians till the 1960s and continues to operate discriminatory entry rules for visitors.*

—Zareer Masani, *Indian Tales of the Raj,* 1987

Jai was not solely responsible for the Rudrakot Lancers being permitted in the Victoria Club, as Ashok had said. It was actually very much an institution of the British part of the Raj, and Indians themselves, no matter what social status they occupied, had been anathema at one time. Ashok would not have known this, neither would have Mila, for they were both very young when Indian officers from the Lancers were admitted into the sacred hallways of the club. The story they told Sam accorded very well with their sensitivities though, and made the Lancers seem quite heroic. What they did not know was that their admiration could have found its home closer to their hearts, in their father.

The club was born for the amusement of the British resident in

131

Rudrakot, sometime after Victoria became queen-empress of India, and hence its name. At the very beginning, only the British were members, and only British men, really. Even the ruling princes of Rudrakot had to wait outside in their limousines when they came by to pick up a government agent who had come to visit them. It was not a tenable state of affairs. The club admitted the vicar, the owner of Pitman's Dry Goods, the clerks in the British resident's office, the publisher of the *Rudrakot Daily News* and two of his senior reporters, the railway stationmaster, and selectively, the resident's chauffer (before 6 P.M.). Even the local *boxwallahs*—young, opportunistic Englishmen who worked in the indigenous industries at Rudrakot, like the block-printing mill and the cement factory—had entry.

In larger cantonments and cities and towns, the *boxwallahs* were banished from the main clubs, seen for what they were, the bottom dregs of society, certainly not on a par with officers of the army, or with the civilians of the ICS who were considered heaven born. The term *boxwallahs* came from the local traveling merchants who carried their wares in boxes from house to house—knife sharpeners, cloth *wallahs*, vessel *wallahs*. How could these *boxwallahs* then even dare to breathe the same social air as the civil servants, how could the ICS wives and daughters be exposed to the ill manners of these lower classes who *worked* for a living, with *profit* in mind? The thinking went thus in the greater towns of the Raj. At Rudrakot, however, the *boxwallahs* were welcomed; there was a dearth of familiar-hued faces.

So the club invited all of these men, but not the prince of Rudrakot. Raja Bhimsen's father, Jai's grandfather, had strolled into the club one morning, sat down to breakfast, and, to start, ordered a cup of coffee. The Indian bearers had dithered, so frightened that the coffee hiccupped its way out of the pot's spout, and a few drops bloomed around the saucer's rim, marring the virginal beauty of the white linen tablecloth. The club secretary, a Mr. Ryder, hovered around this table in acute distress, actually wringing his hands. He had not the gall or the courage to ask a raja to leave the premises. How would he say this? "Your Highness, the club rules state . . ." "Your Highness, I have been informed . . ." "I respectfully beg . . ."

Mr. Ryder had come all the way to India to work at the Victoria Club, and had washed the dust of his common origins off his shoes just east of the Suez, to transform himself into a *pukka* sahib. A tall, thin man with a carefully cultivated pallor that contrasted nicely with his black suits, Mr. Ryder had had no compunction before in banishing miscreants from the club. But damn, it was bloody hard to kick out someone who had to be addressed as being higher than he was in rank. And a prince to boot—a black prince to be sure, but still . . . Mr. Ryder's father hauled coal in London and when he washed the soot off his face at the end of each day, his skin did shine the pearly pink of a pig's backside, but prick him and his blood was nothing special. That morning as he stood there, Mr. Ryder was uncomfortably aware that he had no pretensions to royalty. So Jai's grandfather had finished his breakfast, wiped his mouth with a white linen napkin embroidered with an entwined VC in gold thread, called for his cigarettes and another cup of coffee, and said to Mr. Ryder, "Write out a chit for this, will you?"

From that day onward, there was no stopping the rajas of Rudrakot from availing themselves of the club's facilities. The British resident at Rudrakot, of course, had an automatic membership in the club. And so when Raman came to stay as the political agent, he too could enter its premises when he wished.

When the Fourth Rudrakot Rifles took up residence on the other side of the road from the Rudrakot Lancers, its officers were, as a matter of course, admitted to the Victoria Club. Raman insisted that the officers of the Lancers, hitherto not given access because they were Indian, had equal rights.

It took a minor *hartal*, a strike, to achieve this. Jai, who was then only thirteen, but prince of Rudrakot nonetheless and so a member of the Victoria, and Raman, sat cross-legged on the concrete steps of the club for two days in protest of this unfair policy. They held up placards that read ADMIT THE LANCERS. It was a huge embarrassment for the civil servants of Rudrakot and the Rifles regiment.

The British resident himself took the senior officers of the Rudrakot Lancers to the club on the evening of the second day, and gave them dinner at his table, along with a victorious Raman and a delighted Jai.

This story Mila and Ashok did not know, for Raman never talked about it, and Jai had long forgotten the thrill from his first attempt at civil disobedience.

Once thus invaded, the no-longer-sacrosanct and weakened Victoria Club began admitting women also. They were only allowed in certain rooms, not in the smoking room, not in the billiard rooms, only in the bridge rooms and the main dining hall. An additional wing was built behind the club and dubbed their special province, with its powder rooms and salons, as the blasted *murgikhana*—the henhouse.

Mila struck the gear into fourth and drove the jeep into the gateway of the Victoria Club. The watchmen's loose beards flew in the wind raised by the whizzing past of the jeep, and they had barely raised their hands to their foreheads in a salute before it disappeared in a whirl of dust and flying gravel. Once inside, she shifted down abruptly, and banged on the brakes. A long, waist-high hedge lined the enormous drive down to the clubhouse. Beyond the hedge was also club land, and most of it was bare, dotted with trees, skirted by desiccated attempts at sprouting a lawn in the hard ground. The lake was to the right, and the driveway, after going straight down the line of hedge for half a mile, curved around the huge white building, lakeside, to end under a pillared portico. The blinding sun harassed them all the way to the clubhouse, undulating in waves of heat across the building until the green of the hedges, the browns and reds of the earth, the white of the clubhouse all melded into a haze.

They arrived in the welcome shade of the cool portico, and a bearer came running down the stairs to take care of the jeep. Mila gave him the key and said to Sam, "The *mela* is set up on the lawns, Captain Hawthorne. I have to go find Mrs. Sexton, but Ashok can show you around."

"No, thank you," Sam said. "I'll find my way."

"We will leave in two hours," Mila said, though it was not necessary to remind him of that; they would see each other. But she thought that their guest, being American and unused to India, would not realize that they would not be able to converse much with each other at the *mela*.

"Thank you. I'll look for you before then." Sam turned and began to walk toward the lawns, and then he paused and seemed to ponder something. When he turned back, his face was disturbed. "Mila, what does the phrase 'four *annas* to the rupee' mean?"

Mila and Ashok were struck into stillness at first, their expressions similarly stunned for a moment. They cast a sudden, synchronized glance at each other, but for the sake of politeness, it was over even before it had begun and they were again facing Sam, their expressions stoic.

"A rupee has sixteen *annas*, Captain Hawthorne," Mila said carefully.

"Has someone been cheating you of your money? I would have thought you would be conversant with our currency by now."

"I am," Sam said. "But I did not understand that phrase."

"Where did you hear it?" Ashok asked. When Sam did not reply, he held up his hand, palm forward. "It doesn't matter, but it sounds very much like something quite a few people here would use."

"I see."

Mila sighed, and lifted an arm to brush hair from her forehead. "No, I'm afraid that you don't see, Captain Hawthorne. It's a derogatory term, humiliating."

Sam nodded. "I guessed that much."

"The Anglo-Indians . . . ," Mila said, hesitating, trying to form an explanation that was succinct, "are born of both the British and the Indians. It has become . . . shall we say fashionable, to refer to the amount of British blood they have in them as *annas* to the rupee." She was red in the face by now, uncomfortable at having to talk about this, but when she lifted her gaze to his, it was direct and uncompromising. "Your girl, or boy, was one-fourth British."

"Thank you," Sam said. He had started to move again, hands in his pockets, when another thought struck him. It was a simple thought, one he voiced in an instant, without giving it too much weight, but it was one he would remember repeatedly for the rest of his life. So thus, casually, standing under the portico of the Victoria Club, Sam asked, "And this terminology . . . does it apply to everyone who has some mixed blood in them? I mean, does the prejudice stretch beyond just Anglo-Indian alliances, to no matter what your parentage is?"

"You mean European . . . or even American?" Mila gave him a hard smile. "But it is a prejudice on all ends of the world, Captain Hawthorne. We are as inflexible as anyone else is. Mixing of bloods, as you say, is frowned upon." When she voiced this truth, an ache blossomed within her. There were a few alliances between the Indians and the British that existed because of love and affection, but the prejudices existed also, and without an overwhelming, sweeping love, Mila could not imagine anyone opting for such a life in India. For the most part, the British held themselves remote, and those who moved away from these strictures to find love, and marry Indians were cast out of their own communities and were considered to have horrifically "gone native." They were no longer "us" and had become "them." Even if Indians had been accepting of mixed alliances, the xenophobia of the British warranted no other response to Anglo-Indian alliances, and if for nothing else than as a defense against the xenophobia—Indian communities were now as prejudiced as British.

Sam rubbed his face thoughtfully. He then raised his hand to say goodbye and went out onto the lawns toward the *mela*.

They watched him leave, and in both of their hearts there was the same yearning, though they had known Sam Hawthorne for such a short time. Mila was troubled by Sam's question, and worried in an illogical way that perhaps her answers would have prejudiced him further. Ashok thought so too. They did not want Sam Hawthorne to turn out to be ordinary, just like everyone else they had known who had spent some time in India and, in the end, become what they had abhorred when they had first gotten here. Mila and Ashok had heard that argument too many times from the so-called British socialists who had come to India full of ideals about the nationalist struggle, equality of all men, and who, in the end, succumbed to the prevalent British belief in India that Indians could not rule themselves when they could not control their beggars, manage their monsoons, battle the heat.

Mila rubbed Ashok's arm lightly. "What are you going to do?"

"Get a drink first," he said. He put an arm around her shoulder. "Were we rude, Mila?"

"I'm afraid we were."

"I like him though."

She was silent for a while, pondering this statement. "I do too."

Ashok said, "Who is he? Why is he here? What is a U.S. Army officer doing in Rudrakot of all places?"

"I don't know," Mila said slowly. "I doubt Papa does either. How do you know he is from Seattle?"

"Sayyid," Ashok said. "It's on his uniform, sewn into the neck of the shirt."

Mila leaned against her brother. He had grown in the last two years, was no longer just a little brother. She had taught him to drive, and still sat with him at his lessons, although this was his last year in school. In a couple of months, they would have to decide where he was going for further studies. But they still had this summer here in Rudrakot, since Papa had decided not to send them to the hills for the hot season. She clasped her arms around his slim waist and looked up at him.

"The mustache is taking shape nicely; you might even grow one like Jai's."

He touched his upper lip. "There's no chance of that at all. To grow one as refined as Jai's on my face, I would have to drink like him, smoke like him, drive like a lunatic, sleep in the saddle, and dream of polo balls in the night sky instead of stars. At least that is what he thinks grew the hair on his chest. Have you seen his naked chest? Well, his overgrown chest?"

"Of course I haven't, Ashok. Don't be silly." She pinched the skin under his ribs. "Get your drink and eat some *paan* so Papa does not smell it on your breath. I'm off to battle with Laetitia."

She watched him leave and raised a hand in farewell. This was Ashok's last year at home, his last few months, really, and then he would thunder out into the world to become his own man. Papa and she could no longer tie him to them. It would be Kiran all over again. Kiran who was home now, who had failed his ICS examinations for the second time, whose two years in London had been a torrid waste of Papa's money and of Papa's energy. What would he do now? He was twenty-four, and the civil service was what he had been brought up to do. Kiran was not an army man, like Jai, although Jai had his princely title too, more than enough of a fallback option. Kiran had Jai's tastes, but none of Jai's resources.

She climbed the stairs and entered the club's cool front hall. A chest-high reception counter stood against the far wall. Two four-feet-by-six-feet portraits in oil hung on that wall, both of Queen Victoria. One was painted around the time of her coronation. In this one, she was a sylphlike figure with a minute waist, an enormous billowing pink skirt, and a tight bodice, jewels glittering around her slight neck and on her wrists, an ethereal crown of diamonds floating on her dark hair. Her shoulders were bare, dabbed by light from above somewhere, and her hands clasped the scepter and the orb. The second painting was also of the queen, only she was much older, and time had taken some hair away and lent gray to the rest, added heaviness around the eyes and in the cheeks, fattened the shoulders and thickened the waist. The gown was as resplendent as in the first portrait, the jewels as glittering and enchanting, the majesty even more so. *This was our empress,* Raman had said to Mila on the first day they visited the Victoria Club. Mila was seven that year, they had come by in the afternoon, before six o'clock, after which time no children were allowed at the club, and no members were allowed without their neckties and dress whites. *How large is the empire, Papa? Many, many countries, on many continents.* Mila had tried to imagine this much land belonging to this little woman. How had she managed all these lands and these people? Where had she lived? Had she ever come to see this corner of her empire, this country that people now called the jewel in the imperial crown?

Mila had refused to believe that the two portraits were of the same woman at different times of her life. Surely, it was just an aunt or someone like that, a wicked, older, uglier aunt of the princess on the left. She had spent many hours here, in the doorway, the light behind her falling upon the portraits. There was something fascinating about the oils, something so much more intimate than a mere photograph. It was also the size of the canvases, so mammoth and so colorful across the back wall that the effect was astounding. True, Jai's palace had paintings of that size and bigger, but Mila had seen his gallery only once; here she could visit as often as she wanted. And since she was Raman's daughter, no one denied her right to stand in the doorway and gaze at the paintings.

There were pictures along the walls on the sides—the one in the center was of the governor-general's visit to Rudrakot when Raja Bhimsen was alive. It was a typical, crowded picture, everyone seated in chairs in two rows, one row higher than the other, their legs crossed from right to left on one side of the governor-general and from left to right on the other side, like well-coordinated cancan dancers frozen in motion. Raman was the reason for the visit, not the official reason, of course, but the great man himself had to come and see who this young whippersnapper was who had Raja Bhimsen's ear. Raman was at the very left in the front row, and, apart from Bhimsen, the only dark face among the whites.

There were two doors on either side of the club's main hallway, which led to the ballroom and the main dining room, and two doors behind the counter that went into the club secretary's office. Mila went past the clerks at the counter with a nod and they said good afternoon. The way to the *murgikhana* was through the main dining room, which was empty now, the tables laid for dinner with white tablecloths, napkins, and cutlery. The windows were opened early every morning and late every evening to air out the dining room. And when "God Save the King" was played to announce dinner, it was accompanied by bearers carrying tiny coal braziers with smoking sandalwood chips to freshen the air. Yet the dining room held the hinting aroma of long-gone food—turned milk used in a pudding; a scorched chicken curry; the stale scent of after-dinner cigars.

The powder room was empty and Mila slid into it with a feeling of relief. She unwound the sari *pallu* from around her hair, set her sunglasses down on the dressing table, and went to the sink to wash her hands and her face. When she returned, the *ayah* offered her a towel and a hairbrush. She then switched on the row of bulbs over the mirror on the wall. Mila sat down on the stool and smoothed her hair back from her face. She opened her purse, took out a little vial of perfume, and brushed it against her wrists and on her neck. The cool bite of the perfume chilled her heated skin. She patted some talcum powder against her neck and forehead, not too much, for she was sure to sweat outside and the powder would just congeal into a white mess eventually.

The mottled glass windows of the powder room faced west, infused with the glow of the sun. The *ayah* sat in the shadows somewhere, knitting, Mila thought, for she could hear the quiet click of needles. Water gurgled in one of the toilets, wasteful and melodious. Brushes and combs guarded the surface of the teak dressing table. Pink tins of talcum powder were arrayed on a silver-embossed tray, now dusted with the powder that Mila had used. There were sanitary napkins in the drawer, along with cigarettes and hairpins. Despite the lavatories, the pleasant aroma of countless sprays of perfumes and the smoke of cigarettes tarried in the air. Mila, still at the mirror, was strangely lethargic, unwilling to move and go back outside. But she had to. She pleated the end of her sari again, put it over her left shoulder, pinned it into place, then gathered one end, swung it over her right shoulder, and tucked it into her blouse. Picking up her purse, Mila left the powder room to go battle the heat and the *mela* crowds.

# Eleven

*So far as I was concerned, I cannot give any satisfactory answer to the question why I should have sought to enter the [Indian Civil] Service after my reactions to the activities of Sir Michael O'Dwyer and Brigadier-General Dyer. Certainly it was not with any idea of ever supplanting the British, since in 1924 the latter showed no indication whatsoever of being supplanted . . . there must . . . have been the youthfully egotistical desire to prove to all that I was as good as the next man (English, of course!).*

—N. B. Bonarjee, *Under Two Masters*, 1970

My name is Pithamber, Agent Sahib," the old man said. "I come from the Nodi village and have lived there all of my life. I do not know how old I am, Sahib, but the year I was born, the monsoon rains failed."

The man paused to wipe his eyes with the clean cotton towel he carried slung over his left shoulder. He cleared his throat, bent his head, and spoke into his chest, "There was a story, when I was a boy, that I had brought bad luck to Nodi because of the misfortune the year of my birth. I could have gone away, sometimes the teasing became very hard . . . but where could I go? I was my parents' only son, the sole sustenance for their old age. And they had lived in Nodi all their lives. How could I move them?"

His voice fell silent in the cool room. The westward windows had their *khus* mats rolled down; the east windows were open to the backyard and the garden beyond. A little breeze, bearing a sudden and welcome dab of coolness, wafted in through the windows, birthed from the waters of the lake near the Victoria Club. Above them, the green ceiling fan clanked and shuddered, making a sharp, twanging sound at every fourth revolution. With the room quiet now, Raman listened for the next twang.

He was in his office, but not seated behind his mammoth and gleaming desk, for he would not have been able to see the old man from behind it. He had pulled his chair out to the side when the petitioner had insisted upon sitting on his haunches near the door. Raman was a short man, much like his ancestors from southern India, and his feet barely touched the floor. Actually, only his toes touched the floor if he sat up straight in the chair, so he slouched a little, arms on his stomach, the old man's voice pleasantly sonorous to his ear. The Turkish carpet in deep reds and black separated them; the man would not even sit upon it, preferring the cool of the mosaic floor.

Why he had come to the political agent's office, Raman still did not know, and it would be a while before the old man would tell him. For Raman first had to listen to the story of his life, his birth, his marriage, the petty squabbles of the village—it was a process of gaining trust, this listening. And over the years, even before he had become a civil service officer, Raman had adopted this skill of paying attention to stories, for they told him more about the situation than the facts could.

Raman heard him say that the rains did come the year he was married, drenching the village lushly. His wife was an incarnation of a goddess the day he married her, fiery eyed, with a sharp tongue. She had been dead for ten years now, but she had done him well, giving him three sons and three daughters. The sons were long gone from the village, the daughters were all married . . . he saw them sometimes . . . he missed his wife. He did not know how old she had been when she died, or how old she had been when he married her; he knew only that she was two years past puberty.

"What do you do for a living?" Raman asked when the man had fallen to quiet again. He was quite old, perhaps seventy or eighty, and yet Raman knew that he would still work. To this peasant, not working meant to invite the God of Death, Yama, into his home, noose in hand. His dark, desert skin stretched tightly over a thin frame, his shoulders were bent with age, his bare feet calloused and the nails cracked, the soles thick as shoe soles.

"I build wells, Agent Sahib," the man said, and smiled for the first time since he had come into the office.

And so he had redeemed the misfortune of his birth, Raman thought.

So he had stayed on in Nodi, not just to look after his parents, but because he had honor in the village. The old man's tale was otherwise not so different from countless other stories that Raman had heard since he had come to Rudrakot. All lives in the desert, he had realized, revolved around water. Births were marked by the monsoons—the year they came, the year they did not; superstitions swirled about water—the first rains of the year were beneficial to the health; marriages were conducted after spring because a mating after the rains would result in the blessing of many children.

The villages in Rudrakot were too poor for the villagers to own wells—or those would have been marked out as assets in wedding negotiations—but almost every village in Rudrakot now had a communal well, at least one. How far away are you from the village well? was now the question prospective brides' fathers asked. The farther away, the lesser the dowry, for their daughters, newly brought into the family and so low in its hierarchy, would be the ones who would hike to the well for the family's water.

The door to his office opened, and the old man, startled by the noise, scrambled to his feet. Sayyid looked in.

"Yes, Sayyid?"

"Sahib, Kiran Sahib wants to talk with you."

Raman shook his head. "I'm busy now. Afterward."

Sayyid lingered in the doorway, and the villager half-bowed to him, his hands raised together in a greeting. Sayyid nodded back briefly before saying to Raman, "When"—he paused to be respectful—"do you think you will be able to see Kiran Sahib?"

Raman clicked his tongue in exasperation. Was Kiran finally awake, then? He had been away late last night, and Raman had not even seen him for lunch, with Sayyid covering up for Kiran's lateness at both ends of the night. What was he to do with this son of his? He had to see him. He *wanted* to see Kiran. It had been what, four, maybe five days since Raman had seen Kiran. And they lived in the same house.

"In half an hour, Sayyid," Raman said finally, in English.

The butler nodded, stepped back beyond the door frame, and shut the door.

The old man turned and Raman said, "Please sit down again."

"Are you sure, Agent Sahib? I can come back later, when you are less busy."

The man had walked three days from Nodi and had waited four days outside the political agent's office to see Raman for a few minutes. He had spent the nights at the railway station, sleeping on the platform. Yet he was willing to go back outside and wait for his turn again. It was an inbuilt patience, Raman thought, an inbuilt persistence even. The villagers knew that the sahibs had their vagaries, but they were their Ma-Baap, and would in time tend to their needs.

"Please sit," Raman said. "I have nothing else to do. Tell me why you are here."

As the man began to talk again, Raman wondered whether, after all these years, he was fit for the job of an ICS officer. It seemed as though no matter how many little matters were taken care of, others cropped up just as fast as those were resolved. Raman had wanted to be an Indian Civil Service officer because the officers who had visited his village when he was a child had been a source of awe and wonder to him. Sage and even tempered, and so all knowing. They had descended from their mansions in the cities to mediate, scold, fuss, and settle issues. *I am your mother and I am your father* was their credo. They were here to look after the people. The ICS was the backbone of the Indian government, why, the ICS *was* India.

"They do not listen to me, Agent Sahib," the old man said. "I tell them, I built the rainwater well; I know how it works. If they wash their clothes on the surface and bathe the children, it rots the water. And we have to drink that water."

"You build rainwater wells?" Raman asked, looking at the shriveled old man in front of him with a new respect. The rainwater wells were a Sukh desert construct; Raman had seen these nowhere else in India. They were actually enormous brick-laid saucers that sloped gently toward the middle, capped in the center by a six-foot-high dome. The dome had eight or ten iron *jalis* along the bottom, screens that filtered the rainwater into a well beneath. The brick and mortar saucer sluiced up the rains and rushed them into the well; the dome kept the precious water from evaporating under an unsympathetic sun.

Raman knew that building these wells was laborious and tedious work, requiring the finely honed skills of a well-trained engineer. The saucer had to be sloped at the right angle, the dome had to sit right, and the well below the surface had to have channels for possible overflows. This old man who had brought bad luck to his village by staunching the monsoon rains in the year of his birth had more than made up for it by providing precious water for his village.

"Do you have enough water if the monsoon fails this year?" Raman asked.

"Enough with what is in the ground, Sahib," the man replied. "Even if it is not replenished, it will last and will not bring disease. But the villagers sleep on the well at night; children throw stones into it; cows graze and defecate too close to it. The water will not keep fresh."

"This is," Raman said finally, "a matter for the resident sahib. Nodi does not lie in my jurisdiction."

"I did go to the resident sahib, Colo-nel Pank-hurst," the man said, Pankhurst's name coming out with hesitation. "He sent a *munshi* to talk with the villagers; the *munshi* ate and drank with us; we even slaughtered a goat for the meal. But in the end, he left without talking about the well. If you could come to Nodi, Agent Sahib . . . they would listen to you."

"I cannot come," Raman said automatically. "I do not have the time."

"Yes, of course, forgive me, Sahib." The old man sighed and scoured his head with a gnarled hand. His hair was all white, barely dotting his dark skull.

In the early days, when Raman was a new ICS officer, he had spent most of his time in camp, living out of a tent, traveling over his district on a horse, with only three servants and Sayyid by his side. This was an un-stated ritual of investiture into the civil service. And so Raman had come to know the land and the people intimately, listened to all of their prob-lems, big and small, learned where the pulse of the district lay. Since com-ing to Rudrakot, his geographical boundaries had shrunk to his house, his office, Jai's palace, of course, and the Victoria Club. Raman was at Rudrakot to look after Jai—there was nothing tacit in this understanding; so he had been told when he was posted to Rudrakot at Raja Bhimsen's in-sistence. In all else, the agriculture, the taxes, the issues of land rights, the quarrels over livestock, the lack of water, or, rarely, the surfeit of it, Colonel Pankhurst, the British resident, had command.

Much as Raman loved Jai—as a son, as his prince—he missed his early nomadic days in the ICS. It had been a harsh life at times, with rocks for chairs, and sheets on the hard ground for a bed, no conversation around the campfire, the hunger for the scent of a woman, the sudden noises of the jungle night, predators in human and animal form. But it had been the ICS that he had dreamed of when he was a child. Present where the villagers were, at their homes, there to settle squabbles minor and petty, to scold, to mollify, to pet, to rule. He was, to the villagers, their Ma and their Baap. *I am your mother and I am your father.*

Now he warmed a chair behind a desk, he saw only pane-size chunks of land outside; his world had shrunk to the confines of his office and to much conversation about what went on beyond.

Nodi was a day's ride from his house. Both Jai and Colonel Pankhurst were away right now, Jai at the Imperial Cadet Corps on a teaching assignment, Colonel Pankhurst at Delhi on the invitation of the viceroy. He should not go, Raman thought, he *could* not go . . .

"I will come tomorrow," he said to the old man.

The man smiled, his lower jaw deepening toward his toothless mouth. His blurry, cataract-smeared eyes filled. "Thank you, Agent Sahib."

"Stay here tonight," Raman said. "Sayyid will find you a place to sleep. We can ride together in the morning."

"I do not ride, Agent Sahib. I have never ridden a horse; a water buffalo, once, when I was young, but never a horse."

But of course he would not ride a horse, Raman thought. He could not ride a horse, only lead it and walk next to it. Horses were for the privileged few in India, the sahibs and their wives, the princes and their consorts, the landowners—all floating above the old villager in a social class rife with the rarified air of advantage. Raman looked at the old man's feet, bare and cracked at the heels, fissures of dirt crawling upward, his soles hardened into a hooflike quality. He had never worn either shoes or *chappals* before and wouldn't know what to do with them if he was given a pair. His feet, spread out and flat from the weight of his thin body, would not fit into them. Seeing the old man's feet, Raman's foot ached and he slid his left foot out of its sandal, and ran his toe around the rim of his right heel, smooth and pale from Sayyid's nightly massages with sesame oil. There was an immense gulf between the two men in that room, measured in terms of their right to ride a horse, to clad their feet in the skin of animals, to sit on furniture. Such were the rules of their world. Raman was a sahib, here to serve the old man as a civilian—a member of the Indian Civil Service—but the old man was a commoner, served and scolded, and in turn, kept in his place.

"We'll find a way to get there then." Raman hoisted himself off the chair and went to the door. Sayyid was standing just beyond. He listened to his master's instructions and beckoned to the old man.

"Ask Kiran to come," Raman said.

For Kiran's talk, Raman dragged his chair behind the desk and sat down. Earlier in the afternoon, he had heard Mila zip out of the drive in the jeep with Sam and Ashok. Raman arranged his pens on the blotter in a straight line and wished his daughter would not drive as though an army of *asuras* was chasing her. Pallavi disliked Mila driving the jeep, driving at all or being out on her own, without an escort. She should be married, Pallavi said to him often, too often sometimes, until he would snap back at her that she *was* going to be married, so what was the hurry anyway?

In another, more ideal world, Raman would have wanted to invite Sam into his life, perhaps even as a husband for Mila. But he was not Indian, though Raman felt that in another life Sam must have been Indian, else why this affinity between them? Why was Sam so knowledgeable about his community, about the names people carried upon themselves? His daughter would like him very much, as much as he himself liked him. Raman saw Sam's charm, he even saw his physical attraction in his long and lean body and his gentle hands—Mila would like him. There was a centuries-old wisdom in arranging marriages in India, something the Western world often overlooked, thinking all such marriages to be based on economics and pride. But no father or mother would willingly give their child to a man or a woman who did not fulfill all needs—economic, physical, emotional. Since such depth of knowledge into a person's character came only after a lifetime of learning, and since marriage negotiations did not allow for this amount of time, the parents learned to judge character upon first or second meetings. Raman had not considered any of this when he'd had met Sam earlier that morning, but as the afternoon had passed, as he heard Mila drive away to the club, he had been left with a feeling of comfort and affection for this man who had strayed into their home, carrying on his demeanor fatigue and an underlying fear—what that was Raman did not know. It was almost as if Sam was searching for something in Rudrakot; he had an air of anticipation, of expectation, of trepidation at the outcome of his search.

For Raman, Sam was an easy read, almost too easy. The excuse of his being here to rest his shoulder was just that—an excuse. Raman swiped his broad hand over the smooth wood of his desk, once, twice, feeling the coolness under his palm. His hand came away smelling faintly of polish. He would have to find out who this Sam Hawthorne really was.

April 1942, a Month Earlier

*Somewhere in Burma*

$\mathcal{T}$he opium hangs around them in the stagnant, moisture-laden air, and they breathe that sweet, almost cloying smell into their lungs, over and over again. Sam drifts in an amicable opium smog. Ken's face is indistinct to him, he seems to be asleep, but his eyelids flutter spasmodically. Sam pats his chest, hoping to ease the uneasiness there. Surely he must have imagined that transformation in Ken when he had talked of that girl . . . what was her name? Marianne begins to speak and he turns his attention to her as she tells of her last few days in the Kachin village.

It was, in many ways, an idyllic existence. A peaceful one, fueled by the opium that every Kachin smoked—men, women, even the children. Fed by the drug, they ate little, worked hard at tilling, plowing, keeping their poppy fields lush with pink and red flowers. The Kachin were opium farmers; they had not always been so, of course, but in the last century or so, British colonists had encouraged them to convert their rice fields into the more lucrative poppy fields.

It was here Marianne and Joseph Westwood had come to preach their mission of Christianity, to talk of their God, to convert where they could, mostly, to live and work among a people so unlike themselves. To learn from them. Humbly. As few missionaries did. They were not new to Burma; Joseph had taught for one year at the American Baptist mission school at Rangoon University, Judson College. They were new, though, to the Kachin village they came to. Strangely, the Kachin here, along the overgrown dirt track from Burma to Ledo, in India, where white men were most likely to stray, had not seen many white men. But they took to the two new members of their village, and made them theirs, made them wanted.

The Kachin were friendly, smiles painting their faces, tempers evened and stamina nurtured in an opiate smoke. Marianne and Joseph settled into a *basha* standing cranelike on stilts above the swampy water at the edge of the village. That first day, and for months afterward, the Kachin brought them potable water in bamboo poles of different widths and lengths and stacked these poles against the side of their *basha* like a pipe organ. They brought them eggs. And hens. Joseph built a church with their help; it had a bamboo cross on a bamboo steeple. It collapsed the next year, the year they ran out of malaria pills, the year the mosquitoes fed on Joseph's blood and killed him.

Marianne could not leave. There was nothing to keep her, with Joseph gone; she could only speak English to the walls of her *basha* and she knew she would not see a white face for months. But she could not leave. For here, among these half-naked tribesmen of Burma, Marianne Westwood forgot that she was from New Jersey, from a different land, forgot even the more modern, more convenient pleasures (such as they were) of Rangoon, and found her peace.

And then late last year came rumors swirling up from Rangoon and Mandalay that Pearl Harbor had been bombed. There had been a war, somewhere in Europe, this much Marianne had known, but this bombing changed the trajectory of all things peaceful, and this she discerned almost immediately. America would go to war. Join forces with Britain, become her ally. What Hitler had been smart enough not to do—compel America into the war—and therefore had kept Britain without the help of its most powerful friend—the Japanese had unnecessarily precipitated. Too early. What, Marianne had thought, that December morning in her *basha,* would keep the Japanese from invading Burma? It was their closest link to India. And sure enough, a few months later, she heard that Rangoon was to fall. Then she heard that *that* was all just a silly rumor; the British troops would hold out. Burma? Fall? Ridiculous. And then Rangoon fell.

Then began the frightening panorama of the flight from Burma on the dirt track that led to Ledo in India, passing by their Kachin village. Huge hordes of refugees at first, civilians, British and Indian, some traveling most incongruously with bedsteads, chairs, footstools, even a baby grand, the keys frittering music at every bump in the road. The refugees stopped at their village; they were fed, they rested, they moved on. Some looted rice from the *godowns* that the Kachin were hired to build to store Burma's precious rice supplies farther north, nearer the Indian border. Some raped the Kachin women. Most left their diseases among the Kachin. The dreaded cholera, something the Kachin had never been exposed to before. It devastated their population. Confused and numbed by this, the Kachin withdrew the hands of friendship they had so eagerly extended to the white strangers who looked and spoke like their beloved Marie-anne. As the flood of evacuation continued, RAF planes flew over the village so often that when the first Japanese planes came, the Kachin literally forgot to duck, thinking the new planes to be friends too. The first bomb ate out a chunk of the swampy earth, the second denuded the hillside, and in the next morning's rain, mud sluiced downward to bury the remaining *bashas* and the poppy fields.

"Why didn't you leave then?" Ken asks, his eyes still closed. So he *has* been listening, Sam thinks. They are all relaxed now, no longer tired, not afraid, hunger at bay. If the village sends its death reek toward them, they can no longer smell it. They have not forgotten, but they are engrossed in Marianne's story.

"I wanted to leave," she says. "I begged them to leave. I knew the Japanese army would follow the planes. But where would they go? North and west toward India on that dirt track?"

"We are here now." Sam points to the muddy road below, along the slope of the hill, carved and gutted into deep ruts with bullock-cart tracks, imprinted with the footsteps of thousands of men and women. They avoid the track, follow it only within the jungle, staying away from its obvious lack of cover. Burma *has* fallen, absolutely and completely. Japanese troops are in front of them—hence the devastation in the village they are to go into—and behind them and around them.

The edges of Marianne's mouth lift in a wan smile. "This road leads to India through the Naga hills. My Kachin had not had very . . . shall we say bonding experiences with the Nagas?"

Ken chuckles as he cups his hands around the opium pipe's bowl. "The headhunters? Surely, that's a joke? Who hunts heads in 1942?"

"The Nagas are said to still prey on white men, Ken," Marianne says. "And we have to travel through their territory to India." Then she smiles. They both smile. Only Sam is grim, watching them, no longer mesmerized into lethargy by the opium. When he was given his plastic-coated map and his orders in Assam to rescue Marianne, Sam was also told about the Nagas. Like Ken, he had been disbelieving at first. And then he was told that last October, a Naga tribe had gone on a rampage (perhaps for them, with all this encroaching civility toward fellow humans and just plain civilization, a *last* rampage) and acquired a bounty of a hundred and fifty heads. Whose heads? Sam had asked his CO. Just anyone around. They were not very particular. He lets Ken and Marianne grin at each other somewhat asininely and then says softly, "We must go now."

"Noooo . . . ," Marianne begins to sob. "No . . . ,"

Sam digs his fists into his eyes, fits his head into the curve of his arm, and wishes he could rest, just for a little while. He knows how obstinate Marianne is; it is because she is pigheaded that she did not leave Burma when she was ordered to evacuate. And it is because she did not leave that he is here to take her out. Oh, for some relief, Sam thinks, from this constant argument. If only they would listen to him, follow his orders, be reasonable, so he can do his duty. If only he can shake off the sight of Ken swamped with the hurt and pain this girl Rosalie has caused him. Sam shrugs to loosen his skin. Marianne is still crying, her voice growing louder and louder in the silence of the forest. The monkeys have stopped their interminable shrieking at last. Sam ignores Marianne's tantrum, like an ostrich, *his* head though, buried in the crook of his arm. The letters from Maude and Mike lie heavy against his chest. Sam wishes he could cry too.

# Twelve

*. . . I was slow to realize that the free and easy attitudes of the British in England stiffened somewhat imperially east of Suez . . . the social life of Anglo-India was very narrow in its outlook and restricted in its scope . . . there appeared to be no intellectual life whatsoever . . . which, I think, was a pity, since . . . an occasional free and open discussion on what was going on in the world around one,* might *have brought about a greater understanding between the two races, or at any rate reduced . . . misunderstanding.*

—N. B. Bonarjee, *Under Two Masters,* 1970

*I*t was ten minutes before Raman woke from his pleasant musings about Sam. He sighed. What foolish thinking this was for him, Mila could never marry Sam. His society would not allow it or accept it, and neither would any American society. Besides, it was futile to look any further for a husband for Mila.

It was at these times, when he thought of Mila's marriage, or of Kiran or Ashok, which was most of the time, that Raman missed Lakshmi with a huge, gaping ache in his heart. She would not have railed against his decisions about Mila and Kiran as Pallavi did.

He laughed aloud, his voice cutting through the silence in his office. His mother had chosen Lakshmi for one reason alone—the color of her skin. In all other factors—caste, background, dowry, family status—she had been vetted and approved by the elders. But at the girl-viewing ceremony, when Raman first saw Lakshmi, he remembered that his mother had taken her to one side on the pretext of a talk, and clasped her arm at the elbow. Raman's mother had been the fairest in their family for generations—no other daughter-in-law could match that virtue. She had been brought in (other things being equal, of course) quite specifically to breed color into the line, or to more specifically breed a *lack* of color into the line. But Raman had taken, quite perversely, after his father's family and had come out like charcoal.

So Raman's mother had laid her arm next to Lakshmi's and glanced down surreptitiously at their touching skins on the inside of their elbows, where the real color was, and found them to match. Actually, Lakshmi had been just a shade lighter, but it boded well for future children.

Mila and Ashok took after Raman, lighter hued than their father, but still dark enough to be called coffee colored. Kiran had delighted his grandmother and his mother.

Raman knew that a lot of his ideas about Lakshmi were long dead, that they would not have fit the living woman, that had she lived, she would probably have been very much like Pallavi in restrictions imposed on Mila. But he had been in love with the idea of Lakshmi—of a wife, rather—before he married her. On him had not been the onus of choice, the fear of disappointment or subsequent distress; that responsibility belonged to the elders of the family who had decided whom he would marry. Lakshmi had satisfied his ego, for all love—despite popular opinion—is not selfless at its very beginning. Raman fell into love with his wife because she took good care of him, tended to his wants before hers, and thought of him at every turn. He reciprocated with a gentleness and intensity. Over the years she loved him deeply too, in every sense of the word, for what had begun for her in an emotion tied to duty blossomed under his care.

He had known, when he married Lakshmi, that she was not particularly intelligent, in the way that men were taught to be; nor educated—she had failed her fourth standard exams and had never tired her brain after that; that she would not fit into his ICS world with its so-British drinking and clubs and parties. He had still loved her, knowing all of this about her. It was a simple love, based on joy and laughter, and few expectations. Lakshmi might not have known how to drink a gin and tonic at the club and still keep her head, but she knew what made Raman happy.

Yet he wanted Mila to be different. He wanted her to ride and read and drive and make her own choices. It was a radical way of thinking. Raman had not been brought up thus—he had been taught to respect his elders unquestioningly, to defer to their judgments, to believe as they did. But he had also seen too many men make the sudden leap from believer to elder when their time came, with no originality of thought, no allowed period of transition, no making of mistakes, and certainly no redeeming of them. Raman wanted Kiran, Mila, and Ashok to make their own mistakes.

"Papa."

Raman looked up. "Come in, Kiran."

He watched as his oldest child came into the room and sat down on the chair opposite him. Kiran swung his legs over one of the chair's arms, leaned his back against the other, and smiled at his father. Raman had always wanted a daughter, always, even though his society told him that it was important to have sons as a crutch in old age—someone to set light to the funeral pyre to send his father's bodily remains to heaven, someone to perform those sacred rituals that would help his father's soul gain eventual absolution. Even so, Mila, his second child, had been the fulfillment of a desire. But Raman had not been ready for the ambush of love he had felt when Kiran was born. He had taken after Lakshmi in everything, his huge, heavily lashed eyes, the moonlight sheen to his skin, the gloss in his hair. He had looked so different that Raman had felt as though he was a caretaker to an adopted child, not one made from his body. But the force of love had come that first morning.

Now Kiran had grown into a tall (another facet of Lakshmi's family) and handsome young man, and Raman felt that same sense of early surprise that he had made this child.

"Where were you last night?" Raman asked. "You came home late."

Kiran straightened in the chair, and a bit of stubbornness firmed his mouth. "With the Rifles."

"At their club?"

"Yes."

Raman began to shake his head and stopped himself in time, but he could not seem to stop his words. "Kiran, you must think of doing something. How long can you be here? What do you want to do? Tell me, we can figure this out together."

"I did not come here for a lecture, Papa," Kiran muttered.

"Why then?" Raman asked. "For money? Have you run out?"

A flush began on Kiran's neck and rushed upward to the roots of his hair. So he *had* come for money, Raman thought. Why could he not make some on his own? At his age, Raman had been married for a good eight years, had a child already, Mila was on the way, and he had been well settled in the ICS. Kiran had returned from England after failing his ICS examinations for the second time. The money, the expense, was nothing compared to the shame of failure, and Raman felt it keenly. More so than Kiran, he thought with a prick of irritation, who spent all of his time drinking beer and gimlets at the Rifles' clubhouse or at the Victoria Club. It was not just Kiran's reputation, it was *not* Kiran's reputation—Raman amended in his head—that was at stake. It was Raman's. Kiran was too young to possess something as lofty as a name; his only designation was as the political agent's son; why could he not have passed his examinations? Kiran was not stupid.

"I hate to beg, Papa—," Kiran began.

"Then don't."

Kiran reddened again and his body grew slack in the chair. He did not even know how to sit in front of his father, Raman thought. Perhaps he had been too easy with his children in giving them choices in their lives. Perhaps the old ways were right after all. For Raman there had been no option other than the ICS. But it was ridiculous to talk of the ICS as though it was the *last* option; it was the *best* option in India. The civil servants were the heaven born, nominated by God to rule the common. For Raman it had been the fulfillment of a dream. He was finally a sahib. A brown sahib, but a sahib nonetheless. How could Kiran not have wanted this?

"You are not unintelligent, Kiran," Raman said slowly. "How did you manage to fail the examinations?"

"I didn't fail the written examinations," Kiran said, finally heated enough to swing his legs back on the floor and sit up in his chair. "It was the damn viva voce, to test my 'alertness, intelligence, and general intellectual outlook.' What a bloody crock that was. It was one chap who did me in. The others were kind."

"Don't swear," Raman said. "Who was he?"

"I can't remember his name now. Some history master from Balliol. I don't think he had ever been to India, and only knew of it academically. But he had connections and that got him on the board."

"What did he ask you?"

"How does it matter now?" Kiran's voice was bitter. "There's no going back, is there?" He went on. "He wanted to know if Jai was truly loyal to the empire's interests, if Raja Bhimsen wasn't a manipulative bastard in getting Jai instated as heir, if he wasn't a bigger bastard in getting you to Rudrakot. He wanted to know if I had my finger on the pulse of Rudrakot's politics. I told him where I thought my finger should go."

They were silent for a long while and Raman felt a flood of anger inside him. In the end, it had come to this. Because Kiran was his son, because there was still a great deal of upset over Raman's appointment to Rudrakot, Kiran had not passed his viva, his interview. In all fairness, Raman thought, even in the midst of his rage, Kiran did not know how to control either his tongue or his emotions. Vivas were meant to be chatty and polite. A little deference, a great deal of platitudes, some answers that sounded intelligent, whatever they might actually be, a shaking of hands. Do your job there, get out of the room, become an ICS officer. The viva was a formality at best, not meant to fail candidates for the ICS. He let Kiran's last sentence pass away, mostly because he did not quite understand it, and because he thought it was something rude that he did not want explained. Where had Kiran learned such language?

"What are you going to do today?" he asked in a gentler voice than he had so far used with his son.

Kiran shook his head sullenly, a heavy cast of dark over his face. "I do not know."

"Mila and Ashok have gone to the *mela* with our guest. You should go too."

"It's at the club?"

"Yes, the Victoria."

Kiran glanced up at his father. "Who is this Sam Hawthorne?"

"He is here to recuperate from injuries sustained on his flight from Burma last month," Raman said. "I know little else about him. He has been quiet so far."

A little smile lit up Kiran's mouth and eyes, and Raman felt a deluge of love. How lovely he looked when he smiled, more now than ever, since he smiled so much less. "You took him in, then, Papa? You have always had a propensity for sentimentality and nonsense. This Hawthorne chap could have stayed at the club."

Raman shrugged. "I like him. He is different somehow, engaging."

"When does Jai return?"

"In a month, I think. I heard from him yesterday."

"I'll go," Kiran said, rising from his chair. He leaned over and offered his hand to his father and Raman clasped it with his own and then, briefly, held it against his chest and patted it with his left hand.

"Ask Sayyid to give you something from the money box," he said.

"Thank you, Papa."

When Kiran had left, Sayyid came in with the tea tray and a plate of scones with butter and orange marmalade. Raman ate and drank slowly, not minding that the *chai* cooled in its cup, for it was only his morning coffee that got his heated devotion.

At least, he thought, there were no further embarrassments to come from his children. Kiran would find his way; he would help him. Would Ashok eventually consider the ICS too? How splendid it would be to have two sons, both his sons, in the service. How his fellow officers would admire him. Then, perhaps, Kiran and Ashok would have sons too who would follow their grandfather's example and join the service. They could be a family of ICS officers with a lengthy tradition.

Raman put his teacup down and bit into a scone. He had little idea of how his own years in the service were going to come to an end. Here they were, in 1942, but a few years at most from independence from the Raj. The ICS was comprised mostly of British officers, and they would all leave when India wrenched herself away from British rule. Who would be left then? A few old-timers like him, a new bunch of upstart recruits with nothing like the *pukka* sahib's love for the country, or sense of the people, or immersion in their districts' problems—it did not bode well even for Raman, let alone Kiran or Ashok.

This life, *his* life, was built by a British institution, nurtured and nourished by it; Raman had become a sahib in this best of traditions in India, which was, after all a British construct—how would it restructure itself in an independent India? The ICS upheld India, it *was* India, he had always thought. Who would take the places of those who would leave? And never once, in all of his years in the ICS, had he felt an intruder or a misfit on the basis of the color of his skin. He knew his presence was resented at Rudrakot as a political agent, but only because he sliced away a part of the resident's duties, because it was unusual for a princely state to have both positions serving the same need. The British *were* fair masters though—else he would not be here in Rudrakot. Why did the freedom fighters not see all this change, why did they insist upon complete freedom?

The truth was, Raman thought sadly, that Mr. Gandhi and Mr. Nehru were hurtling them all toward an ideology, a dogma that sounded and seemed nice enough but would not translate quite so easily into practice for all of their rhetoric. Raman's loyalties lay with his king, in England, and to India, which was after all a part of the crown, *the* jewel in Britain's crown, according to Churchill. Why couldn't they just remain as they were? Why insist upon independence? There *was* some semblance of equality. Raman had achieved this, after all.

Raman did not think India was ready for democracy, not yet anyway. He did not consider the masses to be educated enough to make their own decisions, in any democratic fashion, without being influenced by one source or another. The well builder who came to him today had had a very specific and seemingly trivial request—keep his well water clean—but to him it was a problem of gargantuan proportions. Why would he care in the future about the value of his vote? Or that it would elect a leader for his thronging country? His entire life had been lived in Nodi, and his allegiance would extend only to those who administered his village; for him, the geography of India *was* Nodi.

In the most honest moments of this wrenching discourse in his head, Raman also had to admit his greatest fear was that democracy would shatter his carefully cultivated bureaucracy.

Now there were mild rumblings of the nationalist movement in Rudrakot also, in the shape and form of earnest young men and women who went, ostensibly, to an "exercise camp" for their health, but in reality to gather and rouse each other in the name of Mr. Gandhi.

At Annadale College a few months ago, Raman had watched a demonstration from inside the grounds, along with the principal, Mr. Stokes, and the chief inspector of Rudrakot. The shouts rose and died out over a period of two hours. Send them home, I say, a young man had called out, and was answered by a huge *yes*. India is for Indians; we do not want their like here. And Tilak's doctrine, taken and adopted firmly into the freedom movement: *Swaraj is my birthright*. Self-rule. Self-rule, they shouted, let us rule ourselves, by ourselves. Go Home. *Quit India,* would come later that year, but those latter two phrases were already in the consciousness of all Indians. Then they had begun to sing "Vandemataram" in praise of India.

> *I bow to thee, Mother*
> *Richly watered, richly fruited, cool with the winds of the south*
> *Dark with the crops of harvests, Mother!*
>
> *Nights rejoicing in the glory of moonlight*
> *Lands clothed beautifully with trees in flowering bloom*
> *Sweet of laughter, sweet of speech*
>
> *O Mother, giver of boons, giver of bliss!*

Their voices had been hoarse and sweet together, mostly men's voices, a few higher-pitched women's voices interspersed in between. Raman, enclosed in Stokes's office, the windows open toward the gates so they could hear what was being said, even if they could not see or be seen (for security reasons), was overwhelmed as his heart swelled to stifle within his chest. Tears caught in his throat when he heard the words, made him feel whole with the crowd outside. Then the song died down, the man on the gatepost began to yell invectives, the police constables toppled him off into the crowd, and then the students went home.

But they had all learned something that March morning in Rudrakot from the thousand-strong throng outside Annadale College—that the nationalist movement was here to stay in 1942, that it had been growing unfettered in the exercise camps without their knowledge, that it was a threat needing to be checked.

At least, Raman thought, his children were not involved. Kiran, with his self-imposed idleness, was in danger of having his head turned, but Kiran was too much like his father; he would never join the movement. Mila and Ashok were enigmas of sorts—idleness would not draw them into nationalism, conviction would. But they were safe for now . . . unless that boy Vimal, who was tutored with Ashok, approached him. But there could be little opportunity for a meeting, Raman hoped.

Putting away all this, he sat sipping his cold *chai* and munching on his scones. He would leave early tomorrow morning, while the night was old but not yet dead, at two o'clock or three o'clock, and he would ride in the dark to catch what little cool there was in the air. As the sun rose, they could stop for a breakfast. When Raman had been a young assistant collector on tour, Sayyid had thrown fabulous curry omelets on a smoking cast-iron *tava:* eggs whipped with a fork with milk and a pinch of sugar; slivers of red onions; whole leaves of coriander; one garlic clove, plump and pungent when crushed; a sprinkling of cumin powder; ground peppercorns. His mouth watered. Sayyid would toast the bread slices in the same *ghee* used to cook the omelet and bring the whole, hot and steaming, to Raman. This is what he remembered most about being in camp, the breakfasts under a canopy of fading stars accompanied by the song of birds. Surely, Pankhurst would not mind if Raman took over this little duty of his.

So Raman ruminated with pleasure on the next day. Many, many years later he would know for certain that he should not have gone from Rudrakot to Nodi, that he was needed at home, that Pallavi would not be strong enough to resist Mila's pleas or Ashok's tantrums. That his children, because of that one night and day, would hurl the paths of their lives away from him, break that umbilical cord that connected them to him as surely as if a midwife had gnawed through it with a knife. Raman would never regret knowing Sam Hawthorne, and so would never be remorseful that he had invited him to stay in his house when he could very well have bunked at the Victoria Club. Raman believed in karma, in a fate that etched the lives of men and women into stone well before they were born. Sam Hawthorne, he considered a karma for them all. They were meant to know him.

But he did wish in later years, when he was old and grizzled, confined to an easy chair in the verandah, two grandchildren on his lap, their fragrant heads resting on his chest as he told them stories, that the gap left by Mila's child could be filled too. That the granddaughter he had known for only a short time after her birth would come to lay her face against his, wind her arms around his neck, kiss him and call him *thatha*—grandfather. If she had stayed on with them, they would have used one of her Indian names, but in America, she was called Olivia.

Unknowing of how fate was to unravel all of their lives, Raman put down his teacup and called Sayyid into his office to talk with him about packing his clothes.

# Thirteen

*They didn't come from very good families at all. They married for the sake of marrying, I suppose, and companionship. And they became very haughty. They had dozens of servants, though they never had one servant in England; and they thought every one of us was servant class . . . I remember once at a gathering one Englishwoman turned to me and said: "Oh, what beautiful English you talk." I said: "Really? I'm surprised you acknowledge it. After all, we educated Indians talk English all the time. Thank you for noticing, but it's not a compliment."*

—Zareer Masani, *Indian Tales of the Raj*, 1987

*For many years after the death of the Raj, my dear Olivia, British writers would pen long tales about Raj childhoods, Raj service, the might of the empire, the necessity for it, why it benefited India. Indian writers tell of sacrifices made and horrors undergone in the name of that ultimate mother, India. Neither opts to be deliberately untruthful, but as much as the passing of the years has brought a clarity about the characters and attitudes of the rulers and the ruled, the distance has also created a fog. The Indian writers can sometimes be overly vehement, and the British look back wistfully upon their* pukka *sahib childhoods with memories clouded by sentimentality and twaddle.*

*But there was no losing sight of the fact that, friendly or not, sympathetic or not, the British were the masters and we were . . . They were unwelcome, and would be asked to Quit India in a few short months.*

*So back then, my dearest Olivia, back in 1942, on that 28th of May, the differences were sharp and clear, as though newly cleaved into being. As Sam moved down the lawns toward the* mela *at the Victoria Club, he did not see these differences or realize what they could mean—why, he was in love with Mila, how could he separate her from her people?*

Sam looked out in the direction of the lake. From here he could not see the *mela* itself, but a path, fringed with a short hedge of jasmine bushes led out between the lush lawns. Everything was neat, trimmed to precision, mowed to perfection, the blades of grass short cropped, as though with the razor of a skillful barber. He glanced back over his shoulder and saw Mila and Ashok on the steps to the club. Nothing had taken away his own surprising attraction to her, and this rush of feeling startled him anew. He found himself thinking of the drive here, of the way her hands rested on the steering wheel, the folds of her sari around her waist and the curve of her thighs, the obvious affection she had for young Ashok, the fact that both of them thought deeply about matters that had little to do with them.

A loudspeaker boomed somewhere near the lake just as Sam lit a cigarette. "Two fat ladies, eighty-eight!" "One short of my age, twenty-nine!" A shout came out into the air. "You saw thirty at least a decade ago, mate."

"A pair of hockey sticks, seventy-seven," the loudspeaker went on. "Housie!"

There was the sound of laughter, both men's and women's voices screaming to check the results. Sam went down the path and came out into a clearing that sloped gently to the lake. There were rows of stalls set in a ring around a central tent, topped off by striped red and dull gold *shamianas* with fringe in the front, in the colors of the Rudrakot Rifles. Wooden poles held up the *shamianas* at regular intervals, wrapped in red and gold ribbons that climbed up in dizzy diagonals. The tables at each stall were covered with immaculately white tablecloths, their edges dragging on the grass. One huge wooden pole had been dug in at the very center, like a maypole, and strings of triangular flags swung down over the grounds and up onto the *shamiana* poles. The flags simmered limply in the still-lingering May afternoon heat.

A castle gate loomed over the path, complete with battlements and pointed merlons, the large stone slabs painted in blacks and grays of undulating color on canvas stretched across a wooden frame. The gate was meant to evoke the chilly black stone of Home fortifications, of knights in armor, of maidens in distress, of mists across moors and muffled horse hooves and flying capes. But the artists—one of the bearers at the Victoria Club and a gardener—had not been able to comprehend all this foreignness, even though it had been explained with a great deal of patience and some eventual asperity, by both the club secretary and Laetitia Sexton. So the castle was now both English and Indian; the main gate had blue-and-white-tiled Persian and Hindu inlay, mimicking most of the forts in Rudrakot; the stone slabs had furtive dabs of ocher, for the artists had never before seen black stone, only the red sandstone from the local quarries. What little English part remained on the canvas sweated reproachfully in the heat, the paint melting in spots.

At the ticket booth, Sam counted out four *annas*. He held the coins in his palm for a fleeting moment before handing them over. The last time he had looked at money in his hand was at the railway station. Four *annas* bought entry into a church *mela*. Three further eroded the innocence of a little boy, made him think that all adult men were predators. Life was cheaper in India than music organs.

Sam put the rest of the change back into his pants pocket and stepped onto the grass that squished damply under his feet. The recent watering, the moisture on such a hot day, had brought out little clouds of mosquitoes hovering around in patches. The insects did not follow to swarm about him, but it was less than an hour to sunset, and that was when they would begin their seeking of light from unnatural sources and the seeking of flesh and blood without discrimination, both Indian and British. The biggest crowd, the most people, drifted in and out of the main tent, which had the legend bearing the letters TEA. Sam paused at the entrance.

He saw them in a tableau—the Indians seemingly on one side, the British on the other. Hands froze toward mouths, glasses slanted precariously, the lemon slices in the gimlets nudging the rims. Smiles and half smiles widened mouths. In every gaze, there was a question. Sam was new, he was unusual, he felt it to be so, and yet he was aware that they must all know that he was in Rudrakot. The Indian women were in a mass of color, saris that were of all fabrics, silk and cotton, chiffons with a sheen, glittering embroidery. The English ladies were in deliberately muted pastels, their legs cast in stockings, bows on their shoes.

Eventually, the tableau disintegrated, as it had to, for they had all stood regarding each other for a while. The lines shimmied, coughs arose in throats, an elbow itch was scratched. An officer from the Rudrakot Rifles came forward.

"Second Lieutenant Sims," he said. "Fourth Rudrakot Rifles."

"Captain Hawthorne," Sam replied. He did not flinch from either the handshake or the gaze leveled upon him—there was nothing to show him as the afternoon's *mali* outside the barracks. Now he saw Sims clearly. He was a young man without the shadow of hair on his smooth cheekbones and palely lashed eyes that blinked in the light.

"You're an awfully long way from home, aren't you?"

"Not that far away," Sam said easily, "Third Burma Rangers."

Now the other officers came up and introductions swung around the circle. Blakely, Marriott, Patton, and Miles. Sam strained his memory for a mention of the new names in Mike's letters, but could remember little. If Mike drank in the mess with these young men, if he played bridge at this club, if he even had an altercation with another officer, his letters had said nothing about it. Instead there were reams of prose on Rudrakot, the town, the cantonment, the bazaar, and the freedom movement. Mike had come to India for India, and for the war, and though he had not expected to be stationed in Rudrakot, so far from any war front, there was India everywhere around him, and little else had engaged his attention when he picked up his pen twice to write to Maude. They were all curious, he saw that, but too polite to ask anything more, until one young man said, "How long have you been in this infernal country?"

"Three months," Sam replied, even as a slow burn began within him.

"And Burma?"

"Just a little while," Sam said. "I'm glad to be here. I had not realized there was a regiment quartered at Rudrakot."

"Have a drink?" someone else said. They parted to let him through to the chairs ranged around a wood table, and as he came up to the table, he was introduced to the ladies sitting there. The final one, when his eyes came to rest upon her, was Mrs. Stanton.

"Why, we are old friends," she said. She spoke with the assurance of a long friendship, though theirs had been a mere acquaintance, tinged by something very akin to loathing in Sam. "We shared a coupé from Palampore last night," she said to the listening ears around her. Even the officers of the Rifles had stilled, waiting for more, watchful. She tittered and raised a hand to hide a smile. "Nothing inappropriate, I assure you. There was simply no other place in the bogie. Captain Hawthorne has been in the war, at Burma. I had no idea that your business in Rudrakot was at the Victoria, Captain Hawthorne."

Two of the Rudrakot Rifles officers wistfully slid their hands along the brass buttons on their uniforms, a sharp red, with dull gold epaulets. Only in India, Sam thought suddenly, would even men wear the red of ripe cherries—a color so bright as to almost be naughty—with no effect on their manhood. Here everything was so shamelessly hued—countenances, clothes, hair, even the languages, rich with ribaldry that Sam had not even dared to understand. For he knew that all such ribaldry would suffer in translation into English and become, from the colorful, merely banal. The khaki, *his* khaki, represented the war, any other color, especially red, which was difficult to camouflage, meant a regiment in waiting, a rear guard, and one perhaps never to be called to the front, never to glory in victory, never to die a stupid death.

Mrs. Stanton had made everything worse, as women would when they meant to be clever but ended up being merely shrill. Envy rose and sighed above them all, onerous, souring the sun-fired air—it extinguished some of the goodwill around Sam and he wanted to say to these young men, not so much younger than he in age perhaps, that wars were messy, deflating exercises, that life never returned to normal, that the only way to survive was not to feel *anything*, especially not regret at a well-ironed red uniform.

"There's no business as such, Mrs. Stanton," he said. "I'm here, as I said on the train, to rest my shoulder. On leave." He paused. "I'm not at the Victoria Club either."

They waited.

"I'm staying with the political agent."

Mrs. Stanton raised her thinly penciled eyebrows. "You mean the resident, surely. But I did not see you in the house. Is he with us, Amelia?" This last to the young woman next to her who wore a wide-brimmed hat even under the *shamiana*'s shade, and lifted it and her head with an effort. Sam transferred his attention to Amelia Pankhurst and felt a slight surprise when he saw her. For she was young, younger than he had expected the wife of a British resident to be, perhaps not even thirty. She had a conventionally pretty face, with eyes, nose, and mouth at the right places, and a sleek head of golden hair. Her eyes were blue, but the blue of newly blown glass, without any character behind them. Amelia Pankhurst had slung her long and thin body on the easy chair, arms on the armrests, a glass of something cold casting drops of condensation upon the wood. Her expression did not change, the smile remained the same, no life came to her eyes. Mrs. Stanton surreptitiously nudged her in the ribs. "My dear, is Captain Hawthorne with us?"

"I'm sure I don't know, Adelaide." Her voice held a little bit of child-ish petulance. "I was lying down after lunch; perhaps he is in the house, but I wouldn't know that." She caught Sam's gaze eventually and said, "Welcome to Rudrakot, Captain . . . er . . . Captain. We hope you have a good stay with us." And then she subsided into her loose, flowered dress and allowed it, in doing so, to fall in becoming folds around her body. Amelia Pankhurst was not quite as detached as she seemed; she knew how to be picturesque in the best of ways without seeming to think about it.

Sam bowed his head. "Thank you, Mrs. Pankhurst."

"Lady Pankhurst," Mrs. Stanton corrected, and Sam acknowledged that with another nod and continued, "But I am staying at the political agent's house."

"Ah . . ." That came out in a rush of whispers from almost everyone around him.

"By special invitation?" Mrs. Stanton asked. "Surely not, Mr. Raman would have no reason . . ."

The underlying implication was that if Sam was at all important enough to have been invited to stay with the political agent, when he could, as all other visitors did, have just as easily stayed at the Victoria Club, then Mrs. Stanton had very poorly judged her traveling companion of the previous night. Sam saw her dust something invisible off Amelia Pankhurst's shoulder and saw Mrs. Stanton for what she was—not a rela-tive, not an aunt or an elderly cousin, but a hired companion. Engaged for the special purpose of keeping Amelia Pankhurst connected with the real world. Mrs. Stanton oversaw the myriad duties of a resident's wife; she wrote out the elegant dinner invitations at the end of which Amelia scrawled her pretty name; she scolded the servants into obedience.

Colonel Pankhurst had escaped the arrows of Kama, the Hindu God of love, all over the length and breadth of India for thirty years, only to fall prey to Cupid on his last Home leave three years ago. He had met

Amelia in London and had been charmed by her aloofness, her exquisite grace in smoking cigarettes, even by the crimson lipstick imprints on her wineglasses when she set them down on the table. The war was but a few months away, trouble rumbled all through town, but Amelia was untouched. So strong, so brave, Pankhurst had thought, while they were all in such a dither. So he married her after a very brief courtship; *she* married him because she was told to do so and thought it would be jolly good fun to go out to India and ride on an elephant or watch the races at the gymkhana in her best hats. It took Pankhurst two months to realize that his wife was unruffled all the time because very little meant anything to her, but he was still in lust with his her, and still envied for the perfection of her complexion and the gloss of her hair. He was a practical man— even reasonable at times or he would not have been inculcated from the army into the more hallowed Indian Political Service as a diplomat stationed in princely kingdoms—so he'd hired Mrs. Stanton from the ranks of old, widowed army wives who had stayed on in India.

Mrs. Stanton then was the unofficial wife at the residency, and she made sure the real wife, the woman who carried Pankhurst's name, sailed through her days with relative ease, that she came down to the parties on Pankhurst's arm correctly dressed, that she kept up a semblance of social obligations and danced with the officers from the Rifles and the Lancers in the correct order.

Sam could not have known all of this upon his first introduction, but he sensed most of it anyhow; since coming to Rudrakot earlier this day, he had suddenly become aware, suddenly started to see this society in India. It wasn't just Rudrakot, of course, Sam had been in India for three months, and now the sum of all of his experiences slowed into an ultimate comprehension, all the pieces, noticed blatantly or absorbed only by his subconscious, began to fit into place. He also saw why Mrs. Stanton considered herself so important.

Before this job as a companion to Lady Pankhurst, she had been reduced to taking quarters on a monthly basis at a hotel run by a slovenly Indian who never looked at her without seeming to want to rip off her starched collar and bury his head between her sagging white breasts. His mouth had always watered when he talked to her, his saliva stained red with *paan*. Mr. Stanton had been a mere *boxwallah*, a clerk at the local cement factory for twenty-five years, and when he died, there had been no home for Mrs. Stanton to return to, no children to impose upon, and she could only afford the rent at the second-class Indian hotel and all the travails, real and imagined, the lustful owner put her through. Here, she could not pay for the whole-meals plan, so subsisted on tea and dry toast for breakfast, the odd curry pounded into blandness for dinner, a stringy leg of chicken bathed in a squishy white sauce when her purse ran full. But for all the poverty, the shame and embarrassment at her reduced circumstances, her tongue had been cutting, her gaze keen, her sense of propriety stupendous, her person neat and presentable, every frock darned in pearl-like stitches, every stocking reused until the silk feathered and disintegrated upon touching. Colonel Pankhurst's choice had fallen upon her, among the various other women who could have had this job. In all of her fifty-eight years, this was the best thing that had ever happened to Mrs. Stanton, and so enormous was her self-confidence, so little her humility, that she thought it only her right—after all, she had spent an unnecessarily penurious life as a wife with Harold; she had been born without either looks or money; something that was *long* owed to her had come due.

Sam could not resist his irritation at Mrs. Stanton, could not help being petty, even though he knew he was being petty and saying, "Colonel Eden at the governor-general's office in Calcutta suggested that I stay with Mr. Raman. He has been most welcoming."

There was something about stringing of those words . . . Colonel Eden . . . governor-general . . . that became a matter of awe and respect, just as Sam had intended. Now he was ashamed of having been so blatant, but he was tired of all the talk even without having talked very much. Sam had no drawing-room manners, not because he had been brought up without any, but the minuets with words, the fencing, the possible thrown daggers sidestepped, the chatter bored him. His mother had never asked much of him other than a few minutes of politeness when they had company and some respectful silence that could be taken for assent when it was necessary. Mike would make faces, or sometimes retching noises that would disintegrate into coughs to cover them up, and fooled no one really but the guests, but Sam had learned to hold himself courteous on a razor's edge, and had never been pushed over that edge to make a cutting remark. Until now.

"Of course they would have been," Sims said, raising his glass and looking at Sam through it. "It's an honor to be commanded by anyone in the governor-general's council. Do you know Colonel Eden, I mean, personally?"

"I've only met him once," Sam said.

"You must come and stay with us," Mrs. Stanton said, swiveling her head this way and that until she saw Mr. Abdullah at a table near the cakes and the tea. She waved at him and he ignored her a couple of times and then, forced to respond, rose from his chair, dabbed at his mouth with a napkin, and came to stand by her. Surprised by this supposed intimacy between them, surprised even to see Mr. Abdullah at the *mela*, Sam had begun to shake his head, but Mrs. Stanton would not allow him the luxury of speech. "Mr. Abdullah," she said, "I have invited Captain Hawthorne to stay with us at the house. Will you see that arrangements are made, please?" Then to not seem too nice, for Sam was just beginning to become more astonished at all this civility, she added, "Right away."

Mr. Abdullah unbent his back—he had been leaning over Mrs. Stanton—and cleared his throat. He brought his hands around his stomach and clasped them together, cracking the knuckles of his thumbs as he did so. He raised his head, his gaze fixed solemnly on the tablecloth, and nodded a couple of times. Sam began to smile. It was the entertainment in the bogie all over again, with a different twist this time, for this time Mrs. Stanton had deigned to talk to Mr. Abdullah, or she was somehow forced into it by circumstances. Who was he to her? A servant in the house? Impossible then that he should sit under the shade of the same *shamiana* as his masters, sit even at a table, drink tea from the same cups and saucers, wipe his mouth with the same linen napkins. Sam looked around, hoping Mila or Ashok was nearby for an explanation.

Mr. Abdullah glanced at Sam, smiled faintly into his mustache, and directed a short bow toward him. He said firmly to Mrs. Stanton, "I will do so if Lady Pankhurst wishes it, but I believe Captain Hawthorne to be staying at Mr. Raman's house—it would be churlish of us to take him from such good company, to provide him with merely ours. Am I not right, Captain Hawthorne?"

Glad to finally be given an opportunity to speak, Sam said, "Not entirely, Mr. Abdullah. I will be glad of your company, but I have accepted Mr. Raman's invitation and am quite comfortable there. Thank you, nonetheless."

"There," Mr. Abdullah said to Mrs. Stanton. "The matter has been settled. Now I will go back to my tea." He turned around and walked back, and they were left with Mrs. Stanton's splutterings.

"Really," she said, a flush rising on her face. "Really!"

"Adelaide," Lady Pankhurst said sedately, "you must leave poor Mr. Abdullah alone. Edward has told me, in no uncertain terms, that he is his *diwan*, his right-hand man, and not here for our purposes." She giggled. "I really *must* listen to my husband, Adelaide. He quite demands it, this obedience." She reached pink-frosted fingertips toward her cigarette case and all the officers snapped open their lighters and stood around her, little flames glowing over their fists. Amelia Pankhurst surveyed each of them and their lit flames pulled upward in the still, hot air before placing the cigarette between her rouged lips and leaning toward a young man with a pronounced Adam's apple and a weak, blubbery chin. His hand wobbled noticeably as he held the light under her cigarette. She held it to steady and guide the flame with one finger, cool against his heated skin, and fluttered her eyelashes in thanks. "Captain Hawthorne," she said, exhaling a long plume of smoke. "Welcome to Rudrakot. You will find yourself very well accommodated at Mr. Raman's home—he is a charming man, with much conversation, and I'm afraid we might just be lacking there. I hope your stay here is very pleasant."

It was all said with a little shade of superiority and some condescension, for no matter what personal sentiments might be, no matter what their jobs or duties were in India, no Englishman or Englishwoman could help being unaware of the fact that if Mr. Raman had conversation, if he was charming, if indeed, he was intelligent—it was all born of them, *their* language, *their* charm, *their* methods of refining minds in Oxford or Cambridge, at the latter of which Raman had read history and economics before appearing for his ICS exams.

But nothing that Amelia Pankhurst said was offensive to Sam, not immediately, not even later when he had reflected upon her words. For she had tact, and diplomacy, and not quite such an empty head as everyone imagined. Amelia Pankhurst was no fool, but they none of them around her saw it except Sam, because he was not so taken by the delicacy of her profile or the slenderness of her neck, or the length of her legs. The officers hung over her, enamored. The young lieutenant who had lit her cigarette cradled his lighter in the palm of his hand with the attention of a new father about to smother his newborn with kisses. Mrs. Stanton had regained some composure, her feathers smoothed down. Sam saw that Mrs. Stanton had a place of convenience at the residency, she took care of matters that Lady Pankhurst could not be bothered with—those matters that Amelia really cared for, she handled herself.

So he was to stay on at Mr. Raman's, he thought, though not all the weight of society or etiquette would have made him change his residence. The group broke up as the waiters brought more tea and cakes. A plate was pressed into Sam's hand. The officers of the Rudrakot Rifles left their places by Lady Pankhurst as she got up and wandered away in a vague manner. When she passed Sam, the sleeve of her dress brushed his arm, and she lifted her shoulder in a tranquil shrug. That little touch was deliberately done and she left Sam bemused and wondering. He saw Mila enter the tent and began to call out to her, but she just smiled quickly and made her way to the other side where more officers were ranged around a table in white uniforms with light blue facings, their shoulders braided, as with the Rifles, with gold epaulets. These were the officers of the Rudrakot Lancers—Jai's regiment. The regiment that was commanded by, in Mike's words, some sort of a prince. Discomfort began to inch its way under Sam's skin as he watched Mila laugh at a joke, take the seat warmed for her by a young man with a magnificent mustache. He saw their division now, for the first time.

There was a clear demarcation between the Indians and the British even within the tea tent. Something tacit and understood. Here and there, a few of each color strayed to the other side, but this was mostly to say hello, to nod, to complain about the heat, or to feel thankful that it had cooled down. The groups formed cohesive units, each person at rest only while belonging to their own species, and imperceptibly bothered while on the other side, hands in motion, backs rigid with protocol, manners in check. Though many people from Sam's side wandered to Mila, they did not stay long, and she, he noticed, never rose from her seat to come to him. She did talk with Lady Pankhurst, but they met somewhere in the middle of the tent, each on the pretext of the search for a thinly sliced cucumber-and-butter sandwich. They shook hands, spoke for a very little while, and then wandered away from each other.

It was magnificently done—this comedy of manners. Mila was her father's hostess, Amelia Pankhurst was the resident's, and, as such, they had equal footing in Rudrakot's society because each man was equally important, the colors of their skin notwithstanding. At every dinner where they were both present, the two women rose to lead the way out of dining rooms (to leave the men to their port) alternatingly, so there was no impropriety.

Sam knew that Mila was not stupid; he now saw that Amelia Pankhurst was not either. Whatever Amelia might think inside of herself, however she viewed her position, she had grace and diplomacy. His admiration for Amelia Pankhurst was brief; he looked at Mila longer, until he was afraid that he was beginning to stare. What was she saying? And why?

There were two little Indian boys, about ten and eight years old, dressed in suits even in this heat, their faces scrubbed clean, a glitter of coconut oil in their dark hair. They looked alike, though with the indiscernible features of childhood, and it was difficult to estimate if they looked like their mother or their father, or both, for they resembled none of the keepers around them. Each boy had on a light blue tie with diagonal muted white stripes, their cuffs came halfway down the backs of their hands, adorned with three tiny diamond links, and as they sat, their trousers creased at the knees and pulled up to reveal thick white socks and black patent leather shoes that gleamed with polishing.

Mila stopped by their table and the two boys rose with immaculate courtesy to shake her hand, to speak, to bow and almost click their heels. The boys had half-eaten slices of cream cakes in front of them, and they had laid their little forks at an angle on their plates and swabbed at their mouths with napkins. For all their grace and elegance, they were, in the end, little boys, and the older one had a starlike pattern of yellow cream on the right side of his mouth. Mila rubbed this from his face with her thumb and said something. The boy blushed. Sam pondered who they were, and if he had had the time to think about it at all, he would have realized that the little boys' ties were the same blue as a summer sky bleached into paleness—the same blue as the trimmings on the uniforms of the Rudrakot Lancers. The regiment commanded by HRH Jai, prince of Rudrakot.

Ensconced within that circle of men who had at one time been Mike's friends, or, at the very least, his acquaintances, Sam answered as many questions as he could about his purpose at being here, how long he was going to stay, what he was going to do for the next few days. As he talked, his mind and the corner of his eye followed Mila's progress around the tent. He kept that pond water green chiffon sari in sight; if she stopped to talk with a man, he wondered who he was. And so Sam did not notice that Sims was watching him over the rim of his gimlet glass, lighting one cigarette from another.

And then this finally penetrated Sam's consciousness, this phrase that would tell him that they knew of Mike, that they acknowledged his presence, which Sam had been wondering how to bring into the conversation without evoking suspicion.

Sims said in an exaggerated, Western-movie-learned drawl, "By golly, damn if we don't have another Yankee in our midst."

April 1942, a Month Earlier

*Somewhere in Burma*

$C$ ome," Sam says, holding out his hand for Marianne. She wipes her eyes and gives him a half smile. Now—in the dull gloom of afternoon forest light, with her white hair sparkling with wet, her eyes liquid, the age lines on her face muted—Marianne looks like an elf. Sam suddenly does not like the way Ken looks, though. His face is too wan, his brow too blemished with streaks of pain. The opium they have smoked has helped dull everything—the pain they carry, the sorrow, the fear, and even, when they allow themselves to feel it, the hopelessness of their quest for India. In one piece, all alive.

"Come, Ken," Sam says, helping him to his feet and grasping his arm tight as Ken puts weight back on his shattered ankle. "We must find some food."

"We cannot say no to you anymore, can we, Sam?" Marianne asks. She heaves her haversack onto her shoulders and leans with it against the trunk of a teak tree so that she can adjust the straps.

They lumber down the hillside and come upon the clearing that once housed the village. Again they stop to absorb what they see, but distantly, for the opium has cut away the keenness of their observation, so Sam, Marianne, and Ken see what they see, but they do not react to it. The *bashas* are black skeletons staggering drunkenly on crisscrossed stilts. The trees of the village are stumps of charcoal. The bamboo poles used for water lurch against the sides of broken walls, lie heaped on the ground like a pile of matchsticks. At the far end of the village are three new and pristine palm-thatched silos, like inverted weaverbird nests. They are untouched, but even from here, they look helpless and empty to Sam. The silos once housed rice, brought up here to the Kachin villages from southern Burma, to be kept safe from the Japanese army. But the Japanese army has clearly been to this village; Sam knows the silos are empty.

They step into the village's main street. All of them, even Sam, lucid as he is at this moment, glide on their opium haze, and so willfully do not see the bodies of the villagers scattered around them as they walk toward the silos. Arms and legs chopped off, skin charred into dust, a thick section of black hair untouched by the fire. A little boy on his side, legs curled up to what was once his stomach. A man lying on his back, two gaping holes in his ankles, his feet hanging onto the rest of his legs by severed tendons. All these people, shells of humanity, are now blessedly and gratefully dead. They feel no pain, no humiliation, no fear anymore. And Sam, Marianne, and Ken, stepping around their bodies, feel no pain either. The opium has eaten away their capacity to feel.

They enter the hollow silos and scramble through the dust for the precious, pearly grains of rice that gleam in the light from the one window set high up. They dust off each grain and pile them into Sam's handkerchief until they have almost two handfuls. Armed with the rice, they search through the village for other stuff, a vessel to cook the rice in, water to wash it and to drink, a moldy green gourd from a garden that Sam reverently slices with his *dah*. As the rice cooks, its starchy aroma wafts over them, the white meat from the gourd glistens and softens in the heat from the fire, and Sam sits away from Ken and Marianne, his back against a tree. They are still in the vicinity of the village, for seen from here, a wisp of smoke from their cooking fire will not be suspicious, as it would be if they were somewhere else in the deep jungle.

Sam takes out his map for what seems like the hundredth time, spreads it out, and traces their route. He does not know exactly where they are; there are so many Kachin villages here, they all just meld into a motley bunch of squiggles on the map. Even Marianne does not know; she has been singularly narrow-minded and focused during her years in Burma, and knows little of the tribes and habitations beyond her village.

Ken comes up to him and points at a patch of emptiness on the map. "We should head this way," he says. "There's a trail here, I've seen it from the sky."

Sam peers at the spot Ken's grimy finger indicates. It strays from his originally planned-out path. He shakes his head doubtfully.

Ken shrugs. "Suit yourself. If we don't go that way into the wilderness, we might well encounter the Japanese on the marked trail." He wanders away to sit by Marianne, leaving Sam to ponder his suggestion until the greens in the paper swim into one color in front of his tired eyes.

He puts the map back into his pocket and takes out his tin of cigarettes. There are only ten left. He rubs his fingers over their long and smooth lines, sniffs at the tobacco smell, shuts the tin and puts it away too. Marianne lifts the green banana leaf over the pot of cooking rice and gourd and its fragrance swirls up to Sam. His mouth begins to water and he swallows his saliva, and forces himself to wait. To share, when the rice is finally cooked. To not be greedy, for he knows his two other companions are rabidly hungry too. And then, after this, they have cherries and cream for dessert. *What about tomorrow?* Damn tomorrow, Sam thinks, as soon as that thought comes to his mind, tomorrow they will find other food. Today, they will feast. He shuts his eyes, allows the saliva to fill his mouth again and wonders what it will be like when they reach India. What it will be like in a world where there is no want of anything, where food is aplenty, and where, though he does not know it yet—love awaits.

# Fourteen

*. . . the average Indian makes very little difference between the Americans, the British or any other European nation, as long as their skin is white . . . He approaches all white men with the same extreme caution, and treats them all with the same self-conscious, rather theatrical courtesy in his efforts to impress them.*

—Louis Hagen, *Indian Route March*, 1946

*A*nd so that day slipped quietly into the arms of the night. There was no twilight to speak of, at one moment the sun still burned hotly above Rudrakot, as though unwilling to restrain its ambush, and in the next it ducked below the horizon, pulling all light with it. For a few minutes, a glowing blue stained the air around the *mela,* faces grew indistinct and blurred, whether from the lack of light or the speedily dispatched gimlets and beers, it was hard to tell.

Rudrakot had one mosque, and from the slender concrete minaret on one corner of the mosque rose the muezzin's deeply melodious voice. *Allah u Allah u Akbar. Ya Allah* . . . The sound of his call to the faithful for prayer swung out over the town, aided by a loudspeaker, floated through the cool of the shaded Civil Lines, skittered over the waters of the lake, and caused pause in the conversation around Sam. In Raman's home, Sayyid pulled out his prayer mat and faced toward the front of the house, and west toward Mecca. Temple bells rang out from the hundreds of temples in Rudrakot, as the priests' voices rose in chants of Sanskrit *shlokas,* welcoming the presence of God within. It was the time to light the hundreds of *diyas* and lanterns in and around the town.

As Sayyid prayed in the back garden, kneeling on his prayer mat, so Raman did too, seated cross-legged in the verandah, his sacred Brahmin thread, worn slung across one shoulder and under one arm, held between his fingers. He had not been entirely truthful when he had spoken to Sam earlier that morning about abandoning his caste—Raman had given away his name, but kept the other marks of his caste in the thread worn across his chest, under his clothes where no one but he knew it existed. Part of owning that thread, of being of the Brahmin caste, was to pray three times a day, morning, noon, and evening, and this Raman did because he honored where he came from and honored his ancestors. Sayyid and Raman were separated from each other by a few feet, master and servant, each with his eyes closed, his mind immersed in prayer, appealing to two different Gods without any sense of irony.

And while his father completed his evening ritual with the Brahmin sacred thread, Kiran rubbed his hand over his stomach, where his thread should have reposed, but it had been many years since he had discarded it, although he had been invested with it in a thread ceremony that marked his coming of age, his advent into life as student. Mila bent over Jai's children at one of the tables, three aides-de-camp standing stiffly to attention since her approach, their only job to guard the boys. Somewhere on the periphery of the *mela*, Ashok stood near a *rath-ki-rani* bush, the Queen of the Night, which had just begun to unfurl the sweet white buds of its flowers, and gazed with surprise at the young man who had jumped up from behind it and called his name. For a moment, Ashok gazed dumbly at Vimal Kumar. They had been friends about four years ago, studying in the upstairs drawing room with Father Manning as their tutor. Now Vimal had changed, had grown into a very handsome young man, but then he had always been blessed with pulchritude, even as a child. Ashok moved around the bush to clasp Vimal's outstretched hand.

Kiran walked across the lawns and watched the circle of Rifles officers around Sam. These men he considered his very best friends, even though this friendship was transient in nature. They were soldiers serving in the army, and while Rudrakot was their permanent home after a fashion, the army beckoned its servants away far too often and to distant lands. The war fumed beyond them and they were curiously untouched by it, but it was just a matter of time before the Rifles would don their uniforms and sling on their armor and weapons. The Rifles officers drank their nights away in the mess or in the clubhouse, threw *anna* coins at *nautch* girls brought in to sing and dance prettily, took a few of them to their beds, or visited the Lal Bazaar. But they spoke the king's English and they were his only friends in Rudrakot who could do that. He tarried at the outside edge of the *shamiana* and touched his back pocket where the rupee bills that Sayyid had given him reposed. What a bother old Pater got into, he thought, over a bit of money, and why, really, he had chunks of it lying around. Well, not chunks of it perhaps, but enough. They had their house, and Papa had a job that would last him until he had to retire, for Jai would never let go of him. How did it matter if he, Kiran, did not get into Papa's cherished ICS?

He moved forward and touched Sims lightly on his shoulder, thinking that for tonight and the next few nights he had enough money to pay the bills at the Victoria Club. What was to happen after that, he would worry about later.

"Where have you been?" Sims demanded.

Kiran felt a flush of happiness at the question, for it showed him that Sims had been aware of his absence. What a good chap he was.

"Here and there," Kiran replied with nonchalance. "Had a bit of a run-in with the Pater."

Sims grimaced and patted his slick blond hair. "Sorry to hear that, old chap. Fathers can be the absolute worst sometimes."

Kiran nodded, and then indicated Sam. "That is our hallowed guest? Captain Hawthorne?"

"Yes." Sims turned to follow Kiran's gaze. He rubbed his finger along his weak jaw. "Something is not right though."

"What?"

Sims shook his head. "I don't know. It's not his uniform"—and they peered at the Third Burma Rangers badge sewn on Sam's sleeve along with the red, white, and blue China-Burma-India theater of war badge— "or his demeanor. He's not regular army, that's for sure, corralled in for the war. And I seem to have seen him somewhere before . . ." Sims shook his head again. "It will come to me in time. So, are you going to return with us to the mess tonight?"

"Of course," Kiran said eagerly, then remembering his afternoon talk with Raman, he sobered. "But this may well be the end of more such out-ings. Papa was furious when I talked with him."

"Tough luck," Sims said sympathetically. "Then don't tell him; you're not a child anymore, Kiran."

"I am not," Kiran said with determination.

They were silent for a while as Sims steadily drained his glass and a passing bearer brought a fresh gimlet for him and one for Kiran.

Then Sims said, "Mila is particularly lovely tonight."

"Oh?" Kiran turned to look at her. She was standing alone now, near the tea tent's exit that led to the coconut shy, which she had promised Laetitia Sexton she would tend until the end of the evening. As they watched her, her eyes fell upon Sam and a glow crimsoned her cheeks. Sam caught her gaze at the same time and raised his glass to her.

"What was all that about?" Sims asked, his tone tinged with spite and speculation. "Did they know each other before? Something's afoot be-tween them."

"Of course not," Kiran said in a heat. "Sam Hawthorne is a guest in our house; naturally Mila would look after him. Don't be filthy, Sims."

"Sorry, old chap," Sims said, "I forgot that she was your sister. It's easy to do that, you know; I think of you as one of us." He put an arm around Kiran's stiff shoulders. "Let's go up to Sam Hawthorne for a minute here; I need to ask him something. I think I remember where I know him from."

He dragged a reluctant Kiran with him past the tables to the spot where Sam was talking with a few of the Rifles officers. Kiran went along, flushed himself now and uncertain about Sims. It was the first time he had even made a comment about Mila, and damn, his sister was pretty, but it seemed like something dirty when Sims spoke of her. Kiran had spent enough hours at the Rifles mess and here at the Victoria Club with Sims and Blakely and the other chaps to know that their talk was not always the most refined or polite. But then it had seemed like a lark to make fun of the women they knew, talk of who slept with whom on which afternoon, be mirthfully irreverent. Sims had spoken of Mila in the same tone he used at their drinking sessions, and Kiran felt a wave of disgust.

But at the same time he remembered that Sims had said that he was *one of us.* One of us—there could be no higher compliment, no higher honor than those words from a British officer. Delirium and blissfulness infused

Kiran's veins and he floated behind Sims. He was both mollified and still troubled somewhere at the back of his head about Mila. He heard Sims say, "Damn if we don't have another Yankee in our midst."

Sam waited for five seconds before responding, and when he did, it was in an overly casual and disinterested manner. "You have another American visiting? An officer or a civilian?"

Sims, still belligerent, said, "You must know of him, Captain Hawthorne."

Sam shrugged and borrowed a phrase from Mila. "America is a big country; I could not possibly keep track of who comes here."

"Who are the Third Burma Rangers anyway?" Blakely asked.

They had gathered around him again, breaking once to let Sims in, and Sam saw that there was a young Indian man within that circle. He was slim and pale and quite tall, taller than Sims and Blakely. Like Ashok, he was impeccably dressed in trousers with a sharp crease running down the front, a silk shirt in white, a slender red tie with tiny black polka dots. He seemed to be like one of them, not uncomfortable outside the circle of Indians, though a slash of discontent had come to mar his face in knitted eyebrows. He held out a hand to Sam. "I'm Kiran Raman," he said.

Then it all fell into place, for he looked like Ashok and Mila and yet did not look either like them or their father. This then was the elusive son who had come home late the previous night and not woken up until very late this morning, details Sam had garnered from the time he had spent at Raman's house—from Mila, from Sayyid, from Raman himself earlier that morning. Kiran and Sims stood shoulder to shoulder as though they were fast friends. Sam, who had begun to loathe Sims after his encounter with him earlier this afternoon, found their apparent friendship to be a strange and repellent thing. Surely Kiran was aware of Sims's bigotry, his intolerance—how could he find anything amicable about this man who denigrated Kiran's own countrymen?

"Where are the Burma Rangers garrisoned, Captain Hawthorne?" Kiran asked.

"In Assam," Sam replied. "We are newly commissioned to help in the retaking of Burma."

"We need no help from the Yankees," Sims said slowly.

Sam turned to face him with a level gaze. Where he had been willing to overlook the earlier disrespect in his voice, for he was used to this by now, this time he could not. "We all need help, Lieutenant Sims," he said. "We are all on the same side, fighting the same enemy."

"Are the Third Burma Rangers all from the U.S. Army?"

"Most of us are," Sam replied. "But tell me about the other American you have visiting here. I'd like to meet him."

"Why?" This from Blakely. And they were all watchful now, breathing softly and in unison. What *had* Mike done?

"No particular reason."

"He has defected from the Rudrakot Rifles, Captain Hawthorne," Sims said. "Gone AWOL for a little more than a month now. I doubt he is going to return."

"I'm sorry to hear that," Sam replied easily, though he searched through all their faces for a sign of deception and found none. Unless he was wrong, these men did not know what had happened to Mike. They were belligerent toward him, unwelcoming even, suspicious of his regiment and who he was—all of which Sam had anticipated and encountered in Assam. Whatever the politics might be between America and England, at a personal level, all of their prejudices welled up and spilled out into uneasy encounters like this one. Sims, Blakely, and the other officers had been far more polite than Sam had expected. And if they truly believed that Mike had gone AWOL, then they would not be kindly predisposed toward another American in Rudrakot.

"The next round of drinks is on me," Sam said, raising his hand to signal to the bearers. He smiled at Kiran. "Can I repay a part of your father's hospitality by getting you a refill?"

Kiran grinned. "Thank you, yes, Captain Hawthorne, I'm drinking a gimlet."

As the darkness enveloped the *mela* grounds, the lights strung around the lawns and the tents came to life in bright glitters. For the next two hours, Mila was kept busy at the coconut shy with an unending stream of visitors. For two *annas*, each person received a set of three white tennis balls to throw at the coconuts resting on specially constructed wooden stakes with cupped platforms. If they knocked more than two coconuts down, they received a treasure from underneath the booth's counter. The regimental wives had crocheted and embroidered antimacassars, table runners, napkins, and tablecloths in pink and blue thread as prizes. These Mila gave out as fast as she could, amused by the ease with which the coconuts came tumbling down; either the stakes were too close, or the coconuts too wobbly, or the players too skilled.

One by one, as the night wore on, people drifted back into the tea tent for some more *chai,* cakes, sandwiches, and hard-boiled eggs sprinkled with chili powder and mustard. Across the lawn from Mila, the lady at the weigh-the-cake booth left her post and went wearily to the tea tent also, leaving Mila gazing wistfully after her. She forgot to take the glass jar with her, which was crammed to the rim with slivers of paper bearing guesses on the cake's weight upon them. The cake itself, an enormous cream-and-coconut concoction, sweated on the booth's main table, the icing slipping down the side and onto the wood. Under normal tradition, the cake was the prize for guessing the correct weight, but this one had lost its shape and had pulverized in the heat. The other stalls began to close also, the hoopla stall, the fancy goods stall, and even Mrs. Sexton put a board outside her tent that said, GONE TO TEA. The vicar's wife had dressed in voluminous pants, many bangles, dangling earrings, a multicolored scarf, and black eyeshadow to transform herself into Esmeralda, Queen of the Nile, the fortune-teller.

As Mila was desultorily counting out the money at her booth, she saw Sam approaching her with two martini glasses of pink champagne.

"Are you thirsty?" he asked with an engaging smile and a tilt of his head to keep his hair from his eyes.

"Thank you." She put the box of money away and accepted the champagne, suddenly overcome by thirst. The liquid fizzed and bubbled on her tongue, and Mila put a hand over her nose to sneeze. Just for a moment there, when Sam came toward her, backlit by the lights strung over the *mela* grounds, she had thought he was Jai. There was something in his gait, the way he swung his arms, the fact that they were both tall, both had dark hair . . . but they were two different men, there were no similarities between them at all. Papa would have laughed at her and as usual called her too imaginative. Mila sighed.

Sam leaned against the booth. "Are you done for the night?"

"Almost," Mila said, indicating the box of money. "I'm two *annas* short of the target Laetitia has set for me; one more player and I shall be done. Are you having fun, Captain Hawthorne?"

Sam gave her a curious look, his blue eyes bright and deepening in color the longer he gazed upon her. "I thought I might not enjoy my stay here because, of course"—he touched his right arm—"but I find myself enchanted in Rudrakot."

"Oh," Mila said, feeling a smile widen her mouth, filled with a strange happiness.

"Let me try," Sam said, putting a hand into his pocket and drawing out some change. "Here." Instead of putting the money on the counter, he gathered her left hand in his, laid the coins in her palm, and covered it with his other hand.

At that moment, the rest of the world faded away for Mila. It was such a simple gesture on Sam's part, a mere holding of hands, but that was when Mila fell in love with Sam too. Not simply because of the gesture, of course, but it brought to a culmination all of her thoughts about this stranger who had come to Rudrakot to stay in their home, whom her father liked so much.

For all her little obstinacies and rebellions in driving the jeep, in riding the horse Jai had given her, in drinking pink champagne or smoking the odd cigarette, Mila had been brought up traditionally, in the shadow of her father and her brothers. It was the men who made decisions, who changed the courses of other people's lives with their actions. Mila would never have thought of Sam if Raman had not been delighted with him, and so it was Raman, with his enthusiastic welcome of Sam in the morning, who had inadvertently placed a morsel of affection within his daughter's heart—a fragment that blossomed eventually into love. Mila knew nothing much about Sam other than what she had gleaned from their conversations; she did not know if he had a father and a mother, brothers and sisters. She knew that he came from Seattle because Sayyid had rummaged through his bags and found, beneath the tailor's label behind his collar, the words *Seattle Sam*—a nickname the army had bestowed upon him.

Sam, who was cautious and pondered every deed before he took a step in the direction of *anything*, had clasped Mila's hand without thought, and once he held that small and slender hand within his, he did not want to let it go. What he wanted was to bring that hand to his chest and hold it against his heart, but he stayed that action, his fingers shaking with want over hers.

At that moment, Mila looked down on their hands and thought it was an intimate act, unlike a mere shaking of hands to say hello upon meeting. She saw the fine hairs on his knuckles, a little tremble before he increased the pressure and wove his fingers into hers. The cool of the metal from the coins flooded her palm. There was a tiny scratch on the back of Sam's hand, and this Mila touched fleetingly.

"Does it hurt?" she asked.

"No."

She had not been cognizant of the sound of her own voice or even that she had spoken aloud, but when she heard his voice, Mila realized that they were at the *mela* grounds, in front of everyone. Men and women simply did not touch in public, no matter how long they had been married, or how close their relationship. Indians certainly did not, and neither did the British; if anything, distant pecks in the air, accompanied by a *"darling"* was the closest one came to one's husband or wife. The noises at the *mela* pervaded her consciousness—the laughter, the music from the orchestra, the click of women's heels on the wooden floor laid out on the lawn for dancing. But every sound came from a fading distance. Mila finally broke the grip, and it was with a reluctance that she recognized but refused to acknowledge, for it meant nothing, surely it meant nothing.

"I could not possibly take your money, Captain Hawthorne," she said, "Someone else will come along soon to make up my quota."

"Please do," he said, "I want to play."

"All right." Mila put the money in the box and placed the three tennis balls on the booth's table. Then she finally looked up to meet his smile. This close, with just the table separating them, she could see the oncoming sheen of dark hair on his chin and cheeks. Mila glanced around quickly, almost with guilt, to see if anyone else had been watching and saw with a growing fear that Lady Pankhurst, Mrs. Stanton, and Laetitia Sexton were grouped in a threesome just a few booths away.

When Sam picked up all three tennis balls with one hand, she said, "You are to throw them, one at a time, at the coconuts and knock as many down as you can."

"How many tries do I get?" Sam stood back from the counter and took aim.

"Just the three."

The first ball went sailing past the coconuts and thudded into the canvas backdrop of the booth.

"You need to try just a little harder, Captain Hawthorne," Mila said, "it's really quite easy." She put a hand up to her mouth. "Oh, I didn't mean to say that . . . I meant . . ."

Sam grinned. "I must try harder."

He stood even farther back from the booth and made an elaborate pretense of first closing one eye and then the other to take aim at the coconuts. He juggled the tennis ball from one hand to the other. He turned his back and made as if to throw the ball over his shoulder, twisting his body. As he tried this last antic, a grimace of pain swept over his forehead and he straightened up and turned around to face her again. "Sorry. I had forgotten that I was not quite back in shape again."

Despite this, Sam nudged an imaginary cap on his forehead with his knuckles, lifted his left leg, drew his right arm back, and sent the ball thundering out of his hand to knock down first one coconut, and then a second in quick succession.

Mila clapped her hands. "You were joking that first time. This is wonderful."

Sam bowed to her and she smiled at him, forgetting all of her worries. He had showed off to Mila with a preening of his feathers, with his pitcher's stance, his pitcher's throw, even his sham attempt at evoking sympathy from her by openly demonstrating his reaction to the pain from his injury.

As he stood there, his shoulder throbbing, the pain beginning to creep up his neck, Sam felt glorious, and they gazed at each other under the string of lights. Mila first broke that gaze, everything within her floating and delighted. It was as though nothing else mattered right now but Sam—the patches of night on his face where the light did not touch, the darkened blue of his eyes, the sweep of hair across his forehead. He stood rubbing his shoulder.

Mila ducked under the booth and ran her fingers along the wooden boards searching for a prize. She began to giggle, imagining Sam's surprise when he was given a neatly crocheted set of six napkins. She searched and realized that the prizes had all been given away. In one corner, long forgotten from some previous *mela*, was a little cardboard box.

Mila pulled it out and set it on the counter, her head almost bumping into Sam's, who had been leaning over to see what she had been doing.

A cloud of dust rose into the air when Mila thumped the box down and Sam coughed. "I'm afraid there are no other prizes left, Captain Hawthorne, but I found this instead. Whatever is in it is yours."

"Wait." Sam's grip on her wrist was strong this time and he yanked her hand away from the box. "Let me look. There might be a snake or a scorpion hiding inside." He pulled a pen out of his shirt pocket and gingerly flipped open the box's cover with one end. There was a pile of straw inside, quite flattened out, and on that straw rested three tiny monkeys, chopped roughly out of a light-colored wood.

"The Mahatma's monkeys," Mila said. "They speak no evil, they see no evil, they hear no evil." She picked them up one by one and set them on the table, facing Sam. "Are these good enough for a prize?"

"Yes," Sam said. "But let me give them to you. I want to give you something."

"Oh no," Mila said. "You have rightfully won these monkeys. They are yours, Captain Hawthorne."

"Are they made of sandalwood?"

They bent their heads to the carvings. Mila studiously kept her face away from Sam but was aware, with every breath and every sense, that Sam's head was thus so close to hers. She could smell the wood-sweet aroma of the sandalwood and the sharper cut of Sam's cologne in the air around her. She knew he was looking at her and wanted desperately to clasp his hand again. Perhaps if she made as if to place the monkeys in his hand . . . Mila straightened up. As she did, she saw Lady Pankhurst drifting toward them, the chiffon from her skirt trailing along the grass.

"Mila," Lady Pankhurst said, waving her white arms around languidly to mean nothing at all. "Please do bring Captain Hawthorne to see me at my 'at home' tomorrow. How fortunate it is," she said, turning to Sam, "that you are here on a Thursday. My 'at homes' are usually tomorrow afternoon. At two o'clock."

Mila felt her heart still and die and all that silly euphoria of a few minutes ago come to a clean end. Three years ago, when Lady Pankhurst had first made her appearance in Rudrakot on Colonel Pankhurst's arm, she had arranged Friday afternoons as her "at homes," and these solely for Mila. *For you know, my dears*—she had told the civilian and regimental wives, somewhat suspicious that this exclusivity was a sign of favor not bestowed upon them—*I must get to know her. We are to be at the same level, Edward says, though how I do not see. I must find out.*

Mila had visited Lady Pankhurst at two o'clock every Friday after-noon and sat for an uncomfortably long time in the drawing room at-tached to her bedroom. Mila was only eighteen when these forced "at homes" began, and she went because Papa had suggested to her that they might well be a very good idea. Until then, all of Colonel Pankhurst's parties and balls had occurred without a hostess, and suffered as a conse-quence. Lady Pankhurst was decorative in the best of ways, and Raman was man enough to appreciate this. That she was friendly to his daughter was simply wonderful.

The first three Fridays, Mila did not see Lady Pankhurst at all. She waited for two hours in the lush and hushed drawing room until she could recall everything in it from memory. There were long-stemmed dahlias in silver and porcelain vases; the poor stuffed tiger Colonel Pankhurst had shot in a past *shikar* with Jai gazed at her with a frozen stare; Dresden dolls lounged on the occasional tables. This waiting, this lack of attention from Lady Pankhurst, was all very bewildering to Mila, but she did not com-plain, or even, in the innocence of her youth, consider what it might mean. On the fourth Friday afternoon, the door to Lady Pankhurst's bedcham-ber opened and a lieutenant from the Rudrakot Rifles came out, buttoning his collar. He stopped and flushed when he saw Mila, but did not recognize her as the political agent's daughter; otherwise his momentary discomfort would have been more acute. When he had left, Lady Pankhurst emerged with a gin and tonic to talk for the rest of the afternoon with Mila. Or rather, she talked, Mila listened.

This ritual continued for the next three years, with only minor changes. Mila visited Lady Pankhurst promptly at two o'clock, sat in the drawing room, and read a book while a slew of young officers entered her bedchamber. Then she would hear the soft, singsong murmur of Lady Pankhurst's voice, unending and boring, and Mila would be thankful that all she had to do was wait outside, not listen to that voice. By now, Mila knew what was happening and once had even dared to flatten her ear against the door to listen. She heard a soft thumping of flesh on flesh, and Lady Pankhurst saying, "That was marvelous, darling. Hand me a ciga-rette, will you?" Lady Pankhurst's bedchamber did have another door leading to the outside verandah and the back gardens of the residency, but she had very soon deemed it necessary for her young men to leave through the drawing room to the outside in case anyone was around to see this or ask questions. She could always tell Edward that she had been having a nice little chat with Mr. Raman's daughter and the young man.

Heat and anger crept under Mila's skin at the *mela* grounds. She watched a thick and large moth flap lethargically around Lady Pankhurst and settle on her thin shoulder, and wanted to slap at that shoulder with a newspaper, ostensibly, of course, to kill the moth. Mila's face seethed with warmth, and she wondered dispassionately, in the midst of all that rage, where this loathing had come from. She had never before *hated* someone as much as she hated Amelia Pankhurst right now. She had never even cared that she had assisted in Lady Pankhurst's randy "at homes," and when Raman asked—as he invariably did—how her afternoon was, she would reply noncommittally and he would be satisfied.

Lady Pankhurst held out a hand to Sam and he took it in his. To Mila, it seemed as though he held it for an unnecessarily long time, but it was Lady Pankhurst who left her hand in his, opening her mouth to talk a few times, but seeming not to succeed with the words until this came out somewhat coyly, "So I will see you tomorrow then, Captain Hawthorne?" It was a command, not a request.

Before Sam could answer, Mila said, "I'm afraid that will not be possible, Lady Pankhurst. Captain Hawthorne wishes to visit Chetak's tomb; we have a picnic planned for tomorrow."

Lady Pankhurst sighed and withdrew her hand from Sam's. "I think," she said, turning now to face Mila, "you must have misunderstood me, dear Mila. I would very much like to see Captain Hawthorne tomorrow. I'm sure he wishes to come too."

Sam finally cleared his throat and said, "Thank you, Lady Pankhurst. But we do have a prior engagement. It is a pity that your 'at homes' are only on Fridays, since I am not going to be here next Friday."

An immense hush then descended upon them. Lady Pankhurst's back grew rigid. To Mila, the band seemed to play American jazz unnaturally loudly and she watched the dancers twirl on the floor, their skirts flying, their mouths open and toothy. Sam looked away, his shoulders shaking. He was *laughing*, Mila thought with outrage. Laughing at them both. She should let him go to Amelia Pankhurst's lecherous afternoons and let him be ensnared by her in an iron web. But she did not want that, really. She wanted Sam Hawthorne unsullied by anyone else here at Rudrakot. That was a thought that lurked unacknowledged somewhere inside; on the outside Mila considered that Sam was their guest, and Papa had said that she was to look after him. And tomorrow just happened to be a convenient time to take him to Chetak's tomb.

"Well then," Lady Pankhurst said. "So it goes." She shrugged gracefully and nodded at them both. "I will see you next Friday as usual, Mila?"

"Of course, Lady Pankhurst," Mila said, "as usual."

"When does our dear Jai return?" Lady Pankhurst said this with a shard of malice, and it was a question that required no answer from Mila, for by the time the last of those words had been spoken, Lady Pankhurst was well out of earshot.

For a long while, Mila and Sam did not speak. Something had happened between them, hurtling them toward a future that was still indiscernible, and there was the real fear of that unknown that kept them silent. Mila gathered the coconuts in a box, placed the money on top, and Sam carried it for her across the lawns to the tea tent.

They walked carefully apart from each other, uncertainty marring their brows. From his table, Kiran watched them with foreboding, thinking that this surely could not be, dreading that Sims could be right in his estimation. He was well on his way to getting drunk and saw everything through a gimlet smog that was surprisingly clear and lucid. Come tomorrow, he would not remember all of the evening, but this one moment of a sudden dread would return, repeatedly. Sam and Mila could not be. Kiran knew that Sims, much as he extended a hand of friendship, even brotherhood toward him, would not look kindly at Kiran if he coveted a white woman. It was as simple as that, obvious to all of them, obvious, really, to everyone but Sam and Mila.

Sam excused himself briefly to visit the men's washroom just beyond the billiards room, which was off-limits to women. The stalls in the washroom had been built with rich brown chin-high mahogany partitions. The toilets, known affectionately as thunderboxes, were little more than holes in mahogany seats with deep galvanized tin trays beneath to accumulate the waste. Sweepers emptied these trays; they were a special caste of men who came in the dense of the night, their skins charred and darkened by this dirty work. The men's washroom was more primitive in its fittings than the women's washroom with its wicker furniture, talcum powder on trays, and gurgling, new, flushing toilets.

Kiran followed Sam and occupied a stall near his. Their eyes met over the partition but they said nothing. More than once Kiran dragged words from his sluggish brain, but he could not speak them, for all he had was a suspicion. How did one voice that?

Sam left first and paused quite by chance to glance at the map of Rudrakot on the far wall of the billiards room. He traced his bearings with his finger—the Victoria Club, the Civil Lines, Raman's home, the residency, and striking out into the desert was Chetak's tomb, where Mila said they were to go tomorrow. That would not happen, of course; he had to return to the Lancers' headquarters and talk with Sims and Blakely, find out what they knew. His finger idled over the contours of Chetak's tomb and then strayed out into the wilderness. A little building was drawn on in pencil, and somewhere in the sands were the words, *Field Punishment Center, 1930.* Sam snatched his hand away with a thudding heart. He looked around. There were a few officers lounging around the room, a few more playing pool, leaning on their cue sticks.

Almost casually, without another glance at the map, Sam nodded to the men and sauntered out to meet Mila and Ashok. On the drive back Ashok chattered away. At another time, Mila would have seen that his eyes were feverish with excitement, his speech was impassioned and frivolous, and she would have been worried. She had noticed him at the hedge, talking with Vimal Kumar, the man they had passed near their house who had stood and stared at them in all of his glorious beauty, the man who had studied mathematics and English with Ashok. Mila had never been able to rest easily in Vimal's presence, and now the rumors were that he was involved in the nationalist movement and she did not want Ashok pulled into the snares of nationalism. Mila herself was ambivalent about the movement, and whatever her private feelings, she could not, would not, voice them in public because that would mean going against Papa and his life's work. Her loyalties lay with her father.

On another day, Mila would have fretted about Ashok renewing any friendship at all with Vimal. Now it was Ashok who caught the uneasiness in their silence and fell quiet himself, thinking, as his brother had done, that something was not right between Captain Hawthorne and Mila.

May 29, 1942

*Rudrakot, India*

# Fifteen

*T*wo missives passed each other that night, neither read until the morning, when it was too late to do anything about the information contained within. By the time Mila, Sam, and Ashok returned home the previous evening, it had been late. Not perhaps late in the calendars of the officers who went to the soiree at the residency and danced away a good portion of the night, but Raman was in bed and well asleep before nine o'clock.

Mila paused outside her father's door for a long while, listening for a sound from within. She heard him sigh in his sleep, turn over in his bed, but then his breathing settled into evenness. She went back to her room and sat down at the little teak desk that Papa had bought for her when she was six and wrote out a short note for Raman that they—Sam, Ashok, and she—were going to Chetak's tomb early the next morning on a picnic, that they would be out the whole day and return perhaps for dinner, perhaps not until much after. She did not ask Raman for permission. He would not have denied it, though he might have hesitated and thought about the propriety of their leaving like this and being away for so long without him as a chaperone. But there was no impropriety really in what Mila was going to do, just a hesitation, a cautiousness. She expected that they might well be out of the house before Papa woke up in the morning, so she wrote him a letter in her own hand without leaving a message with Sayyid.

She stepped out of her room and felt against the wall for the switch to turn off the corridor light. Now light seeped from under the doors near hers—Ashok at the far end, Sam right next to her, only darkness from Kiran's room to her left, and a disapproving peel of light under Pallavi's door, next to Kiran's. Papa's side of the house, opposite her, was dark and silent. He was still asleep. She switched on the light again and went across to slide the note under the door.

When she came back to her room, she unwound her sari, threw it on the chaise longue, stepped out of her petticoat, and unbuttoned her blouse with a great weariness. Then, in just her bra and underpants, Mila sat at the dressing table and dabbed some lotion into a piece of cotton to clean away the lines of kohl under her eyes and wipe away the big red *bindi* she had painted on the middle of her forehead. She heard Pallavi's soft footsteps in the corridor outside as she walked up and down the length of it in bare feet.

Mila let her hair loose from its plait until it fell around her shoulders to her waist and began to brush it until it shone. Her movements were jerky until the knots had come loose from her hair and then the brush slid in smoothly. Her arm tired, but she would still not ask Pallavi to come in and do this for her. This was the first time Mila could remember that Pallavi had not helped her prepare for bed, combing her hair and plaiting it again, even rubbing her forehead gently until she slept. A tear formed at the corner of her eye and slid down her cheek and she wiped it away, deafening her ears to Pallavi's striding in the corridor. She knew Pallavi would continue this for at least another two hours, until she was able to contain her anger, until fatigue forced her to bed.

The idea of going to Chetak's tomb had come in a moment to Mila, upset as she had been with Lady Pankhurst's machinations to get Sam into her boudoir. But this was not something she could explain to Pallavi. What could she say? That she wanted Sam Hawthorne for herself, and so she had made up an excuse with Lady Pankhurst? It sounded so stupid even in the coolness of the night, Mila thought, even now when she was free from any provocation, that it must be untrue. She was just being solicitous of their visitor. Let him leave Rudrakot after having visited and seen all they had to offer. He was, after all, *their* guest, not staying at the residency. Why should Lady Pankhurst take up any part of his time here? But none of this would have even remotely mollified Pallavi, who had been on the edge of being scandalized when she heard of their plans. Her reaction had been unnerving, stunning.

"Tell your papa," she had hissed, pulling the *pallu* of her sari close around her.

"Why?" Mila asked in exasperation. She hoped both Ashok and Sam had gone up to their rooms after they had parted at the front entrance and were not anywhere nearby to listen to this conversation. "I mean, I will tell Papa. What do I do in this house without Papa's knowledge, Pallavi?"

"Tell him *now,*" Pallavi said. "And see if he gives you permission to leave like this tomorrow."

"Sam Hawthorne is our guest, Pallavi."

"He can find his entertainment at the Victoria Club. Why does he not stay there? Would it not suit him better, all the parties, the women who dance and drink and smoke? These women who speak English?"

Now Mila had to grin. "You speak English too."

Pallavi was pleased by the compliment and so her face lightened but was soon replaced with a frown again. "Mila, this is not right. I have not seen you all day long. You were away riding in the morning, at the *mela* since late afternoon, and now it is so late." She gestured at the grandfather clock in the dining room, which obligingly began to chime out the hour of ten so that Pallavi had to raise her voice to speak over the sound. "When are you ever at home? A woman must find her amusements within the walls of her house. Here you must supervise the servants, tend to the kitchens, embroider and knit in the afternoons, wait for your husband to return in the evenings. Your mother never went to the club, even after she was married and had the right to go. She never stepped out of her house before she was married."

"My mother . . . ," Mila began and then grew quiet. What could she say about a mother she barely remembered? Pallavi knew more about Lakshmi than she did; Mila had been five years old when Lakshmi died.

This much at least was true about her, though. Her mother had been traditional and conservative, and had she been alive, a vast number of Mila's
activities would have been confined. Papa might still have had his say in
her education, but her mother would have influenced him in some way or
the other. Mila's memories of her mother were hazy now; she could remember the scent of sandalwood on her soft skin, the white of her teeth
offset by a mouth stained red with *paan*, an arrangement of jasmine flowers threaded into a garland, bowing down the weight of her slender, fair
neck. But when Mila had been sick with a fever, it was Pallavi she recalled
as sleeping by her side, and it was Pallavi's hand that had wakened her in
the night, brushing softly against her brow as she checked periodically to
see if the fever had risen. It was Pallavi who was here now, scolding her
with a mother's insistence, but without a mother's authority.

Mila began to yield and then hardened her resolve again. If she had
lingered to ask herself why, and if she had been truthful about it, she
would have told herself that it was because she wanted to spend some
more time with Sam Hawthorne before Jai returned from Meerut. Now,
all she felt was a stubbornness, an assertion of her pride and her right.

"My mother did not speak English, Pallavi," she said. "She was a different woman, and I am different now. Why is that so difficult for you to
understand?"

Pallavi shook her head. "We are never as different as we would like to
be. The changes are little, subtle, but in the end it is all the same. I will say
this once more," she said, rising to leave, "you must ask your papa for his
permission, talk with him, and tell him what I have said." And so saying,
she left the room.

In her bedchamber, Mila put down the brush and plaited her hair.
When the length had grown beyond her shoulder, she brought the plait
forward and continued until the end. Then, without donning her nighttime sari, Mila climbed into the bed and reached over to switch off the
lamp on the bedside table. She thought she saw a piece of paper on the
mosaic floor, scrunched under the edge of the door, near the hinge, but
that impression was fleeting before the room plummeted into darkness.

It was not until the next morning as she rushed out of her room to the
waiting jeeps that she saw the paper again. Mila picked it up and slid it into
the pocket of her pants, and did not open it until they were well on their
way. Raman had already left that morning, two hours before them, on his

way to the village of Nodi for the day and the night. He said that he would
return on the morning of the thirtieth of May. There was no mention of
their trip to Chetak's tomb; her heart filled with guilt, Mila realized that
Raman had not read the note she had slipped under his door.

In a strange series of coincidences, Raman too had missed Mila's letter,
but Sayyid had seen it as he went back into the room to bring out his
master's bags, and he had tucked it into his turban for Raman to read later
that night.

The desert had a music of its own; all sounds did not expire into its vastness. But to listen properly, one had to tarry in an absolute and complete
silence, in a void where there were no human voices, no ants clicking and
chewing, no flies buzzing, where even the wind was holding its breath. All
had to be still as death.

It was in one such instance, for a whole three minutes, that Sam found
himself later that morning. They had driven out of Rudrakot in two jeeps
on a slim, macadamized road that even that early, 6 A.M., had begun to
throb and waver with a black heat. The road left Rudrakot and vanished
into the horizon, heading away from Chetak's tomb, which Sam could just
discern on his left. At some point, he assumed, it would lead to the tomb
or they would have to cut through the scrub and dirt of the Sukh to get to
it. And so it had been. After heading south for two hours, the road had
curved and swiveled east again, and now as they neared, the tomb began
to grow in size and in Sam's imagination. Each time he thought that they
had come to the tomb, the heat haze shuddered and reformed itself and
pushed the tomb farther away. At times, the tomb would be a blurred edi-
fice of red sandstone, at times as clear as though he were viewing it
through a magnifying glass and it was but a palm length away.

Then, incongruously, they had come upon a stand of trees, a jungle,
Mila had called it, a sumptuous patch of green. Trees grew here thickly,
elbow to elbow, their undersides dense with a murkiness that did not allow
even a tiny slice of the sun. A tower rose majestically in the center of this
forest. It was a square building of red sandstone blocks, and the mortar
that held the blocks together was seamless. It was capped by merlons
much like the ones Sam had seen on Jai's fort in Rudrakot. As they approached this forest, Sam thought that he was dreaming, for all the way

here all he had seen were the rusts and umbers of the desert stretching endlessly around him, and they were but half a mile from the jungle before the light shifted and revealed the tower and the trees.

They sat down for a break in the shade at the very edge of the forest. Looking inward, Sam saw that it was almost impossible to penetrate the undergrowth of tall grass, and the only way to the tower was by a path carved out of the foliage. A servant unpacked a tray and four glasses, filled the glasses with sugared *nimbupani*, limeade, spiced the drink with black salt and mint leaves, and offered it to them.

When that first coolness from the *nimbupani* and the shade of the trees had come to bless them and loosen his tongue, Sam asked, "Is this a mirage of some kind? There's a forest here, in the middle of the Sukh desert?" Just beyond where they sat, the desert stood vigilant guard—the trees ended, and the desert began in dust, dirt, and hard-packed ground where it was difficult to imagine that anything could ever grow.

"This is Jai's hunting forest," Mila said. Her voice was low and strained, more so since she had opened and read a note that she had taken from her pocket. Her thin hands, with just that one little silver pearl ring, rested on her lap. Today, Mila was dressed much as she had been when Sam had first seen her, in pants, a brown snakeskin belt, a white shirt open at her neck, and tiny diamond earrings in the lobes of her ears. The pants were tight, fitted around her little waist and curved over her hips and thighs. She had pockets sewn down the length of her legs and a row of dull brass buttons climbing up the cuffs. The shirt was loose and woven from very thin cotton, so translucent that Sam could see the muted colors of her skin underneath. It was a simple outfit, even with its Russian hussar undertones, but it took Sam's breath away. He wanted to touch the place where her hips arced out, place his hands on the edge of her waist . . . he looked away, fraught with yearning. The palms of his hands tingled as though he still held her hand in his.

"Behind you," Mila continued, "is a magnificent stock of partridges, deer, *nilgai*, which is a kind of blue bull, and lions."

"You are joking." Sam turned hurriedly to look into the forest and was met with only a cool and thick dimness, and silence.

"They are well fed, Captain Hawthorne. The keepers make sure they are not too hungry."

Something Mila had said stuck in Sam's mind. "There are no lions in this part of India," he said. "There haven't been lions here for a few centuries at least."

Mila raised an eyebrow. "Who told you that?"

"It's an accepted notion."

"The villagers have seen plenty of lions in this jungle; Jai has killed a few, he has the skins hanging in his palace."

Sam shook his head. "But that can't be. Lions do not exist here; perhaps the villagers have confused the lions with tigers?"

Mila laughed. "And Jai did also? He shot an animal thinking it to be another animal? He's not an idiot, Captain Hawthorne. *I* have seen one myself, only glimpsed his back and tail, but there was no mistaking the plume of golden mane around his head. Your authorities are wrong; before they make such statements, perhaps they should travel and live in India and see this for themselves."

It was incredible, Sam thought, could an entire slew of scholars on this subject be wrong? He leaned back against the trunk of the tree behind him, drew out his tin of cigarettes, and lit one. The smoke traveled out of the shade to linger in the still, hot air and the heat bent in waves in the horizon. In the distance, Sam saw the lion Mila claimed roamed this jungle behind him, in a majestic slouch under the shade of a spiky *ber* tree. He swiped at the smoke hanging in front of him, and when it cleared, saw the figure of the lion dissolve into the background. Sam flicked ash from his cigarette and closed his eyes.

The air was invigorating and newborn around them. They were all struck by the same lassitude, draining their *nimbupanis,* setting down their glasses, stilling their hands and legs. Even the servants, farther away from them in the shade of the trees, seemed to have fallen into indolence, and in this sudden quiet, Sam heard the desert's music. It began as a low, keening wail, like a mourning dirge, and the sound then shifted and formed itself into a melody and came across the heated land, surrounding Sam, enveloping him, filling him with a happiness and peace he could not pause to even think about. He saw no one else there but Mila and himself, and though she sat at a little distance from him, he felt her lean into his chest, felt the sleekness of her waist when his hands went around it, inhaled the aroma of her skin. It was for a long time thus that he held Mila in his arms, with no fear of the future, no anticipation of troubles ahead. Somewhere, behind him, he heard a soft purring and a grunt, the sounds of contentment from a big cat. The lion, he thought, the lion that the naturalists around the world considered to have been extinct here for the last two hundred years. Mila's voice finally brought him out of his dreaming and she spoke as though they had been in the middle of a conversation and the break had not happened.

"Jai brings Colonel Pankhurst here on a *shikar*, a hunt, four times a year. Papa has been here, and so has Kiran, but Ashok," she said, and turned with a smile to her brother, "is yet to hunt with Jai."

"Next year," Ashok said, his eyes bright and feverish. "Jai has promised me that next year, just before the hot season, I can go on my first *shikar* with him. What do you think, Vimal?"

Sam leaned out from next to Mila to look again at the young man seated next to Ashok. He remembered him, strangely enough, as the boy with the intense gaze whom they had passed on the way to the Victoria Club. Today, Vimal was dressed much as he had been yesterday, the same white *kurta* and the same loose pajamas. His curly hair was mussed and disorderly, but his skin shone like the inside of a delicate shell, smooth and iridescent, as though lit from within. A thick red thread encircled his leanly muscled wrist, and when Sam's gaze fell upon it, Vimal said, in impeccable English, "From the Kali temple, Captain Hawthorne, I received it as a blessing from the Goddess over all of my future endeavors." His voice slurred over Sam's name, *Haw-thorne*. It was deliberately done, for Vimal Kumar knew something, and he wanted to let Sam know this.

Mila tensed and scowled. She did not like Vimal, Sam thought. He did not like him very much either, but Ashok seemed to. When they had started out this morning, just before the break of dawn, Vimal had presented himself at the front door, crisp and clean in his clothes, his hair still damp from a bath. He seemed to have come by some prior arrangement with Ashok, for the comedy they had played out had fooled none of them. Mila had been taken aback by his presence, he had himself merely been curious, until Vimal had spoken to him on the way to the jeep. What he had said had astounded Sam.

Pallavi had stood behind them, sniffling as Sam came downstairs. Was she crying, Sam had asked Mila, but Mila had not responded, her attention caught by Vimal.

"Have you come to visit us, Vimal?" Ashok had cried, a little too joyfully, a little too theatrically.

"If I may," Vimal had said, shaking Ashok's hand. "But . . . I see you are on your way somewhere." He stepped back, spread out his arms in a gesture of ruefulness, and raised his voice so that it reached Sam and Mila, near the front door. "I would hate to intrude upon your entertainments. I know you cannot want me here."

"But no," Ashok cried. "We are merely on our way to Chetak's tomb. You *must* join us. *Mustn't* he, Mila? We have plenty of place in the jeep, here," he said, pointing to the backseat, "you can sit next to me. We are taking Captain Hawthorne there. Come, meet him, Vimal."

Sam watched Ashok orchestrate the whole invitation with ease, heaving aside Mila's polite suggestions that perhaps Vimal did not have the time to spend the entire day with them, that perhaps he had other engagements. What could Vimal have to do, Ashok had demanded, and Vimal had gracefully shrugged to say that his time was theirs, with such friends as these, no demand on his time was too great. The place problem in the jeep Ashok had solved almost immediately, and the food would, of course, not present any difficulties at all—they always took more than they needed. And . . . at this Ashok smiled a little slyly; Papa would be glad to hear that they went in a larger party than originally planned.

In the end, Mila had agreed, exhausted by Ashok's enthusiasm. Sam had been bemused, wondering how Ashok had managed to send word about their picnic plans to Vimal that late at night.

As they had waited for the bearers and servants to load and pack the jeep they were to travel by and the extra jeep that had been borrowed overnight from the Rudrakot Lancers regiment, Vimal had stopped by Sam and said casually, "It is indeed a great pleasure to meet you, Captain Ridley." A flush, on cue, had darkened his face and neck and he had said, "You must excuse me, you are Captain Hawthorne, of course. Only . . . you have the look of someone I once knew."

April 1942, a Month Earlier

*Somewhere in Burma*

*T*he rain dulls into a light misting around them; the *drip-drip* they hear is from its past thunder, as teak leaves slant downward, dropping beads of water toward the forest floor. The early afternoon light is wet with moisture, blurred as though seen through frosted glass panes. Where the tops of the trees break, Sam can see no sky, no blue, just the mutinous gray of clouds. Sam muddles through his tired brain in search of passages from the Burma booklet he had been assigned, but which he has long buried in the forest floor, for even the slim ten pages it contained, bound between thin leaves of cardboard, had become burdensome on his back. January to June are called the hot-dry season; it is April, the monsoons are already here to belie that phrase. They are officially in Burma's hot-wet season. There is another season, with warm days, cooler nights, no rain—the simply lovely season. The trail winds to a hill, and they march up it in silence, their boots sinking into the mud.

They crest the hill early in the afternoon and look down for a brief, surprised moment before flinging themselves down into the mud.

"What is that?" Marianne asks.

"A plantation owner's bungalow," Sam says in a whisper. "I'll be damned if I knew it was here."

"Isn't it on your map?"

"It should be," Sam says, "but I did not notice it."

"You missed an entire plantation on the map, Sam?" Ken lifts his head cautiously over the ridge of the hill. "Says something about your map-reading skills."

"I know."

They crouch behind a tree and peer out, hoping they are not visible from below. The rain has settled into a steady drizzle. At least it is a warm rain, Sam thinks, unlike Seattle rain. He waits for the next drop of water to fall on the sliver of skin on the top of his skull, where his hair parts. Inhaling deeply, his lungs draw in the damp air of the forest, the scent of days-old perspiration. The rain brings some relief from the heat of the relentless sun overhead; the forest provides cover too, but a dense, cloistered cover that gathers the heat and water within it and refuses to let go.

The hillside is bare here, sparsely planted with teak, and there is little to give them cover. But they have to get nearer to be able to see anything. Sam's binoculars was shattered when he stumbled in the mud two days ago, and he buried its remains in the ground. He keeps the pieces of glass from the lens in the wrapping of a chocolate bar inside his haversack. Perhaps he might need the glass to create a fire if his matches run out.

Below them is the plantation, or what is left of it anyway. A huge bungalow sprawls all over the ridge in sharp right angles. It seems as though room after room has been added on haphazardly over the years, creating courtyards and semienclosed gardens. How has he missed seeing this on the map? Sam wants desperately to reach into his pocket and pull out the map, if for no other reason than to satisfy his academic interest, but this is not the time.

They wait. It is hushed here, quieter still near the bungalow, and the red tiles of its many roofs glisten in the rain. Parts of the bungalow are still smoking, there are gaps in the tiles where the roof has fallen in, and a deathly placidity lies over the whole.

"Let's go and explore," says Ken, pleading in his voice. "I can't stand being wet anymore. We can spend the night there."

He begins to move and Sam shoves him behind the tree again. "Wait. It's too quiet—"

"Because there's no one there, Sam," Marianne says. "I agree with Ken, let's go in. The Japanese are done with the bungalow; they've moved on."

"And they won't come back again?" Sam asks.

"Why would they?"

"For the same reason as us—shelter for the night."

Ken and Marianne groan together and slide down below the hill's crest. They lie on their backs, breathing slowly into the moist air, hands clasped across their bellies. Sam stays where he is and lifts his head cautiously so he can peer over the foliage. He lets his eyes glaze over after a while, but is still alert to the possibility of any movement in the bungalow below him. After half an hour, Sam turns to them. "We can go a little closer if you like."

They fall onto their stomachs along the steep slope and begin to inch forward, slowly, until they are halfway down the hillside. The bungalow is enormous. It has a red-tiled portico in front, a covered teak walkway leading to a driveway, lawns on either side of the walkway fringed by rose-bushes. The sloping roof has an embellished fringe with scalloped wooden overhangs all around, painted white. One of the courtyards is actually a swimming pool, with the verandah jutting out onto the translucent pea green water. The edges of the verandah's floor are inlaid with lime green tiles and it gives the effect of the verandah dissolving into the pool.

Sam drops his face into the mud, and digs his toes in to get a grip and not go sliding down the hillside. This is like a dream, a movie set, a scene out of Orwell's *Burmese Days*—the lush plantation, the gently misting rain disturbing the glassy surface of the pool, the plantation chairs on the verandah, the roof with scalloped edges, for pity's sake. He's waiting for people to stroll out onto the lawns, gimlets in hand, the women's hats wide-brimmed in colors of pale greens, blues, and yellows, skirts swishing about their knees, their . . . Are they all dreaming? Would the Japanese leave this lavish bungalow and go elsewhere?

"It's a trap," he says softly. "Look, the western half of the bungalow has been trashed and burned; the rest is still intact. They are waiting for us."

"They don't know we are here, Sam," Marianne says. "You are just being morbid."

"Let's go." Sam lifts his head to look at each of them. "We are going to skirt around the plantation. No stopping here."

Ken, his shoulders lodged against a vine to give him stability on the slippery mud, shakes his head stubbornly. "I want to get dry. I hate this. I want to get dry, Sam. I feel like moss; things are growing on me."

"Ken . . ."

Marianne reaches out for Sam. "He's right. We deserve this rest; we have been pushing ourselves too hard. How much will one night under a dry roof slow us down? We need to sleep, in any case."

Sam looks down at the bungalow. This is his decision; he is responsible for Marianne and Ken. But . . . a sudden and intense longing fills him too. He wants to be under that roof, to air out his shirt and pants, to take off his boots and let his feet dry. His toes feel turgid and swollen, beyond aching, and surely there are leeches feasting inside on the skin of his ankles. He turns and finds Marianne and Ken watching him, heads raised from the ground. Teak trees slant behind at an unnatural angle; Sam realizes that the trees are not aslant, he is. A big drop of water splashes onto Sam's head, right at the part of his thick hair. It cuts a line through the middle of his forehead and divides into two thin streams of water on either side of his nose. Perhaps he can wash inside the bungalow, Sam thinks, perhaps even swim in the lovely waters of that pool. Hibiscus bushes, with great, green, glistening leaves, throng the path around the pool and drop their brilliant white and yellow flowers into the water. Although it is not raining anymore, merely misting, it is still deadly hot, and damp and sweat are all mingled upon their bodies. They no longer know the smell of clean; they have been filthy for so long, bloodied by leeches, muddied by dirt.

"We wait," he says finally. "Right here. No movement at all, is that understood?"

"How long?" Marianne asks.

"Till nightfall, until I'm sure there is no one inside the bungalow."

"Hooray!" Ken says in a whisper.

Sam settles his elbows into the mud and rests his chin on his hands. He tries not to think of the maddening drizzle, of the damp dirt beneath him, of the stench of rotting vines and insects in the mud. He hopes that no one from the bungalow is looking up the hillside, for they have so little cover here. Their skins are cured into a muddied brown, their uniforms and boots covered in slush and filth; they must meld into the hillside. No one will notice them if they do not betray their presence with a movement.

A little part of Sam is still suspicious of such a bounty as this below them, and an idea forms in his brain then. The plantation bungalow is not on the map, but Ken must have known of its existence—he is the one who has prodded them from the marked trail and into these lands. How could he have missed this building from the air, if indeed he has flown over this area as he said he had? Sam's belly rumbles; he is ravenously hungry. If they lay siege to the bungalow for the next five hours, perhaps there will be food to be found there, and definitely shelter and dryness. He struggles to keep his eyes open. The sound of the rain lulls, the wet sludge under his stomach is no longer a discomfort, his body aches and now slows into sleep.

# Sixteen

*All kinds of magic are out of date, and done away with except in India where nothing changes in spite of the shiny, top-scum stuff that people call "civilization."*

—Rudyard Kipling, *Plain Tales from the Hills,* 1899

*F*rom half a mile away, the real dimensions of Chetak's tomb took form, almost piece by piece and stone by stone. It was erected on a sandstone platform with a flight of fifteen stairs leading up to the entrances, of which there were four. The four sides of the square structure faced north, south, east, and west and each side mirrored the rest, so they looked the same, no matter where one stood to view the tomb. Built only a hundred years ago by Jai's great-grandfather, this style of the building, equally symmetrical on every face, was copied from the Mughal emperors who had ruled India until 1858, when Victoria became queen-empress. The Mughals in turn had brought into their architecture elements of Persian and Turkish influences. So Chetak's tomb, in a much-convoluted path from many centuries ago, was built in a Persian style, imitating the Mughal and Muslim emperors, and was constructed by a Hindu king for his much-beloved horse.

If a horse could have been said to profess a religion, and during his lifetime the majestic Chetak had been adorned with many a *tikka*—a red vermillion streak of protection on his forehead—then Chetak had been a Hindu too, like his master.

The black-tar road had given way to wasteland a mile back, and the jeeps now bumped and jolted over the dirt path to the tomb. As they approached, Ashok, the most keen-eyed among them all, pointed forward through the dusty windshield and said, "There's someone there."

They peered in the direction of his finger. Sam was driving, and he reached out with his right hand and rubbed some of the dust from the front of the windshield so that he could see better. It did seem like there were two or three human figures in white in front of the tomb in the shadow of the eastern side, their *dhotis* and *kurtas* aglow with ambient sunshine.

"A ghost!" Ashok cried out, and then facetiously, "Chetak's ghost."

"Don't be silly, Ashok," Mila said. "Chetak was a horse, not a human being. Are they though," she asked worriedly, "human ghosts?"

Sam began to laugh, gave her a quick glance, and sobered. Fine lines of worry marred her brow. Mila clasped her arms around herself and shuddered. She was afraid of ghosts that walked abroad in the middle of the day? Her anxiety transferred itself to him and a tingling crawled up Sam's spine. Later, many years later, Sam would look back upon this time in Rudrakot as a dream, as something that had happened and had not, a jumble of impressions, ghosts and beloveds, blood and heartbreak so mingled that he could no longer tell where one began and the other found its end. Everything in India acquired a magical quality; nothing was impossible, nothing even improbable.

Through the clouds of dust, Sam saw one of the figures drag a cow to the front of the tomb, or what appeared to be a cow; it could very well have been a horse from this distance. Mila gasped when the man lifted his arm and brought it down upon the animal's neck; he did not seem to be holding a knife or a sword, he merely used the edge of his palm. The cow seemed to move its head about once, and then twice, before its knees crumpled and it collapsed to the ground, its head hitting the dirt first, before the rest of its body.

Sam pressed on the accelerator and the engine began to protest. What was going on? And who were those men? For Sam, of course, did not believe in ghosts or consider that those figures ahead of them were not real men. Mila had a hand over her mouth, and behind them Ashok and Vimal gagged and coughed. If it had been a cow that had been sacrificed, or even slaughtered for meat, the men would have to be Christian or Muslim, for no Hindu would commit such a sacrilegious act. If it had been a horse . . . for some reason, at this thought, Sam felt a sickening in his gut. If it had been a horse, it would have been a foul ritual, some sort of sacrifice offered to that entombed horse that had once been so adored by his master. Had he been driving alone, Sam would have thought that the desert was playing tricks on his eyes as usual, here, because the spaces were so large, the horizon limitless, objects formed and melted without cause, as though to provide the mind with some relief from all that immensity.

They heard a chattering and a pointing of fingers from the jeep behind them that carried the servants and the food. The driver of the second jeep began to honk. Sam waved to him.

"We should stop, Captain Hawthorne," Mila shouted over the scream of the engine. "It doesn't look safe there."

"It's nothing, and there's nowhere to stop, no shade from the sun. It's an illusion, that's all," Sam said with determination, although he did not believe this himself. He had seen *something*—they all had—that much was true.

They drove on, nearing the tomb, and all the while their hearts crashed against their ribs. Their skins seemed to exhale fear, turgid and fermenting in the air around them. Sam bit his lower lip to taste blood and shake himself out of this strangeness. Ghosts did not bother him, and yet . . . it had all been so real, for all of them had witnessed it. The cow, or the animal, was dragged away by its legs around the tomb and the two men in white finally looked in their direction. One put a hand up to protect his eyes from the sun and stared at them for a long while, unflinching. Sam drew his foot away from the accelerator, almost involuntarily, at that long stare. Then the man moved unhurriedly and they watched his figure and that of his companion disappear around a corner.

There was no approach left to Chetak's tomb; it simply rose out of wasteland, a monolith of red sandstone, its edges buffed and buffeted by the hot winds that yowled through the Sukh desert in May, just before the monsoons. The dirt path ended abruptly just in front of the tomb and here, facing west, the jeeps arrived under the burning rays of the sun. Sam switched off the engine and a thick, heated silence descended upon them.

"There was nobody here," Sam said. "There's nothing to fear."

No one moved. The servants in the jeep next to them had fallen silent also, their faces blanched with dread, knuckles intertwined in prayer. Their driver had his fingers wrapped around the key, which was still in the ignition.

"Wait," Sam said. He drew his Colt .45 out of the holster at his belt and swung his legs out of the jeep.

"Would you like me to come with you, Captain Hawthorne?" Vimal asked.

Sam shook his head. He moved slowly toward the tomb, looking into each arch in the verandahs on both stories, but there was no movement, no suggestion of human inhabitation. The ground was smooth dust and strewn with pebbles, small and large, but there were no footprints there, or indeed even hoof prints from the animal. On the rest of the short drive over, Sam had thought that the men they had seen could have been nomads, taking cover in the tomb. This was common all over India. There was no fear among the many poor about sleeping where death had slept and they found shelter where they could, whether it was with the living or the dead. The dirt was crisp around the tomb and Sam's boots crunched as he walked around, the Colt held loosely against his thigh, his forefinger on the trigger. But there was no one around, no sign even of the fantastic tableau they had witnessed, the sacrifice of the cow, the brooding men in white—there was nothing.

Sam climbed the stairs to one of the entrances to Chetak's tomb. From here, he could see through the entire structure, as it was built in an open floor plan. Three steps led down to a sunken rectangle, and the horse's sarcophagus was raised in the center, its white-marble-inlaid cover level with the floor on which Sam stood. The verandah on this story let in shards of light from the outside. Sam froze for a moment when he saw an enormous varan, an iguana-like creature five feet long and barrel thick about its belly, sunning itself in one of the arches. It slept undisturbed, eyes closed against the sunshine, its prehistoric scales glinting with iridescence. A steep set of stairs, its stone banister crumbling, led upstairs, and Sam took these two at a time. Here he was in another open gallery; in the center the floor opened to the story below and a view of the sarcophagus, and around the outer edges was another verandah with a low wall and cusped arches. Here also light streamed in, shadows leaking in long, black strips from the verandah's pillars, in patterns of *champa* flowers from the latticework of the outer walls. There was a faint, musty odor, and a smell of rotting bones. But here too there was no one to be seen. Sam ran around the long, outer verandah, looking out into the desert that stretched in an unbroken swath of bleached brown on all sides. Nothing again. No sign of the men, no sign of *anything* out in the wilderness. If the men had been here with their sacrificial cow, they had disappeared into the rays of the sun.

Sam put the cool, long barrel of his Colt against his forehead. India was strange, he thought, with its ghosts that disappeared, a lazy lizard downstairs large enough to eat them all, buildings that existed on maps and not on the earth. He went back to the jeep. Sam offered his hand to Mila to help her out, as though it was the most natural thing to do. He wanted to tell her of his attraction for her but there was no time. He had to be back in Calcutta and Assam soon, back in Burma. For a moment last night, when he had held her hand at the *mela,* Sam had almost asked Mila to dance with him to the music the band was playing, but something had stopped him.

Ashok and Vimal scurried away, shouting with delight as their feet pounded over the sandstone floors of the tomb. They came to a halt by the slothful lizard.

"A *baran!*" Ashok shouted. "A colossal one. Look, Vimal, he's moving."

Mila shuddered and retreated to the other end of the tomb. "Get it out of here," she called over her shoulder. "It's disgusting."

Sam watched as Ashok and Vimal knelt by the varan and stroked its thick hide. It swung its tail about, thwacking at their legs, and then lifted itself on powerful thighs and arms and waddled away. Greens, blues, and reds undulated under its skin as it slid over the edge of the verandah and fell onto the ground on the far side, raising a fine plume of dust.

Then, the two boys climbed on the sarcophagus and lay on their backs on the dusty stone, gazing up to the roof of the second story. Here they had the best view of the ornate, carved ceiling. At the very center was a huge lotus flower, etched into the stone, the petals lush and creamy. Peacocks danced in full form at the four corners of the ceiling, each detail of their feathers cut patiently into the stone. Other flowers—jasmine and hibiscus—abounded; a *nilgai* nibbled on grass, its blue neck bent as an offering to a hunter's musket. A black buck stared out for all eternity, its ears pricked for a sound it would never hear, its eyes large and liquid. Once he

realized what Ashok and Vimal were looking at, now in a complete silence, Sam lifted his neck and bent his head backward.

Despite everything, he was overcome by a sense of awe and peace at
the sight of the ceiling. This was the real and hidden beauty in Chetak's
tomb. In everything else, it was simple to the point of being austere,
straight Persian lines for the shape of the inside and outside verandahs and
corridors, smooth, unembellished curves on the pillars. The sarcophagus
was like a gleaming jewel in the center of the floor, its top and sides carefully inlaid with the purest of white marble in patterns of hexagons, trian-
gles, and squares. This inlay work, called *pietra dura*, traced its origins to
Italy, but was now ensconced firmly in Indian architecture. The work was
as flawless as it must have been when the tomb was constructed more than
a hundred years ago. The tiny marble slices had been embedded in the
sandstone with glue and mortar and then the whole was polished and
smoothed until it looked as though the sandstone was born that way—
seamless to the touch. For the rest of the stark tomb, the only adornments
were the striations of cool beiges in the sandstone, everywhere the eye lit.
The stones had been chosen to match, color for color, slab for slab. The
ochers, rust-golds, and browns harmonized perfectly, melding, until the
whole tomb looked as though it had been cut out of one mammoth piece
of stone.

But Sam had not come to admire the beauties of Chetak's tomb. He
looked around. Ashok and Vimal had disappeared from the top of the sarcophagus, and Sam could hear their deep-timbred voices in the upstairs
verandah. He caught a little glimpse of Mila's brown arm wrapped around
a pillar at the far entrance of the tomb; she was leaning against it, facing
north. Sam could see her shoulder, the curve of her cheek, and a wisp of
her hair lifting in the gentle, heat-laden breeze that flew through one entrance and out the other. Sam moved to the east-facing verandah, reached
into his shoulder bag, and brought out a pair of binoculars. The contours
of the desert swam and rippled through the glass. Here and there, a lone
*khejri* tree spread out its irregular, thorn-ridden branches. Its leaves were
sparse and it was selfish with shade, proudly lifting its spiky arms into the
furious blaze of the sun.

He lowered his glasses and gazed out into the distance, shading his
eyes with his hand even though he was not standing in direct sunlight.
The map that Sam had glanced at on his way back from the men's wash-

room at the Victoria Club had upon it a building east of Chetak's tomb. Written in an uneducated hand were the words *Field Punishment Center, 1930.* Even fainter than that, mixed in around the artist's fanciful rendering of a gallery of trees and shrubs in the barren reaches of the Sukh, was a cheap little rhyme: *Beware, all ye who enter here. For once ye do, give up all that ye hold dear.*

Sam closed his eyes from the strain of having stared too intensely into the horizon and listened hard. But all he could hear was the raucous chatter of the servants as they prepared the afternoon's lunch, the clatter of the vessels, the tinkling cooling down of the jeeps' engines. Where was the field punishment center? According to the Victoria Club map, it was somewhere close by, and yet he had seen nothing through the binoculars. *Mike,* Sam thought, suddenly overcome with a terrible fear that threatened to break his heart, *are you there?* He listened more intently, sifting out the sounds near him, yearning for the miraculous sound of Mike's voice calling out to him, knowing it was stupid to wish for something so strange, so unreal. But everything had been unreal to Sam for the last few days, even Mike's disappearance. For people did not simply vanish from the middle of a regiment without any reason, without a trace. Sam rubbed the weariness out of his temples and lifted his gaze to the horizon. Nothing. Nothing but a slow swirl of sand, a waver of radiance. He began to raise the glasses up again and saw, without the aid of the binoculars, that the light had altered, cleared, magnified in the distance. And in that shifting a low building of red sandstone crystallized into being.

The field punishment center was less than two miles from Chetak's tomb.

# Seventeen

*I had begun to understand and sympathise with the problems of the white man in India soon after my arrival, when I reached the phase that everyone goes through of thinking of the Indians as Wogs. When this happens, all your preconceived ideas seem to go sour on you and then melt away in the hot sun; you see the Indians as a lot of hopeless degenerates and the Soul of India as backsheesh."*

—Louis Hagen, *Indian Route March*, 1946

*A*t two o'clock in the morning, Raman had risen from his bed, bathed and prayed, eaten a light breakfast to keep hunger away, and then set off on his way to Nodi. The old villager had slept at the back of the house, on the steps leading down to the garden. It had been his best night's sleep in the last ten days, since he had left Nodi to come in search of Raman. The old man had stopped under a few banyan trees, terrified by every rustle of the leaves (for ghosts of the ill-treated lingered there), on the roadside, in the verandah at Chetak's tomb, in the bazaar, and finally, spent the last three nights on the platform in the railway station, using his cotton towel to cover his face from the gaze of others. When they left from Rudrakot, Raman rode his horse, fancifully named Sans Reproche by Jai (after he had spent a summer in Paris), who had reared this horse in the regimental stables. Sans Reproche was a gentle, doe-eyed creature, with a propensity for nuzzling his warm and wet nose against Raman's neck each time he dismounted. The old man had been convinced to ride a donkey, and he had agreed to mount this lesser animal only because it was not a horse. The donkey's lead was tied to Sayyid's horse's saddle and the three of them set out with two other servants to run ahead and light their way with kerosene lanterns held aloft at the end of a pole.

Sayyid had laid his head down for only a brief rest the night before because Mila had returned from the Victoria Club to say simply, "We are going to Chetak's tomb for a picnic, Sayyid, about six o'clock. Will you see to the arrangements, please?"

"Of course, Mila," Sayyid said. He had been with Raman for twenty-eight years, since he was sixteen years old, and looked upon Raman as a brother, and his children as his own nephews and niece. But at no time in the last three decades had Sayyid forgotten that he was a servant. Raman, he addressed as "Sahib," and Lakshmi as "Memsahib," for they were his masters. With Pallavi, the situation had been fraught with tension and difficulties—for Pallavi too had been a servant when Raman had first married, and had grown into adulthood and the status of the children's mother, a fact that was still questionable to Sayyid. He ignored Pallavi. He had called her by her name, or "girl," when she was young, but as she grew older and more assertive in the house, at times daring to order him around, he began to grow deaf and had by now quite forgotten that she even had a name. Sayyid was respectful, but always found an opportunity to materialize under her nose before he spoke so that he did not have to use any form of address.

The children he called by their names. Though rightfully, when they were young, Sayyid should have called Kiran and Ashok something like *chota baba*, or little Sahib, and Mila *missy baba*, which had no translation. This he had not, and one day three years ago, suddenly mindful of his place in the house as a butler, and his duties, he had said Chota Sahib to Kiran in the course of a conversation. And Kiran's response, in his impeccable public school English, had been, "Come off it, Sayyid. *I'm* a Chota Sahib now? Don't be ridiculous." Kiran had gone chortling to Raman's room to tell him of this latest joke.

Sayyid had then retreated into a dignified silence on that matter and continued to address Kiran, Mila, and Ashok as he always had, all the while bemoaning their too-familiar ways with the household help. Not done, he thought. The masters ought to keep their distance from the servants, and so he had learned from the other butlers in the Civil Lines, especially the British one, imported to the residency to add pomp in the front portico with his elevated nose and his dour visage.

At Mila's request for a picnic lunch at Chetak's tomb, Sayyid had balked, but within himself. Where Pallavi could ask, no, demand that Mila talk with her father about the proposed trip, Sayyid kept quiet, not even telling his master the next morning. But he had his duties to the child of his master. Mila did not think about the lateness of the hour or any inconvenience to Sayyid from her request, and neither did Sayyid. He telephoned from the hall phone to the quartermaster of the Rudrakot Rifles, caught him at home as he was sitting down to a late dinner with some friends, and asked for an extra jeep for the next morning. The quartermaster merely asked how far the jeep was to travel in order to write out a chit for the petrol. By midnight, the jeep was parked in the driveway of Raman's house, its driver asleep on the backseat in twenty minutes.

Then Sayyid went about meticulously arranging for the picnic lunch. He took care of every little detail himself, and finally lay down on his *charpai* under the brilliantly starred night sky, the near-to-fullness moon hanging pendant above him. When he woke, Sayyid checked on the arrangements again, wishing all the while that he could have gone along with Mila on the picnic to be sure that every element of his preparations was attended to, but he had to, *wanted* to, accompany Raman to Nodi.

At Chetak's tomb, the servants began making the first round of drinks with a care that belied Sayyid's absence. They shook out ice cubes from the thermoses into another, insulated container and set this aside in the shade of one of the pillars. A cocktail shaker was placed within this ice, to cool to freezing. The servant then poured in cognac, pineapple syrup, orange curaçao, a dash of Angostura bitters, and some ice chips and then capped the shaker and shook it gently. The ice hissed and splintered within the cold shaker, and when the servant poured his version of the Royal Bombay Yacht Club cocktail into the shining martini glasses set upon a carved wood tray, the drink frosted the outside of the glass upon contact. He carefully lifted his tray and went around Chetak's tomb in search of his masters. Mila he found leaning against a pillar at the north entrance. She held the delicate stem of the glass between her thumb and index finger and drank a good portion of the cocktail even before the servant had turned to leave.

"Bring me another one please."

"*Ji, Memsahib,*" the boy said. He hesitated. "Right away?"

"No, take the drinks to the others. Only two, maximum, for Ashok Sahib."

The boy nodded and went off. He found Ashok peering under the stone stairs that led up to the tomb, hoping for another glimpse of the varan. Like Mila, Ashok drank his cocktail in one mouthful and reached for another glass.

"Only two, Sahib," the boy said gently.

"All right."

The servant found Vimal standing a few paces behind Sam, at the east-facing verandah of Chetak's tomb. Heat rose in waves and gusted toward them. It hung in the air, clawed its way into their lungs until they could not breathe, dragged perspiration out onto the surface of their skins. Sam did not know yet that Vimal stood behind him; he had his binoculars raised to the view of the field punishment center. The building dozed in the midday sun, bare and unembellished. It was constructed with slabs of sandstone glued together with mortar, and on the side that faced Chetak's tomb was a wooden gate with an arched top that mimicked the arch of the gateway. There were no windows on this wall, or perhaps on any of the other walls, Sam thought, for this was a prison. Four square minarets rose out at the four corners, topped off by a stone pavilion with a stone roof. The minarets, guard towers, were empty. Even if a prisoner was foolish enough to escape in the middle of the day, he would be seen for miles in this deserted land, and if he was not caught immediately, the sun would kill him. At night other dangers, human, inhuman, and animal, awaited. Rudrakot was the nearest place of habitation and it was three hours by car, and innumerable hours by foot. The field punishment center was literally in the middle of nowhere.

As the servant approached, Sam turned to see Vimal. They both accepted the cocktails gratefully.

"Will lunch be soon?" Sam asked.

"In an hour, Sahib," the boy replied, bowed, and padded his way to the tent that the servants had erected to cook the food. A little spiral of smoke and the aroma of wood and charcoal wafted over them to signal that a fire had been started.

Vimal sipped his cocktail and looked out eastward. "The walls of the center are twenty feet high, Captain Hawthorne, and sheer. The gate has no footholds in the planks of wood; in any case, two sentries stand guard all night on the inside of the gate. The guard towers are usually manned on every night except for the nights before and after *purnima,* the full moon. There is a common superstition in this part of the world, and I'm not quite sure where it came from, but Chetak is said to rise and ride through the desert on the nights before and after the full moon, and one of those," he said, turning to look at Sam, his skin glistening with a thin sheen of perspiration, "is tonight. Tomorrow the moon swells to fullness. It is considered to be bad luck to lay eyes upon the horse's ghost, so the guards stay inside."

"Does it matter if there are guards in the towers?" Sam said, wiping the sweat from the eyepiece of his binoculars against his shirt.

"Not really," Vimal replied. "They are a bunch of lazy buggers. There is not much excitement in their lives, Captain Hawthorne. The men they watch over are on their way to meet death in any case—no one has ever escaped from Rudrakot's field punishment center." He put his empty glass down on the verandah parapet's ledge and almost at once, a line of red army ants came marching up the latticework stone, swirled around the base of the glass, and then swarmed into it. Vimal knocked against the glass and the ants shuddered, fell to the stone, regrouped, and marched up again.

By his side, Sam sweated in silence. Vimal knew somehow that Mike was his brother, and knew also that he was at the field punishment center. As he watched the building, it evaporated again from sight and the sun whitened into horizontal lines in front of his eyes. Ghosts and disappearing buildings, Sam thought, how was he to battle all of this to find Mike? His shoulders bent under the weight of this entire burden, and the pain of loving the woman who now stood silhouetted in the entrance archway. Nothing seemed possible suddenly.

"How did you know?" he asked finally.

Vimal did not answer for a long time and all Sam heard was the ragged intake of his breath. He had asthma, or some other breathing disorder, and Sam wondered if he was aware of this.

"You have the same face, Captain Hawthorne," he said finally. "Or should I say Ridley?"

"It does not matter, the name does not matter," Sam said. "Michael is my brother." But Mike had sandy hair that bleached to a straw yellow by the end of the summer. His lashes were light too. Sam had never given much thought to their physical resemblance, he had supposed, as one always took for granted that they looked alike, that perhaps they spoke in the same way, had the same mannerisms. They had grown up in the same house; they must be alike. Yet they were physically different and Vimal was the only one who not only had seen the likeness, but had made connections with that knowledge and had come to him. By now Vimal's martini glass was completely covered by the brown and red bodies of the ants, thickly layered like treacle. He knocked on the glass again, and the ants fell off, only to climb back again.

"They have a great deal of determination, Captain Hawthorne," Vimal said. Then he looked upon Sam, a faint dusting of red on his cheekbones. "But so have I."

"Is Mike at the field punishment center?" Sam asked.

"Yes." The answer came too quickly.

"Why?"

"He was"—Vimal spread his hands out—"sympathetic to us, to our cause."

Sam leaned against the verandah's parapet and crossed his arms in front of his chest. "Others have been, and not everyone is incarcerated because of harboring sympathies toward the nationalists."

"Bravo, Captain Hawthorne," Vimal said softly. "You know who I am then."

Sam inclined his head. There was much he did not know about Rudrakot and its residents, but Vimal Kumar and his nationalist supporters had been on every page of the report Sam had read in Calcutta. So far, Vimal had only led a few student demonstrations at the local college and somewhat alarmingly filled the front compound of his "exercise camp" headquarters with a throng of supporters to listen to his vehement speeches. There was also mention of a bombing and the authorities suspected Vimal was involved in it. It was only on the drive here that Sam had finally recalled who Vimal was; until then his name had merely been familiar.

"Four months ago," Vimal said, using the palms of his hands to heave himself onto the parapet so that he was no longer facing Sam, "a British schoolteacher died in the schoolhouse she had set up on the outskirts of Rudrakot. Her name was Jane Crowley. Or rather"—he grinned and his face lit up with a beauty an artist would have envied—"as you say, names are not important. Suffice it to note that Miss Crowley was a dried-up old bird who had been born in Palampore to a major in the Indian army, never married, and had grown meddling and troublesome—there are a thousand Englishwomen like her in India." Vimal's voice dropped, even though Mila and Ashok, and the servants, were nowhere near. "We wanted the schoolhouse and the land it was built on as a base for keeping our fleeing freedom fighters safe from the police. I went and offered Miss Crowley a very large sum of money for the property, but she refused. The ornery old bitch." Vimal said this last without any inflection or change of tone, as though Jane Crowley ought to have succumbed to the money if not his overabundant charm.

"We courted and wooed her for seven months, Captain Hawthorne, and all the while the freedom fighters were sent to safe houses elsewhere in the country because we could not look after them properly here." Vimal tilted his martini glass and it wobbled for a moment on the edge of its base before falling through the hot, still air to the ground where it broke into tiny, shining pieces. "Because of Jane Crowley, I could not meet the great men of my time, could not host them, and look after their needs."

To Sam's astonishment, tears pearled at the edges of Vimal's eyes and came rolling down his well-formed cheeks. He did not bother to wipe them away. "The old bitch," he said again, and this time there was a murderous intensity to his voice.

"And so what did you do?" Sam asked.

"We set a bomb in the schoolhouse on a Sunday afternoon when no one was to be there, but Miss Crowley had decided to correct term papers at that very time. The bomb," Vimal said matter-of-factly, "blew her into little pieces. But we bought the land and the remains of the house and rebuilt the structure."

Sam felt an overwhelming wave of pain sweep through him. He could barely bring himself to form the words, but did eventually manage to say, "Did Mike light the fuse?"

Vimal smiled. "Of course, Captain Hawthorne, that was the point of my story."

"He was punished for that?"

"Well . . ." Vimal paused and considered his next words. "I cannot lie to you, it was not just for that. Your brother, Mike, was involved in a month-long argument with one of the officers of the Rudrakot Rifles; I'm not sure what that was about, some stupid *bawarchi* who had been thrashed . . . something like that."

"Sims," Sam said, his whole being crushed with rage. "That bloody Sims."

"Ah, yes," Vimal said. "That was the name of the officer. Well, so they managed to send Michael Ridley . . . er . . . away."

"Is he in the field punishment center?" Sam asked quietly. Again.

"Yes."

Sam looked out into the shaky landscape that shimmered in the heat. They would have to return to Rudrakot without him since he was going to the field punishment center.

Vimal put a hand on his arm. "I will take you there tonight, Captain Hawthorne. It is not an easy fortress to storm. Let me show you the way."

"Go back to the others. I will handle this myself."

In response, Vimal jumped off the parapet, dusted his hands, and dragged Sam to the west-facing verandah. He pointed out into the distance. "Look," he said. "We will not be able to return to Rudrakot this afternoon."

Sam peered where Vimal's finger was pointing, his eyes crinkling for clarity. He could see nothing but the hot dust and a thin, ailing tree. He began to reach into his bag again for his binoculars, but Vimal stayed that gesture. He dipped his head past the shade of the tomb into the sunlight. Every curl on Vimal's handsome head glittered, his eyes gleamed with delight, and a tiny smile arched the bow of his lips, as though he was going to make an important announcement. "It is not visible yet," Vimal said. "But it will be, and soon."

At Sam's next intake of breath, a fine mist of dirt entered through to coat the inside of his lungs and he coughed. Vimal stood aside, watching and smiling more fully now. When Sam finally looked up, bleary eyed and irritated, Vimal said, his finger again flung out into the horizon, "A dust storm approaches, Captain Hawthorne. We call this the Lu, the heated wind. It will come in a few hours, last for a few more. There is no question of returning to Rudrakot tonight."

Sam rubbed his eyes, gazed out again, and saw now, for the first time, a fine smear of red dust at the very point where the washed-out blue sky met the burning, red earth.

"When will we leave?" Sam asked, his heart beginning to bang and crash within his chest.

"After everyone is asleep," Vimal said.

Sam walked back to the eastern verandah and reached out in his mind to the myth of his brother in the field punishment center. There was no guarantee that Mike was still there, or even that he had ever been there. He would be a fool to trust Vimal. And yet . . . when at the Victoria Club he had looked at the map and had seen the pencil drawing of the center, Sam had been assailed by an unshakable conviction that Mike was there, that he was alive, that he had called out to him for help. Until now, Sam had been sure that he would go to the field punishment center and find Mike, but having seen its mammoth, impenetrable face, and hearing Vimal's account of it, he was no longer sure that he could get inside without assistance. And Vimal had offered himself up as a . . . friend, no, as someone who would help him. But why?

His face inscrutable and stony, Sam finally turned to the young, hand-some man by his side and said, "What is it you want in return, Vimal?"

# Eighteen

*The air was heavy with dust and sand from the bed of the river, that*
*filled boots and pockets and drifted down necks and coated eyebrows and*
*moustaches . . . The wind seemed to be picking up the earth and pitching*
*to leeward in great heaps; and the heat beat up from the ground like the*
*heat of the Day of Judgment.*

—Rudyard Kipling, *Plain Tales from the Hills,* 1899

*L*unch was a desultory, somnolent affair, exhausted as they all were
by the incalescence of the day. Sam had thought that he could not
bear to put a morsel in his mouth, and yet when the food was being cooked
and the aromas came eddying toward him, he found himself suddenly ravenous.

Sam and Mila sat on the side of one of the verandahs, watching a servant make *rumali rotis* with practiced movements. He patted the dough
into a large circle, turned his hand over, palm facing down, and draped
the dough over his fingers. Then he flipped his hand in the air, with each
flip flinging the dough out into the sky, and with each flip the circle of
dough swiveled outward until it became thin and almost translucent.
Handling this waferlike dough carefully, the servant swathed it over a
*kadai,* a scoop-bottomed pan that rested upside down over the wood
fire. The *kadai* had been roasting over the slow fire until its surface was
crimson hot. The *roti,* thin and airy as it was, took less than minute to
cook. The man peeled it from the surface of the *kadai* with a pair of iron

tongs, layered its many folds on a plate, dabbed it with some fragrant *ghee*, and deposited the *roti* into a porcelain dish with a lid. The dish was fancifully wrought with a detailed painting of a peacock, the blue of its skin iridescent in the sunlight, a tree in bloom with white flowers in the background. Sam watched as the servant's thick fingers held the lid's handle with delicacy and elegance. The dish was a Sevres china dish. Only in India, he thought, would there be such a study in contrasts, only here would Sevres china be used at a mere picnic, amongst the dust and dirt of a centuries-old tomb built to celebrate the life of, and then mourn the death of, a horse.

He glanced to his left at Mila. "I will never quite get used to the fluidity with which you can settle into this life in India—servants a plenty and no work to do."

"And yet," she said deliberately, "the British do not really want to be here."

Sam raised a quizzical eyebrow. "I thought they did. Isn't that what the nationalist movement is about? Them leaving India?"

Mila sighed, her fingers twisting into each other. She had been fretful for a long time, seated by Sam's side. "Oh, they want to be here because India is a conquered country and they are the conquerors. But every Englishman I have known has always talked fondly of Home."

In one way or the other, Sam too had noticed this particular quality of speech among the British ever since he had come to India. He had encountered officers of the Indian army who had been in India for four or five generations—always marrying into the British community, bringing up their children in an insulated India made to seem like that elusive Home.

"Have you heard Mrs. Stanton speak Hindustani?" Mila asked.

"Yes, her English accent slips when she does."

"And she speaks then like one of us, like a native. Mrs. Stanton grew up in India; she has always lived here, so she strives harder to not seem too much like an old India hand. She learned her Hindustani from the servants in her father's house; but early on she learned her English from them too."

Sam began to laugh as the full import of that last line sank in. "Why?"

"Children, by a very Victorian standard, are meant to be seen and not heard. They are meant to be kept away and brought out on special occasions to be shown off to company. So Mrs. Stanton's childhood nurse-maids were Indian ayahs, her playmates were the *malis* who took time off from watering gardens, her guardians during afternoon rides were native syces—all of whom, doubtless, insisted upon practicing their smashed English upon the *missy baba*. So she originally spoke English in that same *chee-chee* accent that she now deplores, that set her apart, made her almost Indian."

"A pity indeed," Sam said, no sympathy in his voice. "How did her parents get around it?"

"The servants were forbidden from speaking English with her, only the native languages, where the accent did not really matter. She had a British governess"—Mila paused and looked out into the distance—"as did I, once; Papa thought it necessary. The governesses are usually girls seeking marriage among the many eligible officers and civil servants in India, for you see, alliances between Indians and the British are forbidden by society." She shrugged. "I learned how to say, 'thank you' and 'toodle-oo,' and comport myself at high teas, but I can never forget that I am Indian. If my papa had to arrange a marriage for me, it would not be with someone who was not . . . Indian."

Sam had no reply to this, and did not know how they had transitioned from one conversation to another so personal. He could not argue with that statement, so simply offered as an indisputable truth. For too many years now, since 1858, the British in India had claimed a superiority over the Indians because of the color of their skins. That prejudice had given birth to a dislike, an antipathy, a feeling among Indians that everyone who was white held the same chauvinistic opinions. Mila rose and walked away and Sam let her go, his heart thumping with pain.

He turned his attention to the servant who had fashioned a *chula*, a stove, out of three bricks that had come loose from the stairs leading to the tomb. Sam lit a cigarette and watched through the smoke as the fire under the *chula* licked the sides of the *kadai* in which there was a chicken curry. Sweat poured down Sam's forehead and he wiped it with the back of his hand. How did the servants keep cool enough to bend over a living fire in this heat? They squatted in the sun, bareheaded, the skin on their arms browned and charred, not a drop of perspiration on their faces or necks. The curry cook's movements were as deliberate as the bread maker's, even though he managed to make it look casual in the way he hurled pinchfuls of salt, and scattered cumin and coriander powder. The gravy in the *kadai* simmered and Sam's mouth watered. The servant chopped fresh coriander leaves on a wooden cutting board and stirred this into the curry. Then, holding the two handles of the *kadai* with the cloth towel he had draped around his neck, he took the pan off the fire and looked up at Sam.

"Lunch is served, Sahib," he said. "Come. Sit. I will call the others."

"No," Sam said, flicking his unfinished cigarette to one side. "I'll do that."

The servants' gazes swung to the still-smoldering cigarette on the ground, and they waited, hands frozen in midair, for Sam to leave so that they could pounce on that precious, remaining one inch, dab out the cigarette and store it away carefully for a future smoke. Sam saw the lust in their eyes, and quietly took out a handful of cigarettes from his tin, laid them on the ground, and went away to call Mila, Ashok, and Vimal for lunch. When he returned, the cigarettes he had left had gone, along with the half-burned one he had so carelessly tossed on the ground.

Sayyid had packed white china plates, cups, and saucers in sheets of old editions of the *Rudrakot Daily News,* and these had been carefully unwrapped, rinsed in water, and laid out on a red-checked tablecloth on the floor of one of the verandahs. By the side of each plate was a gleaming cut-glass tumbler of water, choked full with ice cubes. The hot *kadai* with the chicken curry rested on a folded-up kitchen towel, and the Sevres dish with the *rumali rotis* was to the side of it. There was also a *kachumber* salad—thick slices of cucumber, onions, and tomatoes, tossed with lemon juice, black salt, and coriander leaves. There were no forks and knives, and Sam realized that he was expected to eat his food Indian style, with his right hand only. He had learned to eat with his hands as politely as he could, smearing the food only up to his knuckles and no farther. The process was still a trial, but, somehow, he felt as Indians did that food did taste better when eaten without the metallic medium of cutlery.

The servants brought steel bowls with tepid water and a piece of lime for them to wash their hands, and then they all sat on the floor, cross-legged, in front of the plates. Each of the finely wrought *rumali rotis* was as flimsy as air, and Sam devoured nine of them, mopping up the chicken within their delicate folds. The food melted in his mouth, spiced as it was with the heated desert air, the tiny flakes of desert mud, the desert wind. A strange lethargy seemed to have come over all of them, and though they were all hungry, they ate in silence, not even meeting one another's eyes but staring out into the distance instead.

At the end of the meal, Vimal said, "The Lu is coming. I can feel it in my bones."

Mila said without raising her gaze, "How old are you, Vimal? A doddering eighty? You can feel it in your bones?" Then she flushed, knowing she had been rude, but her mouth firmed with determination.

"He only means to protect us all, Mila," Ashok said.

"I can feel nothing," Mila replied. She washed her hands in another bowl of water with lime and wiped them on the towel the servant proffered. "Thank you, that was delicious. Quite the best picnic we have had in a long time. Will you please pack up everything so that we can leave from here in an hour? And don't forget to eat lunch."

"*Ji*, Memsahib," the servant said. He made to go, and then turned back resolutely. "What that sahib says"—he gestured toward Vimal, who was leaning back against a pillar, twirling an unlit cigarette held between his lithe fingers—"is true, Memsahib. It is the day before *purnima,* the Lu will come, either today or tomorrow and blow for fifteen days."

"From where?" Mila asked.

"The soothsayer in the Lal Bazaar says from the west."

They all turned around to face west. The sky and the earth were framed in a rectangle of space down the long length of the verandah, its pillars throwing streaking shadows across the floor. Where there should have been blue, there was now, most definitely, a mottled burgundy daubed across the sky.

Mila looked at her wristwatch and frowned.

"When?" Sam asked.

"It will catch us in an hour, or maybe two. Have you been in a dust storm, Captain Hawthorne?" she asked, and when Sam shook his head, she continued with a sudden wash of fear in her voice, "We will not be able to get back to Rudrakot tonight."

In the Sukh desert, heat began to take life by the end of February. There had been no rain or even the slightest hint of moisture in the air for the last three months. Instead, each morning the sun had scorched a steady trail across the thin blue sky, dipped into the horizon at night but left its searing embrace upon the earth. The red sandstone rocks and boulders sizzled and roasted all day long and many a lizard and snake hid in shad-

owy crevices to sleep at the height of the afternoon, only to be cremated
to death by nightfall. The land emanated heat in huge gusts and all this hot
air rose skyward, day after day, until May when the relatively cooler air
rushed in to replace this boiling air. And that created the Lu. Although sci-
ence said the Lu was cooler air, to the inhabitants of Rudrakot, the Lu was
as dry as cracked, unused farmland, and as hot as the heart of a burning
*chula*. This thick Lu came in many colors, depending upon where the
wind had a mind to wreak havoc—mustard-flower yellow where the wind
picked up and sifted the very top layer of the Sukh dirt into the air; raven
black where days were turned into night when the wind brought clouds to
kill the sun; and hibiscus red where the earth spat into the sky, encouraged
by the wind.

The storm that came upon Mila and Sam at Chetak's tomb on that
twenty-ninth of May 1942 raged red. Before it arrived, they finished their
lunch and helped the servants pack the rest of the food and the dishes into
the two jeeps and then lash down the contents with a sheet of tarpaulin
and jute ropes. The jeeps were then driven to the east side of the tomb and
parked nose first in the triangular space under the stairs, their backs jutting
out. And still the storm that they waited for did not come.

Mila tied one end of the red-checked tablecloth to her wrist, swung the
bulk of the cloth around her back, and then tied another end to her other
wrist until it dragged behind her like a cloak slipped off shoulders at a
party. Ashok and Vimal had disappeared, where she did not know. Mila
raised her voice to call out to her brother, and he answered from a distance
saying that he was all right, and that he was with Vimal. At the head of the
stairs Mila paused, knowing that she should get Ashok to be with her while
the storm blew over them, but her feet took her instead to the east-facing
verandah of Chetak's tomb where Sam Hawthorne stood against the parapet, his gaze eastward, fixed upon the lines of the field punishment center.

Mila went up and stood next to Sam. "Why the interest?"

Sam shrugged. "It's nothing."

"What is that place?"

Sam turned to search her face. "Don't you know?"

She frowned. "We've been here many times, but never really paid
much attention to that building. One of the Rifles officers said that it was
abandoned when Lady Pankhurst asked to go there, full of snakes and
lizards and such."

"He's probably right," Sam said slowly, dragging his attention away.

Mila moved closer to Sam, almost imperceptibly, and laid her wrists upon the parapet and leaned forward until she was supported on her hands. Sam took one edge of the red tablecloth and pulled it over Mila's back and head.

She smiled, looking up at him. "We will need something to cover us from the storm."

"When will it get here?"

They both turned to the west entrance. The sky was now fully red, more a terra-cotta red, the red of clay lightly fired in a kiln. Behind them, the heavens still glowed palely blue, in front of them claret. "The storm has begun to chomp at Rudrakot," Mila said. "I give it twenty minutes."

"Listen," Sam said, an arm around Mila's shoulder as he pulled her into his chest.

Her heart almost gave way at the closeness. The khaki of Sam's uniform shirt was pleasantly rough under her cheek, and she could smell the aroma of his body, a cologne of musk, the scent of soap from the morning's bath, the faint undertone of clean perspiration. His arm stilled, as though he was waiting for her to pull away. But Mila did not want to. There would be time for guilt later, even for atonement, if that was demanded of her. For now, she wanted to be in Sam Hawthorne's arms. She did not reach out to embrace him though; all she did was to bring her own arms up and around herself until she was wrapped in the red-and-white checks of the tablecloth.

At first, she could hear only the shuddering thud of his heart in his chest, and then she heard that complete silence that came before a dust storm. There were absolutely *no* sounds. The hum of desert life had melted away—the flies had disappeared into cracks in the walls, the varan was doubtless resting on Vimal's lap (he had caught it and put a leash around its neck after lunch), the tomb's breeze had stopped, preparing also to give way to the larger onslaught of the Lu. Even the heat, more sultry now than before, had slowed itself to stillness. It was as though a giant presence surrounded them, muffling everything else.

"Come," Mila said to Sam. "We must not linger any longer; if the world dies around us, the storm is sure to come soon. We must take cover; there will be no chance later once the storm is upon us."

She put out her hand and he placed his trustingly in hers.

"Ashok . . . ," he said reluctantly, not wanting to have to worry about the boy, much as she herself felt.

"He's with Vimal," she replied. "They will be safe."

They walked down the corridor in that dense and unnatural tranquility, their boots hushed and heavy upon the slabs of sandstone. At each corner of the tomb were little grottos; here the floor was clean, there were niches in the walls for oil lamps, and the walls were solid, twenty-inch-thick sandstone. Mila knelt on the ground and indicated that Sam should do the same. Then she flung the tablecloth into the air and it ballooned out, still captive at her wrists, and came to settle gently over both of them.

Within, they drew closer to each other, sitting down now, their knees touching, their heads together, converging along their hairlines. When Mila lifted her eyes to look into Sam's, all she saw this close was a blue haze. Their breaths mingled. Mila could not speak and so they waited in the red-and-white light that drenched them.

The storm came in five minutes, and until the very last moment, the absence of sound persisted, and then, suddenly, there was a huge roar of noise, like the breaking of a tidal wave, and the wind whipped through Chetak's tomb with a velocity that yanked the tablecloth from both of them. Mila's hands flew out as the cloth flapped outward, and Sam caught her wrists and pulled them into himself.

"Now I see why you tied the tablecloth to your hands," he shouted. "I will hold you down, Mila. Let the Lu battle both of us."

She laughed into the screaming of the wind. Strands of her hair came free from the plait and lashed across her face. Sam, with a serious cast to his face, put a hand behind her head to undo her plait. It took him a while to do this; first he had to untie the green ribbon that held the bottom of the plait together, and then dig his fingers into each strand, pulling one and then the other loose. Until in the end, the black shawl of Mila's hair hurled out from her head in all directions.

"I must look like a ghost," she cried.

"You look beautiful," Sam said. He wrapped the sheet around them more tightly now, until they were in a little island of calm, the wind buffeting the outside, lifting the edges of the cloth, trying to sneak in. The light in their makeshift tent had a curious, transparent quality, as though they could run their fingers through it and it would sift through their skins and vanish into the distance. And in this red, glowing luminosity Mila saw

Sam more clearly than she had before. She was at once fraught with fear and exhilaration and a desperation to feel Sam's skin beneath her fingers. She touched his face lightly and the pads on her fingertips scrubbed against the day's growth of beard on his chin and his cheeks. She traced the arch of his eyebrows, thick and lush above his intense blue gaze that she would not meet. Sam leaned in and kissed her.

Mila had been kissed before, not many times, but enough to know what it was supposed to feel like. There was the touch of lips upon lips, the scent of the other person, the slick feel of their teeth. With Sam, there were none of these specifics. He opened her mouth to devour her, there could be no other word for such passionate action, and she accepted, feeling her heart fly out of her chest and settle somewhere within Sam. He lay back against the wall and pulled her onto him. For the next two hours, the storm raged and ebbed around them, hurling itself against Chetak's tomb, lifting its red veils to reveal flashes of false lightning streaking across a preternaturally darkened sky, hurling handfuls of red dirt over their exposed boots and legs. Mila and Sam did not notice any of this. They kissed, they drew back to gaze upon each other, they drowned in each other. Although they were both trembling with need, Sam knew that Mila was holding herself back from him, and he refused to take only part of her. He wanted everything. They talked after a while, their voices clear to each other above the indignant yowls of the wind demanding attention.

Sam told Mila of his mother, and father, of Mike, though he still did not tell her why he was here, and that was only to protect her from him or any consequences of what he was about to do. Sam told her stories from his childhood, told her of the snows of Mount Rainier capturing the last golden light of summer evenings, of dripping rain forests upon the western coast where the trees were clad in mosses of every conceivable green. Here we have browns, Mila said, the browns of the earth. Every conceivable brown. What do so many greens look like, Sam? He tried to explain them to her—the green of grasshoppers, newly born pine needles, glistening rhododendron leaves, pond water.

Mila talked then, in her turn, of her mother, Lakshmi, whom she had barely known, of Lady Pankhurst's "at homes" and Sam's fortuitous escape from her, of her father whom she loved more dearly than any other man. At this she hesitated. Mila was also keeping one most important secret from Sam, something she hoped he would never have the opportunity to learn before he returned to Assam. Even that thought was instinctive, for she had deliberately shut out the world, reveling in this flood of happiness. What tomorrow would bring, no, even how the next few hours of reflection would shape her actions, she did not know or care about. Everything was in this moment. Guilt could wait.

The storm eventually died down, and caught in their little oasis under the red tablecloth, Mila and Sam did not notice its demise. For Sam had begun to kiss Mila again, and through the fog of their want, they finally heard the servants shouting to ask if they were safe. They emerged covered with infinitesimal particles of red dust, so minute that they had crept in through the very weave of the tablecloth to coat their eyelashes, their hair, and to turn Mila's brilliantly white shirt into a shade of pink. Ashok and Vimal came running up to them, Vimal still carrying the enormous varan as though it were a baby, its massive head leaning against one shoulder.

Sam met Mila's eyes and he smiled only for her. He made a movement to put out his hand and to ask for hers, but she shook her head imperceptibly. A misery began to grow within her until her whole chest hurt.

# Nineteen

*No farmer ever existed who does not grumble sometimes. . . . As their own*
*proverb puts it, "He was given a bundle, and he asked for a mule, after*
*that for a man to lead it, for another to put the bundle on the mule's back,*
*and then for a third man to take it off."*

— Lady Wilson, *Letters from India,* 1911

Raman, Sayyid, and the old villager had arrived at Nodi at ten o'clock
in the morning after riding for eight hours into the scrub of the
desert. Or rather, Raman and Sayyid rode their horses; the old villager
had pleaded instability and dizziness and dismounted from his donkey to
walk the rest of the way. Raman and Sayyid slowed to a steady trot and
listened as they rode to the clip-clop of their horses' shoes and the accom-
panying flap-flap of the villager's thick-soled feet. Two miles from Nodi,
they had come upon a little boy asleep under the shade of a *dhokara* tree,
his herd of two scrawny cows chewing away at the lower foliage. He woke
up and a laugh burst out of him when he saw them, so full was he of happiness at the presence of the *burra* sahib, the big sahib. The boy ran
screaming toward Nodi, shouting that Raman was here, that the old villager had made good his word and brought the *burra* sahib to their village.
His cows he left foraging around the *dhokara*—they would eventually rest
under the shade of the tree and wait for him to return to lead them home.
For a long while, almost a mile, Raman could see the tiny figure of the boy
as he raced through the deflated land of the desert, and even hear his jubi-
lant wailing as it cut through the sheer air.

It was a reception he had missed in the years he had spent as Jai's advisor. Jai, though always happy to see Raman—sometimes he would be petulant but always polite—had never been *this* ecstatic. The entire trip so far had been glorious, Raman thought. Riding through the cool of the early morning, the servants' footsteps in accompaniment, their lanterns held untiringly aloft to light the way and to warn of snakes and scorpions. The stop for breakfast in the shadow of a tomb, crumbling and in ruins. No one knew whose tomb that was, who lay there in eternal rest, and travelers did not care, for the structure provided shade and coolness from the midday heat and a partial shelter at night for those who dared to sleep where ghosts walked. It was a tiny building, the inside walls blackened with smoke from a hundred breakfast, lunch, and dinner fires, and to this soot Sayyid added his own, cracking open eggs for a savory egg toast— thick slices of bread doused with whipped eggs, garlic, coriander leaves, and chili powder and fried on a pan. Sayyid then cut green mangoes for a sour chutney on the toast. This last was Raman's private affectation, when the mangoes lay heavy and green on the branches of the trees, sap smearing their sides, he ate his egg toast with mango chutney. Sayyid also served Raman with his hot cups of coffee and wedges of golden muskmelon to finish the meal. For the next two hours, Raman rode in aimless musings, a smile painting his face without his knowledge.

At sunrise the thick earth of the Sukh desert turned from indigo to gold. In two hours, the heat became almost unbearable, but Raman affixed a *sola topi* upon his head and sweated his way in the saddle, relishing the waves of heat from the ground upon his face, and the tiredness that had begun to creep into his limbs.

Half a mile out from the village, what seemed to be the *entire* village had turned out to meet him. Some of the men had garlands in their hands, made from knitted mango leaves, and these they insisted on putting around Raman's neck even before he dismounted from Sans Reproche. His neck and chest grew heavy with the weight of the good wishes and blessings upon him. They led him to the main village square, which was no more than a brick platform built around the burly and growing roots of a banyan tree. The main shops were arranged around the tree—a green-grocer with withered vegetables baking in the heat, a dry-goods merchant with small mounds of multicolored lentils and pulses, a blacksmith with his smithy fire and cinder-blackened face, a cloth merchant with a few cheap voile saris hung under a jute awning. Nodi was a poor village, like too many villages in India. He saw a few of the women glance at him shyly from under their *ghoonghats*, the veils only pulled over their heads to their noses, saw that a few more had their hands folded in supplication, and that yet others had tears in their eyes. They kept wiping the tears, more fell in their place, and Raman felt an ache flood his heart.

It must have been too long since any administrator had been here at Nodi to listen to their complaints, seek out their wants, pacify their needs. Colonel Pankhurst and Raman's primary duties were to Jai. In other parts of the British Raj, the villages would come under the jurisdiction of the Indian Civil Service. In Rudrakot, because it was a princely state and the ICS had no authority here, Jai was in charge of the land and the people, collecting agriculture taxes, putting that money to good use. Raman now saw that they had all been lax in their duties. He had held Jai's hand for so long, mentored him into adulthood, taught him right from wrong as much as he knew himself and as much as he could that he had forgotten the common people in the kingdom of Rudrakot. It took him only a few minutes into one such visit to realize all of their folly.

Raman sat down in the shade of the banyan, in the *best* shade of the banyan, for its leaves were sparse in some areas, and as the sun shifted to pierce through the tree's canopy, the villagers insisted that Raman move from one spot to the other so that he could be the coolest of them all. He listened to the men speak for hours about the vagaries of the monsoon rains, the failing of crops, the lack of water, the fights over land rights, whose cattle strayed and foraged in whose land, and so on. Some of the women talked of squabbles from their front doorsteps where they spent the afternoons knitting for the cooler, winter desert nights, and soon Raman found a pattern among them all. If their husbands were engaged in a spat, inevitably the women found something spiteful and petty to say about each other. *Her voice is too loud. She brays like a donkey. She has teeth like a horse.* To each complaint, Raman sat and listened with patience. He kept his place under the banyan tree all morning and afternoon long, eating his lunch and drinking his afternoon *chai* right there in front of hundreds of eyes.

Finally, the old villager, who had been attending to Raman's every word, scuttled over on his haunches as close as he could get to Raman's knees and coughed to attract his attention. Then Raman spoke to the villagers in his gentle voice about the possibility that they must all face, that there might not be a monsoon this year, no matter how much they prayed or propitiated their Gods. That the well this villager had built had sweet and clean water inside it, that its vicinity was to be kept pristine if the water was to maintain its freshness. That to sully the land around it, to defecate and shit there would mean taking away the only source of pure water for all of Nodi. That even if the nights were immeasurably hot—and they were hot now and were going to continue to be—the villagers must show resilience and strength and not seek the temporary coolness of the well's saucer-shaped brickwork.

Because Raman had stayed under the banyan tree, listened to them speak, showed a concern and consideration they had not had from any other administrator, his words were taken as gospel. The villagers nodded their heads respectfully, made promises to do exactly as Raman said, and even told him the words he was always thrilled to hear at the end of one of these village sessions. *Aap hamare Ma-Baap ho, Sahib.* You are our mother and you are our father.

The Lu came roaring out of the desert and exploded around them a minute later, just as Raman was wiping a surreptitious tear from the corner of his eye, using a cloth towel to ostensibly mop his face of sweat. The villagers and Raman had all been somewhat mesmerized by each other and no one had noticed that the atmosphere had become laden with the stillness that heralded the coming of the Lu. And no one had remembered that the Lu was always prophesied around the time of *purnima*, the full moon, which was tomorrow.

As the wind snarled and clamored around them, they all ran, shouting with laughter at themselves that they could have been so ignorant of its approach. Sayyid brought a towel to wrap around his master's head, and they both wrestled with the piece of cloth, Raman screaming that Sayyid should take cover himself, Sayyid shouting back that he would be where Raman was. After the villagers had taken their very old and their very young away and tucked them under the shelter of *charpais* and huts, two young men came running across the village square with torn and ragged blankets and offered them to Raman and Sayyid.

"Come to our house, Sahib," one man said above the bawling of the wind.

"We are all right here," Raman replied, "Go, take cover yourself. Are our horses safe?"

"Yes," a man said, "we led them to the mango grove behind the village; they will be safe enough there."

Raman and Sayyid stayed crouched under the banyan tree, the wind whipping up red dirt in swirls and eddies as they each huddled in the relative comfort of their blankets. The dust flew in to sting Raman's legs and his stomach through the rents in the blanket, but he was thankful for the little protection it provided. Every now and then, he put out a hand blindly to feel for Sayyid's shoulder and to make sure that he was still near him. And so he rode out the storm. Conversation was not possible, so, ensconced within the tough roots of the many-armed banyan tree, Raman allowed a lassitude to overcome his body and immersed himself in his thoughts.

Sayyid had shown him Mila's note at breakfast that morning, and Raman had read it briefly and put it away, more because he could do nothing about it, could not turn back to Rudrakot, and did not really want to either. He was a little discomfited by the tone, what was it . . . she had not been disrespectful, Mila would never be that, *could* never be that. But she had always before, in all of her conversations with him, made her desires seem like requests. Not this time. *Dearest Papa,* she had written, *Captain Hawthorne has expressed a wish to visit Chetak's tomb, and I will take him there tomorrow. Ashok comes with us and I wanted to let you know of our plans in case we leave before you waken in the morning.*

Shutting his ears to the blast of the wind, Raman admonished himself not to be too fanciful and too imaginative, just as Mila always was. She could create stories out of little beginnings, and give them legs, torsos, heads, ears, eyes, and noses to make them complete. She must have been tired last night, and yes, there was something different in the way she had written that note, but it was nothing, surely it was nothing? Then, because he had little else to do, thoughts about the suitability of Mila's going away on such a pleasure visit with a man they knew so little about came to Raman. Normally, busy as he was with a hundred myriad troubles during the day, he would give very little credence to such proprieties. But he had nothing to do during the dust storm. He was physically exhausted from what had already been a long day for him, and the queries and complaints of the villagers had mentally taken his strength too, but Mila, Ashok, and Kiran were still never far from his mind. Ashok was with her; if only Sayyid could have been too, Raman thought. He reached out to pat

Sayyid's shoulder again, and felt a reassuring press of fingers upon his hand in return. Sayyid was the very soul of goodness and decorum—his presence would have stilled all gossiping tongues if they had even thought of wagging in that direction. Sayyid should have gone with Mila.

But he was being unnecessarily stupid here, Raman thought. For he had liked Sam Hawthorne, immensely, more in the short time he had known him than any other man. And Raman was used to being confident in his ability to judge men's characters upon first acquaintance; it was one of his best and most finely honed skills. Sam Hawthorne would be properly solicitous of his Mila. Raman sighed. It was not Sam Hawthorne he was worried about, it was the ladies at the Victoria Club. Well, at least they would return later this evening, and safely, and even as he thought this, the wind flattened him against the banyan's roots and knocked his head against the bark. Raman pulled the smelly blanket closer about his face with a sense of dread. The storm would have reached them too, and if it lasted any longer . . . Mila, Ashok, and Sam would have to stay the night at Chetak's tomb.

"Sayyid," he said.

He heard Sayyid reply, his voice muffled by the roar of the wind and the blanket over his mouth, "*Ji*, Sahib, I know. But they will be safe for the night, at least that."

"Did you send the telegraph?" Raman asked, bending close to Sayyid's ear.

Sayyid nodded and Raman sat back again. It was curious that Captain Hawthorne was an officer in a regiment called the Third Burma Rangers, more curious that the Americans had already formed, trained, and sent out an entire regiment to help in the retaking of Burma. Why, Burma had just fallen. Were the Third Burma Rangers a regular army unit or . . . what else? Who was this Sam Hawthorne? Why had he come to Rudrakot? The telegraph he had sent to Calcutta last night would answer some of these questions for him.

# Twenty

*T*hey departed when the moon had just begun to ascend, cutting a newly hewn gold arc into the horizon. When it finally rose, perfectly round and enormous, it would take on a honeyed cast, like a harvest moon.

Sam stepped down the stairs from Chetak's tomb and into, literally, another world. For the next few minutes, his breath stilled as the glorious silver-blue brilliance of a million stars percolated into the air around him. There was so much light that the desert was better illuminated at night than it had been at midday. When the sun was out, its rays had seared Sam's retina, almost blinding him; now there was a clear and cool ultramarine light that bled right into his skin. His fingernails were shadowed half-moons, the lines on his palms, normally brushed lightly, stood out indigo black, and Vimal's eyes glowed with a fire. Sam could see for what seemed to be miles to the extremity of the earth, with no obstructions or fuzziness in the images imprinting themselves into his brain. The field punishment center was discernible in every detail, the empty guard towers, the mammoth walls, the closed gate. For just a moment, Sam hesitated as he stood there. If he could see so far, and so lucidly, they could see him too.

"Tonight is the night Chetak rides out, Captain Hawthorne," Vimal said softly.

And that meant no one would dare to linger outside for fear of seeing the horse. "Let's go," Sam said. And they set out.

The desert air was fresh, cooled and scoured of the day's heat. It had even cooled enough in the last two hours to necessitate a fire in Chetak's tomb as they ate the last of the provisions the servants had brought for their dinner. Cold grated-egg sandwiches with pepper and salt, thick slices of cucumbers, tomato juice or warm Bloody Marys (their ice had long since melted and puddled into the sawdust in the ice coolers), coffee and tea, and a platter filled with Indian sweets—coconut *burfis,* sweet *samosas* stuffed with jaggery and lentils, *mysorepak,* a chickpea-flour bite-size cake.

"*This* is our dinner?" Sam had asked, incredulous; he had expected much less when Mila had sent Ashok to warn him that they might not have enough to eat since they had not come prepared to spend the night.

"Sorry it's so little," Mila replied. "This was to be for our tea, and Sayyid would not have expected us to have to stretch it for dinner."

The sweets were almost too sweet, and Sam felt a rim of sugar still coating his tongue as he walked beside Vimal. There were no sounds in the empty desert night. Nothing but the rhythmic flap of their shoes upon the hard dirt, Vimal's feet dragging more than Sam's as he struggled with the weight of the giant varan he had strapped across his back like a rucksack. The varan slumbered, undisturbed by the jolting ride it was being given. Its head lolled this way and that, slapping against Vimal's neck.

"Why do we need that thing?" Sam asked in disgust. "Couldn't you leave it back at the tomb? Ashok would have looked after it for you."

"Oh no," Vimal said, reaching around to pat the varan's back and to stroke its long tail. "We need him." He glanced at Sam with a lambent smile, his teeth ultrawhite in the light from the stars. "You'll see." He looked ahead of them. "It's not very far, Captain Hawthorne, and here in the desert, sound travels vast distances. We must no longer talk and must keep our noise to a minimum."

Sam nodded and paused for a minute, allowing Vimal to trudge ahead. He turned to look back at Chetak's tomb, black and gloomy in the starlight. They had already come enough of a distance that Sam could no longer see the orange glow of the fire left burning on one end of the verandah. At the other end, Mila had given instructions to the servants to make up beds for them with the tarpaulins they had brought. She lay down next to Ashok, her hand linked through his. Vimal was to be across the stone floor at the other end of the wall and Sam could sleep anywhere he wanted. Sam and Vimal had waited for Mila and Ashok to fall asleep and, even thus, she would not let go of Ashok's hand. She did not like Vimal, Sam had thought again, watching her through the cigarette smoke. He had not lain down or even rested, merely sat against a wall and looked at her, smoking one cigarette after another.

Night had come rushing in on them even as the mighty Lu wind had died and departed. At one moment, there had been the murk of the storm, at the other the gloom of night, and so returning to Rudrakot was out of the question. It would have been madness to seek out a path in the dust storm, and even greater lunacy to attempt to capture that thin, metallic ribbon of road in the night. With everyone else around, Mila had retreated from Sam. She would no longer even look at him; when she talked, it was with a stilted affectation, as though she was being a little too polite to a stranger. Sam, his nerves still throbbing from the encounter under the red tablecloth, had been bewildered at first, had sought her out only to be rebuffed, and had finally become angry. What had he, they, done wrong? Ashok and Vimal chattered all through dinner. Mila ate little and once asked Sam for a cigarette. She put out a hand to steady the lighter as he held the flame for her and then flushed at the contact of their skins. Why? Sam wanted to ask, exhilarated.

She had stared at Vimal, at his overfamiliar gestures toward Ashok, the touch on the shoulder, the rubbing of his forearm. Ashok's eyes glittered; he was in the throes of some excitement and was jittery. At various times during the day, Ashok had accosted Sam and asked him for a cigarette, and he did so again after dinner. Then Mila and Ashok began a spat. She harangued him for his smoking; Ashok was astounded at first, saying that she *knew* he smoked, she even stole the odd cigarette from him every now and then. Come off it, Mila. She would not listen and insisted that he put out the cigarette right away or she would tell Papa. Now. Ashok's lower lip began to tremble, and soon Mila too was in tears and they both ended up bawling in each other's arms. Sam had stared at them, bemused. Why all the fighting? Why would she not look at him? Why was she so distraught?

Only Vimal was unaffected. At the first signs of the quarrel, he had risen, taken himself to the other end of the tomb, and only returned to hear Mila giving orders to the servants about the sleeping arrangements. Ashok and Mila lay down almost immediately and held hands, the ankles of their opposing feet looped around each other. At one point, well after Sam had thought her asleep, Mila had turned to her side, toward him, her face cushioned under her left hand. She opened her eyes and looked at Sam for a long time, as though she was memorizing the features of his face. Neither of them spoke, and this was what Sam remembered the most—the lingering scrutiny from Mila, filled with an intensity, a yearning, even a *want,* and behind it all an aching sadness. Why? Sam wanted to ask, but he had been too mesmerized by the flicker of the fire's gold over her smooth cheek, the length of iridescent hair along her chin. The linen of her pants was stretched tight over the bow shape of her hips. She had taken off her boots and her feet were long and narrow, her toenails painted with a clear varnish. Her hair flowed behind her. Sam's hands hankered for a touch of that hair, of that skin, but he did not make a move. His gaze kept returning to hers and he tried to seek out what she would not tell him in words. Finally, Mila slept.

Sam reached Vimal easily, even without lengthening his stride, and saw that the boy had begun to slow his steps to a crawl.

"I'll carry that monster on your back," he said in a whisper.

Vimal nodded gratefully and unslung the vapid varan from his back and helped Sam tie him on. The varan's skin was cold and a little slippery, and its feet and hands came to clench at Sam's shoulders and back with a surprisingly puissant hold. Sam almost shouted from that sudden pain and Vimal quickly peeled the varan's fingers from Sam. He spoke to the animal softly, his voice breaking into song, and the animal quietened. It relaxed and laid its head against Sam's neck.

"You experienced his hold on you, Captain Hawthorne," Vimal said as they moved on. "That is why we need him."

They reached the outside of the field punishment center thirty minutes later. The sandstone walls loomed before them whittled and chiseled into a smoothness by twelve years of ferocious Lus. It looked as though the building had been there for centuries, embedded in the ground, beaten into the earth by the sun and the winds, glossed to a shine by the stars in the sky. Sam put his hand on the stone. It bore some traces of roughness, of nicks and slips from the stonemason's chisel, but the mortar used to bind the stones together was thin and hardened to a shiny patina. There were no footholds on these walls; it was an effective prison. Even if it had not been birthed in the middle of nowhere, in the middle of a desert, miles from any vestiges of civilization, the field punishment center would have been a formidable fortress.

Sam put his ear to the stone and coolness seeped into his skin.

"They all sleep," Vimal said. He glanced up at the moon, which had risen to a quarter of the sky and was now the gleaming white of seashells. "Twelve o'clock. The witching hour in your literature, Captain Hawthorne. In our legends, the ghost of a horse will walk now."

A fissure of uncertainty crept up Sam's spine. He looked back over the sand and dirt to the stout outline of Chetak's tomb. "Will they be all right?" he asked, his voice rife with worry.

Vimal laughed. "So you believe me now, do you?"

Sam rubbed his hand over the stones on the wall that went up twenty feet into the sky. "There is no way up. We will have to get in through the gate somehow."

"Wait," Vimal said. He untied the varan and pulled it from Sam's back to set it on the ground. Sam massaged his neck and reached down to peel his shirt from his skin where it was glued with sweat. A rank odor of fish and rotting offal pervaded the space around him. The varan was not particular about its personal hygiene, or it had emptied its bowels upon his back as he had carried it. He cringed at the thought, but did not even bother to shrug his wet and stinking shirt from his back, so spellbound was he by Vimal's actions. The boy unwound the length of rope he had carried looped around his arm and fashioned a halter on one end. He slipped this halter over the varan's neck and threaded its short arms through. The other end of the rope he coiled loosely and flung on the ground. Vimal hefted the varan into his arms and laid his head close to the gigantic head of the lizard. He crooned to it, sang to it in Hindustani, called it "darling." The animal began to shift its fluid neck, its tongue slicking out into the air.

"He will get you up the walls, Captain Hawthorne," Vimal said, his eyes luminous. His face was drenched with sweat, the stench emanating from him matched the one from Sam, his hair stuck to his head in unruly curls, and yet Vimal possessed an undeniable beauty. The giant lizard licked at his arms with its thin, liquid tongue.

"How?" Sam asked, enthralled by the sight of the varan twisting its weight in Vimal's arms.

In response, Vimal bent low to the ground with his knees and heaved the lizard on the wall. It slammed against the stone, moved its arms and legs about and slid down the wall into a flaccid heap.

"It is too heavy to carry its own weight," Sam whispered.

"No." Vimal picked up the varan again and threw it upon the wall, and again it slipped down. "You try, Captain Hawthorne," Vimal said, "I am not able to throw him high enough; he's too big for me."

With a thudding heart, Sam bent to pick up the animal and cradled it in his arms. On the second try, it had flailed about as though it finally knew what was expected of it. Could it really scale these walls? They were immense and so sheer. No human could climb them, surely. What harm was there in trying? Sam only hoped they were not making too much of a ruckus on the outside walls but did not realize that the walls were five feet deep all around the perimeter of the field punishment center; a cannon blast would, perhaps, wake the inmates and the sentries, nothing less than that.

He slid one hand under the varan's neck and the other under the root of its enormous tail and stepped back a few paces from the wall. The animal began to squeal, its throat undulating unpleasantly under Sam's hand, and before it could protest anymore, Sam leaned back and threw it as hard as he could against the wall. His shoulder screamed with pain and he waited, panting from the effort. The varan scrambled fervently as it hit the wall, slid down a few yards, and then its tail snaked out to catch a slender gap in the mortar and simultaneously its fingers and toes burrowed into the stone. It started to climb.

Sam and Vimal stood on the ground, their mouths open with wonder at the speed with which the black figure of the varan moved up the wall. The rope began to unravel on the ground. Vimal bent to pick up the other end and loop it around his wrist.

"You must follow him quickly, Captain Hawthorne," he said. "When you get to the top, reel him in. He will stay where you leave him; when you return you can climb down the rope again."

Sam flexed his hands and clasped them around the fast-slithering jute rope. As he started to climb, entrusting most of his weight to his left arm, he looked down at Vimal, who stood with a faint smile on his handsome face. "Will he hold me, Vimal?"

"I don't know. I have only read of a great hero in Indian history who did this once to scale the walls of a fort, but I've never tried it before myself." The boy chuckled. "Good luck, Captain Hawthorne."

The top of the wall was built similarly to a fort's rampart, with a slender pathway from one end to the other, leading to the guard towers and to four sets of steep stairs down to the ground. Sam crawled on his belly along the path until he found the varan half-dangling over the other edge of the rampart, its breathing harsh and uneven. It shuddered when he touched it and then turned its huge head to run its tongue over his hand and his face. He dragged the lizard to the place where he had ascended the wall, moving laboriously on his knees so that his figure would not be outlined against the starry sky to anyone looking up from below. At the wall, he put his head over the rampart cautiously, and thought he saw the murky white of Vimal's *kurta* and pajamas against the impenetrable black of the earth. But he was too far away and Sam had climbed a very high wall.

Sam unbuttoned his holster and took out his Colt. Patting the varan once to reassure it, he crouched down on his knees again and crept to the staircase along this wall. The moon was still low in the sky behind him and its light along the far side threw this set of stairs in shadow. Still, Sam did not dare to stand as he went down. He found himself in a deserted square courtyard. On every wall were tiny cells fronted by iron bars that gleamed dully in the starlight. A well covered with wooden planks dominated the center of the yard. There were no trees, nowhere to take shelter from the sun, no verandahs even. There was also no sign at all of human presence. If there were men in the cells, they slept, drugged or tired. No snores cleaved through the still air. The inside of the lone gate leading into this prison was unguarded, as were the guard towers.

The fetid odor though was a living presence. It seemed to permeate the air, clot it, and hang over the chunk of sky over the field punishment center. It was the smell of unwashed human bodies, the stink of excrement, and the acrid tang of cigarette butts.

Sam stifled a cough, leaned back into the shadow, and waited, the Colt held ready. His own breathing slowed until he could barely hear it, and finally he could no longer smell anything, his nose charred and deadened to the stink. A faint roar swept over the field punishment center and goose bumps ran up his back. What was that? The roar came again, bigger now, the sound cutting over the flat earth and meeting the walls of the prison. A tiger, Sam thought. There was a tiger on the prowl outside. As he began to move, a door was pitched open to the right of the gate and a rectangle of light threw itself upon the dirt in front of the doorway.

"Damn lions!" a man shouted from the inside. His figure appeared in the opening, framed by the kerosene lantern's glow, and he stood there with his legs apart and his hands placed on his hips. He was wearing shorts and no shirt and was barefoot.

"Come back inside, you old mutt," another man drawled. "You are begging for a bloody krait to bite you in the bum."

The first man reached inside the doorway and pulled something out. He threw it against the far wall a few feet from where Sam stood. The beer bottle crashed on the stone and split into a hundred tiny pieces, and one of the glass shards nicked Sam in the arm. But he did not move, his pistol still held steadily at the man's figure. He knew he could not be seen in the shadow, that the white light of the moon probably blinded the man, but he had sensed Sam's presence somehow. The guard still lingered in the doorway, and then, with one last, hard look at the staircase near Sam, he backed into the room and slammed the door shut.

All at once, a series of moans rose to rend the air around Sam. The noises came from everywhere. There were groans of pain, the scratching of uncut nails along the sandstone floors of the cells, the thumping of feet against the walls, yelps that sounded unreal, inhuman.

The guard threw his door open and stepped out, a rifle in his hand. He had pulled on his boots by now, the laces untied. Striding out to the center of the yard, he aimed the rifle into the sky and pulled the trigger. The sound of the shot exploded in the courtyard and ricocheted from one wall to another, its last echoes taking a painfully long time to die away. Sam's ears rang. He pushed his shoulders into the wall behind him, but did not take his eyes away from the guard, who was shouting now. "Shut up, shut up, shut up, or one of you bastards is going to take the next bullet. Get it?"

The moans died into silence. The guard remained where he was for a while and then went back into the room and shut the door.

Sam began to shake. Mike was here. He *knew* Mike was here. He could feel it, he could smell him, he could sense his presence. His gaze began to whiten with anger when he realized that this was how Mike had lived for the last two months, since he had supposedly gone AWOL. That no one had attempted to find him, that everyone had taken him for dead. That bloody Sims had somehow used Mike's involvement in the bombing of the British woman as an excuse to send him to this piece of hell. But how did that bastard possess so much influence?

He stepped out into the starlight, keeping the guard's room in the corner of his eye, and walked along the string of cells, peering inside with the help of his torchlight. He kept the beam masked under the fingers of his left hand, in his right he held the Colt. The men inside the cells were shadows of their true selves, some so close to death that they merely lifted their heads to whimper as Sam passed, like beaten dogs. Sam began to whistle, softly, so that only the man he was passing could hear him.

> *I really can't stay—Baby, it's cold outside*
> *I've got to go away—Baby, it's cold outside*
> *The evening has been—*

"Sam?" a feeble voice said, so faintly that he almost did not hear it. Sam retraced his steps unhurriedly, his heart banging in his chest, and went back a few paces until he came upon the emaciated figure of a man stretched out on the floor of the cell, his head shoved against the bars. The man's fingers reached out beyond the bars, clawing at the air. Sam placed the cloaked glow of his torchlight against the man's face, lighting his features one by one. The man's eyes blinked even in that dull light, one of his eyebrows had been singed from his skin, his hair was muddy and dusty, his cheekbones jutted out. Sam switched off the torchlight and bent to kiss Mike's rancid fingers. The third finger of his right hand was broken, bent at an unnatural angle, and Sam cradled this hand gently even though he knew that the break was an old one, that Mike felt no pain there anymore.

"I'm here," he said softly.

"Sam," Mike said and he put his matted, lice-ridden head on the floor. "This is a dream." His voice rose to a wail at the end of the sentence, and Sam put a hand on his neck to quiet him, feeling the scabs and rashes that had bloomed on his skin.

A quiet descended around Sam. He could see a few hands protruding beyond the bars in other men's cells, could hear their labored breathing and also hear breaths being held as the men tried to listen in on their conversation. But no one made a sound to call out to, or attract the attention of, the guards. They must all want a chance at freedom, Sam thought, but not enough to destroy the opportunities of another man?

"I have to go now, Mike," he said. "I will be back in a day or two."

Mike did not respond, and then finally he lifted his head and a streak of tears cut through the grime on his face and sank into his beard. "This is a dream," he said again.

"No, not a dream anymore, Mike. Mom sent me to find you." Tears choked Sam's throat and he thought that his heart would be eviscerated.

"Mom," Mike said. "Mom."

Sam bent and kissed his brother's hand again. "Soon," he said and rose to run across the courtyard to the stairs that led up the wall. At the top, he tugged on the rope three times and when Vimal answered with a tug of his own, Sam slid down the wall, arriving at the bottom with a thud. When he had reached the ground, Vimal began to sing his curious song in a low voice and, after a minute, the varan hurled itself down the smooth wall of the field punishment center and came to a rest, panting with devotion, at the young man's feet.

As they walked back, Vimal did not glance at Sam or ask him what he had seen inside the center, or what he was going to do about it. Overwhelmed by his brief encounter with Mike, at the burnt umber of his brother's skin and the crooked finger on his right hand, Sam could not talk. He rubbed his chest as he trudged ahead of Vimal, hoping to ease the pain. Sam could not even cry, for anger and hatred had come to lodge within him. Then came many minutes of clarity and a sense of calmness. When they neared Chetak's tomb, he stopped and waited for Vimal to catch up with him, and watched dispassionately as he struggled under the complacent weight of the varan.

"Can you get me a couple of horses, Vimal?"

"When?"

"Tomorrow . . . no make it the day after."

"Just that, Captain Hawthorne?"

"Yes." Sam turned to stride away again toward the tomb. Vimal made a little noise like a muffled cough and Sam stopped, still facing away from the young man.

"You must remember your part of the bargain, Captain Hawthorne."

May 30, 1942

*Rudrakot, India*

# Twenty-one

*. . . you captured my fancy, and since*
*That hypnotic moment I felt like a*
*Prisoner dragging his shackles and*
*Impelled into an unknown place . . .*
*I became intoxicated with your sweet*
*Wine that has stolen my will, and I*
*Now find my lips kissing the hand*
*That strikes me sharply. Can you*
*Not see with your soul's eye the*
*Crushing of my heart?*

—Khalil Gibran, *The Enchanting Houri*

*T*hey left for Rudrakot ten minutes before sunrise, when the sky was a pale lilac along the edges of the horizon and they could see little beyond their outstretched hands.

They had all woken when the night was still dying and the fire in the verandah had burned out. Sam lay in his corner in a swirl of coldness, blinking and rubbing his eyes, wondering if the night had passed as he now remembered it. A few hours ago Vimal had released his varan in the desert, but it had found its way to him in the darkness, led by the scent of his skin, and slept again by his side. Once Mila and Ashok had woken, their hands still clasped, their ankles still touching, they had wanted that very instant to go home.

It took them less than an hour to rouse the servants, pack their belong-
ings into the jeep, and drive out into the gloom, toward Rudrakot. As they
fumbled and bumped their way over the rocks and the dirt, the night train
passed by in the distance, its clean, hooting whistle blasting across to
them. Was it only one day, no, two days ago that he had taken that train
into the kingdom? Sam thought. How much had happened since; the days
had stretched into an eternity.

Then in two hours, when the sun was blazingly hot, the first jeep collapsed on the road, spewing puffs of steam in all directions. Thirty minutes later, the second jeep overheated.

They limped into Rudrakot a little past noon, tired, irritable, and hungry. As Sam turned the jeep into the half-moon driveway of Raman's
house, Mila put a hand on his arm and said, "Do stop here, Captain
Hawthorne. Vimal will get out now." Then she turned to him and said,
"We've enjoyed your company. Quite enough. Thank you."

Vimal sighed theatrically, swung his legs over the side of the jeep, and
jumped down. "I'm sure I'll see you all again. And you too, Captain
Hawthorne," he said, raising his hand in a mock salute, "why, we are now
old friends."

"Mila," Ashok said, and pointed to the front of their house.

A shining white Hispano-Suiza, the color of clotted cream, with
gleaming bumpers and polished window glasses stood near the front
door. It had a long and sleek running board clothed in black rubber, con-
trasting with the spokes on its white-walled tires, aglitter like silver. Sam
leaned around the dusty windshield of the jeep and his breath stilled when
he saw the car. It was a masterpiece of luxury, with persimmon-colored
leather seats and a lengthy front bonnet under which, surely, reposed a
V-12 engine. Its top speed would be a hundred miles per hour and it would
take a mere twelve seconds, a flicker of an eyelid, to reach sixty from a
state of rest. You could drive those speeds in the desert, Sam thought, especially on the flat road that led to Chetak's tomb. Sam had only seen pictures of this car before and he was astounded by how gorgeous it actually
was. A man leaned against the Suiza's front hood, his legs crossed at the
ankles, arms laced near his waist. He was holding a swagger stick—in
leather, knobbed in silver with the Lancers regimental badge carved on the
head—and had it tucked under his armpit. He was dressed in crisp white
to match the car; even his shirt buttons and his cufflinks were silver. His

turban was white, and its sash swung over his shoulder and down his back. He had a dark and strong face, a well-trimmed mustache, an arrogant chin. He made no move toward them.

"Jai!" Ashok screamed, jumped out of the jeep, and pounded down the driveway.

Mila got out more slowly, stood for a minute by the jeep, and then began to run too. A few feet away, her footsteps slowed and she turned to Sam, her face miserable, her eyes bright with a hint of tears. She continued to walk backward, her hands tucked into the back pockets of her trousers so that her elbows jutted out. It was, for all its bravado, a vulnerable stance. She had left her hair loose after Sam had undone her plait the previous afternoon, but had worn a pink silk scarf around it during the drive back. Now she reached up to her head and with a graceful gesture pulled the scarf from her hair, so that it fell in a sweep of ebony around her shoulders.

She said, with the steadiest gaze upon his face yet, "Sam." A pause. "I'm going to marry him."

April 1942, a Month Earlier

*Somewhere in Burma*

*W*here the hell is he going?" Sam hisses, raising his head.

Ken has lifted himself and is plodding down the slope with great deliberation toward the plantation bungalow.

Sam glances at his watch. One hour to sunset; they've been here for four hours now. It's too early, there's still too much light, and the rain has stopped. Dammit.

"Ken," he calls.

But Ken just keeps on going, slip-sliding down now, dragging his shattered foot behind him. Sam shakes Marianne awake, scrambles to his feet, and plunges after Ken.

"Ken!" he calls again, in a voice that is little more than a whisper. He follows as fast as he can, ungainly and inept, his loaded haversack slowing him down. Ken is almost at the bottom of the hill by now. He begins to laugh and the sound fractures the silence around them. Sam slips off the straps of his haversack, flings it aside. If only he can get to Ken before anyone sees them or hears them. What an idiot he is, Sam thinks, tripping again and beginning to slide. His head bangs against a rock, but it does not slow his pace. He keeps falling, stars shattering before his eyes, until he comes to rest at Ken's feet.

"What?" Ken asks, grinning. "I want to get inside the damn bungalow, that's all."

Sam pushes himself up to stand on shaky legs. "You're going to get us all killed, you idiot."

"We've waited long enough, Sam. It's okay now."

From where he stands on the slope, Sam is below Ken, looking up at him. Ken sports a curiously self-satisfied expression. He seems to have forgotten his crushed ankle. Sam encounters that prickle of unease again, but his attention is distracted when the mud of the hillside loosens as Marianne picks her way down. The skin on her left cheek is patterned with the twigs and leaves that glued themselves to her face as she slept. She is disoriented, her eyes bleary with fatigue. She drags Sam's haversack behind her.

Ken starts to laugh, his teeth starkly white against the mud brown of his face.

"Shut up! Shut up! Shut up!" Sam shouts, and slaps Ken with an open palm.

In the sudden quiet that follows, they all hear the sound of a door creaking open on unoiled hinges. Sam turns toward the bungalow. Fear stops his heart for a brief second and then his training kicks into gear and his hand drops to the .45 Colt in his belt holster. The front door is ajar, a scrabbling noise comes from within, and the three of them stare at the opening, frozen where they stand.

There is a gentle clucking, and then, a skinny little face with a pointed beak looks out from behind the door. A hen comes out into the front yard of the bungalow, continues its cluckings and nibbles industriously at the ground.

Sam almost dies. There is a *hen* in the bungalow. A hen. A chicken! He drops his hand from the pistol. Saliva inundates his mouth. His stomach cries out and his hands tremble with wanting.

He begins to pant and knows that Marianne and Ken are also gazing at the busy little hen with the same rapt attention. They all begin to laugh and shout. Food for dinner. Not scavenged cold rice, not ferns or berries. A cooked chicken. A roasted chicken perhaps. A plantation house will have a kitchen garden. They can wrap the meat in plantain leaves, garnish it with coriander, some mint, chilies even, and bury it in coals. Perhaps a few cloves of garlic, pungent with aroma. Now Sam gets greedy. He hopes there will be some *ghee* in the kitchen, just a few tablespoons, just enough milk fat to rub onto the chicken, to roast it golden and crisp, to keep the meat moist and flaky. He still has ten tablets of salt in his haversack; they are to replenish what he loses in sweat, but powdered, crushed, they could still substitute for table salt. He can use three for the chicken just to take the edge off of bland and give it some taste. Oh, how is his stomach even going to adjust to this feast after all these days of near starving? Neither of their last two supply drops has come through, for each time they had made it to the meeting points, they had heard the drone of Japanese aircraft close by; it would have been madness for the RAF planes—or the ones from the AVG, the American Volunteer Group, of which Ken is a part—to come by with their food.

Sam, Marianne, and Ken wrap arms around each other, a triangle of hands on waists and shoulders, heads bent and touching at their tips, matted hair mingling. They rub cheeks. Their tears mingle with their laughter, curve around the widest parts of their mouths.

The sharp retort of a rifle fissures the air. Their voices still. Oh shit, Sam thinks, as his mind roves over his body—arms, shoulders, back, legs. There is a burning on his back, on his shins, but that is an old sensation, leech wounds not yet healed. His head is surely all right or his mind would have been blown away and could not travel over his limbs. He feels no pain. His grip tightens on Marianne and Ken, propping them up. He nudges their heads with his, hears no sound from them, no more laughter, not even a whimper. All of this happens in a few seconds and Sam feels a huge wash of relief. His fingers slacken. They are all right too. They still stand.

And then. Ken crumples to the ground.

# Twenty-two

*. . . an Indian woman strayed into the lines where we were barracked, and she got into very serious trouble. I don't know whether she'd come in by mistake or whether she was looking for business, but things must've got out of hand and she was passed from bed to bed and finished up as a dead body on the incinerator in the morning . . . There'd been about twenty-four to thirty fellows involved, probably a lot more than that . . . The thing was that she had come in of her own accord and that was the result . . .*

—Anton Gill, *Ruling Passions: Sex, Race and Empire,* 1995

*J*ai did not move even as Mila neared. Ashok flitted around him, almost too happy to see him. He shook his hand, patted his shoulder, and now, almost hung on his arm rife with questions—when had he returned, how was the ICC, how long had he been at the house. To all of which Jai gave, what seemed to Mila, noncommittal replies. His attention was all hers. She jogged down the driveway, and then, suddenly overcome with shyness, stopped fifteen feet away, her breath searing her lungs.

His mouth lifted at one corner and Jai brought his swagger stick forward to touch it to his turban in a salute.

"You remember the story," he said, with a fuller smile now that irradiated his face with charm.

She nodded, and still waited where she stood.

A few years ago, the maharaja of Kurvi had come on an official state visit to Rudrakot. He was an older man, with three grown daughters who were potential candidates as a second wife for Jai. Raman and Colonel Pankhurst had discussed the possibility of an alliance between Rudrakot and Kurvi for many months, ever since Kurvi's *diwan* had flung open hints about this at Raman's last visit to the hill station of Mussoorie, where they had all been members of the same club. It would have been a politically gainful union for Rudrakot for two reasons—Kurvi was a neighboring kingdom, with two-thirds of Rudrakot's boundaries abutting it; and it would finally mean the end of a sometimes torrid, sometimes indifferent war between the two princely states.

The origins of the disagreements came from a woman, naturally, and in the lands around Rudrakot, *all* disagreements stemmed from water, women, livestock, or land. What had happened was that about a hundred years ago, a daughter from the house of Kurvi had been given in marriage to a reigning Rudrakot king. She had only been a third wife, and had been so unfortunate as to have been born ugly—a fact the king had only realized upon lifting her veil within the seclusion of his bedchamber on the wedding night. The marriage remained unconsummated, and finally, the much-beleaguered wife admitted the shameful fact. Her husband had since taken another wife, a French woman, and had lustfully begat two half-caste children with her.

The king of Kurvi came roaring into Rudrakot to haul up his errant son-in-law and demand that his daughter be impregnated so that she could bear an heir for the kingdom. And Jai's ancestor had lazily said something that loosely translated into, "I'm sorry, old chap. No can do. She makes my skin crawl." It was an unfortunate set of phrases to speak to a father about his, admittedly, ungainly daughter. The Kurvi king spluttered and shouted, but he could not very well launch an all-out war because he had been well aware that his daughter was unprepossessing (and had hoped the Rudrakot king would manage somehow); and, the East India Company had offered the services of its armies to Rudrakot by then. That began a century-old official policy of the two kingdoms blackballing and ostracizing each other until finally, a few years ago, the current maharaja of Kurvi decided to offer one of his daughters to Jai to bring the feud to an end.

Jai did not intend to marry any of the Kurvi girls, but well aware of this history, he still demanded, and got, three photographs of each of them—one full length (to check for deformities), one seated, and one close up. Even though they were blessed with a minor amount of pulchritude, Jai had already decided against an alliance with Kurvi, for two years ago, when Mila was nineteen, he had fallen in love with her and could think of no other woman as his wife, not even the one he currently had.

Raman and Colonel Pankhurst were understandably thrilled by the offers of friendship from Kurvi, for management of the land around the boundaries between two warring kingdoms had been a difficult task for them and for Kurvi's political agent. They cajoled and pleaded with Jai to let the maharaja at least come for a visit, whether it led to a marriage or not—there was no sense in saying no this early in the negotiations. Jai agreed, with a great deal of reluctance.

Arrangements were made for the maharaja of Kurvi and his 150-strong entourage to be housed in the hunting lodge that Jai's foster father had built on the outskirts of the town of Rudrakot, four and a half miles from the fort and the palaces where Jai lived in his own stately splendor. The maharaja came by train, even though his kingdom and his palaces were only a day's ride on horseback and eight hours by car and jeep. The Kurvi maharaja wanted his own bogie, much like Jai's, shunted onto the Rudrakot train and wanted to travel in style, much as he had heard Jai did. He also wanted his bogie to rest in the train yard in Rudrakot, so that all the citizens could marvel at the green-and-gold embellishments and the pure brass fittings and bars of the carriage windows.

For four days after his arrival, Jai waited for the maharaja of Kurvi to pay a call upon him. He did not come. Raman and Colonel Pankhurst, in their official capacities as diplomats of the Indian government and of Rudrakot, went over to beg and beseech and importune with the maharaja, and finally realized that *he* was waiting for Jai to come and pay his respects to him. The hunting lodge in Rudrakot, *Jai's* hunting lodge, had become, temporarily, the maharaja's property and it was here Jai had to visit since he was younger and Rudrakot was a smaller kingdom than Kurvi. This went back and forth for another week, while Raman and Colonel Pankhurst began to grow weak with fatigue from all the running trips from the palaces to the hunting lodge and back. Finally, they all reached a compromise. The distance between Jai's palace and Jai's hunting lodge was measured and found to be four and a half miles. *Diwans*, ministers, and sycophants paced this off on each side until an exact midpoint was found, and here, eleven days after the maharaja of Kurvi had first set foot upon Rudrakot soil, Jai and Kurvi met. Then, Jai took Kurvi back to his palaces so that the official visit could begin.

The whole incident had vastly amused Mila and Ashok for months and Kiran too, when she had written to him in England about it. They had all laughed at Jai and the maharaja, and Mila had been concerned that Papa had been too harried and too ill rested during the whole of the official visit. To her surprise, Jai had laughed at himself too. He had the capability of being self-deprecating and honest about himself, and had admitted that the whole exercise had been one steeped in silliness and idiocy. But Mila had known, even though Jai had said nothing and neither had her father, that it was the *appearance* of anything remotely like impropriety that had to be battled, whether it was silly or not. She had asked him once why he had not married one of the princesses of Kurvi, and he had said, "Because I am in love with another woman. If I take another wife, it will be her and no one else. If I had known I would be in love with her, I would not have married my first wife."

Mila stood fifteen feet away from Jai in the front driveway of her father's house, and waited for Jai to come up to that imaginary line between them and meet her halfway. Ashok had begun to accompany Jai when he turned to him, put a staying hand on his arm and said, "Wait, Ashok. Please," and sauntered toward her, the swagger stick tucked under his right arm, his hands in his pockets. With much the same attitude, outwardly, as he had employed with the maharaja of Kurvi, but the difference was—and Mila was well aware of this—that Jai had not cared about Kurvi, but he cared about her.

Now Mila knew that she was the woman Jai loved. His offer of marriage had come, scrupulously, after he had asked Raman for permission two months ago, after he had received his king's commission in the army. He had said nothing of love at the time he made the declaration, but an anxiety had assailed him, and his gaze, normally bold, had dropped to the points of his shiny boots. "Will you be my wife . . . sometime in the future, whenever you want?" She had said yes, because his offer was irresistible, because she had been wondering if she would ever meet someone she would want to marry so much that nothing else would matter in her world, and because, after all, she had known Jai since she was seven years old and she had been in love with him, in some fashion or the other, for that long.

He came up to her now and stood staring down at her. His hands moved, only once, to brush against her hair and follow its lines down to her waist. "It becomes you," he said. The same words Sam had used a few hours ago.

Jai shook Mila's hand and held it for a long while. He would not lean in to kiss her on the cheek or put his arm around her. Doubtless, there were people watching even this encounter, Sayyid and Pallavi, the other servants.

Mila was equally formal. "How was your visit at the ICC?"

A fine spasm of pain flashed across his eyes. "All right. I will tell you about it later. Will you have dinner with me tonight?" Jai turned to look toward the house. "Ashok can come too, as he always does, to be a gooseberry between us, because your papa will not let us dine alone. Will you come?"

This last was said almost hopefully, as though he was afraid of a negative response, and Mila's heart went out to him. "Yes," she said.

"Thank you." Jai let go of her hand and walked back with her to the Hispano-Suiza. "I will send the limousine for you. Remember, tonight is the White Durbar—"

"I will wear white," Mila said. "Thank you, Jai. I must go in now, we had to spend the night at Chetak's tomb because of the dust storm, and so we weren't able to return yesterday evening." She fumbled over her words, smitten with pain again, thinking that if she could only cleave herself in two, then all of her would be satisfied. It was impossible to think that she was in *love* with Sam Hawthorne, and yet there was nothing about him that she did not like; his presence made her yearn for the comfort of his arms, he listened as she talked, even about the most inane things, and in the end, her attraction for him, if it could be called by so mild a word, was indefinable. She was almost embarrassed by her desire for him, by how much she had been lost in his kisses, how fascinating were the lines of his mouth, his face, and the bones under the skin on his chest. And yet here was Jai whom she loved for who he was, because he was charming and could be funny (though not very often, because his sense of duty often overcame any humor), because he loved her with a devotion that she would not find anywhere else, in any other man. Perhaps not even Sam Hawthorne.

Mila was miserable. She dragged her steps up the three short stairs to the front door and turned to Jai to say good-bye, her voice broken and laden with tears that she could not shed yet. "I'm sorry," she said. "I am tired, and hungry."

"Yes," Jai said. "Do go in, my darling. Tell me, was your guest, this Captain Hawthorne, with you last night at Chetak's tomb?"

Mila nodded.

"I'm glad to hear that; you must have been safe."

She went into the house and up the stairs to her room, thinking that perhaps if Sam had not been at Chetak's tomb, she would have been safer. At the landing, she looked out as Sam came up the driveway and met Jai. The two men shook hands and spoke before Sam also came into the house and Jai got behind the wheel of the Suiza and drove away. When Mila heard Sam's footsteps on the stairs, she slipped into her room, but held the door ajar a few inches so that she could see him pass by.

By the time Mila left for the Lal Bazaar, later that afternoon, she had made two decisions that she intended would hold good for the rest of her life. But nothing could be held true for the rest of one's life, every coveted thing in the end was *maya*, illusion, a myth, and this the great sages of India had always understood—little was real. We were put on this earth transitorily; we deposited our genes in offspring; deluded ourselves that we would be missed when we were gone; pretended that money, wealth, titles, and land were to be desired. But every such thing was ephemeral, prone to change. The only reason to live was love.

That afternoon, Mila thought about Jai's love for her as unconditional, but also capable of outrageous jealousy and demanding assertion. She was aware of his devotion though. If Mila had wanted or indicated a need for anything—jewelry with rubies and diamonds, silks spun so thin as to be made of cobwebs, wines and furniture from the reigns of dead French kings—Jai would have acquired it for her somehow. Instead, he would come to visit her with a rose from his famous conservatory within the fort, or a silver dish with one slice of *rabadi* in it, layered with sweetened cream, flavored with golden strands of saffron, drizzled with a dusting of finely ground pistachios. He had invested thought in every gift, knowing somehow that she would not, could not accept an exorbitant gift from him before marriage.

When she had finished her bath and sat on her bed eating her lunch from a *thali* she had ordered from the kitchens, Mila read through all of Jai's letters. Before that, when he had not yet declared his intentions, there had been no question of a correspondence between them, and even so, Raman had hesitatingly given his permission, wishing within himself that they were already married so he would not have to meditate over the propriety of this. In each of the letters—and there were only eight, a restrained eight—filled on four pages with handwriting reduced to a tiny scrawl, Jai had included a gift. A *champa* flower he had plucked and pressed in his copy of *The Memoirs of Baron de Marbot;* the leaf of a mango tree; the wispy seeds from a dandelion glued to a sliver of parchment; a sketch of the horse he had given her, Ghatoth. It was a funny name for a horse, taken from the name of the demon king Ravan's brother from the Ramayana. Why, Mila had asked once, would he name his horse for a demon? And Jai had replied, Do you remember what Ghatothguch did for six months of the year? He slept, Mila replied. And when he woke up, he ate a lot. Right, Jai had said, running an affectionate hand over the horse's glossy rump, this Ghatoth likes to eat and to sleep, but he is gentle, unlike his namesake. It still astonished her that Jai loved what he loved so passionately, that he had watched and learned of the horse's personality before naming him.

He had called her darling when they parted earlier that day, and it was the first time Mila could remember him employing that word. He had always used her name, or come up to her elbow to say something; once he had bent close enough to her ear so that she could feel the warmth of his breath upon her skin.

Jai had kissed her four times. Despite all of Papa's injunctions, it was easy enough to find solitude for an embrace. Ashok had to be with them at all times, and Jai was not above bribing him with what was most denied to him—cigarettes, a ride in the Suiza, a walk in the corridor that led to Jai's *ʒenana* for a possible glimpse of the ladies who kept *purdah*, the veil. Before the first kiss, on the verandah leading out to the enormous indoor swimming pool in Jai's Neel Niwas, the Blue Palace, Mila had been afraid, knowing what was to come, yet not sure if she wanted it. But Jai had been so gentle, he had kissed her hand first, then the inside of her wrist, the curve of her elbow, touched lightly upon her collarbone with his warm tongue before working his way up to her mouth. She remembered the smell of him, the feel of his mouth on hers, the absolute fit of her body against his. He had been considerate, loving. But none of the four kisses had compared to the explosion of love and lust Mila had experienced with Sam.

But how could it be? Mila thought over and over again all through the afternoon. With Jai, there were little histories that went back in time and built upon each other to form an entire whole, with Sam, there was no history at all.

When the household descended into its midafternoon slumber, Mila slipped out of the house and rode her bicycle, under the frenetic blaze of the sun, to the Lal Bazaar. Sam Hawthorne was a fantasy for her; Jai was real, and here, where her life lay. It was a blessing that he had returned from the ICC now, for they would be together more often and she could keep Ashok away from Vimal by asking him to come to their dinners and outings. These were Mila's two decisions—she would only visit with Jai, and she would take Ashok with her and keep him by her side also. Having made up her mind, the only feeling of unease that remained in Mila was because she had neglected her duties in the Lal Bazaar in the past few days and a letter from Father Manning had come yesterday to lie on her bedside table and reproach her.

Father Manning was the only British Catholic missionary in Rudrakot, or rather, he had remained, in his semiofficial capacity, well after the Catholic Church had pulled its mission out of the kingdom. The reasons had been varied, but mostly because Rudrakot was too small a state to require the ministrations of both the Catholic, and the Anglican church, represented by the vicar and Mrs. Sexton, and all of their good deeds liberally forced upon the poor. Father Manning had chosen not to leave when the two other missionaries had departed, for in the time he had been here, thirty-five years, his soul had melded into the light and heat of Rudrakot. He loved its people—the children of the bazaar; the women with torn spirits who used their bodies as barter; the old, toothless men nodding in the sunshine; the young, brash men who teased him for no cause at all. Father Manning, born George Manning, had no family left in England he could even remember—his parents were dead; his sister had faded into a life of comfortable domesticity and still advised him irregularly on how to deal with the "savages" he worked amongst; the church had loosened its ties upon him when he had refused to leave the kingdom.

The mission house was a senescent building tucked behind a *chai* shop and a brass and copper shop, with a narrow alley leading to the gate of the house and the inner courtyard within. It was the same mission house the church had used, and when he was left on his own, for just a brief while,

Father Manning had worried about finding rent for the place. He had mentioned this, casually, to the *chai* shop owner, Ramu, during his morning cup of *chai*, which he always, companionably, drank with the young man. By afternoon, four hours later, one of the little vagabond boys of the bazaar had come up to Father Manning and thrust a gunnysack in his hand. Inside was crammed a *khazana* of money—soiled and damp rupee notes, glittering *anna* coins, and even the odd British shilling. Just enough, to the last *anna*, for his monthly rent and food for the kitchens.

The mission house, fittingly called Prem Nivas—the Abode of Love—was always rife with the rich sound of children's laughter, their sometimes frightened cries at night, the soothing croon of Father Manning's bedtime songs. Almost all children of the women of the Lal Bazaar found their way at some point or other during the night to Prem Nivas, honing in to the shelter of his home. Each evening at twilight, Father Manning would drag out fifteen jute-knitted *charpais* into the courtyard under the emerging stars and wait. And each evening, as their mothers went to work, the children would leave the brothel houses and come to the Father. At night, if one of them had a fever, it was Father Manning who would stand vigil by their bedsides, dipping cloth towels into the water from the courtyard tap and laying it on their foreheads to bring down the temperature. In the morning, he wakened his brood with a touch, a word, a smile, a tickle under the ribs for the littlest ones and fed them *khichdi* and a dry potato curry—the only things he knew how to cook.

The gunnysack money came every month to Father Manning, but he always needed more for his children. There were school uniforms for those whose mothers did not mind a little learning, lunch boxes, slates and chalk pieces, medicines from the bazaar apothecary whose generosity had already been stretched beyond enduring in the cause of these children. So Father Manning taught extra lessons of mathematics and English to the more privileged children whose parents lived within the Civil Lines in Rudrakot. And there, five years before, he had met Mila because he had gone to Raman's house to tutor Ashok and, incidentally, Vimal.

A year ago, one of the women from the Lal Bazaar, who was really a child herself, perhaps not even sixteen years old, had come in copious tears to Father Manning about having been defrauded by a traveling cloth merchant who had given her back less change for a transaction. He had taught her numbers then, how to add, and subtract, how to ask for the correct change, how not to be cheated in the future. The very smallest of the children who slept in the courtyard of his mission house could now calculate those numbers in their heads—without the aid of their fingers and toes—and the prostitute's ignorance deeply saddened him. He accosted the madams of the white side of the bazaar and the black side of the bazaar and pleaded with them to allow him to teach the women, but they were adamantly against it. A man, even though he called himself a man of God, could not be allowed into the brothels under any pretext without paying the requisite fees. Finally Father Manning saw Mila ride past him one day on her way to the Rifles regiment's *maidan* for her daily ride on Ghatoth, and asked her if she would mind teaching the women some basics—the letters of the English alphabet, a few Hindustani words, some mathematics and numbers.

Mila always rode her bicycle carefully, keeping her legs well away from the pedals and her sari border away from the greasy chain. Pallavi had clucked with irritation, shouted, and wanted to know where she disappeared to in the afternoons every now and then, and why it was necessary to ride the bicycle instead of taking the jeep. At this last thought, Mila smiled and wiped her forehead under the brim of her *sola topi*. Pallavi never wanted her to drive the jeep because she thought that was unwomanly, but at least the jeep had some status, whereas if anyone saw Mila cycling through the bazaar, they would not stop to consider that this was the political agent's daughter. And that was exactly why she took the bicycle. She pedaled furiously as she broke out of the trees in the Civil Lines and into the flat expanse of land that led to the stand of trees that shaded the two regiments. As she neared the trees on the farther side, she heard the squealing slowness of the chain and felt it yank at the border of her pink cotton sari. Mila reduced her speed, groaning, and pulled at her sari border gently, hoping to release it before it became more entangled. After a few tugs, the sari came loose, and there was only a small smudge of grease at the bottom, hardly visible at all. She continued on, thinking of Pallavi's next complaint, that she could very well wear her jodhpurs if she *had* to use the bicycle, again a departure for Pallavi, but in this one instance, Mila could not enter the Lal Bazaar in anything other than a sari, her head covered and bowed, so as not to attract attention from any lascivious man on the street.

Father Manning's unusual request a few months ago had been surprising and somehow stunning, for too many reasons. Mila had heard of the Lal

Bazaar, of course, from Jai and from Kiran, but they were always vague about the specifics. She only realized what occurred there after the officer had exited Lady Pankhurst's bedchamber, buttoning the front of his coat. Mila was eighteen that year, old enough to have been married herself and to know what happened between a man and a woman. But she had kept herself deliberately obtuse, not curious, not even interested. The Lal Bazaar came as a shock when she passed through it. The women had called out to her, their language rich with phrases and sentences she could not understand; at times, she did glance at them furtively and saw strident mouths, brightly colored saris draped unbecomingly, manlike stances with legs apart, and a tautness to their bodies that came from belligerence. None of this was appealing and she kept her eyes from them as much as she could.

Father Manning was the first man to talk openly with Mila about the women of the Lal Bazaar, and it was with a great deal of embarrassment that she could even listen to what he had to say. They were poor, uneducated, in need of help. He asked her to teach in his stead since he—being a man—was forbidden to.

Why? Mila had asked. Why did these women deserve anything, need anything other than the life they had chosen?

Mila flushed with regret when she thought of this question now. Hers had always been a privileged life because Papa, though not rich, had access to the perquisites of the wealthy. They did not own their home or even the Morris or the jeep, but these would not so soon disappear from their lives; they were on extended loan until death. Mila had an *almirah* full of saris and pants and jodhpurs, shirts in silk, enough jewelry to weigh down two brides, and now, with her marriage to Jai, even all that Papa had given her would be inconsequential. For Mila there had always been a choice, even in the choosing of Jai to be her husband; it was not a decision Papa would ever have forced her into. She had thought that the women of the Lal Bazaar had chosen to do what they did. Father Manning had said simply that such a life was never a choice.

At one time, early in the days when Father Manning had given lessons to Ashok and Vimal, Raman and he would sit in the upstairs verandah under the jute matting and take their afternoon *chai* and scones together. Mila had listened in on these conversations too, intrigued, and most of their debates had been about religion. Raman talked of the philosophies of Hinduism, and Father Manning talked of his Lord Jesus Christ. They had

found many similarities, many differences, much to ponder, even asking
Mila what she felt or thought at the time. Until now, Mila's only encounters with missionaries had been the proselytizing type, with every conversation invariably ending in an exhortation to cleave unto their God or to
disdain her own. But Father Manning had been content merely to discuss.
He did not assert the superiority of his religion, why, he had even agreed
that its policies of forcible conversion were unbecoming of Christian val-
ues. If it had not been for these series of talks with Father Manning on the
afternoons of the tutoring sessions, Mila would never have agreed to visit
the Lal Bazaar with him that first time.

Somewhere in the back of her consciousness was also the thought,
never fully enunciated, that of all the British in Rudrakot, Father Manning
was the only one who was not . . . well, *British*. He did not consider himself a master, a member of the ruling race, did not attempt any condescen-
sions. Father Manning had come to Rudrakot because of the empire, true,
sent here to proselytize and protect a people considered to be in need of
religious succor and reassurance, but he was not *the* empire.

Mila reached the edge of the bazaar, near the tailor's shop, and tucked
her bicycle under the tattered tarpaulin awning that shaded him as he
stitched clothes on an ancient, clanking Singer. He had an understanding
with Father Manning that Mila could leave her cycle with him and he
would look after it all afternoon. Then she pulled the *pallu* of her simple
pink sari over her hair and walked into the bazaar, toward the section that
housed the brothels, her head bowed, her steps measured, a cheap cloth
shopping bag hanging on her bare arm. The man seated at the entrance to
the brothel grunted at her, but Mila did not answer back. Her heart thudding with an unnamed fear, one she always experienced when she came
here, she left her *chappals* inside the front door and then climbed the concrete stairs to the main corridor.

Rooms lined the whole length of the corridor, with most of the doors
thrown open. Mila did not glance either to her right or to her left as she
walked to the room at the far end, her skin bristling with discomfort and
something so acute in her chest that it was almost painful. There was the
smell of old, used perfumes; cheap attar; the lingering essence of sandalwood and myrrh. All the entertainment rooms were garishly done with
toffee pinks, copper sulfate blues, and parrot greens on the walls, and covered with frescoes of dancing girls in tight bodices and flaring skirts. The

accompaniments to the women's singing, the *tabla*, the harmonium, the violin, the *sitar*, sat in their cloth housings at one end. The mosaic floor was thick and padded, first with a layer of jute matting covered by a thin cotton mattress, this covered with a thick cotton sheet of the purest white. The *nautch* girls danced on this padding, performing for private audiences of soldiers from the Rudrakot Rifles regiment, who would be seated against one end of the room, under a satin and gold canopy, propped against silk bolsters and cushions.

The women who serviced the white soldiers, officers, and NCOs of the Rudrakot Rifles practiced their singing and dancing in the afternoons. At night, they performed, and later still, well after midnight, they took the men into private rooms, which led off the corridor, where the only furnishing was a curtain on the window and a bed against a wall. Nothing more was necessary or needed, for these women had no conversation and only one skill. The doors to these rooms, now unused, were also open since they were empty, and Mila could not help looking into them as she passed, filled with a sadness and an aversion at the same time. In some of the rooms, she heard the clearing of a throat before the girl or the woman rehearsed her night's recital, or the tuning of the *sitar*, or the gentle *thump-thump* of the *tabla* player's fingers upon the smooth skin of his drums. When she entered her room, she saw that her students, three girls ranging in age from fifteen to eighteen, were already there, heads bent over their slates, laboring over their Hindi alphabet.

"*Namaste, Didi*," one of the girls said, folding her hands in front of her in salutation.

They called Mila thus, *didi*, or elder sister, and it was in its own way a mark of respect. They had called Father Manning *Bapu*, the same appellation that was now being used for Mahatma Gandhi, but for these girls the priest was in the place of a father. In the very beginning, Mila herself had been incredibly shy with them and then had realized that under their loud and coarse voices were hearts that were wounded and shattered. That they had lost the ability to trust and had no capacity for believing. The girls had been suspicious of Mila at first, and had stared at her, eyes open very wide, mouths sometimes agape to deliberately show how ignorant they were, seated on their haunches, with their saris wrapped around their knees as though they were sitting over a latrine. Their writing had been indifferent, their attention span minimal. And then, something had fallen into place with all of them. Mila learned to keep the horror out of her face and her expression, and the girls learned that she did not consider them entirely with disgust, as most of the other memsahibs did. Mila had returned home and cried until she thought her heart would break that first afternoon, and then remembered how young most of them were, how afraid, how maladroit behind all the bluster. And so she had returned.

If Raman had known of these visits, he would have put a stop to them. If Pallavi had known, she would have taken a whip and flayed the skin on Mila's back and then locked her in a room. If Ashok had known, he would have been thrilled and would have wanted to accompany Mila, just to see for himself. Kiran would have been ashamed to have his sister anywhere near the Lal Bazaar, for he had been here before, often enough, once even with Sims and Blakely. Jai would also have locked Mila away, covered up any impropriety, and asked her to contribute her charity in other, much cleaner avenues. Knit a scarf, he would have said, or crochet a table napkin. Organize a *mela*. So Mila told no one and did what she wanted to do. She assumed—and because she was young she could assume so and consider that it would be true—that not one person of her acquaintance would *ever* find out.

But even as she bent over the black slate of one of the girls, wiping it first with a dampened piece of cloth, a man walked by the open door to the room, looked in as he passed, and then came back to stand in the doorway. His footsteps were almost silent, because he too had to take off his boots inside the front doorway to the house—it was a rule the madam, Leelabai, was very strict about. He stood in the rectangle of the doorway for a while, his face filled first with surprise and then chased by cunning and malice. He rubbed at a chin that did not exist, for he had only a weak bone under his thin mouth. He moved away for a bit and then came back with a friend. The friend, also an officer in the Rudrakot Rifles, pursed his mouth in a whistle, but a warning hand on his arm stayed that sound.

And so Mila never looked up from her work or heard the men, for the girls had begun chattering, telling her stories of their childhoods, of how many goats one of their fathers had, how the village idiot had made eyes at one. Her sari *pallu* fell off her shoulder once, revealing the satin skin of her neck and the shadowed cleavage of her breasts in her blouse. She draped it up again, almost absently, but not before Sims and Blakely had gaped in surprise and then, smiling, retreated down the corridor again.

# Twenty-three

*The bee, the lotus, the cloud, the conch-shell, the fish, the deer, the bow, the leaf of the banyan tree, the stem of the plantain tree, the yet unopened flower, silver moonlight and golden goblets—all these must dwell in harmony on my beloved.*

—K.P.S. Menon, *Many Worlds: An Autobiography*, 1898

Mila returned exhausted from the Lal Bazaar and sat in an armchair in her room, watching the ceiling fan revolve overhead. She had shed her sari when she'd come back and had piled it on the floor. Her blouse, its armpits dampened with sweat, she had peeled off and thrown on the floor also. So she lounged now much as Kiran had in front of their father, her legs over one arm of the chair, her back resting against the other, her head flung back. She put a hand out into the air, and then slowly tucked one finger and then another into her palm, counting aloud all the while, "One . . . two . . . three . . ." How easy that was to her, and to numerous other people in the world. When had she learned to count? When she was a year old? Two? What did it really feel like to look upon the writing on rupee notes and see nothing but indecipherable gibberish?

She let her hand fall back beyond the chair and drag on the floor, not left with any energy to even hold it up again. The girls she had taught had names, Chameli, Radha, Richa, and some others, names that they told her with a great deal of pride, but none of those names was actually bestowed upon them at birth. They were the property of the madam,

Leelabai, who sent the officers of the Rifles regiment *the* Chameli they
had so enjoyed the last time, and substituted one girl for another with a
great deal of ease. The rooms were darkened, and Leelabai assumed that
the white men could not tell the difference, and in any case, it was not
their *faces* they cared about. Mila thought that the girls did look the same.
They had the same long hair, just beyond their shoulder blades, the same
artificial arch in each of their eyebrows, the same mole dotted on the right
of their mouths (to ward off the evil eye), the same heavily powdered
faces, thickly rimmed eyes, lush painted lips. And the same frightening
mixture of innocence and artifice. The girls had been brought to the
brothels and kept there with threats and whippings; this was to be their
life, for now no reasonable man would marry them or provide them with
another home.

Still saddened, Mila went to bathe and dress for the dinner with Jai.
The water was tepid at best, almost on a par with the temperature of the
room, but the soap bar dissolved into a mint green foam, the shampoo
lathered her hair richly, the towels were thick and clean. When she came
back into her room, still dripping from the bath, she saw that Pallavi had
left a tray upon the table by her bedside with a teapot in a tea cosy and a
plate of *nankatais*, sugar biscuits baked an hour ago in the outdoor oven.
Mila ate and drank slowly, watching the movements of her mouth in the
dressing-table mirror. By the time she had finished, she had driven all
thoughts of the afternoon's happenings from her mind and rose to dress
with the simple anticipation of what the night was to bring.

Pallavi had laid out a white silk chiffon sari upon the bed. The sari was
almost plain in its simplicity, no borders, no patterns, just the vibrant
sheen of the weave, but hand-embedded in that weave were thousands of
tiny, glowing, white crystals set less than an inch apart over its entire six-
yard length. Her tight blouse was plain white cotton, closed with three
strings at her back, revealing the rest of the skin there. Her sleeves though
came all the way to her wrists and her waist was bare under the shimmer
of the sari's *pallu*. Mila left her neck undressed and looped large silver
hoops inlaid with diamonds all along their rims into her ears. She wore
three diamond bangles on each arm and slipped her feet into a pair of
high-heeled *chappals* studded with crystals on the heels so that as she
walked and as the edges of her sari lifted, the light emanating from her
person continued in a glitter to the ground.

It was still too hot to make up her face too much, so Mila merely dusted on some powder, lined her eyes with kohl, and painted her lips pink with one of the lipsticks Kiran had bought her in England. She pondered a long time on how to dress her hair, whether to gather it into a bun, or pin the sides and let the rest loose, or plait just a few strands and tie up the rest and finally, as she was running her comb through her hair, she decided to leave it the way it was.

Her hair lay thick and lush across her shoulders, over her breasts. It had no curl in it at all, and fell in a shining long sweep to her waist. Even caught up behind her head, it was more than a mere handful. At every small movement, even the merest breath, the light from the sconces on the wall frittered over the crystals in her sari so that she seemed to be on fire.

She wondered if the sun had completed its journey of the day already, for Jai had said that he would send the limousine at ten minutes to sunset, and Jai's chauffeurs were very rigid with times. She wondered if she should go to Ashok's room and make sure that he was ready. And then she heard the soft click of a cigarette lighter in the verandah beyond her room and the flare of the flame and Mila moved toward that sound to find Sam. She told herself, even as she walked, that she was only going to look out into the sky to see if it was time for the car, but that thought and all others disappeared as she stepped through the doorway.

Sam had his back to her and when he turned to face her, it was with an expression so filled with despair that she almost went over to put her arms around him. He had just begun to dress and had donned only his white pants and his white silk shirt. His feet were bare, his collar unbuttoned, his hair still sodden from his bath, even his cigarette was damp as he held it between wet fingers.

"The *darzi* has done a good job," Mila said.

Sam ran his hand over the front of his shirt and around the waistband of his pants. It had been only seven hours since he had met Jai and been invited to the White Durbar later that evening, and already, since he did not have the appropriate clothing for the occasion, a tailor had been hired from the bazaar to sit in the downstairs back verandah and sew him a new set of clothes. The shirt and pants had then been washed, flung on the clothesline in the backyard for an hour to dry, ironed into a pristine crispness by Sayyid, and laid out in readiness upon his bed before he had stepped into the bathroom.

"I'm still amazed by the speed with which I have these," he replied. "But why the insistence on white?"

"Tonight is the night of the full moon, Sam, and Jai holds a White Durbar . . ." She paused. "It is a meeting of his court in the moonlight. There are no colors but white, to mimic the essence of the moon. The durbar itself is a practice of old, when the feudal lords in the kingdom would come on the night of *purnima* to pay their respects to the Rudrakot king. The rituals are in some ways similar. In the olden days, the *thakurs*, the lords, would lay down their arms in front of the king and bow to him; now it is merely a bow and a knock upon the floor with a sword. You will enjoy it immensely, I'm sure." She finished in a rush, with a pounding heart, knowing that she had been talking too much and to no purpose.

He beckoned to her with a hand, and she obeyed, if only to get closer to him. When she was near enough to feel his breath, he said, "I thought Jai was married. I saw his children at the *mela*."

"Yes," Mila replied. "He has three actually, a little girl also, but she's in *purdah* in the *zenana*. She is kept behind a veil, in . . . in the women's quarters of Jai's palace, because his first wife"—and here she hesitated again, stumbling—"his first wife was brought up in *purdah* herself and so thinks it right for her daughter to be so to."

"I will not ask if Jai can marry again and if it is not against the law," Sam said wryly.

But he had asked, so Mila said, "The law, such as it is, is fluid and flexible around the princes and their kingdoms. I will have all and as many legal rights as the First Her Highness after I marry Jai." She reached out to Sam's cigarette, and he gave it to her as though she was a child, putting it carefully between the index and middle fingers of her right hand. Then he guided it to her mouth, his palm cupping her chin as she dragged on the cigarette. His touch was gentle and just hovered near her skin, but Mila could not breathe. She saw now that Sam was not angry with her. The kisses at Chetak's tomb had been something they had both wanted. Mila did not reach up to clasp Sam's hand, but she did not object when he continued to hold hers.

"What will you be?" he asked.

"Second Her Highness."

"And will you be in *purdah*?"

She shook her head. "I don't keep *purdah*."

And then he asked her the question she knew he had wanted to ask all this while. "And why are you going to marry him?"

But he had still sidestepped the real question, Mila thought. The smoke from the cigarette in her fingers curled gently between them. Sam took the stub from her hand and threw it over the ledge of the balcony. He wound one strand of her hair around his finger and tugged at it and then raised it to his nose and inhaled. Mila felt herself melting into Sam and swayed toward him, her gaze riveted upon the lines of his mouth.

"I am betrothed to Jai," she said.

"That is not enough of an answer," Sam said. He lifted her chin so that he could look into her eyes and rubbed the line of her jaw with his thumbs. His hands then traveled down her slender neck, twirled in the circle of her loop earrings, tucked under the sliver of her blouse that stretched tight across her shoulders. Then he pulled her close so that he could touch her back, his fingers sliding under the three tenuous strings that held her blouse together. His fingertips were rough against her skin and Mila shivered. She sighed and let her head fall against Sam's chest, listening to the galloping beat of his heart. Her arms lay by her side, and she felt them rise against her will to clasp together around his waist.

"Sam."

"What are your other names?"

"What?"

He buried his face in her hair and said, his voice reverberating near her ear, "You told me you had other names when we first met. I want to know what they are, so that I can choose what to call you."

"Ayesha Olivia Milana," she said, breathing in the clean scent of his skin.

"Why?"

"Papa," she replied briefly. And even the remembrance of her father did not make her pull out of Sam's arms. "He wanted us to have Muslim, Christian, and Hindu names."

"What does Milana mean?"

At that moment, the clean and sharp toot of a limousine's horn sounded in the front driveway. It cut through Mila and filled her with an immeasurable shame. What was it about Sam Hawthorne that made her behave like this? Sam's hold upon her had loosened when he too heard the horn and now she stood in the circle of his arms but nowhere did their skins touch.

She did not move away, not immediately, but when she spoke it was with a firmness that matched the rigidity of her body. "I love Jai," she said.

Sam stepped back.

"I love Jai," she repeated.

She turned to leave and his voice stopped her steps once with this: "I will have a daughter and call her Olivia." The second time, just as she was entering her room, he said, "I want to give her three names too."


Because Jai's limousine had called for her precisely ten minutes before the sun sank beyond the gaze of Rudrakot, it was well dark by the time it drew up in front of one of his palaces in the fort. The drive took thirty-five minutes. The early part, when they were in the Civil Lines, then the cantonment area, and especially the outskirts of the Lal Bazaar had been slow as the car wended through the masses of traffic—cows, bicyclists, a few hens clucking on the road, an army jeep or two, and pedestrians. The Daimler had the Rudrakot arms painted on its front two doors and on the boot behind and passed quietly through the rush as the crowds recognized their prince's car and parted to give them way. Once they reached the fort, it was relatively smooth and easy even though the streets were narrow, at times barely three feet on either side of the enormous gleaming vehicle, and thronging with the tightly knit, three-story buildings of everyone and anyone who had either worked for the royal family, or known the royal family, or were in some fashion related to them. And this relationship, this care of past retainers and present ones, went back too many generations for most of the fort's lower occupants to even recall. This was part of the responsibility of kingship.

When the car went by with Mila sitting in the backseat, the people waved to her from their windows, shouted with joy, or in one instance showered her with rose petals and the petals came floating in to settle on her lap through the open roof of the Daimler. She was going to be Second Her Highness, she was their king's chosen wife; in her was vested a large share of their well-being.

Mila gathered the rose petals that had fallen on her sari and spread them out on the empty seat next to her. At the very last minute, as she stood by the open door of the limousine, its driver patiently holding it ajar for her, Ashok had run down the stairs, half dressed in his shirt and his undershorts, his tie still awry, and announced, "I'm going for a drink to the Victoria with Captain Hawthorne. Papa says you are to go alone. He will see you later in the evening."

"Where is Papa?" Mila asked, suddenly feeling bereft that Ashok would not accompany her. She had not seen Raman since he had returned from Nodi, even though he had been home for two hours by the time they had come back from Chetak's tomb. But their day had been spent apart, and now, even in this chunk of the evening, she would not see him or be with Ashok. "Come with me, Ashok," she said, fiercely jealous. Why should he spend time with Sam when she could not?

"No," he shouted, and opened his mouth in a big laugh. "Papa says I can have my first drink at the Victoria, as long as I drink it with Sam. You go practice your wiles on Jai." And then he turned and bounded up the stairs, taking them two at a time. Ashok had been drinking gimlets, pink champagnes, cocktails, and beer for the past two years now and had a finely developed palate for all of these, but this was his first public sanction from his father and so he was thrilled.

Mila got into the car slowly, both upset with Ashok and worried about him because he had lost any sense of calmness since their time at the Victoria Club *mela*. Every emotion had been stretched finely; at one time he was despondent, at another gleeful, at another, just before they slept at Chetak's tomb, he had clutched her hand so tightly as to leave the marks of his nails on her wrists. And it all stemmed from Vimal Kumar coming back into their lives. She had heard from many people, the maids in the house, her father, even Ashok, that Vimal was abundantly blessed with beauty and that just gazing upon him was akin to being filled with *amrit*, the drink of the Gods. But he did not move Mila to any such devotion. He was handsome, she thought, but with the insides of a snake and, somehow, just as deadly.

She looked back toward the house as they drove away and a longing beset her despite her best intentions. Her hands shook and she squeezed her palms together in her lap until the blood stanched and her fingers turned white. She closed her eyes, not seeing anything as they passed, and her first intimation that they were within the walls of the fort was the soft touch of the fragrant rose petals upon her hands. At that, Mila opened her eyes, amassed the petals, put them away, and became, in her mind and within herself, firmly, the woman who was going to marry Jai.

He was waiting for her at the top of the wide flight of stairs leading to the Neel Nivas, the Blue Palace. Everything was blue here, even the marble outer stairs—which curved gently around the front with marble balustrades and marble lions on two ends—had a brush of sea teal swirled in the stone. As the car drove up, Mila watched Jai. His stance was overly casual, legs apart, arms hanging loosely by his side, only betrayed by a sudden tremor that made him knead his fingers into a fist every now and then. He waited until the very last minute, until the limousine had drawn up in front of him, and then, before the chauffeur had turned the handle of the door, Jai came bounding down the stairs to open the door for Mila.

She gave him her hand, and impulsively, even before she could get out, he put it to his mouth for a kiss. "Come, my dear," he said, bending to her ear. "Or I am in danger of making a stupid exhibition of myself in front of the servants."

But the servants were everywhere of course—lined in a row in their sky-blue-and-silver uniforms at each pillar, the same colors the Rudrakot Lancers bore; along the corridor leading to the outdoor pool; behind the ferns and the potted plants; at doorways; and finally, arranged like toy soldiers, around the swimming pool. And all along the palace, the lights had been dimmed, so Mila sensed rather than saw the servants. They were very well trained, and betrayed their presence only by a mild cough here, covered up by a hand, or an intake of breath as she passed.

Jai was wearing white too.

Later in the night, when he sat at his *gaddi,* his throne, in anticipation of the offerings at the White Durbar, he would don his brocade *sherwani,* a long, fitted coat that extended below his knees. It was made of a hand-embroidered damask, diaphanous silver strands threaded into the fabric by hand, and like Mila's sari, it too had tiny glittering stones sewn onto the cloth everywhere. And while Mila's sari was sewn with crystals, Jai's *sherwani* was made of the purest silk and adorned with diamonds, each perfectly faceted to capture the light of the moon and fling it back onto the audience watching so that it would seem as if he was clad in moonlight.

Now all Jai wore was a pair of riding pants, a white cotton shirt, and white calfskin boots on his feet. This was what he wore all the time, and it had almost become a uniform for him unless he dressed up for state occasions like the White Durbar or to lead a parade of his Lancers.

As they passed through the corridors, the lights around them dimmed further, until they went out completely and at Jai's nod, someone, somewhere threw a switch and millions of little blue lights came on. Mila stopped to catch her breath at the sudden beauty within the palace. The lights went everywhere, strung over the ceiling, around the pillars, along the floor, festooning the plants until it looked as though they were embedded in the very air. And when she stepped out into the marble and sandstone verandah surrounding the pool, it was as though the lights had floated upward and turned themselves into the night sky. There was no moon yet, so all that draped over them was this lovely, icy blue light that cooled her skin. Mila had her arm through Jai's and now she slipped it out to grasp his hand. They stood together just beyond the cusped arches of the verandah, bathed in ultramarine from the heavens above and around.

"Do you like it?" Jai asked.

"Yes," Mila replied. "Thank you . . . for everything."

"No." He began to walk toward the table set on one corner beyond the pool's edge. Mila saw that even the lights in the pool had been covered with a light blue film, so it seemed as though the water had a glowing life of its own. "I am the one blessed"—he paused and laughed self-consciously— "happy that you are here."

He pulled out a chair for Mila at the table and waved the servants away. They turned and marched out in a single file, their feet barely making a sound on the marble paving. "You are here, are you not, Mila?" Jai asked.

"Yes," she said, leaning back in her chair. "I do not want to be anywhere but by your side."

Something, some heaviness and languor, fell from him when she said those words and all of a sudden he was young and youthful again. His teeth flashed in a smile and he said, "How lovely of your Captain Hawthorne to take Ashok to the Victoria Club; I wonder if your father realizes that his youngest son is already a sot."

"I think he does," Mila said, smiling. "There is very little Papa does not know about us, well, about Ashok anyway. Which is probably why he is officially introducing him to drink; it will keep Ashok from sneaking shots of Papa's whiskey. And that sot, as you call him, is going to be your brother-in-law."

Jai groaned. "I suppose I asked for this, didn't I?"

She nodded and thought that she *was* in love with Jai, it was difficult not to be so with the man who sat opposite her, his gaze so adoring, his consideration enormous, his heart so generous. In that moment, Mila was happy, content. Here was her future, in Jai, with him in these palaces, as his wife and his companion. She looked around in the blue light as the servants materialized with a tray of *pakoras* and three chutneys to accompany it. The *pakoras* were light and airy, constructed of chopped red onions thinly covered with a chickpea-flour paste spiced with a dash of cumin, coriander, and *amchur*. The flavor exploded in her mouth.

"I'm hungry," she said to Jai.

"Eat then, my darling. All you want is yours, all that I have"—and here he flung his arms out—"is yours."

The meal was delicious, the *naans* flaky and crisp, the chicken falling off the bone at her touch, the potatoes firm and yet tender, simmered in a tomato gravy, covered in silver foil. There were wines and cocktails to accompany the dinner. Mila and Jai talked for a very long while in the blurred azure light. Until then, all Mila had known about Jai was what Papa had said of him, or what he had said himself, but always with listening ears around. This was their very first private conversation and Ashok's being called away was a blessing.

A shooting star streaked across the sky as Mila lay back in her chair.

"Do you know when you want to marry me?" Jai asked softly.

"Whenever you want," she replied.

He laughed. "If it was only my decision . . . I want you to also have a say."

She turned to look at him. He had pulled his chair near hers and they sat side by side, their backs to the pool and the palace verandah. The moon had begun to rise now and its silver glow cut a swath through the light of the stars. They sat just beyond the parapet, their feet up on the wall. If Mila stood and glanced over the low wall surrounding the pool's verandah, she would look down upon the glittering lights of the town of Rudrakot. But here, just away from those lights, faced away from the servants in the background, they were still in the embrace of just the night.

She said then, "I do not keep *purdah*, Jai."

He nodded. "I know. I would not expect you to. Sheela"—his first wife's name came out hesitantly—"chooses the life, she knows little else; she was in her father's *zenana* too, not allowed to step outside. But you must understand that perhaps your life will change." When she began to frown, he said, "Only as much as a woman's life changes when she marries. I will do everything I can to make this easy."

"I know you will." Mila's voice was subdued. Even the very fact that Jai had wanted to marry her had come under attentive scrutiny from as far as Delhi. When Jai had announced his intentions, Raman had caviled, though only mildly. On a personal level, Raman was both happy and discontented. His happiness had arisen from the fact that Jai was a good match for Mila—a prince could be nothing less than a good match, after all—his discontent and worry had come from the fact that he knew Jai very well, knew his temper, knew his tantrums, knew of his expectation that his authority must always prevail. Yet even Raman had not counted on love. When he had agreed to Jai's proposal, a smile had lit him so brilliantly that Raman had to literally consider shading his eyes, and when he had seen that smile, he had known that his daughter would be cared for and adored for the rest of her life. He had made the right decision for her.

On a professional level, the match between Jai and Mila was *appalling*, and there was really no lesser word for it. After having rejected an excellent alliance from the maharaja of Kurvi for one of his three daughters, Jai was now wasting his princely resources upon a mere political agent's daughter. What worth did she bring to the kingdom? What political connections did she have? Who was she? Who was her father?

All of these questions and their rather pathetic answers Raman was more than aware of. He did point this out to Jai, but Jai just laughed. Colonel Pankhurst was not quite so sanguine, and neither were the kings of the neighboring princely states, quite a few of whom had a gaggle of eligible daughters—well, daughters of childbearing age anyway. A slow storm had begun to stir two months ago, and though none of them acknowledged it in Rudrakot, it continued to blow with ferocity. From what Papa mentioned, every now and then, Mila knew that Jai had been bombarded with letters, missives, even visits from various ministers of state, *diwans*, servants and the princes themselves asking him to consider marrying elsewhere. Even the viceroy, or rather a member of his cabinet who was presumably speaking for the man himself, had written to Jai condemning this action. And if it had not been for Papa, Mila would have known none of this, for Jai behaved as though it did not matter one whit.

If he could stand up and oppose what seemed to be the diplomatic corps of most of the neighboring kingdoms for her, her life would indeed be easy with him. Overwhelmed by an emotion she could not identify, Mila took his hand in hers and kissed his knuckles, much as he had upon first seeing her earlier in the evening. Then she leaned over and laid her head on his chest. *Thank you*, she said silently.

"Will you do me a favor?" he asked.

"Anything."

"Sheela wishes to meet you tonight, before the White Durbar; will you go and see her in the *zenana*?"

Until now, Mila had not given much thought to Jai's first wife, even though she met his children often at parties at the Victoria Club or at the residency. She knew he had a wife, why, her own father had helped in the picking out and choosing of that wife—Jai had in the end married the woman Raman, in his capacity as political agent, had decided was right for him. Jai had never spoken to her about Sheela, who was the princess of Shaktipur, and had come into the marriage with a royal title of her own. Jai's love was all her own, Mila thought, but proprieties had to be maintained. Since she was also going to be Jai's wife, in the parlance of such alliances, Jai's first wife would be a sister to her. They had to learn to be friends, to meet at family functions, to spread their affection among all of their children.

"Where will I live, Jai?" she asked, a sudden fear besetting her.

"Why," he said, rubbing his hand over hers, "with me, in the palace."

Jai's first wife lived within the walls of the *zenana*, the women's quarters of the palace. It was a world populated solely by women, a few children, many servants, also mostly women. There were no eunuchs in Jai's *zenana*, it was a practice he abhorred, and he had retired the oldest eunuch almost as soon as he had gained the crown, at thirteen. That eunuch lived in the lower part of the fort, pensioned for life. There were menservants in the *zenana* now, brought in to move the plant pots, sweep the carpets, mow the lawns, and clean the corridors. But for all this, all the women's lives still revolved around Jai. He would have visited his wife a few times, perhaps more than a few times at night, in order for her to have conceived the children. But even Jai would have entered his wife's apartments in the *zenana* for these nocturnal visits via a set of stairs built in the back of the rooms, and left by them before the sun broke into the sky in the morning. All of his other visits to the *zenana* would be conducted in plain sight of the many other women there—the wives of Raja Bhimsen, the cousins, sisters, nieces, and grandmothers. It was little wonder that he did not love his wife; he did not know her. He had his own array of apartments in another wing of the palace, a series of sitting rooms, drawing rooms, music rooms, a mammoth bedroom built on a miniature lake, a slew of dining rooms of different sizes where he ate if he did not feel like eating in the main dining hall with its seventy-foot-long table.

Mila crinkled her eyes and it seemed to her that the tiny blue lights on the palace walls began to smear their beams in horizontal and vertical lines, as though they were the iron bars of a prison. She would not be able to bear a life in the *zenana*, or even shut away in some part of the palace on her own.

"Where will I be, Jai?" she asked again.

In response, he rose and put his hands out to pull her to her feet. He glanced at his wristwatch briefly. "We have two hours before I have to dress for the White Durbar." As they walked toward the palace verandah, Jai stood still for a moment and inclined his head. A servant came hurrying up and bowed.

"Will you please let First Her Highness know that Second Her Highness will come to visit her in an hour and forty-five minutes? Thank you."

Then, still holding her hand, he led her into the palace's verandah, through a narrow, unlit corridor that Mila had not noticed before, and into the courtyard that led to his apartments. Not all of the rooms were wired for electricity; there were, in fact, so many rooms here, so many tiny squirreled-away inner courtyards and gardens with little pavilions, that even Jai had not fully explored all of these. A servant scurried forward with a petromax lantern and turned the wick on high so that its white light shone with a bright and constant hiss.

"You may go now," Jai said to him as he took the lantern from the servant.

The man dithered. "Your Highness, it is not safe for you to wander here alone."

"Thank you," Jai said politely and waited until the man bowed and backed out of the courtyard. He turned to Mila.

"Do you want to decide where you are to live? Or rather, if you decide to live somewhere too far from my rooms, where *we* are to live? For I will have to move closer to you, you know." He held the lantern up in his right hand and grasped her hand tightly with his left.

She nodded, filled to choking with tears. And so they wandered through all the rooms, some in minor use, some unused, with Mila holding the lush folds of her white sari above her ankles as she walked so that the chiffon would not gather dust.

# Twenty-four

*On April 13 [1919] a peaceful meeting of several thousand men, women and children was held in the walled garden of Jallianwala Bagh in Amritsar, and, under orders of General Dyer, troops fired on the people, who could not get out of the garden because it had only one small exit. Over a thousand were killed and wounded in this infamous massacre, and while General Dyer was applauded in the House of Lords, the poet Rabindranath Tagore returned the knighthood he had earlier accepted from the British.*

—Vijaya Lakshmi Pandit, *The Scope of Happiness*, 1979

*E*ven before he had told Mila that he loved her, in so many words, Sam made a mistake that would make her doubt her affection for him. And he did this knowingly, fully aware that he was betraying the woman he loved. But Sam was on that day in Rudrakot caught irrevocably between Mila and Mike. He loved them both dearly, his allegiance lay with them both, but he was not the type of man who frittered away his word once he had made a promise, however unpalatable it might be.

So Sam lied to Ashok and Raman when he said that he would be glad to take Ashok to the Victoria Club for a drink. It was the only excuse he could think of at a moment's notice after Mila had left him to answer the toot of Jai's limousine's horn and Ashok had come racing out of his room on Sam's left to say, "Is the damn car here already? I'm not even close to being ready. Will you tell Mila please, Captain Hawthorne?"

"Do you want to go to the dinner, Ashok?" Sam had asked.

Ashok's young face folded into all sorts of despair—he wrinkled his nose, bit his lower lip, and knotted his eyebrows. Rolling his eyeballs to the very back of his head so that all Sam could see briefly were the whites of his eyes, Ashok said, "I detest these evenings. Jai will hang over Mila, they will talk stiltedly until he makes an obvious play to get me to go somewhere for a while so that he can kiss her behind a pillar or a fern. Papa has told me not to leave them alone for more than fifteen minutes— I usually give them twenty and make a great deal of noise as I return. I wish they would just get married. And soon."

He said all of this in a light tone and Sam's heart slowly crumbled and crashed to the floor. He saw Jai and Mila together, behind a meticulously maintained geranium in forced bloom, but he could not see them *kiss*— that very word nauseated him. And yet it was possible, Mila had gone downstairs to get into the limousine.

"Would you like to come to the club with me?" Sam asked casually, forcing his voice to be indifferent. Around them as the sun set, the birds of the back garden began to chirp. "Perhaps we can convince your papa to let you have a first drink . . . in public that is."

"Oh, can we?" Ashok was delighted and clapped his hands. "But I have to go with Mila, what will Papa say?"

"Ask him."

Ashok turned and ran into his room again, and Sam heard his room door open into the corridor and then shut as he shouted for his father. Raman's voice answered, more quietly.

Sam lit a cigarette and leaned back against the verandah's parapet to wait for Ashok. He tried not to think of Mila getting into Jai's car. Surely, if Ashok was not allowed to go, Mila would not too? Raman would frown upon it. Surely. Sam wanted to take Ashok with him to keep his word to Vimal, but if it meant that Mila's dinner plans would be thrown into disarray, then so much the better. Dragging smoke into his lungs, Sam held it there and waited, his hands suddenly quaking. He did not believe that Mila truly loved Jai, it could not be, she would not have responded to him as she had if that were true. But she did think she had a duty, and that was not enough for Sam, for he wanted all of Mila, not just the part she was willing to keep from Jai. She had proclaimed in no uncertain terms that she would marry Jai, and that she loved him. When she had left after saying so, Sam had still been exhilarated. Still thrilled. He had not really listened to her. He had said something frivolous . . . about his daughter, about a child he would have, a child he wanted to have with her.

He flung his cigarette away into the bushes below the verandah and watched as the butt glowed and ate at one of the dried branches and then petered out and died in a wisp of smoke. Sam wrapped his arms around one of the verandah's pillars and laid his face against the cooling stone.

"Captain Hawthorne," Ashok said behind him, popping his head from the doorway. "Papa says I can go with you. How splendid!"

Sam nodded, still with his back to Ashok, and his unasked question rushed into the span of space between them and grabbed Ashok by the throat.

"Oh," Ashok said, before disappearing into his room, "Mila goes alone to be with Jai. I'm going to go tell her; she will be thrilled."

Sam waited, listening hard until he heard the soft purr of the Daimler's smooth engine, and Mila went out into the night and to Jai's waiting arms. He felt a layer of hardness form over him. If he had been religious, Sam thought with a sense of irony, still wrapped around the pillar, he could have prayed, but their mother had rarely taken them to church and he had not sought the solace of God when he had learned Mike was missing. And even now, when he was but a day from rescuing him, he would not consider the possibility of defeat or failure, for he had always believed that he could do for himself more than adequately without any help from above. Belief in God had raised too many questions, too much doubt about the existence of any sort of benevolence when there was so much hurt, pain, poverty in the world and when there was this war, which had brought him to Rudrakot. And the Great War before this one, when too many men had died for causes that made little sense to him. Sam had to finish what he had come here for. He had to rescue his brother.

Ten minutes later, Sam and Ashok got into the jeep and drove out toward the Victoria Club. The sun had set by the time they left. Sam drove slowly through the Civil Lines where the houses were almost in complete darkness because even though most of them had electricity, this was visible only by the presence of a lone and weak bulb in the front verandah. But the glass plates were lit in their niches on the gateposts and showed clearly the names of the occupants. Here and there, Sam could see the glowing end of the watchmen's *beedis*. When they passed the cantonment area,

Sam switched off the jeep's headlights and they drove through a wondrous starlight-dappled tunnel of trees, the skin on their arms blue and green, visibility stretching for the entire length of the road. He could feel Ashok next to him, quivering with excitement, and he almost turned the jeep around.

At the *roundtana* where the road branched into many directions, the policeman's box was empty. Sam went around the *roundtana* twice, missing the turn to the road that led to the Victoria Club, until Ashok said, shouting above the jeep's engine, "We are not going to the club, are we, Captain Hawthorne?"

"No," Sam said. "Do you mind?"

"Vimal?"

Sam nodded, and finally, on the last circle cut out of the road, drove into the lane that led to the Lal Bazaar.

When they reached the house where Vimal's freedom fighters had their headquarters, Sam turned off the jeep and stayed where he was, his thumb and forefinger still curled around the key. The front grounds of the house thronged with people, all dressed in white, just as they were, but Sam did not think that they would all be heading for the White Durbar after this. The men and women—and really, some of them were so young that they could not even have accomplished adolescence—were clad in the *khadi* of the nationalists. The *khadi* that Mahatma Gandhi had declared to be the uniform for them all, dull white cloth fabricated by each of the freedom fighters at home, the cotton carded, made into thread, woven in a loom, cut and sewn into clothes. All of this was in defiance of the British Raj, to avoid buying machine-knit clothing made in British mills, to create a boycott of all things British.

The crowd, both men and women, were wearing loose pajamas and tuniclike *kurtas*, short and reaching only to midthigh for the men, and longer, to the knees, for the women. Even in all their finery, their silk shirts and their white linen pants, Sam and Ashok blended in with the crowd and not one inquisitive glance came their way.

A little twinge of regret washed over Sam and he said, "We can leave if you want, Ashok."

"No." Ashok shook his head, the laughter obviated from his face, his excitement more restrained. Something else, something more powerful had taken over and Sam almost pulled him back into the jeep and drove back to Raman's house. But he had brought him here at Vimal's behest, and already, even though Vimal was nowhere to be seen, the young man's arms had reached out and yanked Ashok in. Sam did place a hand on Ashok's shoulder, but he brushed it off with a surprisingly wiry strength. He got down and joined the crowd, lightly touching an arm here and there for them to make way for him so that he could move up to the front of the house. Sam stayed where he was, at the very back, determined that he would not leave Ashok alone here. Even though he towered well over the heads of most of the crowd, no one paid any attention to him. They did not even talk, they barely seemed to breathe. All they did was stare with an intensity at the still-darkened steps that led up to the front door of the house until it seemed to Sam that surely they must all go up in flames if no one appeared soon.

Five minutes later Vimal came out of the door, dressed as he always dressed, simply, in white, holding his hands together in a *namaste*. Sam leaned back against the back wall of the compound and searched desperately over the slew of black heads for the one that belonged to Ashok, but from here it was difficult to tell which one was him. When this ended he would take him back home; his promise to Vimal had merely been to bring Ashok here for this meeting and Sam had seen nothing wrong in that. There was no guarantee that Ashok would become a nationalist because of this one night, or be ensnared in some illegal activity. Sam told himself that they were here because he was himself curious about the nationalist movement. But if he was to be perfectly honest, he had owed Vimal this favor—any favor at all—for having helped him find Mike. Besides, he knew, without having talked with either Raman or Mila, that they would have disapproved of Ashok's being here.

Fifteen Indian policemen led by a British police inspector now slipped in through the front gate and lined up along the wall, blocking the entrance. Sam felt a little trickle of fear. The policemen carried rifles; the inspector, who stood in the gateway, legs apart, rested his right hand on his revolver. Sam moved along the wall as unobtrusively as he could, but the inspector's beady eyes swung in his direction and then away. He had been seen. Sam searched again for Ashok, wishing now that he had not let him leave his side. The crowd of students had, upon the arrival of the police, turned to stare at them stoically, but all too soon their attention was again riveted upon the beloved figure of their leader. And when Vimal spoke, it was only to voice Sam's own fears.

"Do not worry, comrades," he said, barely above a normal tone, but clear and audible, "there will be no repetition of the Jallianwala Bagh incident. The British are now too cravenly to attempt again to massacre an entire population of men, women, and children at a peaceful meeting by blocking off all exits and firing upon a scrambling crowd. The eyes of the world are upon India; they cannot stand up to such scrutiny again."

The crowd began to clap, thumping palm against palm, elbows pumping with effort, sweat drenching brows. "*Jai Hind*!" they cried. "Hail to India!"

Vimal held up a hand. "And our police inspector, Mr. Dyer, though an admirable man in his own right and fortunately thus christened at birth, can make no pretensions to being a *General* Dyer."

A laugh rippled through the crowd and they all turned again, in one body, to look upon the reddening face of the police inspector, who blushed. A tic sprang up on the side of his mouth and he gazed ahead, above the heads of the students. Sam smiled at Vimal's silver tongue and his wit. General Dyer was the man who had ordered the firing upon the crowds at Jallianwala Bagh in 1919, killing hundreds of unarmed civilians gathered for a political meeting. When asked why he had not used the machine guns mounted upon the armored vehicles he had brought to the meeting, Dyer had answered that he could not fit the vehicles through the entrance. Dyer had gone to Jallianwala Bagh with the intention of committing a mass massacre; he had blocked all the accesses to the park so that no one could run out, and without a warning to the people, ordered his men to fire. It had been the catalyst of the nationalist movement in India, and after that, nothing but absolute and complete freedom from the British had been acceptable. And yet, Sam thought, here they were in 1942, more than two decades after Jallianwala, witnessing a similar scenario. He glanced at Inspector Dyer and saw that indeed, Vimal had been right. This man was very well aware of posterity's harsh gaze upon him, this crowd too was peaceful and peaceable, and he would not dare order his men to fire upon them.

The meeting went on then and out of Vimal's beautiful mouth rolled words of fire and strength. "What is the name of Rudrakot's only institution for higher learning, my friends?" he thundered. "Annadale College, named for John Annadale. It admits us now——" he held up his hands and rolled back the sleeves of his *kurta* to expose his skin—"people like you and me, but only for profit. Did you know that it was instated for the use, exclusively, of the children of the Raj? And by that, they did not mean us, the colored, the natives, they meant the children of the whites. But all too soon, they realized that just to keep alive, to barely be able to breathe, they needed the fees we would pay too and opened the doors. And *that* is why you can call yourself students of Annadale."

A murmur began in the crowd. They glanced at each other with anger. Not many of them had known this history because they were too young—when Annadale had allowed admission to Indians—but now their blood was fired by this past impropriety.

"A fine rule that was, my friends," Vimal said, feeding on the wave of discontent that swept through the courtyard. "When our British friends speak of the Raj, they speak only of themselves—we do not figure in any translation of that word at all. The Raj is the British, and yet, where would they be without us?

"Our government advises patience and yet refuses us independence. And here they are"—Vimal encompassed the air with an arcing movement of one arm—"striving to set other people free, defending the Home country against Hitler's ravages, seeking freedom with one hand——" he flung his other arm out—"dominating an entire other people with the other!"

The crowd roared in a massive shout.

Vimal abused the British government of India; he insulted the poor, perspiring inspector; he talked passionately about love for his country and the need for independence. By the end of it, Sam was as swept away as the others. He saw Ashok rapt in the front row, gazing at Vimal with a look of adoration. When Vimal finished, the crowd clapped long and hard, the noise reverberating around the small courtyard while he stood there on the front steps in front of the constabulary of Rudrakot. A policeman walked through the crowd, his khaki uniform like a dab of mud among all that *khadi* white, and wrote down the names of as many people as he recognized.

Sam saw Vimal wilt and collapse into a seated position on the front steps, his chest heaving, exhaustion whitening his face. A hundred arms reached out to him, but he waved them all away and said, "Go. Only he must be here." He was pointing at Ashok.

Ashok went to kneel by Vimal's side, drew out his white silk handkerchief, and mopped his brow. Vimal's breathing returned to normal and the color in his face came back. They both waited for Sam to approach them, and when he did, Ashok said firmly, not even looking up at Sam, "I will stay here with Vimal right now, Captain Hawthorne. You must carry on to the White Durbar."

April 1942, a Month Earlier

*Somewhere in Burma*

*S*o this is it, Sam thinks. This is where his training has brought him. From basic training in Georgia with its interminable and dragging marches. The lessons in camouflage, with shrubs and branches and twigs and leaves on helmets. Night raids on sandbags masquerading as the enemy. The killing of that enemy, sand spilling out for guts and for blood. Then one afternoon, the major puts his head into the barracks and hollers, "Ridley, Samuel! To the colonel's office. ASAP. With your kit. You're outta here."

That day he becomes Sam Hawthorne. That day Sam learns about a fledgling OSS unit. What, he asks? Office of Strategic Services. You are going to Burma. What do I do there, sir? You'll know when you get there, Hawthorne. Why the change in name, sir? So you are nobody. Use your background, just as it is, but be sparing about your past life. You have a brother and a mother? Keep them. Thank you, sir. I will, if you don't mind, Sam thinks with amusement. The army orders his name changed, orders for him a new identity, and orders him to get used to that name so that whatever he is ordered to do during the war will not be traced back to the Ridleys of Seattle, Washington, USA. It seems like an elaborate act of play to Sam at the beginning, but then he realizes that he does not exist at all on any document extant in his country or Burma or India. Even his CO has only a muddy understanding of the backgrounds of all his men in the Third Burma Rangers—all men like Sam, rife with secrets that will save their lives if the Japanese capture any of them. Eventually, in a few months, the Third Burma Rangers will parachute back into Burma and begin to wage a war behind Japanese lines, to weaken the enemy within it-self. But before this, Sam is sent in to rescue Marianne, and finds himself saddled with Ken, who has collapsed after the sound of the bullet from the plantation bungalow.

All this sweeps through Sam's brain in less than a second. Ken has folded to the ground without a sound, and he falls on his face, wet mud slinging out as his forehead hits the dirt. Sam shoves Marianne down. He kicks at Ken's face in the mud so that he flips onto his back, and so that he can breathe . . . if he can still breathe. "Don't move," he says in a harsh whisper, "that's an order."

Sam plunges down the hillside, yanks the safety off the pistol, and runs toward the front entrance of the plantation house. Someone has told him a story of an officer who was caught in enemy fire on a flat land with nowhere to hide, on a tennis court, of all places, and the officer ran at the shooter for lack of anything else to do and managed to lob a grenade into the thicket before he was wounded, killing the shooter and earning himself one of the early medals in the war. Sam gallops toward the house, thinking of all this, but not shooting yet, for he does not know where to aim his precious bullets. He thinks he saw a flash of fire when the gun sent its bullet into Ken, to the right of the front door. Sam reaches the long, covered walkway and clatters down its teak surface, moving so fast that two bullets sing into the stagnant air and then sail into the pillars that hold up the roof of the walkway, right after he passes. Sam hears them, hears the soft thud of metal into wood, hears the pillars creak and moan in protest, but keeps his eyes on the window to the right. The glass is broken, an ugly black rifle nose juts out, wavering as it tries to follow his fleeting path.

To the shooter, Sam is a blur of khaki and green, his arms pumping as he runs, his boots almost silent on the polished walkway, his hair flying. Sam means to kill. If he is not killed himself.

Another bullet bursts into the air, but Sam does not even duck as he runs, his breathing strangely even, unhurried. Everything he has learned in training, every exercise he has performed, every lesson taught moves him through that walkway and toward his enemy without hesitation. He barrels through the half-open door and spins into the front porch. Sam comes to a halt and listens. There is a drawing room to his right, the entrance framed by a brick arch. Light spills in from a window. Even though he has been running, his breathing is quiet enough that he can hear the slither of some kind of furniture (a chair perhaps?) near the wall where the window is. Sam picks up a stool from the front porch with his left hand, and moves toward the arch, his gun held steady in his right. As he nears, he heaves the stool up and throws it into the room. The rifle shots reverberate crazily, and Sam rushes in, his pistol firing also. Once. Twice. He sees a pair of legs behind a sofa and takes aim at both ankles, pulverizing each into a mass of blood and bone.

And then there is silence. And a sound of crying. There is only one person here. Someone left behind. The acrid smoke of their bullets hangs in the air, bites into Sam's nostrils. Still holding his gun, Sam moves around the sofa. The Japanese soldier lies along the back of the sofa, hands clutching his knees, tears plunging down his attenuated cheeks.

"*Tanomuyo,*" he says, waving emaciated fingers in the air. "*Tekidato omottanda. Ore wa kowakattanda.*"

*Please. I thought you were the enemy. I was afraid.*

Sam looks at him, and looks down at the ankles he has shattered. Why, he thinks, he is just a boy. He cannot be more than fifteen years old. Tears gush wetly down his face, an old, decomposed bandage grasps his thin ribs, the coverings mottled with blood and pus, his hair is sweaty and sticks to his head. Sam grabs him by the collar and drags him to the center of the room, kicking his rifle away to the side so that the boy cannot reach it. He tears a white tablecloth into strips, binds the boy's wrists behind his back, and leaves him propped up against a sofa. The soldier's blood pools at his feet and his face pales. Sam surveys him for a few minutes before tearing more strips from the tablecloth and using these as a bandage to bind the boy's ankles. He will never walk again, but he will at least still be alive.

Marianne and Sam bring an immobile Ken into the bungalow after Sam is sure that there is no one else here. There are many rooms, and all of them except for the front drawing room where the Japanese soldier lies in his own blood are trashed beyond recognition—furniture splintered into sticks, sofas and armchairs slashed, brass vases flattened, mattresses and bedding burned and moldering damply. There are big gashes in the red-tiled roof of the bungalow and rain has taken up occupancy in most of the rooms, bringing with it spiders, mosquitoes, innumerable leeches crawling along the stone floors in search of living flesh to feed on. The drawing room is the only safe and dry place in the house. Sam knocks out the door on one end and clears a path from the room to the back of the bungalow so that they now have three exits if they need them—the doorway, the concrete arch leading to the front porch, and the windows along the front from where the soldier shot at them.

Ken's wound is only superficial, and they find this out after Marianne undresses him in one corner of the drawing room as the Japanese soldier watches them, fear blanching his face. The bullet has only singed the skin on the side of Ken's neck. It still takes him a very long time to come around though, and all through this Marianne sits by his side, rubbing her fingers along his temples. She does not look at the Japanese boy, but when her gaze does fall upon him inadvertently, she shudders.

"Will Ken live?" Sam asks.

"Yes," she replies, "there is really nothing wrong with him. I'm not sure why he does not wake up."

At that moment Ken stirs, his eyelids flutter, and when he opens his eyes his gaze is direct and focused, as though he has been awake for a while. Marianne fusses around him and he smiles weakly at her.

"It takes more than a bullet from a bloody Jap to kill me," he says, but he has not yet looked around or seen that the Japanese soldier is in the room with them; he could not have known, Sam thinks, who shot at him.

"Why is he still alive?" he asks.

Sam shrugs. "No point in killing him in cold blood, and when I had a chance he only presented me with his legs, so I crippled him."

Ken seems satisfied with that explanation and closes his eyes again. In a few minutes, his breathing evens and he is asleep. Sam meets Marianne's eyes and the same worry is reflected in them both—Ken is injured on his neck, there is no telling how it will affect him; and they are now guardians of a Japanese soldier who has no capacity to walk. What will they do with him? Leave him here by himself, so that he can point his army toward their direction? Kill him before they leave, to keep themselves safe? Carry him out with them? How will they manage two wounded men? For all the resilience and courage she has shown so far, Marianne Westwood is still an old woman. Sam, who is so much younger, is exhausted already, he only sleeps in fits and wakens drenched in sweat and nightmares; he cannot begin to imagine how long Marianne's strength will last.

Sam digs through his haversack for another pistol, and when he pulls it out, the barrel is rusted through. Three short days ago, it fell into a river they were forced to ford on the trail.

"I will go out and find the hen," he says, "and prepare dinner for us.

And," he says, pausing, "for the boy." Here he glances at the Japanese soldier. "Will you be all right?"

"Yes."

Still Sam lingers, uneasy, not wanting to leave Marianne alone. She waves toward the door. "Go."

The rain has stopped by the time Sam steps out into the darkening light under the moist teak trees. He walks around the perimeter of the bungalow, his boots squelching in the damp grass. What he sees on the inside—a shambles—is mirrored here too, the lawns are blown up with unnecessary throws of grenades, the bushes are hacked down by someone gone mad with his *dah,* the creamy yellow shrouds on the murdered earth are the annual blooming *padauk* flowers. Such destruction, Sam thinks, as his nostrils fill with the fragrance of the flowers. There is a sudden movement in the bushes and the scrawny hen comes clucking out and stops at Sam's feet. He puts out a hand to it and it does not move for a second, then turns around and flees, rending the still air with the sound of its frantic clucks. Sam finally pounces upon the hen on one of the walkways surrounding the house and grabs it by the neck. It flutters in his arms, protesting in a flurry of feathers until he wrings the thin neck with one twist and settles its still-warm body in the crook of his elbow.

Sam comes upon the pool on the side of the bungalow and looks down into the clear, green water, his whole self rampant with longing. The temperature still hovers somewhere over blazing, though the sun is close to setting and the canopy of trees over him has darkened everything to a blur. Water drips from the leaves of the hibiscus bushes and the pool seems to glow as though lit from inside with a string of lights. Sam sets the dead bird down by the side of the pool and strips off his clothes until he is naked. He dives from the side into the water, barely breaking the surface. When he comes up for air after a blessedly long time in the cool water, his body feels clean and strong, the sweat and dirt of the past few days washes away, he can breathe and feel human again. Sam floats in the water on his back, submerging himself until only his nose is in the air. He drifts weightlessly, his arms out, his fingers dragging under the surface to keep his body in balance.

He thinks he feels the smooth and clammy brush of skin against his, for just a moment, but is too lethargic to open his eyes. The feeling passes, but then there is a distinct rising of the hairs along his back and on his nape. Sam does not open his eyes but listens intently, raising himself out of the water just enough for his ears to be revealed. This is no sound from a human being. An animal? His clothes lie in a pile along the side of the pool, by the dead hen, and right on top is his leather holster with his Colt tucked safely in it.

Sam opens his eyes but makes no sudden movements, just gently propels himself toward the rim of the pool. He senses, rather than sees, at first, the gelid pale white and daffodil yellow skin of the snake rising out of the pool. It runs its muskmelon-size head along the edge of the verandah, its forked tongue slithering out for a taste in the air of the dead hen and finds it. The python has begun to open its jaws and slide its body out of the water when Sam ducks his head into the water and swims toward it, thinking only that he is not going to lose his only delicious dinner to a damn snake.

As his splashing sends waves toward the edge of the pool, the python turns around, falls back into the water and races toward him. It comes upon his body from underneath and coils its mighty length over the part it has most access to, his right arm.

Sam suddenly finds himself in the Burmese python's embrace, within the waters of the pool where they have both been swimming. He opens his mouth to call out to Marianne and at that instant, the mammoth snake squeezes and constricts around Sam's arm. And yanks him under.

# Twenty-five

*For seven years, while her son was a minor, she practically ruled from
behind the purdah; a seclusion so strict that even the doctor must look at
her tongue, or the dentist pull out her teeth, through a slit in the curtain
that shut off the inner apartments; and her ladies must follow suit . . . she
triumphed over all imposed limitations; but . . . she could not easily move
about, because of purdah restrictions.*

—Maud Diver, *Royal India*, 1942

*T*he *zenana* apartments of Jai's palace were in a separate wing by
themselves, accessed through a series of corridors. Mila walked
behind the manservant who led her to the *zenana*, a petromax lantern held
aloft in his hand. Here, there was no electricity and this part of the palace
was ancient, perhaps built as early as the sixteenth century by an ancestor
of the Rudrakot royal family. The corridors had huge, cusped arches and
enormous ceilings painted a deep indigo blue. There were gaps in the *jalis*,
screens on top of the arches, from where little bits of twigs and dust came
floating down when a roosting pigeon flapped at the intrusion upon its
night's sleep. Mila heard the deep gurgles of protest from the pigeons'
throats, heard the cry of a peacock somewhere in the gardens beyond the
light from the lantern, saw the colors of the walls intensify and fade as
they passed until it seemed like they were within the embrace of an ocean.

The whole evening had been surreal, the dinner, the flight through the
various rooms of Jai's apartments, startling a lazy gecko here, a nesting

sparrow there; their laughter and an overwhelming feeling of love and affection for this man who wanted to give her so much. She had chosen the
rooms she wanted for her own when she would be married to Jai, three of
them, each opening out onto a marble courtyard with a fountain in the center and a parapet on the far end with a view of the town of Rudrakot and
the Panjari Mountains capping the horizon in the distance. There were two
trees in the courtyard, one a *kinshuk*, now in full bloom with its bright ver-
milion flowers and its dark mahogany-colored bark, and another the pro-
saic *neem* tree, which would soon fruit with its yellow, grapelike, inedible
fruit. The rooms were large and empty, and Mila had stood in one darkened corner—as Jai moved around at the other end of each room—and
listened for the breathing of past occupants, a smell from their presence, an
approval of her wanting this space for her own, for her being here.

When it came time for her to marry Jai and move into these apartments, the rooms would be ready—whitewashed anew, the marble polished and washed, the floors slicked clean of the dust and dirt of centuries,
the niches wired for electricity, carpets laid on the floor, Louis XIV furniture moved in, complete with a four-poster bed in the bedchamber. As it
was, Jai's apartments were on another side of this wing of the palace and
part of the renovation would include his removal from the old rooms to
new ones close to hers. They would sleep in her bedchamber and awaken
to each other every morning. No valets would be allowed to enter the
room, instead Jai would have to learn to rise and go out to meet his
menservants so that they could attend to his needs.

Mila's footsteps faltered at the thought of their sharing a room. She
pulled the *pallu* of her glittering sari around her shoulders and covered
herself from a sudden chill in the heated air. The manservant walking in
front of her paused, inclined his head, and waited for her to make the ad-
justments with her *pallu*. Then he went on, listening for the sound of her
footsteps matching his own.

When they reached the harem apartments, the manservant bowed and
stood aside in front of a heavy teak door painted bright red and studded
with brass fittings, like the outer doors of forts and palaces. He reached
out and thumped on the wood with his fist and the door opened to reveal
another servant, also male, but part of the *zenana*.

The second servant bowed to Mila and swung his hand inward, indicating that she should join him there. His glance fell upon the raised

doorstep and then up to her face and Mila nodded as she lifted her foot to step across the threshold into the *zenana*. As she took that first step, she wondered how many times she would have to come in here in the future and what the etiquette would be then, when she would be officially part of Jai's household. For now, she was merely a guest.

Here also there was no electricity, but the wall niches had been put to good use with oil lamps made of clay, the flames standing upright in the torpid air. The lamps only threw little pools of light within their very tight peripheries, and the rest of the corridor was in darkness, but beyond the corridor were the gardens again and here the stars and the rising moon lit the landscape. Mila went through another set of corridors and another set of doors, and as she neared the heart of the *zenana*, where the most important women in Jai's harem lived, the embellishments on the walls and the doors and the verandahs became more and more ornate. The brass was polished and shiny, the lamps held clean, newly pressed oil with barely the hint of an odor, the floors were clean with wiping, the bushes in the gardens rampant with cloyingly fragrant blooms, the views in the distance, of the town of Rudrakot, like a diamond necklace flung out into the desert night.

And then, from this semidark, glorious world of aromas, Mila stepped into a brightly lit, dazzling room, the main reception hall of the harem. She entered and stopped, her breath taken away by a grandeur she could not ever have imagined.

There were lights everywhere, in the niches in the walls, the candles hung from glass globe chandeliers all over the ceiling, the enormous five-foot floor lamps with a hundred wicks floating in the oil, each one lit to a brilliance. The walls were covered in a light blue mural of arabesques on a bright white background, lotus flowers and peacocks entwined with each other on every surface, and each brush of paint had embedded within it a little sliver of mirror. So the light from the numerous lamps roved around the room and met the mirrors on all sides and returned upon itself until the air seemed on fire. The floors were marble inlaid with turquoise, and of these Mila could see only the portion that she was standing upon, for the rest was covered in thick Persian rugs that led to the other end where there were low, ivory-inlaid wooden tables weighted down with plates of sweets in all colors and surrounded by thick mattresses and divans.

There were four main women, this much Mila saw in a brief glance as she bent down to undo her high heels before stepping on the carpet. Then, barefoot, the bottom of her sari sweeping the floor, she approached the women who were seated on the divans, surrounded by a multitude of other women, members of the *zenana*, and servants. The woman in the center was Raja Bhimsen's wife, the one who had not been able to provide him with a male heir, and though she was nominally Jai's mother in the harem, he had never really liked her because *she* had detested him. There was also one grandmother, one aunt, and finally, on Mila's right, a younger woman leaning against a bolster, smoking a *hookah*.

"Please sit," she said, in Hindustani, her voice rasping. "You must forgive me, for I speak no English. I have no use for it."

"It is not a problem, Your Highness," Mila replied, sitting down gracefully on one edge of the divan in front of the women. She sat alone on this side of the room and looked only at the woman who had spoken to her, though she could not help but be aware of the dark, kohl-rimmed eyes of the others gazing at her.

"We," the princess of Shaktipur continued, waving her *hookah* pipe at the rest of the women, "have been curious to meet you for two years now."

"But I thought——," Mila began, surprised.

The princess shook her head, and the long, hanging diamond earrings in her ears glittered in the reflected light from the lamps. "We have always known, of course, perhaps even before Jai knew, that one day we would be welcoming you into this harem."

"Yes, thank you," Mila said. She sat very straight on the divan and her back had already begun to ache because she was unused to sitting in chairs without supports for the back. The public rooms in Jai's palaces had Western furniture, but here there was no concession to the West, here all was as it must have been a hundred years ago——the same carpets, the same lighting, the same groups of women rife with inquisitiveness, waiting for the first glimpse of a new member of their *zenana*. The air in the room closed in upon Mila.

"I know you mean to have the rooms surrounding the *kinshuk* tree, and that you mean to live there. This is fine with us, but it would be nice if you could come and visit us every now and then." The princess smiled sadly and suddenly Mila saw a loveliness in her that was not immediately apparent, for she was plump, comfortably round in the face, with a button nose and a fast-fading chin tucked in folds of flesh. But now——when her gaze darkened with an ache at having to welcome her husband's second wife, a woman he so obviously loved, into his palace—an attraction had lit her face.

"I thank you," Mila said again. "You have been . . . are . . . most kind." She hesitated, not sure anymore of what else to say. Should she apologize for Jai's choice? Should she even be repentant? She saw that her life would touch these women's lives only gently, for most of the time she would be with Jai.

And this First Her Highness affirmed by saying carefully, "It has been a great disappointment to Jai that I do not speak English and that I cannot accompany him to parties at the residency or even at your father's house. My life——" here she spread out her hands to encompass the room—"has always been within walls, or if outside, merely in the company of other women. I know you are different, you will be comfortable in the presence of the British women with their white faces and their short skirts that reveal calves and ankles, and perhaps you even wear such dresses yourself?"

Mila shook her head. "Not all the time, Your Highness. I wear pants more often; my Papa frowns upon dresses, well, Pallavi, she is . . . she is in our house, she does not like me in dresses either."

"So you have restraints too?" the princess asked. "It is good for a woman to have restraints."

To this Mila could not respond, for her life was constrained as it was, quite simply because she was a woman. With the new wave of nationalism there had been more liberties for women in India, but it was of the strident, masculine type, where even the Mahatma exhorted women to stand up for their Mother India, but in the same way that the men did. In this traditional world, however, Mila thought, it was women like the princess of Shaktipur—and indeed all the women in these *zenana* walls whose eyes devoured her with such burning curiosity—who imposed limitations on other women. Whether out of spite because they had themselves suffered, or because of a genuine concern, it was difficult to tell. Mila said nothing to the princess of Shaktipur because she could not agree with her last statement, but Jai's first wife, young as she was, perhaps only two or three years older than Mila, understood this.

Her gaze was thoughtful upon Mila's face. "If we were to behave like men, then the men would have no one to look after, no one who would help them feel protective and masculine. I know that Jai likes you for your . . . your ability to travel with him to Paris and London perhaps, because you will ride a horse in the regimental *maidan* without fear, because you can read and write. These are all good skills, my dear, but he must not be made to feel less than he is. Or rather, you must make him feel *more* than he is. Let him be the man."

Mila bent her head, unable to even smile. When First Her Highness had mentioned *reading* and *writing* as one of Mila's skills, it was only because she herself was illiterate. And yet what a difference there was between her and the women of the Lal Bazaar. This sort of speaking was the last resort of the *zenana*—the only way the women within it could feel inviolate and sacrosanct, if somehow they were under the impression that they were being guarded from some terrible atrocities in the outside world. She spoke as though she knew Jai very well and yet Mila knew that the princess's interaction with him had been very limited, and if most of it had been her pandering to Jai, pretending a fragility she did not possess, then it was no wonder that he sought love in her, Mila. The other three older ladies were quiet and watchful, puffing at their *hookahs* too until the smoke hung in a fog around Mila and the brilliant light of the room was diffused, as though through a piece of glass. The smoke was sweet, almost fruity in flavor, and Mila realized that the tobacco in the *hookahs* was laced with something else, perhaps opium? Yet the scrutiny on her from the many eyes in the room had not wavered—it was steady and it was questioning. Mila did not intend to satisfy all their curiosity at the same time.

She rose and said, "You are indeed kind to have invited me here, First Your Highness." The use of that title, with the word *first* appended, was a deliberate drawing of battle lines in that if there were a *first* there would be a *second*. They would meet in the future, be polite to each other, but there was no mistaking that the princess of Shaktipur was jealous, perhaps understandably so, that her husband had gone out of the *zenana* for his affections. Mila knew that once Jai married her, he would never return to the arms of this woman, even though she had a right to his presence in her bedchamber. It was a tacit understanding between Mila and Jai, and an agreement without which she would not marry him.


As Mila sat in the *zenana* apartments talking with Jai's first wife, Sam drove from the political meeting at the Lal Bazaar house to the fort for the

White Durbar. He was deeply troubled at having left Ashok there alone with Vimal, but there was no shaking the boy's resolution once he had made it. He refused to leave, and promised, eventually, that he would come to the fort in an hour's time, before the durbar started. And with that Sam had to be grudgingly content.

He drove past the Victoria Club and slowed down at the gates, wondering if he should go inside for a desperately needed drink and then decided against it. If Sam had gone in, he would have found Kiran at the bar with the officers of the Rifles regiment, all of them steadily getting drunk, on their fourth gin and tonics. They were due at the White Durbar also; it was a strict requirement and part of the regiment's rules. When quartered within the boundaries of a princely state, all the officers and men had to present their respects to the ruling prince, irrespective of their personal views on the matter.

Sims downed his fifth gin and tonic, to bolster his stagger across the durbar hall to bow to Jai, and wiped his receding chin. The alcohol had sent a fire into his veins, and the sight of Mila that afternoon in the brothel house had excited him immeasurably. Without thinking, he said to Kiran, turning him around on his bar stool, "Guess who I saw today?"

At that, Blakely, a little more sober on this hot night, clamped a hard hand on Sims's shoulder and said, "No one. You saw no one, Sims."

Sims shrugged off his hold belligerently. "I did."

"Later," Blakely said. "Later."

# Twenty-six

*. . . many of India's marvels . . . must be seen to be believed. In cold print they read like fantasy or exaggeration . . . eleven acres of Palace: an immensity of rose-pink sandstone that would make Versailles look like a cottage, the interminable façade soaring aloft from redder terrace; the vast central saloon furnished with English chairs and sofas . . . bedrooms like reception halls, the bathrooms like ballrooms.*

*In fifteen dining-rooms as many dinners would be served each day on a silver dinner service worth no less than £30,000; the elaborate courses prepared by a hundred and forty-three cooks and kitchen helpers of whom seventeen chefs were dedicated to curries only.*

—Maud Diver, *Royal India*, 1942

It was not until well past midnight that all the grandees were gathered for the White Durbar on the night of the full moon in Rudrakot. The durbar itself, a conclave of the court in the middle of the night, was an ancient tradition, and it had long been forgotten which Rudrakot king was responsible for its inception. But it was an opportunity, as all such assemblages were, to demonstrate the might of the king, the magnificence of his person, his domination over his people, the plenitude of his treasury. In the beginning, the White Durbar was also an event where the vassal *thakurs,* or landholders, came to pay their respects to their king, to swear allegiance to him, to bow before him and establish their unswerving loyalty. But in May 1942, the king was a mere figurehead. He nominally held the lands of his kingdom, he was responsible for the well-being of his people, but he knew that his authority was hollow, the fealty of his subjects merely routine, since he himself was a satellite of the British Raj.

But none of this affected the actual ritual of homage, and all the participants—the king, the vassals, and the audience—comported themselves with the solemnity demanded by the occasion. The British Raj was built as much upon this pomp and circumstance, this open show of might, as any of India's previous other rulers—the Mughals or the minor kings—might have been. The rituals were to placate the masses, to make them think that there still existed some semblance of normalcy, whatever that normalcy might actually be, that nothing had changed from a hundred, or two hundred years ago. The masses, however, were not invited to the White Durbar; they would merely hear of it from the distance of the next day and nod with satisfaction that their king was revered.

The durbar hall in the palaces of Rudrakot was an enormous courtyard with a balcony built into the ramparts of the fort in one end. The balcony was raised only five feet from the ground and cut into the thick red sandstone of the fort's outer wall. It was constructed entirely of an unblemished white marble that fed on the moonlight and glowed like a pearl at the bottom of a dark ocean bed. Around this main balcony, still on the fort's wall, were dotted ten or fifteen tiny marble balconies, higher off the ground, with *jalis*—screens—rising waist high, covered with half domes shaped in the form of unfurling lotus flowers. Here, the women of Jai's harem had gathered to watch the proceedings of the durbar, one or two to each little balcony. A hundred years ago, the *jalis* had covered the entire aperture of the balcony so nothing of the women could be seen from below in the courtyard, but Jai had had the screens cut down so the women could lean over; at least their limbs and their outlines would be visible, because, of course, they would still continue to cover their heads with a veil.

The rest of the courtyard was quite plain—its beauty lay in the inlay of white marble and red sandstone squares over the whole floor, like some gigantic chessboard. The vividness of this inlay work was not lost on the night of the full moon as each man and woman walked up the center aisle to the main balcony where Jai sat and either bowed or curtseyed before walking away, sideways, since it was not done to show their backs to the king.

Since it was the White Durbar, the proceedings only began when the moon had reached its full height in the sky and smiled benignly upon them in all of its silver glory. The white marble of the architecture was lustrous, the white dress uniforms of the Rifles and the Lancers specially worn for this occasion were resplendent, and the women's saris were radiant. There was no light other than the moonlight, and there was so much white, so much silver, so many glittering diamonds and brocades that there was no need for artificial light to discern visages or smiles. Everyone was clad in white, and of them, Jai, in his special *sherwani* and trousers, was the most brilliant.

Before the durbar began, Mila wandered around the line of chairs set flush against the long aisle down which everyone would walk to reach Jai in his balcony and searched for Sam and Ashok. Her father, and Colonel Pankhurst (had he been in Rudrakot on this day), would be arranged in a line somewhere beyond the gates of the palace, waiting to be announced and called into the durbar for their turn. Kiran had never sat with her and she wondered where he was.

As she passed by Sam, he reached out and clasped her wrist gently. "Are you looking for me?"

A flood of happiness went through her and she said, "Yes. But where is Ashok?"

Sam's expression was stolid. "He is here somewhere. He promised me he would come before the durbar."

She sat down on the seat next to Sam. "I thought he was with you at the Victoria Club. Where is he, Sam?"

Sam took a deep breath and held it for so long that Mila began to listen for the sound of his breathing again, and a sudden fear came over her. She did not believe, even then, that Sam would knowingly do harm to her brother, but there was something that troubled him. What? She did not have to ask again, merely to prod his conscience into speech, for Sam knew she would be anxious, much as he had himself become in the last hour. So he told her. Not everything, not that he owed Vimal a promise, or that Vimal had wanted Ashok to come furtively to the meeting, but instead that he himself had taken Ashok to the meeting. He did not tell Mila that this was a fore-planned action, but he felt that she recognized it as such.

"You should not have," she said.

"Why? Is it that you do not want Ashok involved in nationalism?"

She hesitated and looked away over the heads of the people opposite them to the red ramparts of the fort. "We must seem an unorthodox family to you, Sam. I can see that you support the Indian cause for freedom, and being Indian, we should too." She turned to him. "And we do. I do, Papa does, Ashok does when he thinks about it, Kiran does when he wants. Yet it means different things to us all. Here, in Rudrakot, Papa is a representative of the British Indian government, and as such he cannot allow his personal feelings to overrule his commitment to his duty. So not one of us can either. We must be seen to present a united front."

"I was curious about the meeting and wanted to hear Vimal's speech," Sam said.

A wry smile turned up the corners of Mila's mouth. She began to speak and then flushed when she realized what she was saying. "What was it you said in the verandah earlier this evening? That is not enough of a reason." She had to stop, her heart thumping at the remembrance, and it was almost a minute before she could speak again. "It is not just the nationalist movement, for we have our part to do also in this struggle. On the one hand, we are taught not to be individualistic, that fealty to our parents must supersede every other want and every other need, on the other, it is quite simply the question of freedom for my people. I choose to be loyal to my father, not because I am taught so, but because I choose so.

"What I fear for Ashok . . . is Vimal. I do not like that boy, and it is, really, an irrational distaste based on something as stupid as the fact that everyone seems to adore him because he has a slick tongue and a becoming appearance. Perhaps there is more, but I do not like him."

"I'm sorry," Sam said. He could also have said, *I had to take Ashok to the political session; I had promised Vimal.* But he did not, and his silence brought a little wedge of distrust between them, for Mila wondered why, and then thought that Sam must have had a reason or he would not have done something she so disapproved of.

The trumpeters near the gate of the courtyard lifted shining silver trumpets strung with silver tassels to their mouths and a sweet melody floated over the courtyard. They all became silent as the dulcet voice of the *diwan* rang out, first announcing Jai's arrival in the balcony, for which they all rose, and then, one by one, all the men and women who were to pay obeisance to the prince. Lady Pankhurst sailed by, so did the wife of the colonel of the Rifles regiment, the vicar's wife, and quite a few of the ladies from the Civil Lines where Mila lived. The men came next, first the officers of the two regiments and, finally, in the end, Raman, who walked up the aisle and smiled at his daughter as he passed her. Mila covered her mouth with the palm of her right hand and kissed it, sending her love to her father.

Over the next two hours of the White Durbar, the moon shrank in the sky, and when it had ended, strings of aquamarine lights were lit all around the courtyard. Jai stayed in his balcony watching the crowds below, the women of the *zenana* disappeared from their perches, and the audience remained where it was for the grand finale. Bearers in white, with flowing turbans and bare feet, came by with large silver trays on which rested little silver saucers of the specialty of Jai's kitchens, served only on this night, and only to the assembled guests. It was a sweet made from the milk of buffaloes fed only on a diet of almonds and honey. This milk was laced with jasmine honey, boiled for long hours while the top foam was skimmed off and deposited upon the silver saucers. These saucers were then taken into the glass-enclosed conservatory that held the prized roses of the Rudrakot palaces and left there overnight on the cool floor. The dew that formed on the milk was rose-scented, light as air, and sparkled in the moonlight like crystals upon cream.

Each teaspoon of this precious dessert evanesced upon Sam's tongue and soared through his body like an incantation. He knew then that Mila was lost to him forever; how could he even begin to compete with the love of a man who could, so casually, feed four hundred people the sweetened cream of milk drenched with dewdrops? His heart yearned for her, and even though she sat by his side, so close to him, he could not sense her presence. It was as though she were elsewhere.

And Mila was elsewhere. While all the pomp of the White Durbar was meant to awe and impress, on Mila its effect was one of suffocation. She saw herself in this life, in this same life, year after year, perhaps in one of the tiny *zenana* balconies after a while, looking down upon the durbar. There would be little room for spontaneity, not when so many people had to be appeased. She thought of her day and of her evening and how different they had been. The wife of the prince of Rudrakot could not be seen in the brothels of the Lal Bazaar, teaching the girls the letters of the Hindustani alphabet. Her charity, if that is what it was, would have to be more distant, through someone else. Besides, no matter how much she tried to convince herself otherwise, she did not love Jai. Not as she loved Sam.

·   ·   ·

It took a couple of hours for everyone to leave the house at the end of the
Lal Bazaar, but finally it was empty and only Ashok and Vimal remained.
As each person left, they came in their own way to pay obeisance to Vimal
also, just as Jai received respects in the White Durbar. The boy or girl
would bend from the hip, drag their fingers along the floor, near Vimal's
feet but not actually touching them, for he had made it clear that the practice of asking for blessings thus was extremely distasteful to him.

Ashok sat in one corner of the room, still spellbound by what he had
seen and heard. It was difficult not to be swept away by the adulation of so
many, all about as old as he was, fifteen, sixteen, or perhaps as old as eighteen. He recognized a few of them as students from Annadale College and
marveled that Vimal's hold over them was so compelling. As each person
approached Vimal, a tremor seemed to take hold of his or her body simply
with the joy at being so close to their beloved leader. They did not dare to
meet Vimal's burning eyes, which swung every now and then to Ashok
and saturated him with trembling also. Vimal's skin was white on his temples, lines had formed deep grooves around his mouth, his hair was wet
with perspiration, and his breathing was shallow, his chest heaving with
every breath, and Ashok felt fiercely protective toward him. He thought
that Vimal's energy had drained slowly in the two hours that he sat upon
the chair in the middle of the bare room so that his followers could bend,
to speak a tentative word in his ear, receive a smile or a nod. Finally, they
all departed and left Ashok seated in his corner of the room, on the floor,
uncaring that the seat of his expensive linen pants was smudged with dust
and dirt.

"Shall we go up to the roof?" Vimal asked, putting out a hand.

Ashok leapt from his place, ran up to Vimal, and helped him out of his
chair as though he were a very old man. They went up the narrow staircase, walled on either side, with Vimal's arm around Ashok's shoulders,
and Ashok's arm around Vimal's waist.

After the heated closeness of the room downstairs and the stink of
sweat from too many bodies, the terrace was lit with the palely lustrous
moonlight and a sprinkling of stars across the night sky. They sat down in
one corner of the terrace, on the floor, after scratching their feet over the
cement to check for snakes or scorpions their eyes could not see in the
shadow of the parapet. The stone, still warm, retained the blazing heat of
the day, but it was strangely comforting because they were both tired.

Vimal was physically exhausted from his speech in front of his disciples, and Ashok had lost all life from his limbs in the worship of Vimal. He could not stop his hands from trembling.

Vimal took out a tin of cigarettes from the pocket of his *kurta* and lit one, the flare of the flame glowing gold over his beautiful face. The image of that face stayed imprinted on Ashok's brain long after Vimal had blown out the match and thrown it away. Vimal offered the cigarette to Ashok and he put it between his lips, feeling the cool wetness on the tip where Vimal's mouth had closed over it. A shiver ran through him as he handed the cigarette back. They were silent for a long while, listening to the mighty blow of the trumpets at the fort to announce Jai's arrival at the White Durbar.

"You should be there," Vimal said softly.

"I want to be here," Ashok replied, his voice rough and daring.

"Do you really?"

"Yes."

Another silence followed as Vimal smoked his cigarette to the very end and threw the still-glowing butt away, toward the center of the terrace. It bounced and bumped along the floor and came to rest facing them, and then slowly it burned itself out until the only light upon them both was the radiance from the moon swelled to fullness.

Vimal took Ashok's hand in his and pulled him closer, until his head was upon his chest. There was nothing left in the world that Ashok cared about at that moment apart from Vimal. Ashok too, like Mila, would never know another love like this, for the rest of his life.

"An hour before sunset," Vimal said, "I want you to accompany me to the grounds of the residency. They will not let me in by myself, but if you were to come, it would be all right. I am going to put a bomb in Colonel Pankhurst's Daimler. He will drive it himself to the club later in the evening."

It was a testament to Vimal's astonishing power over his fellow human beings that Ashok felt only a fine twinge of guilt, but he also felt almost immediately that Vimal could very well have hidden the purpose for his request and had not. He had trusted him with this incendiary secret. He made a small sound of assent and that was enough.

Vimal put a hand under Ashok's chin and kissed him on the mouth.

April 1942, a Month Earlier

*Somewhere in Burma*

*T*he waters of the pool are suddenly icy cold to Sam. When the python pulls him under the surface with one sweep of its muscular body, he barely has time to register what is happening. His mouth is open to shout out to Marianne, and when he sinks, it fills with water, sending him gasping and choking as his lungs expand and protest.

Sam flails and tries to loosen his right arm from the snake's tenacious grip and feels an immense, shattering pain as it snaps his arm out from its home in his shoulder, tearing tendons and ligaments under his skin. The ache sears its way through his brain and Sam's vision whitens and blurs as everything dissolves in front of him. He can no longer feel the water even, or the lack of oxygen to his veins. If he could think at such a time, he would realize that Burmese pythons are gargantuan creatures, often reaching ten feet or more in length and weighing more than a hundred pounds at full maturity. He would know that once the python begins its crushing embrace, it rarely lets loose until it can feel that its prey has stopped breathing and is completely still. This one, Sam's python, is an adult male, five years old, particularly aggressive and fifteen feet long. The snake has been hungry for twelve days now and has slipped into the pool at the bungalow for the same reason as Sam—to cool off in the immense heat of the late afternoon and to contemplate its hunger in peace. Normally it would not think of humans as prey . . . but there is always a first time.

None of this reasoning is part of Sam's brain the moment it shuts down all other aspects of his body. He can no longer see in the water, no longer suffer from the pain of his dislocated shoulder, no longer even feel the cold of the pool. And in that moment of blankness, comes a sudden clarity, a will to survive, a *need* to do so—the same resolution that keeps his brother alive in the field punishment center in Rudrakot.

Sam heaves upward with a powerful thrust of his legs and hauls himself and the python out of the water like projectiles. He opens his mouth, breathes in deeply before he plunges back into the water, and then strikes out with just his left arm and his legs toward the verandah, dragging the python behind him, still attached firmly to his useless right arm. He opens his eyes finally, and as the water streams from his retina, he sees the figure of Marianne Westwood come into focus. She stands at the edge of the pool, a tiny, pearl-handled pistol held steadily in her hand, aimed at him. She pulls the trigger. The bullet goes cleanly through the python's head and it explodes into a mess of muscle, tissue, sinew, all palely yellow and bloody. Sam reaches Marianne, and just as calmly, she kneels to help him out of the water and unwinds the snake's quivering body from his right arm as though she is unwinding thread from a bobbin.

"There," she says, wiping her hands of the gore from the python on the thighs of her pants, "you're a mess now, Sam. Put on some clothes; you're going to catch a cold."

Sam clambers into his underpants, shivering, his teeth clattering so much the sound fills his ears. He cannot bear to look back at the twitching length of the python by the pool, but before she turns away, Marianne kicks the still-dying carcass into the water with a vigorous thrust from her boot. She bends to pick up the rest of Sam's clothes and the packet of letters from Maude and Mike falls out. Sam lunges for it but not before Marianne has seen the writing on one of the letters.

"What is your connection with Rudrakot?" she asks.

"Do you know of it?"

"It's a small princely state in the Sukh desert, one of the six hundred odd in India. Nothing special, only spectacular for the forts and palaces built in the fourteenth century, where I believe the reigning prince still lives." Marianne's brow is furrowed in thought. Her expression clears. "Rudrakot has a regiment?"

"Two," Sam says, wiping the plastic wrapping around the letters free of water drops against the cotton of his underpants. "My brother, Mike, was in one."

"Was?"

"He might be dead. He's been AWOL for two months now."

Marianne drapes Sam's clothes over her arm, tucks her tiny pistol into the pocket of her pants, and puts a hand to Sam's elbow to nudge him into the bungalow. Sam has begun to shiver. The temperature is nowhere near cold or even cool, but the trembles rack his body as he hunches into his chest. He has not allowed himself to think that Mike might already be dead, but after that encounter with the python, he has used that word, enunciated it flatly, as though it is a fact, not a mere supposition.

"Well," Marianne says in a voice carefully devoid of emotion, "you'll never know until you go to Rudrakot. And you'll never get there like this. Let's go in, get warm, eat that damned bird, and get to India."

When they enter the bungalow again, Sam in agonizing pain from the arm that flaps by his side, they find Ken braced against a wall of the drawing room and interrupt his conversation with the Japanese soldier. Marianne and Sam halt at the archway, both knowing instinctively that this cannot be right—Ken is speaking a laborious Japanese, carefully enunciating each word . . . why?

"Oh, shit," Sam says under his breath.

He bends at the waist so that his useless right arm will have some place on which to rest and with his left, he scrambles for his pistol, which Marianne carries, along with his pants and his shirt, but it is too late. Ken levels a pistol of his own at Sam and Marianne.

"Sit," he says, and when they collapse, he waves at them. "Apart from each other, please. I have a story to tell you."

# Twenty-seven

*Love, when sought out, is an ailment*
*Between the flesh and the bone . . .*

—Khalil Gibran, *The Procession,* 1942

s it happened, only one member of Raman's household slept during the remaining hours of that night, for they were all, in some form or another, engaged in the act of love.

Kiran came home sodden and stewed after the White Durbar because on the way back he had stopped again at the Victoria Club for yet another drink, and again Sims made some maddening suggestions about a secret he held, a secret he would not tell Kiran. They were both drunk, they were all drunk, and it was with great difficulty that Blakely and Forrest managed to part the wrestling Kiran and Sims. They both hurled abuses at each other, and Sims left the indentation of his teeth, a perfect set of thirty-two, on Kiran's back where he had bitten him while they grappled on the floor.

Sayyid opened the door to Kiran and dragged him, none too gently, up the stairs to his room. There, he stripped off his clothes, ran a bath, and forced a staggering Kiran into the bathtub. Once, Kiran cried out, when Sayyid dabbed tincture on his wound to cauterize it, but his touch was firm on his master's son's back. He washed the blood from his skin and put a bandage over it. Then he hauled Kiran out of the tub, dried him as he stood limp and wet in the middle of the bathroom floor, helped him on with his pajamas, and put him to bed. Kiran slept for the next twelve hours.

A weary Raman also came home to Sayyid's careful ministrations and he accepted them with a scolding and gratitude at the same time. They had both returned from Nodi at about ten o'clock in the morning after having been in the saddle for most of the early part of the day. When Raman entered his home, went upstairs to his bedroom, sat in the galvanized aluminum tub, and felt the ache of his aging body, he knew that he could not tour the villages and the districts anymore. That part of his life was over, and with good reason, for he could no longer carry himself for days on end without adequate sleep, and there was no more comfort in the thin tarpaulin sheets laid on rocks that were to substitute for his bed. The exhilaration of the previous day had deflated in the bright light of this one, and he felt old beyond his years. They had come back also to a house that was empty and silent, and Raman knew then that his fears had come true— Mila, Ashok, and Sam had spent the night at Chetak's tomb, unchaperoned. In his head, he said it like this, *Mila, Ashok, and Sam*, as though to evenly divide his daughter's and Sam's names with Ashok's name in his thinking would add propriety to their having been away. Raman did not know then, of course, and would never know, that it was not the night he had to fear, but the happenings of the afternoon, during the dust storm.

Raman returned to Rudrakot and was caught almost immediately in the news Jai had brought from the ICC. Jai was home too from the corps before the end of the session because he had had to expel the maharaja of Kishorenagar from the school. And that had had its repercussions, for Kishorenagar was a princely state with a great deal more importance in the Raj than tiny Rudrakot, and enjoyed the privilege of an eighteen-gun salute to Rudrakot's thirteen. Amongst all of that were some thinly veiled accusations from Kishorenagar that Jai was party to the same habits he had been accused of. There was no truth to the charges of homosexuality on Jai's part, and Colonel Cameron had seen that clearly, but he had also suggested that Jai take a leave of absence from his duties and return to Rudrakot for the duration of the session. Until all of this could be sorted out.

Raman spent the afternoon writing letters to various people. First, he had to let Colonel Pankhurst know at Delhi that a storm was about to thunder above their heads and that he might well be asked about these fictitious charges while he was visiting with the viceroy. Then, he wrote to the two other British instructors at the ICC on Jai's behalf. He pointed out that there was absolutely *no* truth to Jai having any inclination toward homosexuality—Jai was married, had three children, and further, he was betrothed to another woman, Raman's own daughter. *I find this whole affair extremely repugnant and distasteful,* Raman wrote, *and feel somehow, that in asking Jai to leave the ICC, you are lending credence to the tantrums of the young maharaja of Kishorenagar.* He *is the one accused of, and might I add, convicted of these base habits. I would not give my daughter's hand in marriage to a man with such proclivities, even talk such as this, of such unnatural conduct, is disgusting to me, Cameron.*

Jai had been hesitant about convening a White Durbar on that very night; it would be a hastily ordered affair quite simply because Jai was back in Rudrakot unexpectedly. But Raman had insisted upon it, knowing that this was not the time to run and hide their heads in a dark corner somewhere, but to let Jai lead the durbar, accept the obeisances, let everyone see that he was still ruler of his princely kingdom, glorious in his brocade and diamond *sherwani* in the light of the full moon. What of the special dessert served after the White Durbar, Jai had asked. Raman had looked at his watch and measured out a good twelve hours before the sweet was to be served, and had even arranged for the conservatory to be sprayed with water every two hours so that enough condensation could form on the roses to weave into the milk cream.

And so Raman did not have a moment left in the day to see his children, to inquire after them, to find out how they had comported themselves in the last twenty-four hours, or indeed, what they had done with themselves on this day. When he walked down the aisle of the audience at the White Durbar, he finally saw Mila seated next to Sam, and his heart overflowed with love for his daughter whom he had missed in just one day of being away. Tomorrow, he promised himself, he would bring her into his office for a nice long chat. He thought she looked tired, but it might have been a trick of the moonlight. He hoped she was happy, for even if he did not know about her afternoon's activities in the Lal Bazaar, he did know that Jai and Mila had dined together in the Blue Palace without Ashok being there.

Raman came home and Sayyid opened the door to his master, much as he had done to Kiran an hour ago.

"Are you still awake?" Raman asked. "You should have been in bed long before this."

"It is but a little wakefulness, Sahib," Sayyid said. "Now you are home, now everyone is home." Ashok was not in his room, but neither of them knew that yet.

Sayyid helped Raman to bed, massaged his feet with warm sesame oil, covered him with a sheet, and was going to the door when Raman's voice, half asleep, stopped him. "Is it too late to ask for the woman from the village?"

"No, Sahib," Sayyid said. He paused. "She waits downstairs. I asked her to come tonight in case . . . I felt you might want to avail yourself of her services."

"Send her in then," Raman said. "Thank you." He turned on his back and folded his arms behind his head as he waited for the woman. Tonight, exhausted as he was, he wanted a woman's touch upon his body; he wanted to erase the day and start anew the next morning.

And so fifteen minutes later, the woman, who had just one name that Raman knew of, walked down the corridor to be with him. She was dressed in a thick red *ghagara* and a sequined *choli* open at the back and tied with two strings. She wore anklets in silver, the chiming kind, but most of her footsteps were muffled in the folds of her skirt. And had she passed through the corridor just this way, no one in the house would have realized she was there. But Sayyid, who normally accompanied her, had sent her upstairs on her own, and she had forgotten which door led to Raman's room. So she opened the door to Mila's room first and saw the Japanese screen with its embroidered geishas blocking a part of the entrance and knew almost immediately that this was not the spare, masculine room that Raman occupied. She shut the door softly and then went across the corridor to the other side, opened Raman's door, and let herself in.


Mila wandered around in her room, pacing the floor from her bed to her dressing table and back until her head spun. She had returned from the White Durbar in the jeep with Sam, since her father had brought the Morris and come back in that. And during the drive they had not talked. Now she had begun to wonder why Sam Hawthorne was even here in Rudrakot. He had so many secrets from them, it seemed, and they knew so little about him. What had he done today, when she was away at the Lal Bazaar and at dinner with Jai? Why had he really taken Ashok to the political meeting at the house near the bazaar? Though concerned for her brother, all she had done was watch Sam's hands on the driving wheel of the jeep, wished for him to talk with her and dispel this strangeness that had come between them. She imagined herself in bed with Sam, lying side by side, their arms touching. And an immeasurable longing ate away at her heart. What would it be like, she thought, to waken with him by her side every morning?

They had broken away at the door to her room with a few niceties. Mila did not change when she went into her room, she just combed her hair, fanned it around her face, and stared for a long time at herself in the mirror.

She stopped in the center of the room, a tingling running through her limbs, unable to keep still, frazzled from all the pacing. As she stood there, she heard the door to her room open and then quietly shut. Even in that brief space of time, the perfume of jasmine flowers floated into the room. Mila went to the door and opened it so that she could put an eye to the length of the opening. She saw the woman, or rather, only her back, the swirl of her *ghagara*'s skirts, the lush garland of jasmine in her hair, and heard the little tinkle of the bells in her anklets and the fall of glass bangles on her wrist as she opened Raman's door and closed it behind her. Mila waited for five long minutes, but the corridor remained in semidarkness and the woman did not emerge from her papa's room. And then, for the first time, she knew irrevocably that this was the first step toward adulthood—when the love of a parent, a child, a sibling was simply not enough. To be truly loved, to truly love, one must love an equal, share a proximity of skins, indulge a lover. She did not think, as she stood there, that this nameless woman would mean more to Papa than the engagement in the sexual act, for she had recognized also a furtiveness in her being here, and had seen from her gait and her clothing that she was from the village. But those five minutes at the door taught Mila more about her father as a man than she would ever have known about him otherwise.

She went back into her room, crossed over the floor, and went out into the balcony. Sam's door was open too. He had played a gramophone record, but it had wound down and come to the very end, and all she could hear was the scratch of the needle against the record, over and over again.

Mila went to Sam's door and parted the curtains. There was only one light left on in his room, a little, frosted glass lamp on his bedside table. The gramophone was near the door to the inside of the house. Sam sat on the edge of his bed, hunched forward, his elbows resting on his knees. He was clad in only his white pants and his chest was bare. His face was turned toward Mila, hair falling over one part of his forehead.

"I hoped you would come," he said, simply, and she saw in his eyes the fever of desire so strong that it brought a flush to his skin. His fingers twitched against his face and he could not keep his hunger from showing. He seemed to touch her from even that distance, reaching out across the span of the room to caress her waist, run the backs of his fingers under her arms, tug gently at her hair.

"The meaning of my name, in full, Milana, is 'to meet,' " she said. "Or in another conjugation it means 'to find.' "

"It seems appropriate," Sam said. "Now I will not let you go, Mila. You must know this before you take another step toward me, you must know this."

"I do," she said and closed the door behind her.

Sam rose, but he went toward the gramophone instead and plucked the needle's arm from the groove it had made in the record. Then he put another record on the gramophone and held out a hand to her as the music began to play.

"Mike and I have always liked Bing Crosby," he said. "I was surprised to find his songs here."

"Why?" she said faintly. "We have everything. Ashok likes to dance to his songs." She did not move but stood very, very still, her arms by her sides, the chiffon of her sari smooth against her hands.

"I wanted to ask you to dance at the *mela*."

"I would not have danced with you there."

He nodded. "I know why now, but you cannot hide this . . . us . . . from everyone forever."

She came into his arms then, very correctly, as she had been taught by an early governess, a Miss Beasley. Mila had only danced with Miss Beasley and with Ashok, although he preferred to dance alone, in no style at all, just a rabid flailing of his arms and legs.

Sam's hold on her was nothing like Miss Beasley's feeble clutch; his hands were warm, his shoulder muscles flexed as she caressed him and she had to look away from the fierce burning of his scrutiny upon her face. A heat flooded through her and her head drooped, too heavy for her neck. The gramophone scratched through the song.

*I really can't stay*
*But Baby it's cold outside*
*I've got to go away*
*But Baby it's cold outside*
*This evening has been so very nice*
*I'll hold your hands, they're just like ice*

Sam swung Mila around the room, the thick folds of her sari wrapping around his legs, her long *pallu* floating behind them both in a shimmering glitter. She had taken off her high-heeled shoes and Sam was barefoot too, so as they moved their feet made slapping sounds against the mosaic. They danced for ten minutes like this, barely touching each other, barely even breathing. Mila's arm lay lightly upon Sam's injured shoulder, her fingers linked with his, and his hand brushed her waist. They came no closer at all during the music until the gramophone lost its power and died down. Then Sam let go of Mila, took the record out, and put it away in its sleeve.

He went to the bedside lamp and switched it off and they both waited until that first darkness faded and shaped itself around them in light and shadow.

They kissed, and Sam ran his tongue over Mila's face, raising such a hankering in her that she blindly moved her mouth until it could meet his. He undid her sari slowly and she stood where she was as his arms went around her once, twice, a third time, until the pleats had been pulled loose in the front and the sari lay at their feet like a blanket of diamonds. He was shaking with need, but he was gentle, taking off her blouse, cupping her breasts with one hand and then another, bending to kiss them. The frenzy came then upon them both and they fell onto the bed. Sam scrambled out of his clothes. He ran his hands over every part of her body, curving his palms around her feet, sliding them over her knees and her thighs. And where his touch went, his mouth followed until Mila pulled him up to her. Sam buried himself inside Mila as their mouths fused.

Above them the ceiling fan shuddered and clanked, but its noise was not enough and Sam had to muffle Mila's cries with the heel of his hand against her mouth.

May 31, 1942

*Rudrakot, India*

# Twenty-eight

*It was clear to me that Pauline never had any real love for me, and was marrying me simply to be raised . . . to European status. I 'phoned her father . . . and asked if I could call. I intended . . . the interview to last half-an-hour, it lasted six minutes. I . . . said, "I think Pauline and the two of you have been deceiving me all along . . . is there any [Asian] blood in you?" . . . her father flared into a rage . . . ordered me out of the house . . . and I had for one second a fearful sensation that perhaps I was wrong. I turned to Pauline and said, "Am I mistaken? Are you pure white?" She wouldn't answer but looked away, and as I stepped to the door, she said, "You have insulted the whole family."*

—Anton Gill, *Ruling Passions: Sex, Race and Empire*, 1995

"Does it hurt?" Mila asked, her fingers tracing the dark abrasion on Sam's shoulder. She lay on the bed, naked and on her stomach, her hair falling around her to her waist. Sam lay next to her, also naked, his hands clasped on his ribs. He reached out and traced the arc of her buttocks, grasped a handful of her silky, sweet-smelling hair, kissed her bruised mouth.

She smiled against his teeth. "I can see," Mila said, her voice muffled by his skin, "that I will never get a straight answer to anything if I lie here without my clothes on."

He covered her mouth with the palm of his hand. "Never say that."

"Never wear clothes?"

"Not around me, anyway." He took his hand away and slid it behind her hair, seeking the nape of her neck. Sam pulled her down on him.

The night's heat had finally come to rest and become quiet, so it was cooler now, the very nadir the temperature would reach before it began to climb again. There were two hours left for the sun to rise, but Mila and Sam could already hear the birds beginning to stir in the trees outside. Mila knew she would have to leave Sam, and soon, before the servants awoke, or before Pallavi got out of bed. This was like a madness, a joyful intoxication where nothing mattered but Sam. Even as she kissed him, touched every inch of his skin so that her fingers would always remember what he felt like, buried her head in the crook of his arm so that she would never forget the aromas of his body, she wondered about where they would be five years from now. Ten years from now.

"I could not live without you," she said.

His eyes were bright with amusement and glowed in the semidarkness like a sun-washed sky. "You will not have to live without me." It was a simple statement, simply made, a token of Sam's love for Mila. He could not imagine life without her either, but he had no idea that May morning how true this was going to be. He framed her face with his hands and her face was so small, his hands so large that his fingertips almost linked at the top of her head. Sam had to laugh at that, and Mila asked why, so he told her.

She smiled. "You have not been concentrating on my head, Sam."

"No," he said, "I was more interested in other parts of you. But I promise that from now on, I will interest myself in all parts of you." Then he sobered. "I don't do this," he waved around the room and at them with one hand, "very often, you must know that, Mila."

"You do not take women to your bed?" she asked quietly.

"No, not this easily. I mean for you to marry me, become my wife, have my children."

"Is this a proposal?" she asked, and at that moment, for the first time in quite a few hours, Mila thought of Jai. She had now received two proposals of marriage in her life and neither of them had been conventional . . . well, conventional in a Western ideal. In an Indian ideal, Papa would tell her whom she would marry, and she would marry that man and consider herself lucky if she were allowed to meet him before the wedding. A deep and aching sadness came over her when she thought of Jai. Sam rubbed at the lines that had formed on her forehead.

"Tell me," he said.

"Jai."

"When will you tell him?"

"When do you leave, Sam? How long will you be away?"

Sam was silent for a long time; Mila felt something shift between them, and all the old questions came rushing back. She sensed, instinctively, with merely all the experience her twenty-one years had bestowed upon her, that he was an honest man, that whatever furtiveness he practiced now had put him under a great strain. That there was something hidden from them all was equally obvious. Papa knew too, or he would not have sent a telegraph to Calcutta on the very first day that Sam had come to Rudrakot.

"Tell me," she said now, placing a hand upon his heart. "Trust me, darling Sam."

So he told her, finally unburdening himself of three days of guilt and pain. He told her about Mike, who he was in the Rudrakot Rifles, when he had disappeared, why he had been taken to the field punishment center.

"I remember Michael Ridley," Mila said slowly, her forehead patterned with lines of recollection, "although I met him only twice. I liked him. Are you sure that is why he has been interned at the center?"

Sam stacked the pillows behind him on the carved wooden headboard and pulled himself up. "Vimal said that he was at the site of the schoolhouse the day it blew up." He could not bring himself to say what else Vimal had said, but how did it matter, Sam thought miserably, if Mike had been there; he was as culpable as if he had lighted the fuse to the bomb. And yet his imprisonment at the center was nothing short of ridiculous; there had been no trial, no conviction, Mike had just disappeared. As he was going to disappear again, Sam thought grimly.

Mila touched his face and tried to rub the scowl away. "Did you find your brother, Sam?"

"Yes, the night we went to Chetak's tomb."

"So that is where you disappeared to with Vimal."

"You knew?" Sam asked, surprised, for he had left her asleep and returned to find her still asleep.

"I did not sleep that night, Sam."

"I leave tonight, Mila," Sam said finally. "At midnight. Vimal is going to take me to the horse trader at the bazaar and help me get into the field punishment center again. He . . . knows the guards, and says that they will deliberately be lax for a few hundred rupees. I've already given Vimal the money. I will take Mike to Delhi and either hide him there or find him passage on a ship back home. He needs medical care and he needs our mother. And then, I have to go back to Assam."

"Who are you, Sam Hawthorne?" she asked then, sketching the lines of his eyebrows and the bones beneath his skin. Then, not waiting for his response, she went on, "I will tell Jai tomorrow that I cannot marry him." She bent her head. "He will be disappointed."

"I know," Sam said. "I'm sorry . . . sorry for him, not for us. We are meant to be, my love."

"Will you be careful tonight? Are you in any danger?"

Sam shook his head slowly. "I do not think so. I don't believe that anyone will care if I take Mike away from the field punishment center. If they do . . ." He did not finish that sentence, but said instead, "But there is, should be, no danger."

"I will miss you," Mila said, already feeling an emptiness take over her heart at the thought of Sam's being away at Assam. But these were times of war, and any man in uniform, any man at all, had no control over his own life; everything was dependent on the vagaries of the army. There were more questions within her—where they would live, when they would marry, what would happen next, but she did not voice any of them yet, for it was too early to think about a future that seemed so distant. "Will you write to me?"

"Yes," Sam said, and it was a promise he would keep, though Mila would never see any of his letters. "I will send you my address when I get back to Assam. I will have to go back into Burma at least once, Mila, if not twice." He hesitated. "I can say no more than that."

A breeze lifted the curtains of the room on the side of the back balcony and brought with it a thin dusting of dirt. The gritty sand swirled around the room and came to rest upon Mila and Sam on the bed. She ran her fingers through Sam's hair and shook out the dirt, looking deep into his eyes as though she was memorizing every detail of his face so that she would never forget this moment. "A dust storm comes," she said softly.

"Again?"

"Now we will be beset by dust storms until the monsoon rains. They herald the rains."

"When will this storm hit us?" Sam asked, turning away toward the windows where the curtains now lay quiescent, hanging straight down in still folds of cloth.

"In a few hours. Wait for that moment during the day when all becomes quiet, when it seems as though everything is dead, and just after that the storm will come."

"Spend the day with me," Sam said, recklessly. He still had to go and see Vimal in the bazaar, pay for the horses, make preparations for the rescue. There were too many details he had not considered, and yet he could not help wanting these precious last hours with Mila.

"I cannot," she said. "I have too much else to do. I must talk with Papa, see to Ashok . . ." Here she paused and Sam waited, but she said nothing more.

When she left, Mila kissed him once, twice, a third time when she had reached the door to the balcony and had to return for that third kiss before she stepped out to go to her own room.

# Twenty-nine

*. . . My father had dropped me a hint about the bad habits of this unlucky cadet . . . I began to see there that matters were going on too much ahead. Masturbation and sodomy had commenced in the corps.*

*I hear he is still trying to get back in this corps but this is all mere idle fancy . . . These are the results of sodomy. Beware those who practice it.*

—Susanne Hoeber Rudolph and Lloyd I. Rudolph with Mohan Singh Kanota, *Reversing the Gaze: Amar Singh's Diary, A Colonial Subject's Narrative of Imperial India,* 2002

*So you see, my dearest Olivia, that just before the monsoon rains in those four days in May we were all hurtling headlong into an inevitable disaster. I mention the rains because they were the barometer by which we lived our lives, by which we died, after which we celebrated marriages, welcomed our children into the world. We welcome the rain because it brings us coolness, calms our very skins, lets us breathe, feel alive again.*

*I was unaware for a very long time of this love between your mother and your father; in fact, I did not know of it until you were born. I suspected something, but chose willfully not to believe in my suspicions, and yet, when I found out for sure, there was not a sense of betrayal, but strangely, only gratitude to your mother for having given me as much of herself as she did. I'm not being cavalier about this—*

*at the beginning it was a great, thundering shock for me, it rent me apart, brought my world crashing down . . . but all that comes later in this story I tell you, my dear child. Much later.*

*I sometimes wish, even now, that I had been as lucky as your father. To have possessed her love, to have known myself secure in her love, as he had considered himself—for a short time anyway. And that is why I wanted to cause him pain, for I was in the agony of ignorance myself by the time he came back to Rudrakot six months later. But . . . I digress again here, picking up threads to weave my tale from well beyond this point and if I continue to do so, I will leave a gap in the fabric of your understanding.*

*Let me just say this much. I do wish, even now, that Mila had responded to the eight letters I wrote to her from the Imperial Cadet Corps, before she met Sam. Then at least, I would have had a scrap of paper on which she would have put down words that were meant just for me. Just for me.*

The dust storm woke up the town and the kingdom of Rudrakot, and in the parlance of storms, this one was a black one, and vied from moment to moment with the red storm Mila, Sam, and Ashok had encountered at Chetak's tomb. So one minute there was that thick, dense silence when even the birds crept back into their nests, huddled with each other in the trees, silenced their demanding early morning chirps, and at the other minute the wind whistled gently, like a lover calling out to his beloved. The air cooled as if plunged into a vat of ice, and then it cracked and fissured as though it contained body and form, and expanded fleetly over the kingdom. Snakes and varans scurried for cover under the tombs of the dead in the Sukh desert. Horses snickered uneasily in stables and retreated to wedge their heads under some sort of shelter; pariah dogs lay quivering under plows and bicycles.

It was still so early in the morning—actually, the night's skirts had barely swept through the horizon to reveal the mighty sun's glow—that there were few people awake after the exhaustion from the revelries of the White Durbar the previous night. So the dust storm took everyone by surprise. Clouds coagulated across the vast desert sky, carrying within them the seeds of monsoon rains, lightning crawled across the heavens followed by so distant a thunder that not one windowpane in Rudrakot rattled, not one child awoke to wail in his mother's arms. The night watchmen were also asleep all over the city and within Jai's fort and his palaces, fatigued by the heat, thinking that no one would dare invade their domains at the brink of daylight. No one, that is, but the magnificent storm.

It came thundering onto Rudrakot, blackening the sky, blotting out the surprised sun, rousing the dirt and the dust to an ebony fury. On the terraces and in the courtyards across Rudrakot, people awoke screaming, partly with laughter, partly with fear at the tempestuousness of the storm. Girls woke to face the lusty wind, their eyes shut tight, their hair and *ghagaras* billowing behind them like ships in full sail, boys shouted into the storm and heard no sounds from their mouths, their voices snatched and carried away in an instant.

Mila ran to the door to her balcony, which had still been left open and was flapping as if demons were banging on it, and began to shut it, using all the force of her strong young arms. But as she struggled with the last four inches, the door would not budge and she looked down to see why and saw Ashok kneeling in the opening, holding it ajar with his body, his head bowed.

She pulled him inside, yelling that he was an idiot, what was he doing up so early. Then he lifted his face to hers and she almost died. Tears inundated his cheeks, his eyes were red, there were teeth marks on the curve of his shoulder, where his neck met his collarbone, and he shook as though he had been doused in a fever.

Mila shut the door firmly and latched it. She gathered her brother in her arms, half-carried him to her bed but could not lift him onto it, and he had no strength left in him to even raise himself a few feet. He disintegrated to the floor and she collapsed next to him, yanking his shoulders up to prop him against the bed, putting her arms around him fully, so that he could rest his head against her chest.

"What happened?" she said, her heart fracturing as he sobbed. His arms went around her waist and his fingers pinched the skin there, but she did not mind or even notice. "Tell me," she said, much as Sam and she had invited confidences from each other earlier that night. "Tell me, *kanna*." *Kanna*, apple of my eye, my love, a term of endearment Mila had used for Ashok when he was but a child and she had sung him to sleep at night, or sat by his bed when he was ill and when Pallavi did not have the heart to shoo her out of the room.

Mila ran her hands over Ashok's thin body, his head with its sweat-matted short hair, his neck, his shoulders and ribs, his thighs, calves, and ankles. He was all right. He was still in the clothes he had worn for the White Durbar the previous night, but they were soiled, not torn, dirty, as though he had rolled in the dust outside.

"Are you all right?"

So he said to her, I am in love with Vimal, Mila. I love him. As men love women, as women love men.

At first she did not understand and her heart died to a quietude at the thought. She had been afraid of Vimal's influence on Ashok, afraid that he would haul him into the nationalist movement and that that would cause embarrassment for Papa, afraid even of some nameless thing she could not identify. But never this. Never this, she thought. How was it even possible? *What* was it, this love between two men? What would Ashok do now? How could he live? How much more embarrassing this would be for Papa. It would kill Papa.

"You cannot know what love is, Ashok," she cried. "And in so short a period of time. Why, Vimal returned to our lives just two days ago." She said this without much consideration and then the full import of her words came upon her too. She knew what love was, and now, looking back, she knew she had fallen in love with Sam the moment he had held her hand at the *mela* and she had not wanted him to let go. And how long had Sam been with them . . . two, perhaps three days, and he would be gone tomorrow, but her love for him would not die.

"I have done wrong, Mila," Ashok said, wretchedness saturating his face. He plunged his head into his hands and did not have the courage to look at the sister he had always considered in the place of his mother. It was only to her he would dare confess this shameful secret. He had not been able to stop himself, he had not been seduced by Vimal, he had *wanted* this. He had been desperate for the touch of Vimal's mouth on his, for the taste of his skin, for the feel of his body next to his. Desperate with a need that had grown inside him for a few years now, a need he had not recognized, because, like Mila, he did not know what this was.

"Yes," she said heavily. "You have done wrong, Ashok. I do not know what to say, what to do." And so saying, Mila turned away from Ashok.

An anguished cry came from him and he wept harder. She saw the bruises underneath the collar of his shirt with a renewed but almost dispassionate interest. She felt the pleasant tiredness in her own limbs from the hours of making love to Sam; she rubbed the side of her thigh, where she knew Sam's teeth also adorned her skin, much as Vimal's teeth had left their mark on her brother. At that moment, all her disgust fled, for Mila understood what this love was between Ashok and Vimal. Under any other circumstances, given this with any other man or boy, perhaps even with Kiran, Mila would not have comprehended this passion or realized that it could be as strong as, as powerful as the one she shared with Sam. Within the span of one night, three men in her life—Papa, Sam, and Ashok—had taught her how varied and rich love could be, and that in its own way, in each of those ways, these different loves could be enduring. But with Vimal, of all people . . . Mila thought with distress that Vimal would not return Ashok's love; he was incapable of something so unselfish and giving. Her heart grew leaden with grief for her brother because he was sure to be betrayed, and though Mila did not know just then, that betrayal *was* to come, and soon.

She put her arms around him again, this time calmly, and laid her lips against his sweaty head. She rubbed at the grains of sand in Ashok's hair, hugged his slight shoulders, and said quietly, "Papa must never know, *kanna*."

"What shall I do, Mila?"

Once she had said those words, Mila learned within herself yet another lesson, that she had finally grown into an adult, become a woman of her own. It was not necessary to reveal all the details of her life, in this case, of Ashok's life to Papa. She realized that he would be devastated, that it would be a hurt he could not possibly recover from, that she might understand a part of it, but never Papa. Because she was a woman, had been a girl child, there were almost naturally many things she did not discuss with Papa, and this had been easy. On the day when she had glanced down with dread at the first blood in the lining of her underwear, when she was twelve, it was Pallavi she had sought out, ashamed and frightened. Pallavi had told Raman later in the evening, and Raman had merely kissed Mila on the forehead and said to Pallavi, "If Mila does not want a fuss made about this, then there will be no fuss."

"But she has become a woman now," Pallavi had wailed. "We have to conduct the *pujas*, invite the women of the neighborhood to come and visit her, seat her in a special chair so that everyone can see her and bless her."

Raman pulled away from Mila, and held her by her young shoulders. "Well, do you want all this, my dear child?"

Mila was more horrified than she had been at seeing the blood, and gone in that instant were the fears that she would bleed to death, that someone had taken a knife to her insides and had twisted it unmercifully until all of her would leak out through . . . *there.* "No, Papa," she said fearfully, thinking that perhaps Pallavi would triumph after all and put her out in the verandah on display. *Look at the daughter of our house; she has attained womanhood.* Papa had said quietly to Pallavi, "This is one of those instances where my will must prevail. We will let Mila do what she wants. Is that clear?"

And yet even after that, on months when she had been prostrate with cramps or worried about the changes in her body, she had gone to Pallavi with her worries, not their father. Raman would not have been embarrassed at explaining what little he knew, and he understood only very little about women's affairs because even his children had been born behind the closed doors of his house and only brought out cleaned and swaddled in bedsheets, but Mila knew not to go to him then. As she knew now that their father must never learn of Ashok's . . . love for Vimal.

"What shall I do?" Ashok asked again. His tears had stopped and his face had aged with this knowledge of himself. They both wished in that silence as Mila pondered his question for the right answer that time could somehow be turned back and recant the happenings of the previous night for Ashok.

"Nothing. You can do nothing about this. You can never talk of this, and if you are to . . . to meet Vimal again, know that I will not help make up excuses for you or for your absence." He stiffened in her embrace, but she went on doggedly, hoping that he would understand, that he would see things as she did. "No one must know, and no one must ever find out. Be very, very careful, Ashok."

The storm now invaded their consciousness, flinging its winds upon the closed balcony door, thumping against the windows, sending fingers of dirt in snakelike patterns under the door's frame. Fifteen minutes later, it died as abruptly as it had started, and Mila and Ashok heard, just a few minutes later, the crash of a brass pot against the surface of the well's water. They rose without speaking and, still holding on to each other, went out, the cranking of the pulley luring them to the balcony.

Raman had beaten the birds to activity. But as Mila and Ashok leaned over the parapet of the balcony to look down upon their father, the sparrows started their relentless chirping in the mango trees, and the first smoke coughed its way out of the chimneys of the kitchen house, palely white against the dark sky. There was the merest touch of chill in the air, and a half gloom still blanketed everything. The lime-washed wall of the well gleamed dully in the brightening light, and they saw the partly clad figure of their father near the well. His arms moved in a steady rhythm, yanking at the rope, one hand fluidly replacing the other until the brass pot swayed up and over the wall. Still holding the rope with his left hand, he leaned over the vast, yawning mouth of the well and pulled the pot to the well's ledge. Raman tilted the pot to splash some water into a steel tumbler dipped with a spoon. He then heaved it over his head, held it there for a minute, and upended the water over himself.

As the light smeared the horizon, beyond the lake and Chetak's tomb, it illuminated the yard behind the house and the man who stood by the well. A thin rope of thread clung to his bare upper body, looped over his right shoulder and down under his left arm. The thread was a symbol of caste, bestowed upon Raman at the cusp of manhood, and the ceremony he performed now was part of that symbol. He poured a spoonful of water into his right palm and drank it three times. And then, with the practiced ease of years, Raman began the ritual, dabbing his face with his thumb, touching his eyes, his nose, his ears, his shoulders, and laying his fingers on his chest. From where he stood, Mila and Ashok could hear the melodious breathe-and-stop cadence of his voice as he chanted the verses that accompanied his ritual. A dwelling peace came upon both of them then, watching their father engaged in his daily prayer ritual without thought for how the rest of the day, the rest of their lives and his, would progress.

They turned together as they heard a slight movement and Sam came out into the balcony. He smiled when he saw their arms wrapped around each other, Ashok's head laid on her shoulder, as though they had been born that way, fused at the hip. He went to where they were standing, by Mila's side, his right hand resting on the parapet ledge only a few inches from her waist. She inclined her body so that her skin touched his, and this was the most they could do with Ashok firmly affixed to her other side, and even this much was comforting.

"Are you all right?" he asked, in a low voice.

She shook her head briefly, tears filling her eyes, but she said, so that Ashok could hear, "We are fine, Sam."

He caressed her shoulder, and, greatly daring, wiped the tears away with the back of his hand.

"Papa prays," Ashok said. "Perhaps for us all."

Sam leaned beyond the rise of the balcony's wall, cradling his right arm with his left, his palm supporting the elbow. His shoulder hurt, and he had almost forgotten this until reminded as he climbed the wall of the field punishment center and not since then again, but Mila's tears, her unnamed sorrow, brought the ache back. She was in pain, and so Sam was too.

At that moment, Raman glanced up from his meditations near the well, his lower garment of a white *veshti* clinging to him from his early bath, his body beginning to quake from a sudden, unnatural chill. Mila and Ashok both ducked briefly beyond his gaze, behind the low parapet, wiped their faces, and reappeared with watery smiles for their father. But he was not looking at them.

Instead he said, his voice somber, "Will you come to see me in my office, Captain Hawthorne, later today? I have news from Calcutta that I would like to discuss with you."

"Yes, sir," Sam said. "When?"

"Before you leave the house, please." With that, Raman, still shivering in his damp skin, wrapped a cloth towel around his upper body.

Before Mila could even begin to ask Sam what that meant, why Papa seemed so distant with him, what had he done, Pallavi's door opened and she stepped out into the balcony.

She said, her expression hardened and angry beyond anything Mila had seen before, "I want you to take a bath and then come and see me, Mila. Ashok, get to your room and do the same, you are no longer a child and do not need to hang on to your sister like this."

*"Pallavi!"* Ashok began to wail, but she cut him short.

*"Now!"* she said. She did not look at Sam, did not even acknowledge his presence, but she said in very clear, grammatically perfect English, "We need our house to be *our* house now; visitors tend to overstay their welcome."

The first hailstones began then, pelting out of the sky like a sprinkling of flung pebbles and then cannonading down upon them in ten seconds, until everything was blurred into a thick sheet of ice formed over many months of winter somewhere up north, near the arctic. The hailstones were enormous, the size of a ripe *chikku* fruit, perfectly round and incredibly painful when they made contact with their skins.

It was the first of the catastrophes that would come upon them all on that day, and there was nothing they could do to stop them. They would all be deluged with disasters, all of them——Mila, Sam, Ashok, Raman . . . even Kiran.

*And none of this would have happened, my dear Olivia, if Sam had not come to Rudrakot. This I firmly believe. Although that searing pre-monsoon heat was already upon us all, had left us limp and irritable and unreasonable, it was a state of mind we were familiar with, after all. If that spark, in the form of your father, had not come upon the aridity that surrounded us, we would not have been set to flame. And we were burned beyond recognition. It would be many years before we could talk of those four days in May, many years before I could consider them with something akin to equanimity.*

*So many years before I could pick up my pen, write to you, and tell you all of this.*

# Thirty

*On the boat, I had made friends with an Englishman . . . After Port Said,*
*he had a worried look . . . He said . . . last night those senior chaps got*
*hold of me, and they said: "Look, we're just telling you this for your own*
*good, that when you get to Calcutta and take up this job, you musn't be*
*very friendly with Indians . . . this young Indian . . . might have been at*
*Oxford and the rest of it, but still you had better be careful."*

—Zareer Masani, *Indian Tales of the Raj,* 1987

Will you have some more pink champagne?"
"No, thank you, Your Highness." Sam sat back in the chair
and bumped his head against the head rest with its carved head of a lion,
its mane flowing with careful etching, its jaws open in a frozen, unheard
roar, teeth filling its mouth. The rest of the chair was upholstered in silver
and blue, its feet ended in claws clutching wooden balls.

The whole room was fantastic, it was an indoor-outdoor room, and
Sam could hardly have considered it a verandah, in the manner of the verandahs he had seen so far during his stay in India. The room was constructed around the outer wall of a white marble palace perched on the lake
at Rudrakot, and just beyond where Sam and Jai sat, he could hear the soft
lapping of the water against the foundation, gentle, soothing, in an ageless
rhythm. The sun marched sentinel above them somewhere, already tilted
toward the west, since it was late in the afternoon, but the skies were clear,
a blanched blue, no hint of the morning's dust storm remaining in the air.

The room's walls were painted in blue to mimic the sky, and on this background were drawn coconut trees with ridged trunks and ripe coconuts hanging from between their lush leaves, thick grasses hiding the ears of elephants, monkeys swinging from vines, brilliant butterflies swooping across the land. The room's walls were also hung with mirrors with no frames, so that they seemed to be an unending reflection of the mural.

On his way in, Sam had almost tripped over two magnificent stuffed lions, with two perfect gunshot holes in each of their ribs, the only place where their skins were broken. He waited for the servants to bring in the silver tray with two glasses of pink champagne before he asked the man seated in front of him, "Are there lions at Rudrakot, Your Highness?"

Jai took a sip of his champagne, put his glass down upon the carved teak table between them, and said, "But of course, Captain Hawthorne. I shot these specimens," he said, waving a lazy hand behind him, toward the door, "myself, in my hunting forests. I would take you on a *shikar* if you were to be here longer."

"But I can't be," Sam said. His glance swept away into the waters of the lake and then upward to the breathtaking marble ceiling with its carved lotus flower in full bloom. The light reflecting from the lake tumbled in a waterfall across the lotus and surged through the whole room in a burnished glow that seemed to touch both of them.

"Yes," Jai said reflectively, stirring the fizzing champagne in his glass with his right index finger and then putting that finger into his mouth, "it is indeed a pity that we cannot keep you here longer than tomorrow as our guest."

His voice reflected none of this professed sorrow, and Sam wondered if Jai knew already, without being told, that Mila belonged to him. Under normal circumstances, under *any* other circumstances, Sam would never have considered the word *belong* in talking of, or thinking about, the woman who was to be his wife. He had always thought that if he were given the blessing of such an incredible love, then he would worship the woman who bestowed it upon him, and so he still thought. But he had become arrogant, a fine skin of pride blanketing him as he sat in one of Jai's numerous palaces in the kingdom of Rudrakot—this one on the banks of the lake, so pendant over the water as to actually be floating on it. Sam could not give Mila all of this, perhaps not even a fraction of this, well, there was no perhaps about this, for Sam was just a professor of South

Asian languages at the University of Washington in Seattle, and Jai was a bloody prince with a kingdom. For pity's sake, as Mike would say.

Jai had accosted Sam at the outskirts of the Lal Bazaar as he had just finished negotiating for the hire of two horses and a bale of cotton wadding with which to muffle the sound of their hooves as they fled out into the desert. The horse dealer had barely melted away into the bazaar, his smile yellowed, his eyes aflame with greed, fingers still running over a quarter of the agreed-upon amount of rupees (Sam knew better than to give him the whole before he got the horses), when a blue-and-silver Daimler hissed to a halt next to him, the darkened window was rolled down, and Jai slanted his head through the opening to say, "What a co-incidence, Captain Hawthorne. I too was on my way to buy some cotton baling. Do come, have some champagne with me, and escape from our heat for a while. I promise not to ask what you intend to do with all of that cotton."

Sam reddened, not happy at the invitation, but hardly knowing how to say no to the prince of Rudrakot. "Thank you," he began, "but—"

"Oh, but I insist," Jai said, and his chauffeur glided out of the car and opened the door for Sam in what seemed like one smooth movement and Sam found himself in the car next to Jai with the newspaper-wrapped cotton on his lap. The car took them away from the road that led to the fort and toward the Victoria Club instead. There they branched away again and sped along the side of the lake, coming to a halt, finally, in front of a massive marble-and-red-sandstone palace, which Jai introduced to Sam casually as, "One of my hunting lodges." There were guns, muzzle loaders, swords and shields, battle-axes, and gold-and-pearl-handled whips on the wall. The mural in the verandah room, jutting out onto the waters of the lake, was copied in every room Sam passed through. The heads of *chinkaras,* the local gazelle, *nilgai,* the blue bulls, and tigers adorned the walls. The floors were dazzling and impeccably clean and the rooms were cool, picking up moisture and vigor from the lake even under the heated midday burning of the sun.

So Sam thought that at least, at the *very* least, Mila belonged to him, throwing himself back to his adolescence with its willful and unreasonable competitiveness.

He was beginning to think that everyone except Mila abhorred him in Rudrakot and he thought back to his morning's talk with Raman in his office. The summons at the well, and there was really no other word for it than that, had been unmistakably grim and Sam had gone to see Raman with a leaden heart. The political agent had a white-and-blue telegraph sheet in his hand.

"It says here," Mila's father had said, "that you are an OSS officer, Sam. What exactly is that?"

Sam was silent for a long while and when he raised his face to Raman again, his gaze was level and met the older man's without any embarrassment. "I'm not sure what you are talking about, Mr. Raman. I am with the U.S. Army, in the Third Burma Rangers."

"Just that?" Raman said wryly.

"Just that, sir. Nothing more."

"I fear," Raman said wearily, brushing sleep out of his eyes, "that you have come to us under false pretenses. You refuse to admit it, but I too have my resources in Calcutta; I know partly who you are . . . not completely. I'm sorry, but I must ask you to leave my house, and if possible at all, leave Rudrakot."

"I hope to be able to explain, Mr. Raman," Sam said quickly. "I cannot, just right now."

Raman shook his head. "That is not good enough."

Sam had left the office torn in two directions, by his duty and by his heart. He was sworn to secrecy by his government, and even though Raman had, most astonishingly, ferreted out the existence of the OSS by some means or other, Sam could not have talked to him about it. Now he was being ordered out of his house, but he would return for Mila, and this man would be his father-in-law. One day he would tell him all the secrets, reveal everything that had forced him into deceit, beg forgiveness. He could not bear the thought that Mila's father would dislike him so much. But for now that had to be the case, and Sam loathed the creature he had had to become and could not wait to crawl out of this skin and into a more honest, open one when this damn war ended.

Jai hummed a little tune and Sam watched him warily. They had barely spoken in the drive over to the hunting lodge, and Sam knew that this invitation was no offer of friendship. And he knew too that there could be no friendship between them. Jai would grow to detest and abominate Sam in a few short hours, and though Sam would be well on his way to Delhi by then, he would return to Rudrakot to take Mila with him.

"You are very kind to bring me here, Your Highness," Sam said finally, putting down his empty champagne glass. "But I really must leave."

Jai did not answer for a while, and when he did it was with an immovable expression. "I think you have been in India long enough to know that we are—and by this I mean all of us, the British of us, the Indians of us—an inflexible, rigid people, rife with prejudice." Sam opened his mouth to dissent, but Jai put up a hand. "I am not asking for an argument." His tone became gentle, rueful. "Forgive me, I am used to giving orders and at times I forget that I cannot order everyone around. What I mean to say is that I do not make this statement for us to contest the veracity of it, instead I mean it as a truth."

Sam bent his head to look down upon his hands linked in front of him. "I will agree with you then, but I fail to see how this has anything to do with me."

"Yes," Jai said. "Yes." His brows came together on his forehead and he rubbed one side of his face as though he was in pain. "Forgive me," he said again, "I am not quite sure why I said that, if only to assert that we—the British and the Indians—have never really cohered with each other. You see, the color of our skins is an insurmountable barrier to any sort of friendly intercourse."

Sam searched hard in Jai's face for the knowledge of Mila's love for him, or any slight suspicion, and saw nothing. Yet the prince was troubled, anxiety marring his eyes, his fingers interlocking with each other and then coming apart. He did suspect, Sam thought, but in some buried part of his brain, and he was not cognizant yet as to why he disliked Sam. Perhaps they could have been friends too, Sam thought, but not now, not anymore. He could not sit any longer and deceive Jai, and so, very firmly, he rose to leave.

A man came in then, dressed in a black suit with a light blue tie—the color of Rudrakot, Sam realized, the regimental colors of the Lancers, the hues of last night's White Durbar, more blue than white, the tint in the upholstery, the paint on the Daimler. The man hesitated at the entrance to the room and coughed.

Jai beckoned with one hand and the man leaned to his prince's ear and talked for a very long while. Sam watched as pain and sorrow crushed Jai's face and his body shook with some emotion.

"What happened?" he asked, dread filling him.

Jai, white about his mouth, rose from his chair. "You should not have taken Ashok to the political meeting at the Lal Bazaar last night, Captain Hawthorne. You have betrayed the hospitality of the man who extended the use of his house to you, who allowed his children to reach out in friendship to you."

"What happened?" Sam asked again.

"There has been a bomb blast at the residency and a boy was found on the ground near the car where the bomb was put, crying over the body of his cohort. The two boys went there together this afternoon, Ashok and Vimal." Jai's voice grew harsh. "You see, you see now why you should never have let them get close to each other? One of them is dead because the bomb blew up just as they were installing it in Pankhurst's Daimler."

"Which one?" Sam asked faintly, pain shredding his heart. *Oh, my darling Mila,* he thought, *what have I done?* How could he have even known that last night would lead to this?

"The nationalist boy, Vimal. Ashok has been arrested and is in jail now. I have to go and get him out." Jai rubbed his forehead. "Try to get him out, and this is not going to be easy. He will be tried and hanged."

The news of Ashok's arrest reached Jai first, barely twenty minutes after it had happened, for Rudrakot was Jai's realm and he knew of everything that happened within the boundaries of his kingdom, just as he had known that Sam had taken Ashok to the political meeting last night.

In her bedroom, Mila lay on her bed on her stomach, her face turned away from Pallavi, who was seated in a chair beside her. They had been talking too, for two hours now, since Mila had woken. She had not allowed Pallavi to corral her into an argument earlier, and, pleading fatigue instead, Mila had slept away the morning. She knew that all that had done was delay her talk with Pallavi.

Now she lay with a pillow smothering her face, hiding her from Pallavi's fiery gaze. Mila had been crying for such a long time that she felt empty and drained of anything, for everything Pallavi had said was true. She had seen Mila emerge from Sam's room earlier that morning, had seen upon her body the languor of a woman who had been loved by a man, and Pallavi had been horrified. How could you do such a thing, she had asked, repeatedly. And Mila had responded doggedly to that with, I love him, this is no bad thing, Pallavi, do not demean me or Sam with your prejudices.

"What do you know of love?" Pallavi had shouted.

More than you, Mila wanted to say, but knew she could not hurt Pallavi so, even now, when they were in strife, for she spoke not from jealousy or spite but from a real concern for her.

"You cannot betray Jai," Pallavi had said.

But Mila believed that Jai would not want her, like this, with her heart in another man's keeping. It was not a concept Pallavi was even willing to understand; to her, Mila had made a contract with Jai. What would her papa think, Pallavi asked next. To these last two arguments, Mila had no response, for they were the truth. She could not bear to think that Papa would hate her, or even that Jai would hate her. She knew they would both be shattered. Last night she had felt as though things would work out after all. Oh, Sam, she thought miserably, what have we brought on ourselves?

At the thought of Sam, there came to Mila another moment of clarity and she returned to her belief that they *were* meant to be together, that no matter how much her relationship with Sam hurt people's sensibilities, those who loved her would understand, would be supportive. Much as she herself was of Ashok. Alone, she could never have come to such a decision, not because she was intrinsically timid, but because she could not have justified such happiness for herself at such a seeming cost to the others she loved. But Mila had Sam, and with him, anything was possible. She let Pallavi shout for as long as she liked, even let her own tears flow and sheltered her heart.

And then Pallavi said, somberly, "Where do you think you will live with this Captain Hawthorne, Mila? In India? In America? And where will you raise your children? Will they not be half of you and half of him? Who will accept this?"

Mila buried her head between two pillows. There would be difficulties, she knew that also, but did not want to think of them yet. Pallavi said softly, "Remember Grace, Mila."

And Mila did.

Six years ago, when Jai had gone to London for a visit, Raman had accompanied him, in the official capacity of an advisor, but really to keep Jai out of trouble and the titled British ladies from falling in love with him. Prince or not, it would have been bloody inconvenient and necessary to dissolve an unwanted alliance of this sort. Raman was to be away for more than half a year and so Kiran, Mila, Ashok, and Pallavi had traveled with him, stayed at a hotel and taken their studies with privately hired tutors. At the home of her piano teacher, Mila had met Grace Leghorn, and had been charmed by her prettiness and her enthusiasm. They became friends with a speed that youth, indulgence, and a lack of common history grants to most friendships, took walks on Sunday afternoons, drank tea at each other's homes, read Jane Austen together, and promised to write letters if they were *ever* parted again, and write all their lives. Grace gave Mila a little photograph of herself in a locket, with a curl of lovely golden hair tucked under it. Mila pestered Raman to take her to the photo studio so that she could return the favor. And then, just as Raman was to leave England, Grace told Mila that she was to go with them to India; she had been invited to stay with her uncle and aunt in Bengal.

The affection died on the eastern side of the Suez Canal. It was a cruel lesson for Mila. Grace had been her very *best* friend in the whole world, had considered the British in India abominable, had read the papers with Mila about the nationalist struggle, and had claimed to admire Mr. Gandhi and Mr. Nehru. But somehow, in washing the blues of the Mediterranean from her pale hands, and dipping them in the darker hues of the Arabian Sea, Grace Leghorn became the Raj even before she set foot on Raj land.

The irony was that Grace's uncle was some minor official in the textile industry, in some forlorn village *miles* from Calcutta, and Raman was political agent of a princely state that quartered two slapdash regiments. It was no consolation for Mila though. She was fifteen, she mourned deeply the loss that this lesson brought, and in doing so, learned its value very well. She was only fifteen; she recovered from Grace Leghorn, but did not forget her.

"Sam is different," she said finally to Pallavi.

And for the first time Pallavi agreed, but she also said, "You will see, my dear, as you grow older, that you cannot change the way the world will view the two of you, no matter how much you try. Are you willing to fight for the rest of your life?"

The door to Mila's room opened and Raman came in, his shoulders bowed as though he carried a huge weight on himself, his feet dragging, and when he spoke, his voice was hoarse with crying. "Mila," he said, "Ashok has been arrested for trying to place a bomb in Colonel Pankhurst's car." He ran a hand over his face, as though he could wipe away the pain from his skin with just that action. "How can this even be possible?"

April 1942, a Month Earlier

*Somewhere in Burma*

$\mathcal{K}$en talks for an inordinately long time, most of it directionless and rambling. Most of it self-serving. He speaks of a childhood in Colorado, within sight of the Rocky Mountains, of a paucity of food so dire at times during the cold winter months that his mother once boiled the flattened leather of an old pair of boots for a very long time until the leather was soft and almost edible.

Sam and Marianne have both clearly heard him speak textbook Japanese with the young soldier as they came back into the bungalow. Sam sits against the wall, cradling his arm in his lap, and again, just as he had with the python under the water of the pool, he has now also forgotten the pain because there are more important matters to take care of. An immense stillness descends upon him as he searches the environs of the room without seeming to. Night has come upon them a few hours ago, but they do not notice it. Ken lights a little fire in the middle of the room's mosaic floor and the fire smokes damply as it struggles to take a bite out of mildewed and mossy twigs and logs. It is the only light by which they can see each other.

By Sam's side, Marianne sits with a stunned expression on her face that has not abated since Ken pointed the pistol at them a few hours ago. Mingled with that is shock and sorrow and pain, an almost palpable and physical pain—Sam can feel it reach out in waves toward him. He wants to say that she must not mind Ken's betrayal so much—for these are the casualties of war. Ken grew up in abject misery, poorer than he can ever imagine anyone to be, and in Calcutta Ken sees human beings so mutilated by poverty he can finally consider that his life has been better than at least *someone* else's life. There is a strange and pathetic consolation in this to him. His eyes glow with a disturbing glee when he says this to Sam and Marianne and they cannot even turn to each other and show their pity, for they know that any movement could send a bullet their way.

"When did you decide to"—Sam hesitates, picking his words carefully, not wanting Ken to rush into an untimely temper—"approach the Japanese?"

"They came to me," Ken says. "There is a club in Calcutta, the Cardamon Club, in a little alley behind the Grand Hotel. It is a well-hidden place, seems to be exclusive until your nose shrinks at the stink of piss on the walls of the houses nearby. It's a dance hall, really, plenty of half-caste women wanting to dance for a few *annas;* they even allow you to touch them here and there in the alley outside for a few more." Ken falls into a musing. "There was one girl though who was so pretty . . . auburn hair, skin white and luscious, long limbs, a tiny waist." His expression hardens and he wipes the clammy hair from his forehead with his left hand. "I went to the club while on leave a year ago; it was just for fun, nothing more. I expected to throw down a few rupees for the women and the drinks and then come home again, but a man came to me with a proposition. He knew I flew for the AVG, well, he knew that I was a pilot." He falls silent, reflective. "The whole club, though I did not know it then, was for people like me, rich with money from the bloody Japs."

"What did he want?" Sam asks.

"Photographs of the Calcutta docks, as many as I could take while flying over them. I have them here." Ken pats his haversack and Sam and Marianne hear the crinkle of paper inside. Why, Sam thinks, has he not considered all this before? It was almost too easy, even their being here in this bungalow was too well planned, too well thought out in advance. For the nudge toward this part of the map has been Ken's idea, and this Sam remembers now. It had been a very strong suggestion, such as it was. The bungalow is a meeting place, a drop-off point for the photographs. Sam looks upon the young Japanese soldier with a stronger curiosity and a mild regret, thinking that he should have killed him when he first came rushing into the house. The boy had said to Sam in Japanese, *I thought you were the enemy.* He had thought Sam was Ken. The boy was partially right, Sam thinks. For *he* is the enemy, only Ken is not. Now the boy knows and he nods sleepily over his crippled feet, the pain sending him to unconsciousness.

"What did they pay you?" Sam asks.

Ken's eyes light up greedily, for it is more money than he has ever seen in his life, more money than he thinks he will ever see again. "Ten thousand dollars. Five before I even started. Five now, when I give them the photographs."

A little sound of repugnance escapes Marianne, but she says nothing, her head bent toward the floor as though she cannot bear to even look at Ken anymore. The hurt is the most in her, Sam thinks, for he was never quite as enamored of Ken as Marianne was, and she has transferred her grief for her Kachin villagers into affection for him.

"What happened to the girl?" Sam asks.

"She had a pretty name," Ken says, and his face puckers with distress, overlaid with mortification, which seems strange to Sam. "Rosalie. Rosalie Gonzalez. I did not think much about that last name or what it meant, mostly because I did not know. We danced for five months together, she gave me her affections sparingly, she kissed me, she let me take her to a hotel, but that was just once, and it was the best sex I had ever had. I saw her naked in the light of the bedside lamps, in the light of an early morning, and saw not one single blemish on her skin—*that* she carried under her skin, in her tainted blood. But I did not see it, for I was in love with Rosalie. I wonder," Ken says, worry patterning his brow, "if it would have mattered if I had known right from the beginning that she was a halfcaste, that some weird trick of fate had given her the white skin, the hazel eyes, the demeanor of people like us even though she was, in the parlance of the Cardamom Club, just four *annas* to the rupee. One fourth British, and not a drop of blood more." He begins to cry, though his aim at them with his pistol is steadfast. He was in love with Rosalie, Sam thinks, but a little, mean part of his brain is in the end much stronger than any love he might harbor. Hence that malevolence in him when he thinks of her, when he thinks that he has been willfully tricked by her. The Kens of this world are not really made for love; they are too parsimonious.

"I took her out for one last time," Ken says, "and then slashed her face with my pocketknife so that she would not so easily defraud another serviceman." He sobs now, loudly, his nose running, tears submerging his face, hiccups racking his thin body. "Oh, Sam," he says, "I loved her." Then, most incongruously, "It was a true love, a real love, and it was for love that I injured her. Now she is mine and can't be anyone else's lover."

Marianne is sobbing too, her heart atomized into a thousand pieces. Sam knows that her sorrow is partly for Rosalie, but also partly for Ken, who could have been a strong and courageous human being but has lost all his capacity for goodness and, as far as she is concerned, is doomed to hell.

The Japanese boy says this: *"Koitsu wa ikashite okou; yasashii kao wo shiteiruna. Kini itta. Soitsu wo nigashite yare."*

Sam understands what he says, just as he understood what he had said when Sam first ran into the house and blew away his ankles. Sam has known that one of the other two, Ken or Marianne, was going to dupe him, and even from the beginning he has thought it would be Ken because it was a man the Japanese soldier had looked up at when he said, *I thought you were the enemy.* Now this boy is asking for the gift of Sam's life from Ken, he says, *He has a kind face, let the man live.* Why, Sam wonders, was it because he did not kill the boy, because he tied his wrists behind him but lightly, or because he bandaged his ankles?

As the boy's reedy voice, mangled by pain, cuts through the air and hangs between them, Ken raises his pistol deliberately and shoots him through the heart. The Japanese soldier's body convulses once, then twice, and then he sinks with a sigh to the ground, falling on his cheek, his arms akimbo as life ebbs out of him.

Before Ken can turn his attention to Sam and Marianne, another shot rings out in the room and a look of extreme surprise and hurt comes into Ken's eyes even as a round hole, initially bloodless, blooms in the center of his forehead like the red *tikka* that Hindus wear to mimic Shiva's third eye and ward off evil influences. Ken dies, but he does not move from where he sits, only his pistol drops from his hand to the floor.

Sam fleetly drags himself across the floor even before the last echo of the bullet fades away and grabs Ken's pistol, which he throws across the room. It bangs with a tremendous clatter against the wall and bounces before coming to a rest.

"You saved my life twice," Sam says to Marianne, who is staring at the smoking pistol in her hand with something akin to amazement. He had not known Marianne had a weapon until she had shattered the python's head, and neither had Ken. When they reentered the bungalow, Ken had taken away Sam's pistol, but not Marianne's.

"I had to kill him," she says. "You would not have; you would have tried to talk him out of his betrayals and in the process he would have killed us."

Sam, still lying on his left side, holding his right arm tightly against his body, says, "I did not think it was necessary, and I must say, I did not expect it of you."

"This courage?" she asks wryly.

He nods, his heart thundering in his chest.

"Because I am old?"

He nods again, feeling a sense of shame.

"It is because I am old that I recognize evil and poison where I see it, Sam, and I know when to get rid of it, and when to try and placate it. You have to know when to kill, and when to grant the mercy of life."

At this astounding statement, from a missionary's wife no less, Sam has to smile. "Like God?"

She nods, serious. "Yes, like Him. In wars, we must be almost like gods."

They leave the bungalow in the middle of the night, traveling down the dirt path to Ledo in India with the feeble flame of their torchlights shaded by a piece of cloth. They both know they cannot stay at the bungalow for the night because the Japanese are sure to return to keep their rendezvous with Ken. However, Sam, who has so far been the most cautious of them all, the most anxious not to call attention to their presence in the jungles, deliberately skins the chicken with his left hand and roasts it over an open fire. After they eat, they pack the rest of the food in plantain leaves. Marianne attempts to reset Sam's dislocated right shoulder, but she has no strength left and her arms hang limply by her side after just one try. She creates a sling for him though and pads the sling at his shoulder with the cotton stuffing from a damp and smoldering mattress.

Sam still has to carry his haversack, hung over his left shoulder, because the photos Ken has taken of the Calcutta docks are in it. Along with the photographs is Ken's pistol and the fifteen chocolate bars that he has hidden and not shared with them even when they were at their weakest and most ravenous, just outside the Kachin village. Inside also, in a Japanese script that Sam can just barely read (his training only extends to conversational Japanese), are Ken's orders for this meeting. He has deliberately crashed his plane into the hillside so that he can hike to this bungalow, hand over the photographs, and perhaps, if his cover is not blown, return to his unit as usual, a hero in their eyes who marched through Japanese territory in Burma and lived to tell of it.

It has begun to rain again, but this rain, this warm, dripping rain, cleanses them both; it is like a baptism, a new life. They know they will reach India safely, at least now that they do not travel with treachery in their midst.

# Thirty-one

*One of the first distasteful confrontations experienced by Indian officers when they joined a unit was that of blatant racism. . . . Chaudhuri recalls the second in command of the North Staffordshire Regiment who habitually belted out epithets for Indians, such as* wogs, niggers, *and* nig-wigs. *When Chaudhuri politely expressed his discomfort at the major's use of such language, the latter expressed genuine surprise, noting that he did not think Chaudhuri would mind, for he considered him as "one of us."*

—Pradeep P. Barua, *Gentlemen of the Raj:*
*The Indian Army Officer Corps, 1817–1949*

Even as Mila and Raman waited outside the police station for news of Ashok, Kiran was at the Victoria Club that afternoon, not drinking for once, but seated on one of the bar stools and looking outside at the dulling light that heralded the setting of the sun.

He could not remember very much of the previous night; all he could recall was his head swimming in gin, a fight about something with Sims who was being arrogant and a bastard. He flexed his shoulder and felt the tightening of skin over his clavicle where the wound from Sims's bite was just beginning to heal. What had that been about? And why had he even fought with Sims, who had always been a good chap? Kiran blamed himself now that he was sober again and had come to the club to find Sims and apologize. What if Blakely and Sims found their amusements elsewhere, without him? What would he do then?

373

He watched the light slant in a golden arc over the lawns where the *mela* tents had been just a few days ago. Now, all that remained were the holes in the grass where the tent stakes had rested and a few paper flags torn from the strings of flags that had festooned the *mela* enclosure. For just a moment, all of his discontent came back to him and Kiran slouched on his stool, wondering where his life was headed and what he was going to do. It was all very fine for Sims and Blakely, they had jobs, after all, were officers with the Rifles. But he had nothing but Papa's disapproval.

Kiran saw Sims and Blakely cross the lawn in front of him, coming in from a cricket game, their clothes gleaming white, Blakely carrying the bat on his shoulder. As they approached the open verandah of the bar, a man cut across the grass in a steady trot, and, panting, came to stop beside them. Kiran squinted into the sunshine, shading his eyes with his hands. It was the horse dealer from the Lal Bazaar. What could Sims and Blakely have to do with him? Surely they already owned their horses?

He got down from his bar stool and went running down the steps onto the lawn. Sims and Blakely saw him, quite clearly, and just as clearly turned their backs and started to walk away. Kiran paused, struck by a sudden hurt, and then started to run again.

"I thought you meant to ignore me," he said as he came up on them.

"We did," Blakely said deliberately, not looking at Kiran. "Bugger off."

"What?" Kiran stopped where he was, stunned beyond speech.

"Your brother," Sims said, enunciating every word as though he was speaking to an uneducated idiot, "tried to kill Colonel Pankhurst today. You heard what Blakely said, bugger off."

Kiran's heart stopped. "What nonsense is this, Sims? Ashok would never—"

"He did," Sims said harshly, "and your sister is a whore."

Even before he realized what he was doing, Kiran pulled at Sims's shoulder to turn him around, drew his fist back, and bashed it into Sims's face. He felt the bones of Sims's nose pulverize under his hand, and blood and snot flew out to smack him in the face.

"How dare you!" he shouted. Sims toppled to the grass and Kiran had raised his foot to stomp on his chest when he was hit on the back with the cricket bat. He thought he could feel the middle vertebrae of his back crackle and crumble as the air was knocked out of his lungs and he fell, the world blacking out around him before he hit the ground.

Just as he began to lose consciousness, he heard Blakely say, "We saw your sister in the brothel yesterday. She is a whore; why else would she be there?"

Kiran came to ten minutes later and found himself being dragged by his collar to the front of the Victoria Club. A red haze swam before his eyes and the pain in his spine almost knocked him back into unconsciousness, but he kept himself awake with determination. He began clawing on the ground, digging his heels into the hard earth, scratching at the arms that had pulled his shirt tight against his neck until he was almost choking. Then, he felt them release him and he lay on the gravel driveway that led to the front porch of the Victoria Club.

Three bearers came into his view as he lay there, and they were carrying large, galvanized tin trays that looked familiar, but Kiran could not find the words in his brain that matched the function of those trays. He saw Sims, his entire face bloodied, take one tray and upend its putrid contents over his head. It was only when the first rush of excrement came cascading down into his open mouth that Kiran knew what they were doing—they were emptying the thunderboxes from the lavatories over him. He cringed and curled his legs and arms into his body, spitting out the taste of shit, rubbing his blinded eyes. But the stink was everywhere. Maggots crawled over his shirt and made their slimy, fetid way under the waistband of his pants.

Kiran began to cry then, knowing that his whole life in pursuit of these men—men like these—had been a huge, futile waste. He had not thought he fit in as Indian; he had thought he could be languidly English himself, become what he most admired. A small part of his brain told him that Blakely and Sims were not exactly upper drawer, either here or in England, but he had so much wanted to *be* them because there was no one else around in Rudrakot. If he had made friends with men from a better class of society, his class, the class they—Papa, Mila, Ashok, and he—belonged to, this would not be happening. Kiran tucked his head into his chest, the filth and feculence drenching him. Flies came to settle on him as though he were a living carcass. He scraped his tongue with his teeth so that he could dig out the shit and spit it out. He cried, his tears mixing with the slime, knowing that in the end.

In the end, he had climbed a steep nothing.

# Thirty-two

*Our mission is a high and holy mission. We are here to govern India as delegates of a Christian and civilized power. We are here as representatives of Christ and Caesar to maintain this land against Shiva and Khalifa. In that task we shall not falter, we will oppose ideal to ideal, force to force, constancy to assassination . . . If you agitate, you will be punished; if you preach sedition, you will be imprisoned; if you assassinate, you will be hanged; if you rise, you will be shot down."*

—Al Carthill, *The Lost Dominion*, 1924

*T*wo hours after Kiran had been brought home and put to bed, Mila opened the door to Sam's room and stood there, awash in tears. Sam, seated on the floor, leaning against his bed, his clothes and his guns spread out around him, leapt up and went to her.

He shut the door and took her to an armchair, where he sat down himself and then pulled her onto his lap. "I'm sorry," he said. "What can I say or do that will make all of this better? I have wanted to come to you, but did not know how, did not know where to find you."

She could not cry anymore. Mila had spent the whole day in tears, unable to check them even for a little while, and now she was depleted of all energy. And all through the day she had wondered where Sam was, how she could approach him, how to find the shelter of his arms, not knowing anything about his earlier conversation with her father. Even had she known, it would not have mattered, for Mila had always been able to sway her father to her convictions. But . . . now, so much had changed in the space of just one day. Her heart skipped every third beat, in so much pain that she could feel it fill her ribs and rub raw against them. And Sam heard that flutter too, or rather he sensed it against his own skin. He held her face in his hands and licked away her tears until her face was wet with his saliva.

She smiled then for the first time in many, many hours. Mila bent and ran her tongue and her teeth over Sam's face as though her mouth were learning the aroma of his skin and the taste of the bones that jutted beneath his eyes. She undid his shirt and his pants, took off her own sari, in such a hurry that she would not let him touch her until she was naked and straddling him. Then she bent to take his mouth with hers and kissed him, slowly, as they made love. She had not undone her hair, and even though she held Sam's arms against the side of the chair, he dragged his arm away so that he could reach behind her head and pull her hair free until it covered them both.

Against her mouth he said, "I want to remember you like this."

Mila laid her head against his chest. "How long before I see you again, Sam?"

He was quiet, stroking her hair. "Come away with me now."

Mila raised herself and looked down upon him. "Right away? Where will we go? What will we do?"

"We can marry once we get to Delhi. And then . . . we'll work things out. Let me take you away from here, from all this ugliness. Come with me. Wait . . ." He rose from the armchair, still carrying her in his arms, and went to the bed where a little pile of gold glistened against the cool green sheets. Sam returned to the chair, sat down, settled her in his lap again, and opened his fist to reveal the gold chain he had bought for her in the bazaar earlier in the afternoon.

"What is it?" she asked in wonder, lifting one edge of the thin, glittering gold chain with her index finger and thumb and unraveling its length all along her arm.

"I do not know," Sam said. "It's too long to fit around your neck, but you could wear it around your waist," and so saying he threaded the chain around her slender waist three times, until the gold glowed against her warm skin. "Come with me today, my darling."

She rose from his embrace and put on her clothes, first her underwear, then her petticoat and blouse, and then the blue chiffon sari still smudged with Ashok's blood. She did not look at Sam as she did all of this but bent her head instead, as though concentrating on her dressing. Sam watched her intently. He saw that Mila was exhausted, the skin under her eyes bruised from lack of sleep; a cave of emptiness seemed to have grown inside her after the events of the day and he ached to be able to bring back some laughter within her. He had not been able to help her family or her in any way at all; it was even as though they did not want him around. He sat back in the chair and waited for her to speak again.

She said, "I cannot come right now . . . I have to make preparations."

"You will never come unless you come now."

"I will," she said, standing in front of him, her hands clasped at her waist. "I need to say good-bye. I will leave in two hours from now and come with Sayyid. I will meet you at Chetak's tomb."

"Then," Sam said, "I will have to be content with that." He cradled her in his arms for a long while, inhaling the scent of her, listening to the thumping of her heart. Sam let her go and Mila went without a glance backward, for they both knew that they would see each other again—there was no need for a good-bye here.

Sam threw his clothes into his holdall, dressed quickly, and slipped the Colt into his holster. He sat for ten minutes, watching as the hands of his wristwatch moved to form eleven o'clock, and then he went out into the back balcony and stayed against the wall, where he could not be seen, until his eyes adjusted to the darkness. Vimal was supposed to have gone back with him to the field punishment center, but he was dead now. Sam had mourned his loss all afternoon, for even though there had been something he had not liked about him (perhaps just the fact that Mila had not liked him), he had felt a great deal of sadness about the loss of such beauty, such vim, such a lust for life and for his fellow human beings. The students at the Lal Bazaar had been devastated; they had permeated the house there until there was no standing space either within the building or in the compound outside. A makeshift bier had been erected in the center of the front yard, an empty bier to denote Vimal's absence from amongst them. And they had all passed by it, touched it at the foot end, kissed the cloth that would have covered his body, and then most of them had collapsed under the banyan tree and had had to be revived. Sam, kept away from the police station by Jai and Raman, had gone to pay his last respects to the man Vimal had been. He had tarried near the bier for only five minutes, and on his way out saw Jai's limousine pass by with Ashok within. A shattered Ashok, with fresh and bloody nicks and cuts on his face and hands, looking as though his soul had fled, his face plastered against the pristinely clean glass of the Daimler, filled with longing. He had wanted to be where Sam was, by the empty frame that should have held Vimal's body, a body that now lay blown to pieces over the lawns of the residency.

A torchlight came on in the bush and scrub behind Raman's house, once, twice, a third time, and Sam lifted his holdall to his shoulder and went down the concrete stairway. He passed softly by the servants' quarters, but he need not have worried, because the day had depleted everyone beyond relief and they all slept the sleep of the dead. Sam reached the ugly horse dealer, his face spattered with thick black moles and his toothy, yellow smile. When he had made the agreement to buy his horses earlier that afternoon, the man had said, almost casually, "My brother is a guard at the prison house in the desert, Sahib." Sam had ignored him then. But now, when the dealer reached out a wizened claw of a hand for the money, Sam shook his head.

"Take me to the prison in the desert," he said, "and I will give you twice the amount I promised you."

The man scratched his head, and scratched behind one filthy ear for a while. Then he said, "All right, Sahib. But if there are dangers to be found, I will not help you."

It was a strange statement for this dealer to make, when he had so obviously wanted the business earlier in the day, and Sam hesitated, but only for a moment. Two overweight, drunken British soldiers guarded the field punishment center at night along with perhaps a few Indian guards, and they could all be bribed. Vimal had also flung some dark hints about Mike waiting and ready for Sam when he came to get him, for the sum of ten thousand rupees that Sam had paid him. Once these rumors of negotiations reached Sam, he knew that getting Mike out of there would be easy; when money came into play, anyone could be bought. They would no longer need to scale the walls to enter the field punishment center. Vimal's death had thrown his plans off course but only for a while, for Sam still had some more money, the guards would presumably still want it. They did not care about Mike, only Sam did.

"Come then," he said, tying his holdall over one of the horses and swinging into the saddle of the other. "You will not expect me to save your life either if there is danger ahead of us."

"Yes, Sahib."

They rode away behind the Civil Lines, but not before Sam had turned his horse back to Raman's house and dismounted. And Sam, who had prayed but little in his life, never seeing the point of imploring favors from an unknown and unseen God, fell on his knees and bowed his head, mouthing the only words he knew well, *Our Father who art in heaven, hallowed be thy name* . . . The horse dealer waited patiently in the murk beyond the gate. Sam saw a light in Mila's room and thought he saw a woman's figure silhouetted against that light, in the balcony. She moved her hand to her mouth and then threw it in the air. A kiss. Sam waited for it to be borne on the little breeze that swept up from the garden. *Come to me, my love,* he said across the expanse of darkness. *I will wait for you.*

When Sam had left, Mila went back into the house and stood outside Ashok's room. She knocked softly and went in. The room was in darkness except for a little halo of light from a table lamp that Ashok had set on the floor and he lay on the floor near it, his head bathed in gold. He was not asleep, but he was not really awake either, his eyes open and fixed upon the walls. She sat down next to him and touched the cuts on his arms and his fingers. "Does it hurt?" she asked.

He said nothing.

Mila talked then, for ten minutes, telling him of her love for Sam. How she had not expected this, how it had transformed everything she had ever felt or thought. She kissed Ashok's forehead, rubbed her hand against his cheek, told him that this day would pass and that this grief would also die its own death—perhaps not soon, but one day.

"Is this a farewell?" he asked then, still gazing at the wall as though he had not heard a word of what she had been saying.

"You are my brother," Mila said. "There are no farewells between us."

Ashok moved and rested his head on Mila's lap and let her run her fingers through his hair, as she had when he was a child and she was not more than a child herself. She thought of how he had grown up in these past few days, how he was different, how he would never return to the boy he had been. Ashok had learned to become a man within himself, not just an emulation of Papa or of Kiran. He would need all of this strength, because an attempt on Pankhurst's life was not something the government would take lightly. Jai had managed to get Ashok out of the jail for this night and perhaps a few more, only on his word that Ashok would not flee Rudrakot—but there was no guarantee that Ashok would not be jailed. Or hanged for abetting in this crime. A great deal of uncertainty lay in front of them. Mila kissed her brother gently, put his head back on the floor, and went out of the room.

In the corridor, she tarried outside Kiran's door and then opened it, went in, and shut the door behind her. He slept across his bed, his head drooping over one side, his long legs over the other. Kiran slept naked, on his belly, as though he could not even bear the touch of cloth against his skin, and as he slept he moved restlessly, wiping his hair of some sleaze, making hawking noises with his mouth. Mila thought she heard him mumble that he could not stand the stench, that his nose was burning, that he was in pain. He cried out then for their father, *Papa, Papa, come to me, Papa.*

"Kiran?" Raman called from his room.

Mila moved away from the door to one side of the room as her father came running down the corridor in his white nighttime *veshti*, his chest bare, his hair tousled from sleep. He opened the door and came inside to gather his eldest son in his arms. Kiran still slept as though he could not bear to waken and allow space for his thoughts and his shame. He writhed for a few minutes in Raman's arms and then rested, his breathing calmer. What little part of him still remained conscious came to life in tears that trickled out between his shut eyes and down his cheeks. Unable to bear the pain any longer, Mila went to her father and her brother and put her arms around them, and rested her head against theirs. Raman only said, "So you are here too, my dear? We must get him through this; we must all get through this somehow."

"I know, Papa," Mila said, kissing him on the head. She thought she could see the lines on his forehead even in this darkness, she thought she could hear his heart beat with this colossal pain that had descended upon them all. She did not pity herself, or them, or wonder what they had done to deserve all of this, or even think that perhaps they were all paying their dues for some sin they had committed in a previous life. This was life, such as it was, and it had to be borne, it had to be lived. She had Sam's love, and she so dearly loved Sam. And he waited for her at Chetak's tomb.

There was nothing more they could do tonight for Kiran, for that dense, comatose sleep had claimed him again—a sleep from which he had never really awakened. Mila helped her father back to his room and was glad that he used her shoulder to lean on, something he had never done before, always sprightly, always with more of a spring in his step than she. He lay down on his bed and shut his eyes and in a few minutes he was asleep too. She clasped his hands and kissed each one. And then she bent and laid her head against her father's feet, asking for his blessing.

"Mila, my dear," he said, stirring on the pillow.

"Yes, Papa," she said quietly.

"At least you are all right," he mumbled. "At least I can rely upon you. This is why I wanted a daughter all those years ago . . . this is why."

She froze at the foot of his bed, her heart exploding against her skin, an immense pain thronging through her. Her father slept restlessly; perhaps he did not even realize that he had spoken aloud. In the other rooms, Kiran and Ashok lay grieving for different things, their very selves splintered.

She went into her room and sat down on the edge of her bed and thought for a very long while, her fingers linked in her lap, her head bowed with the weight of her hair falling all around her. She saw Sam riding out into the desert, arriving at the field punishment center. She even saw Mike, emaciated and gaunt, but in Sam's arms. He was safe, they were both safe. . . .

Mila rose and went toward the balcony door, and as she walked, deep in thought, she tripped over something and looked down automatically. Her high-heeled *chappals*, the ones she had worn on the night of the White Durbar, lay on the floor, the soles facing upward. Another omen, she thought tiredly, and the *chappals* must have been upside down all through this horrifying day. Perhaps Pallavi was right in her superstitions after all. Without turning them over, she went down the concrete stairway to the back of the house where Sayyid slept under the cooling night sky. She bent to shake his shoulder and awaken him and then told him what she wanted.


There was a moment, an instant in time, all over India, every year, when one knew that the monsoons were here. It was a moment of madness, *pagalpan*, a jubilation so intense that it ate up the whole spirit of the person experiencing it and flung him into the air as though he was formed of nothing but exhilaration. As Mila leaned over Sayyid, she felt this insanity and recognized it for what it was. Every atom of her body was filled with this unnamed frenzy, her brain died to nothingness, and a happiness came flooding over her. She looked skyward and saw the stars blotted out by a canopy of thick, rain-bearing clouds. Lightning crawled across the sky and an enormous boom of thunder followed, shaking the very earth.

"Memsahib," Sayyid said, awake now, looking up at her.

"The rains come, Sayyid," she said.

Halfway across the desert, Sam heard this thud of thunder too and at the same moment Mila looked up into the sky, he raised his head and in-haled that sweet aroma of rain. He thought he had never sensed some-thing like this before—it was not just a lack of heat, it was a lunacy. But the frissons of pleasure coursing through his veins were replaced by a fear and a watchfulness and Sam kept his Colt leveled at Sims, outside the field punishment center.

They were both lit by the headlights of the jeep that Sims had driven into the desert and parked outside the wooden gates of the center. Sam had reached here in relatively good time, considering how long it had taken for them to drive to Chetak's tomb a few days ago, but the horses were fleet and sleek and more sure-footed among the dry dirt and stones of the Sukh desert than the jeeps had been. The horse dealer had thrown a whistle out into the air, and even before it had died down, a door, set in-side the enormous wooden gates, just the size of a bending man, opened and the dealer's brother had stepped out. He had put out his hand for the money, but Sam, one hand on the pistol in his holster, the other holding the rupee notes, had shaken his head. "Bring out the sahib first," he said harshly.

"Bring him out, and soon, you stupid fool," the horse dealer had shouted in Hindustani; he had spoken very fast because he knew that Sam understood the language, but had not realized that Sam understood the language even articulated at such speed. "Do you want to get us all killed? Give him the *gora*, and let me get out of here before that other sahib ar-rives. Get to it, motherfucker."

The guard beckoned and Sam pulled out his pistol and entered through the door to see Mike standing in the center of the square courtyard. He stood with his legs apart, his face awash with bewilderment in the moonlight, his arms and legs loose and flapping, as though he had lost all co-ordination in them. The door to the guardhouse on one side was open, and light streamed out and with it the sound of snores—the British guards were asleep, or drugged.

"Come to me, Mike," Sam said.

"Ah," Mike said, as though he had found his voice after many months. "I thought this must have had something to do with you. Are we going to leave now?"

"Yes," Sam waved him toward the gate, "now."

The guard barred their way out. "The money, Sahib."

Sam wedged his gun against the man's ribs. "When I get out and get on my horse, I will give you the money, not before that."

They had just stepped out of the prison when the door slammed shut behind them with such ferocity that Sam's hair flew out in front of his eyes. He turned around. He had not paid the guard yet, what was going on? And then the hairs at the back of his neck prickled and Sam turned very, very slowly as light bathed the two of them and from behind the headlights of the jeep, Sims said, "Game's up, Captain Hawthorne. Or should I call you Ridley too?"

"Sims, you *behenchoth*," Mike said wearily, pulling himself out from under Sam's arm and falling back on the wooden gate. He had no energy left to even move, but it did not stop a rash of insults in fluent Hindustani from his mouth.

"Shut up," Sims shouted as he came out into the pool of light that had imprisoned them against the wooden doors of the field punishment center.

Now Sam understood the horse dealer's haste at wanting to get away; he had told Sims of his plans. But what did he care? Sims was responsible for Mike's incarceration, and from the colorful invective still spewing from his brother between coughs and pauses for breath, it seemed as though Mike knew it too. They were yelling at each other like fighting dogs, snarling and sniping, but Sam's gun, which kept Sims's stomach steadily in sight, kept him away from Mike. Sims had a gun also, but he waved it around a lot.

"We don't need the lot of you," he screamed. "Go back, go back to America, or better yet, just rot in this land, no one will know."

A branch of lightning flashed across the sky then, turning the pale gold of the jeep's headlights into silver, blinding them all. The thunder followed, the immense madness followed, and it took hold of all of them, even Sims, who began to breathe more easily. Sam watched him carefully, wondering what was going to happen now, how this was all going to play out.

And then he remembered Sims's conversation with Blakely during that hot afternoon, and that filthy little ditty. In Burma, Ken had said, almost indifferently, that the Cardamom Club had been exclusively the province of spies. There could not be two such clubs in Calcutta, or two such clubs with two women who had their faces slashed because they were half Indian and half British, or two women with the same unusual name.

"Rosalie," Sam said, almost conversationally.

"Wha——" Sims stopped in midsentence, a hard coldness seeping into his eyes. "What do you know of Rosalie?"

"Just enough," Sam said, and shot him as he was raising his pistol. Sims crumpled to the ground just as the rains came, at first in big, fat drops and then in a deluge, catapulting the light from the jeep's headlights into a thousand different directions. He slumped slowly, his chin hitting the dirt first, and Sam heard the crack of bones as his jaw fractured, but Sims was already beyond feeling any pain from that.

The horse dealer had disappeared somewhere behind the field punishment center and Sam untied the two horses and smacked each of them hard on their rumps, sending them out into the wet desert night. He helped Mike into the jeep, switched off the headlights to conserve the battery, and they waited, watching the rain form a thick puddle around Sims's inert body.

"What was that about?" Mike yelled, leaning into Sam's ear.

"Something I should have done in Burma," Sam said grimly. "I did not have the courage then, but Marianne——I will explain all that later—— taught me that when the time comes to kill, a man must kill, and not just because he is in danger of being killed himself."

They waited for an hour, until the rain abated and light began to seep into the sky from the awakening sun. Mike asked, just once, when he woke from a light sleep, "Is this about a girl?"

"Yes," Sam said, sending his yearning out into the desert and to Mila. Where was she? Why was she not here, with him? He should never have left her in the house and come away. Sam began to think that he had been right in saying, even though he had spoken then without really considering what he was saying, that if he did not take Mila away with him, she would never leave Rudrakot. He laid his weary head against the steering wheel of the jeep as the rain misted around him warmly. It was a rain much like the Burma rain, like a bath, purging. The rain stopped then, abruptly, and the clouds broke lines to reveal a gently shining moon on the wane. Sam heard the muffled sound of horse hooves somewhere out in the desert and lifted his head hopefully. He could not see very far into the desert, unlike two nights ago when Vimal and he had first stormed the field punishment center and visibility had stretched to the edge of the earth and beyond. Now, there was simply a pool of silver light draining down upon them from the skies and the gap in the clouds and beyond that was all darkness.

Sam saw the figure of an enormous horse emerge from the gloom in front of him and race across the dirt, its muscles gleaming under its black hide, its nostrils flaring from the exertion, its mane silver and flowing behind it. He touched Mike on his shoulder and his brother raised his gaze to the horse. Both their hearts stilled at the animal's beauty, at its ferocity, at its mad dash across the desert night when no one but they were watching.

"Chetak," Sam said softly. "I'll be damned. The legend is true."

Mike's voice had the hidden hint of a smile in it. "All legends are true in India, Sam."

They finally saw the headlights of the jeep flickering and throbbing near Chetak's tomb. It came nearer and nearer and Sam jumped out of his seat and ran to meet Mila.

But only one person was in that jeep, only the person driving—Sayyid.

# Thirty-three

*Something there is that doesn't love a wall,*
*That sends the frozen-ground-swell under it,*
*And spills the upper boulders in the sun;*
*And makes gaps even two can pass abreast.*

—Robert Frost, *Mending Wall*

Mila married me two weeks after Sam left. We were not to marry for quite a while yet, so the shortness of time sent rumors into a frenzy. As for the wedding itself, it was grand, my dearest Olivia, as though it had been planned for years. But I am, was, a prince, you know, and we have our resources, our abilities; money buys speed. Money speedily buys marigold garlands to decorate entire forts; twenty orchestras littered around the city to announce their prince's marriage to the woman he loved; silks in abundance in colors from the center and the edges of rainbows; jewelry for the bride, smelted in two days, fine, shining gold, still warm from the goldsmith's hand and kiln. Did I mention that I was a prince? That I ruled Rudrakot? That I was, for the many denizens of Rudrakot, the kingdom itself?

We found out a month later that we were to have a child and I was ecstatic. There was something of a great sadness within Mila, though, even as the child grew. When she laughed, it seemed to edge her laughter, when she cried (and she seemed to cry very often in the early months and everyone said that it was a woman's way at this time), it was as though her heart would fragment. And at this time perhaps, I began to think that Sam Hawthorne was not just who he was to us, to Rudrakot, to the Rifles regiment, and to Raman. He had meant something to Mila too. It was not a suspicion, but a fear really, one I never voiced or even dared to formulate fully in my own mind. I never talked to her about Sam, and she never seemed to even think about him, or if she did, it did not change her attitude toward me. I loved her, and I felt loved by her. Mila gave you to your father, and she gave me her love.

But before Mila married me, ten days after Sam had left Rudrakot, Marianne Westwood came for a visit. She came on Sam's behest, at his asking. She stayed with me, in the fort, as my personal guest. While we had not heard of Samuel Hawthorne before he came to hurl our lives into disasters, we had, in some fashion, known of Marianne. She was practically famous, and her escape from Burma, with the Japanese at her very heels, her killing of an American soldier who was about to provide secret photographs of the Calcutta docks to the Japanese had been in all the newspapers. Sam came to Rudrakot so soon after Marianne was lauded for her courage and her bravery that *we* did not make the connection between them, and it allowed him for a while at least to keep his identity and his work with the Office of Strategic Services hidden. All we had read was that another American soldier had parachuted into Burma to bring her back to India.

So Marianne was a wartime celebrity, and I took her to my palaces and insisted upon inviting everyone important to meet her in a series of three dinner parties. But it was Mila she wanted to see the most, and she fell upon your mother with such a great affection, with tears in her eyes at the first sight of her, with such love, that it was curious . . . but I gave it no more thought, even after she told me about her trials in Burma. Mr. Raman allowed Mila to come to the palaces more often during the week that Marianne stayed as my guest, and we talked for a long while after all the other invitees had left, sitting out in the terraced verandah under the fading night stars. And that was when we learned of Sam's Burma story and that he was the unnamed American soldier in the newspaper accounts. But even so, only Mila and I knew of this, since Marianne begged us to keep Sam's name out of circulation.

I did not stop to consider then why Marianne was in Rudrakot, or rather why she had chosen a private journey to my kingdom when she could have traveled anywhere else in India and have been feted in a much grander manner. She had come, of course, to find out how Mila was faring, perhaps even to ask her why she had not fled Rudrakot with Sam. He most wanted a response to this question. I was overwhelmed with a little shame, I must confess, at hearing of Sam's heroism in Burma, and was remorseful at . . . shall I say, not having been too welcoming or friendly with him while he was here. But then, he came back to Rudrakot, and I intercepted his letters to Mila, and everything began to make some sense, and I was no longer riddled with even the slightest guilt.

Sam came back for a week, six months later, only to hear that Mila was married. It must have been a shock to him; I wonder how he managed that news, for he had not known, you see, we had heard nothing of him after he left Rudrakot other than the news from Marianne—he had simply disappeared. Did he go back into Burma and into the war? But he came back in December, I remember, for the nights were cooler then and we sat outside for dinners and lunches without being ambushed by mosquitoes as in the days of the rains. I did not see him, but knew he was here, because I know—knew—everything in Rudrakot. He came in stealth, since his exploits had not yet lost their luster; the Victoria Club talked of it, the Lancers and the Rifles buzzed with his rescue of Michael Ridley and the strange and unexplained death of that officer . . . what was his name, ah, Sims. So Sam came into Rudrakot dressed as a peasant, bronzed by the sun, given away only by the tint of his eyes. He seemed to have well perfected the art of this deception by then, had almost become native, something he would doubtless have been immensely proud of—this ability to shed his skin, and to don the skin of another people without the seams showing. He kept his gaze down, mumbled in Urdu and Hindustani, gesticulated, scratched, and spat like a farmer, smiled with teeth stained by *paan*. He played his role well, but I knew he was there. I was not prince of Rudrakot for nothing, even if I may have to seem immodest when I say this, my dear child, but I had my spies, I had my resources.

Your father rowed out into the lake in a little boat he had hired on the other side, the side away from the lawns of the Victoria Club and my hunting lodge. This he did every night, and finally, on the last day of his stay, I took Mila to the lakeside verandah for dinner. Sam had written to Mila, two letters for each of the previous five days he had been here, some of them no more than a note, some long and pleading epistles asking for a glimpse of her, and all of these, quite naturally, fell into my hands. I read only the first one and kept the others, why I did not know then, but I send them to you so you can learn of your father's love for your mother in his own words.

To Sam it seemed as though Mila did not respond to him. But that was not true; if she had known he was back in Rudrakot, she would have fled with him to wherever he had asked her. He only saw her then from the dark waters of the lake, and when she turned in profile he must have seen that she was heavy with a child. *My* child, as he thought then, as I thought then. I could not have let her go, for if she had, what would have happened to me? This then, was my . . . little . . . deception. Your father prevaricated with us; I manipulated the truth just a bit, for the cause of my own happiness. At least he had that sight of your mother. Mila too stood at the parapet and gazed out into the murk beyond for a very long time that night after dinner. Once she said to me, "Do you see a light out there? Is someone fishing?"

I saw nothing when I stood by her, but she sensed your father's presence. She would not leave her place by the parapet and stayed there for three hours, waiting, watching, until the night draped its coldness over us. And then, finally, she consented to come to bed.

Then you came. Two weeks early, not by much really, not early enough to set the gossiping old women chattering, who counted backward on nine fingers, and no less. It cast sorrow upon their brows; you could have been on time, could have come early on your own, not by any design of your mother's or mine—for they thought, of course, that the wedding was hurried because of me, not Sam. Sam did not figure in anyone's calculations, or if he did at all, it was because he had lied to us, misrepresented himself, assailed the hitherto unbreachable—only because it was in the middle of the desert, not because of any effort on the part of the laggard guards—field punishment center, taken away one of its inmates, and doubtless had lived to tell about it.

You had black hair, Mila's hair, mine even, though there is a subtle brush of brown in mine in an ambient light; some ancestor had doubtless dallied with one of our masters. And yet no one would have dared to call me a half-caste; I was born for the throne of Rudrakot. However . . . that is not important, for what was important was that your hair was black and you were well chubby for a month early, fully formed in your mother's womb before your time. But your eyes were blue, like settled indigo in its stewing pot, with a ring of dark iris. Sam's eyes. Mouths fluttered, voicing thoughts that were true, though not evil.

I did not see you again for a whole month after you were born, though I did come to satisfy my curiosity when you first came to us. Sadness, anger, spite, a jealousy that ripped me apart—they all came to lodge within me. Mila died, you see, a few days after your birth. How my hand shakes even now to write those words, *Mila died*. It was then such a colossal physical pain to my heart; I thought I would die too just from the ache in my chest. I did not eat for five days; I saw no one, I talked with no one. I lit the funeral pyre first, as was my duty as her husband, and it was the only duty to her I loathed so much that the torch shook in my hands and fell to the ground three times. She had the best care possible, but something had fled from her when Sam left Rudrakot, something he took with him, and in doing so, took away her will to live. You kept her alive, as long as you were within her, but once she delivered you safely into other hands, she left Rudrakot too. She died because of an infection from the childbirth, that is the official conclusion, but I think she died because she could not live without your father.

That first month passed without my having any sense of its passing. Over the next two months, I visited you often in the *zenana*, searching for your mother in you, finding more of your father. Mila married me even though she loved Sam. I loved her, fiercely, much as Sam loved her, but she loved Sam. Oh, she loved me too, but it was not quite like the love she had for your father.

When you were three months old, Pallavi suggested that we send you to America, to be with Sam and Mike and your grandmother Maude. I did not want to at first, but I agreed in the end because, you see, you belonged more to Sam than to me. You were the gift Mila gave to Sam, that piece of herself.

You might wonder why we did not keep you with us, why you grew up so distant from the land of your birth . . . and . . . how do I answer this without insulting you, my dear Olivia? Know that I mean not to be derisive; we gave this matter a great deal of careful consideration, thought about who we were, where we all were in our lives and where you would best fit—with us or with Sam in America. You see, *we* did not seem very much to belong in our country either, even as full-blooded Indians. One of the reasons your grandfather, Mr. Raman, after one visit, never went to the hill station of Mussoorie to escape the heat of the plains was that although he was accorded entry into the best clubs in the place, the finest restaurants, the homes of the Raj grandees, even the viceregal "at homes" and balls, he could not and I could not enter the public library. On one of our walks through the Mall, when we thought of popping into the library for a book with which to spend our hours of leisure that afternoon, we saw nailed outside on a post a painted board that read: NO DOGS OR INDI-ANS. There was no circumventing the intentions behind that bland statement. It was a blatant prejudice of the British Raj. Remember, my dear Olivia, that while it seems as though your father killed Sims because he was a courier in the pay of the Japanese, Sam actually killed his first man in the war because of that man's bigotry about a girl named Rosalie. And if I could not gain entry into a damn poky library in Mussoorie, you would not stand much of a chance in either a British Raj India or an independent India—for we would retain our prejudices well after the British quit us. So we thought that perhaps America would be best; realize, my child, that we sent you from one family that was very much yours to another that was equally yours—we would have, in making this decision, entertained no other option.

Marianne Westwood took you to America. She had returned also to Rudrakot right after your birth, had seen you, held you in her arms, known from the beginning that you were Sam's child. When we decided to send you to your grandmother, Maude, we could think of no one other than Marianne to entrust you to. I handled all the details of the travel and your passport; I am, if I may be so immodest again as to point out, not without resources. A princely title still counted for much in those days.

I never had the time to grow out of love with your mother. I am told by many, many people that marriages are such—a rush of early passion defined mostly by the need of the body; a mellowing out as visages become familiar, as gestures start to grate on nerves; an indifference and a settling into a life other than the one lived with the once beloved. I never got to that last part, or indeed, even the middle part. I loved Mila's walk, her talk, her limbs. I do not mean to embarrass you by speaking of your mother's beauty and grace and loveliness in the terms a man would use, but know that she had all of those, she was loved for those, and because I had known her since she was very young, I loved her for more.

April 1963

*Somewhere Near Seattle*

*The woods are lovely, dark and deep.*
*But I have promises to keep,*
*And miles to go before I sleep,*
*And miles to go before I sleep.*

—Robert Frost, *Stopping by Woods on a Snowy Evening*

*T*he fire in the stove has long since cooled into a heap of glowing embers turning ashen and gray as each minute passes, and for the last hour of reading, Olivia has had her feet propped against the glass. She wears no shoes, and the soles of her feet are hot and toasted, and there is pain there. She lies on the floor on her back, the pages of the letter heavy and satisfyingly solid against the skin of her stomach. And then she remembers what she has forgotten during the telling of this story, that Sam is no longer here.

"Papa," she says softly, and beside her, Elsa picks up a warm nose from the carpet and lays it in the crook of Olivia's neck as though to say, *I miss him too.* How senseless death is, Olivia thinks, how stupid and uncaring. At one moment she gets a phone call from her father saying that he is coming to visit her on campus, an hour later she hears the hushed, grieving tones of the dean of his department saying that he was hit by a car as he crossed Fifteenth Avenue.

"Did he break a leg?" Olivia asks hopefully. "An arm? Break his damned back?"

But no, nothing so lucky. It takes his life. It is five days before Olivia can raise herself out of her stupor and go to the cabin with the trunk that holds the secrets of her life. Uncle Mike asks if she wants him to accompany her, but as much as she adores him, she cannot bear to have anyone else here but the dog. Grandma Maude says merely this as she kisses Olivia's hair, "Go my dear, go mourn for your papa. We all have our own ways."

And this is Olivia's way of remembering her father, by filling all the silences of her childhood with stories of who she is, where she came from, who her mother was. Why her father never married, why he could not replace Mila in his life, why Olivia was enough for him. Olivia is formed from these silences. There is nothing distant anymore, nothing dissipated and half understood. Jai's story gives her a tale with shape and structure, gives her, finally, her mother and her father. A grandfather. Uncles in their youth. A surrogate father also, who tells little about himself, more about Sam and Mila, and in the telling of this tale, comes through emblazoned in each word.

She knows something of what happened afterward, after Marianne Westwood brought her here to Seattle to be with Grandma Maude and Uncle Mike. It was a little more than two years before Sam could leave Burma and return home. He knew, of course, well before he returned, that Olivia had been born, that she lived with his mother. And strangely, Olivia has a very vivid memory—her earliest memory—of that first meeting with Sam in Grandma Maude's house on Queen Anne Hill.

Sam had come into his mother's arms and sobbed fiercely until it seemed to Olivia so incongruous that this large, lanky man with a thin face and thick black hair streaked with an early gray could be so childlike, much as she herself was when she wanted to throw a tantrum. She had viewed him from behind the paisley print sofa in greens and blues, standing on tiptoe so that she could see over the sofa's back, wearing her favorite patent leather shoes and her prettiest church dress. From the other side, only the tips of her fingers and the top part of her head showed. She had been told that her papa was coming home from the war, but those words, *papa, war,* meant so little to her. "Is he like Uncle Mike?" she had asked Grandma Maude. And they had both laughed so joyously at that and said that yes indeed, he was just like Uncle Mike, only he was all her own if she wanted him.

So Olivia had waited for this papa creature to come down on his haunches by the sofa, and when he still could not see the whole of her and when he could not fit between the side table and the wall, he pulled the sofa out with one strong arm and slid into the gap. Olivia had retreated to a corner when her fort's walls had thus crumbled, and watched him with a tilt of her head. Sam sat down, cross-legged, and waited for her. He let her peer at his face for as long as she wanted. There were sharp cuts of scarred skin, one slashed from under Sam's left eye down to his jawline, two more on the right forehead; the scars were turning white with healing and seemed blanched out of his sun-darkened skin. He put out his hand and waited some more, patiently, telling her he was her father, and that from now on they would be together forever.

Olivia had finally put her little hand in his and allowed him to settle her on his lap so that he could slant her head and gaze down into her face. He kissed her on the forehead and Olivia fell in love with him.

But he had talked so little, all of her life, about what had happened in Burma and what had happened in India.

Sam's stories have been abstract, lovely jewels by themselves, but without the luster of life, as though he cannot bear to talk of the woman he has loved so deeply that what he has considered betrayals—Mila's abandoning him at Chetak's tomb, her subsequent marriage to Jai, even her death—have taken away his power of speech. The most he says to Olivia every now and then is that she looks like her mother when she dries her long hair and spreads it out on her pillow, or when she ponders her homework, tapping her pen against the table, a frown upon her young forehead. And with this she has been fretfully content.

Olivia sits among the garden of colors from all the silk saris, muted and throbbing dully in the abated light from the stove. She has one of her mother's names, and two others, Padmini and Nazeera, from whom . . . ? There are still questions that have no answers.

The monkeys crouch in front of her, the gift her father did eventually give her mother. The black cord in the box strung with gold charms was tied around her waist when she was still a baby, to ward off the evil eye. Jai tells her the significance of each of the charms and that the little gold cylinder contains a sliver of the umbilical cord that had tied her to her mother. To Mila. The box also contains that pile of thin gold chain her father bought for her mother in the Lal Bazaar. Olivia rummages through the trunk until she works up a sweat, but the white sari from the White Durbar is not here. Where is it then? Still in India? Why did Jai not send it to her? She pulls her legs up to her chest and cordons them with her arms, her chin resting on her knees. Jai speaks so eloquently in this letter of a gift for her for her twenty-first birthday—and this trunk of memories, this letter of his dispelling the silence that lingered over her childhood is also his gift to her. Olivia is beset with an unreasonable anger at Sam—why did he have to die before he could open this trunk, read this letter? Would it have finally loosened his tongue?

The trunk arrived on the day Sam died, and he was on his way to her apartment to tell her of it, to take her back to his house and show it to her. And as he crossed the street he was hit by the car. So now only Jai's voice remains, clear and lucid, only Jai remains to speak of the splendor of all the silences. But there are others too . . .

Olivia rises from the floor of the cabin and goes outside into an early dawn. The rain has stopped and it has cleared the air, cleaned it and hung it out to dry, freshly scented and aromatic. Elsa throws herself down the red stairs and Olivia listens to the clatter of the dog's nails on the wood. When the sound stops, a little too soon, she shouts out, leaning over the railing, "All the way down, pooch. No pooping on the stairs." Then she hears Elsa let out a heavy sigh and hurtle down the rest of the stairs to the beach below.

The light from the sun begins to leak into the sky behind the Cascade Mountains. Although the storm is long over, clouds still tarry in the sky, seemingly thunderous and ominously dark blue, edged now with the golden glow of the morning. The sun then finally breaks out from its imprisonment behind the mountains and sends its slanting, honeyed rays out over the cove. It is cold, not bone-chillingly so, but enough that Olivia begins to shiver as she stands there, and she wonders what Rudrakot is like in the month of May. What an enervating, exhausting heat feels like. She lifts the last page of the letter and holds it up to read.

*I write now, dear Olivia, because after so many years we all have a sudden yearning to see you. We want to know if Sam will spare you now to us—at least for a little while. You must be as old as Mila was, shortly before we lost her, and we wonder if . . . there are any similarities. Here, in Rudrakot, are your uncles, your grandfather, and even I—I feel as though I too have some claim upon you.*

*I'm fortunately so circumstanced that I need not talk of money or the need for it, and so I am going to suggest—in what must seem to you to be an uncouth and ungainly manner—that whenever you decide to visit us, if the airplane fare or the passage by ship is . . . too much for Sam and you to handle, a simple word to me will suffice. I will make all the arrangements.*

*Do come. Please come, my dearest Olivia.*

*With all my sincere regard,*

*Jai*

# Glossary

| | |
|---|---|
| *Almirah* | Wardrobe |
| *Amchur* | Dry mango powder |
| *Amrit* | Nectar |
| *Anna* | Raj currency; sixteen annas in a rupee |
| *Asuras* | Demons |
| *Atta* | Wheat flour |
| *Ayah* | Servant |
| *Bawarchi* | Cook |
| *Beedis* | Hand-rolled cigarettes |
| *Burfis* | A sweet, cut into slices |
| *Chapattis* | Unleavened bread |
| *Chappals* | Slippers |
| *Charpai* | Jute-knitted bed |
| *Choli* | Fitted blouse |
| *Chula* | Hand-fashioned stove; usually of bricks and mud |
| *Churidar* | Tight-fitted trousers |
| *Dah* | Burmese dagger or sword |
| *Dals* | Lentils |
| *Darzi* | Tailor |

| | |
|---|---|
| *Dhobi* | Washerman |
| *Dhoti* | Draped cloth; commonly worn by men (similar to *veshti*) |
| *Diwan* | Various meanings; clerk, prime minister, secretary |
| *Diyas* | Oil lamps |
| *Dosas* | Crisp rice and lentil flour crepe |
| *Gaddi* | Throne |
| *Ghagara* | Long, pleated skirt |
| *Ghee* | Clarified butter |
| *Ghoonghat* | Veil |
| *Goras* | Whites |
| *Hartal* | Strike |
| *Hookah* | Water pipe |
| *Huzoor* | Sire; form of salutation |
| *Jalebis* | A sweet; deep-fried and soaked in sugar syrup |
| *Jalis* | Screens |
| *Jawan* | Army rank; a private soldier |
| *Kadai* | Frying pan |
| *Katori* | Cup or bowl |
| *Khazana* | Treasure |
| *Khichidi* | Rice and lentil mixture |
| *Khus* | River reed |
| *Kolam* | Decorative design in rice flour drawn on doorsteps |
| *Kurta* | Long-sleeved tunic |
| *Lathi* | Heavy stick bound with iron |
| *Maidan* | Field or grounds |
| *Mali* | Gardener |
| *Mela* | Fair |
| *Munshi* | Clerk |
| *Murgikhana* | Henhouse |
| *Mysorepak* | A sweet made of chickpea flour and sugar |

| | |
|---|---|
| *Naan* | Leavened bread cooked in a tandoor oven |
| *Namaste* | Salutation accompanied by a folding of the palms together |
| *Nautch* | Dance |
| *Nimbupani* | Lime water |
| *Paan* | Betel leaves |
| *Pagalpan* | Madness |
| *Pakoras* | A savory; deep-fried batter with vegetables |
| *Pallu* | Drape of sari over the shoulder |
| *Puja* | Hindu religious ritual |
| *Punkah* | Fan |
| *Purdah* | Veil |
| *Purnima* | Night of the full moon |
| *Rabadi* | Sweet made of milk |
| *Rajkumar* | Heir apparent |
| *Sadhu* | Sage; mendicant |
| *Sambar* | Stew made of lentils and vegetables |
| *Samosas* | A savory; deep-fried pastry stuffed with potatoes |
| *Shamiana* | Awning |
| *Sherwani* | Fitted coat with long sleeves |
| *Shikar* | Hunt |
| *Shlokas* | Verses in praise of God |
| *Sitar* | Stringed musical instrument |
| *Sola topi* | Pith helmet |
| *Tabla* | Hand drums |
| *Tava* | Flat pan |
| *Thali* | Plate; platter |
| *Veshti* | Draped cloth; commonly worn by men |
| *Zari* | Embroidery; usually with gold or silver thread |
| *Zenana* | Harem |

# A READERS CLUB GUIDE

SYNOPSIS OF *The Splendor of Silence*

In 1960s Seattle, a young woman named Olivia, reeling from the death of her father, receives a trunk from India containing, among other treasures, a letter from an unknown narrator. Olivia reads it, finally learning about her father's time in India and about the mother she never knew—a history that has lived in silence for her whole life.

Thus begins the story of four days in May of 1942 and the events that would shake the fragile peace in the small kingdom of Rudrakot in north-western India, for many years under the rule of the British Raj. It is the story of Sam, an American soldier in search of a missing brother, and Mila, the free-spirited daughter of the local political agent, and of their sudden love for each other, ignited dangerously within the social tinder-box of a country on the verge of change.

Sweeping and poignant, filled with evocative details from a fascinating time and place, *The Splendor of Silence* paints an unforgettable portrait of a rapidly changing society and a love ahead of its time.

DISCUSSION QUESTIONS

1. Though the central story of *The Splendor of Silence* is the romance be-tween Sam and Mila, many other types of love are depicted as well. How does Mila's love for her father and her brother color her relationships with Jai and Sam? In what ways are each of the central characters in search of

or driven by love? Do Mila's familial attachments and Sam's devotion to his brother devalue their love for each other or lend it more depth and meaning?

2. The settings in the novel are described in intricate detail. Does this create a sense of exoticism or more of a sense of fleshed-out reality? How do these physical details juxtapose with less concrete elements, such as the ghosts of Chetak's tomb and the shifting passions of the characters?

3. The central narrative of May 1942 is interspersed with the story of Sam's passage through Burma a month prior and framed by Olivia's perspective in 1963 Seattle. How do the tones and writing styles of these three sections differ? How does the immediacy of Sam's experience in April inform the decisions he makes in Rudrakot?

4. How do the structure of the novel and the repeated foreshadowing tie into the author's themes of karma and fate? In what ways do the future and past exist alongside the present? How does this inform the novel's vision of India?

5. Mila keeps her work in the Lal Bazaar a secret from everyone in her life. What does her work tell you about her character? How is this complicated by her secrecy?

6. In describing Raman's relationship with his late wife, Sundaresan writes that she "had satisfied his ego, for all love—despite popular opinion—is not selfless at its very beginning." (See page 154.) Do you agree with this statement? Are Mila's relationships self-serving? What about Ashok and Vimal, and Kiran's relationship with the British soldiers?

7. The "silence" of the title is a theme that is repeated in several ways, including the physical silence before the windstorm. How does this natural silence operate as a symbol? In which sense is silence seen as a positive force, and in which negative? What, ultimately, is the splendor of silence?

8. The social and political climate of 1940s India is depicted as heated and complex, with issues of race, class, and gender inequality creating daily

tension and upheaval. Does the revelation of Ashok's homosexuality complicate the discussion more than the other issues? If so, why?

9. Why did Mila neither leave with Sam nor provide him with an explanation? Does her death indicate that she made the wrong decision, or was it the only choice she could have made?

10. The novel ends with Jai inviting Olivia to visit India. Continue the story for yourself. What do you think the visit will mean to her? Why is it important for Jai to break the silence and to see Olivia again?

## ENHANCE YOUR BOOK CLUB

1. Interested in finding out more about the author? Visit her website at www.indusundaresan.com where you'll find some of her short works, including an essay on the women of the Taj Mahal.

2. Included in *The Splendor of Silence* are some enticingly detailed descriptions of Indian meals. Why not hold a meeting at an Indian restaurant, or even try some of the recipes for yourselves?

3. Visit wikipedia.org/wiki/Indian_Independence_Movement to learn more about the Indian nationalist movement and the context of the novel.

## QUESTIONS FOR INDU SUNDARESAN

*1. You were born and raised in India. Why did you decide to move to the United States? What was the biggest adjustment you had to make?*

I came to the United States for graduate school, and at the time, I was going to be an economist. The hardest part about being away, in another country, on another continent, was simply that—being away from family and friends of my childhood and youth. I think now, looking back, that I began writing as a means of reconnecting with the past; telling stories on paper was a way to return to the history I had learned, and to relive the time when my father used to tell me bedtime stories.

*2. You have said that your father and grandfather were storytellers and great inspirations for your writing. Can you discuss ways in which they've influenced your work?*

My sisters and I had very few distractions when we were children—an unreliable black-and-white television set, no video games, no cell phones or MP3 players. All we had were books (and so we read all the time) and the voices of our father and our grandfather. My father, especially, loved an attentive audience and loved to make up stories in his head. He taught me that anything that could be imagined could be made credible if only *you* believed enough—and that's an exceptionally valuable lesson for a future novelist, to know that to write with authority and conviction is to be able to make all your stories take life within the imaginations of all your readers.

*3. What drew you to this time period in India's history after having written two novels set in the seventeenth century?*

None of my novels were begun on a whim or completed on a whim (such fancies are hard to sustain for 400 odd pages). I had been thinking for a while about Mehrunnisa and Emperor Jahangir before I wrote *The Twentieth Wife* and *The Feast of Roses*. (In fact, I wrote two other unpublished novels before these two.)

And similarly, I have been thinking about *Splendor* for the last four or five years—sometimes in specifics (I knew Sam's and Mila's names well before I had fashioned a story around the names), sometimes in the abstract (the setting of Rudrakot came to life just before I began a serious draft). *The Splendor of Silence* is a definite departure from the storytelling format and structure of my first two novels, and from purely a craft point of view, it was an important part of my growth as a novelist.

I have wanted, for as long as *Splendor* has been taking shape in my head (and on paper in desultory writings) to explore the Second World War's China-Burma-India theater, and the Indian nationalist movement, but both within the situation of a love story and seen from the viewpoint of characters whose daily lives are affected.

*4. The epigraphs heading each chapter were mainly from historical works and poetry. Can you talk a bit about how you selected them and their significance to your story?*

The epigraphs were chosen to provide setting and background for *The Splendor of Silence*—especially those parts that I did not want to explain in the story. Most of the epigraphs deal with British attitude toward India and Indians—the rulers and the ruled—and the atmosphere they create build eventual tension in Sam's and Mila's relationship; no matter what their personal feelings are on the matter, they cannot escape the embrace of racial prejudice and intolerance. They lived in a time when change, or progress, simply had not been made, and their love was created during four days when people around them faced these very problems under some very explosive circumstances.

So the letter from Jai also has to wait twenty-one years to make its way to Olivia. The epigraph in chapter thirty-three is a short selection from Frost's *Mending Wall*—and I intended that with it, and with the story narrated in *Splendor*, Jai finally breaks down yet another barrier and communicates with Olivia whom he had sent away from India.

*5. The* Splendor of Silence *depicts an atmosphere of magic existing alongside concrete reality in India. Do you believe in mystical forces, such as Chetak's ghost, like your characters do?*

The ghosts at Chetak's tomb were written into the storyline, I must admit, more as an indulgence for myself than anything else; they seemed to fit there, in that part of the story, in that backdrop, in that atmosphere of the slightly surreal. I had a very similar experience in front of an abandoned tomblike structure when I was very young and on a picnic with my sisters and some friends. (They don't remember this incident, but strangely enough I have a very vivid memory of it.) We ran away from this tomb then, but I wanted Sam and Mila to complete that journey in this novel. Similarly, I wanted Sam to hear the lion's roar in a place and a time when lions were considered extinct in India, seen only by the locals and considered only part of village folklore.

Besides, I write fiction—for me, if it can be imagined, it can be real, or rather, going back to my answer to question 2, it must be *made* to feel real. In *The Splendor of Silence* then, I worked hard to create no disconnect between the real, the perceived, and the surreal elements of the story— they are all meant to lend each other credibility.

*6. Your father was an air force pilot. Did he inspire the character of Sam or your military subject matter?*

The military subject matter lent itself to the story because the whole world was at war in May of 1942, and it would have been impossible to take into account any storyline set within that time period and not talk of the military, or the omnipresent khaki (uniforms) of the war. I also needed a reason for Sam to be in India, and his being in a fledgling OSS unit, sent to Burma from the United States Army, all fit the theme.

Raman, Mila's father, is perhaps closest to my father in some points of his character for his openness, his honesty, his sheer delight in learning about and interacting with his fellow human beings. (Though perhaps Sam carries these same traits in *The Splendor of Silence* also, and that is what makes them like each other upon the first meeting.)

*7. Olivia is the most contemporary figure in the novel and lives in Seattle, like you. Is she a character with whom you particularly identify?*

Olivia frames the story told within *The Splendor of Silence*; she is the reason the silence is brought back to life, and the reason why Sam and Mila are revived after all these years. In many ways, she is an amalgamation of her parents, but I think who Olivia is, really, is still a mystery, since she has not had the chance to develop in the story told in *Splendor*. If I do write a sequel to this novel and send Olivia to India in 1963 to meet Jai, her grandfather, and her uncles . . . if . . . then I will truly know who she is.

*8. You've done extensive research for your writing. Is the story developed before you begin the research, or does it color the work as you write?*

Both. I researched the basic framework for the novel well before I began writing, and by that I mean a sense of the time, the attitudes, the atmosphere and environment, not just the politics and social aspects. All of these together gave me the voice and language for the novel—and you will see that this voice is distinct from the one I use for *The Twentieth Wife* and *The Feast of Roses*. All three novels are written from a very strongly omniscient point of view (though in *The Splendor of Silence* you hear Jai every now and then in the first person), and yet the language differs, the rhythms and sounds differ to fit each time frame and each context.

The specific aspects of the story in *Splendor*—details about the freedom movement, the flight from Burma, life in a princely state under the British Raj—all these I researched more thoroughly and factually as I wrote.

*9. You write on page 129 of* The Splendor of Silence, *"Sam was uncomfortable in both roles, of being from a dominating race in his own country and of being considered so impartial—neither was true." You give fair and equal treatment to many political perspectives in this novel. Is moderation in political beliefs something that is important to you?*

It was important for me, as a novelist, as a storyteller, to be able to see both sides of any argument whether or not I actually believed in both sides. And once I was able to get under the skin of characters who thought and acted differently than I would under those similar circumstances, it was my job as a novelist to present their viewpoints in as convincing a manner as I could.

I don't necessarily possess moderate political (or other!) beliefs, but when I begin to construct a story, I need to clear away my own personal prejudices as much as possible before I write, especially if I want to make my characters believable and engaging.

*10. Do you have any advice for budding historical authors who, like you, would like to draw from their own backgrounds and cultures?*

You have to like history! And read a lot. Sometimes there are jewels of stories that lie hidden in folklore and historical tales that can be developed into full-fledged storylines with some exercise of imagination and some creativity. It doesn't matter if the person/time period/event that you write of is well known or famous or easily identifiable; what matters is how you tell the story, with your own unique voice, from your unique perspective and background and experience.